THE
THERAPY

ASHER ELLIS

DEADITE PRESS
PORTLAND, OREGON

deadite press

DEADITE PRESS
833 SE Main Street #342
Portland, OR 97214
www.DEADITEPRESS.com

AN ERASERHEAD PRESS COMPANY
www.ERASERHEADPRESS.com

ISBN: 978-1-62105-323-1

Printed in the USA.

THE
THERAPY

AUTHOR'S NOTE

This story is a direct sequel to my novel *The Remedy*. It is highly recommended that you read that novel before beginning this one. If you have read the preceding book, then let's return to the woods. But be warned: they are dark and deep but far from lovely.

"Hunger is insolent, and will be fed."
—Homer

"Hunger knows no friend but its feeder."
—Aristophanes

PROLOGUE

Dale Preston had not always hated snow. When he was a child, snow was just about the best thing in the world. Snow could mean so many things to children—hours of sledding, epic snowball fights, elaborate forts with secret tunnels and emergency escape exits. Of course, none of these things compared to the monumental importance of what snow *didn't* bring with it, and that was school.

Though no kid ever realized it at the time, the "snow day" would come to ruin any holiday for the rest of their lives. Sure, later in life they still had binge drinking to look forward to on Saint Patrick's Day, and cookouts on the Fourth of July, and that inexplicable day off to celebrate Columbus' accidental "discovery" of America. Nothing, however, would ever compare to that unexpected reprieve after waking up on a post-blizzard morning. Even Christmas, as joyful as it could be, came with a hefty price tag. But snow days didn't require you to buy any presents, or decorations, or send out any cards. Snow days offered a freedom so pure you could practically bottle it.

And now...

Now as the snow began to cover the road outstretched before his pickup truck, Dale could find only two words to describe the white flakes falling from the sky. The first was cold. The second was heavy.

A railroad spike of contempt always drove its way through Dale's heart whenever someone used the phrase, "a blanket of snow." What damn sense did that make? Blankets were warm. Snow froze the earth and killed all the grass and flowers. Blankets were gentle. Snow weighted everything down, slowing transportation to a crawl and piling on roofs until they collapsed. Yeah, snow was a blanket all right. A death shroud.

"God damn it," Dale muttered, flipping the switch to turn on his windshield wipers. This definitely wasn't the first time he'd witnessed such heavy snowfall during mid-November. In fact, this far north into Vermont, it wasn't only to be expected, but appreciated even. According to old weatherlore, a warm November was a sign of a bad winter lying in wait. Inversely, if the first snowfall fell on unfrozen ground, residents could expect a mild winter.

"Bullshit," Dale mumbled again as he turned off of Route 6 onto the unmarked dirt road. Before continuing on, he brought the truck to a dead stop in order to shift into four-wheel drive. The snow had accumulated much more on this road as the town plow trucks didn't bother keeping it clear. More than once had Dale questioned the reasoning behind this decision. Was it to save the trucks' blades from dulling on the various rocks that jutted up from the dirt? Perhaps to encourage people to stick to the main roads during inclement weather?

Or maybe the powers that be just don't give a shit about the people that live up this way.

The cynic, who used to reside in the far reaches of Dale's mind but crept closer and closer as the years went by, believed the last to be true. That was the thing about racism: though sometimes it was as blatant as ethnic slurs scribbled on a bathroom stall, most often it occurred behind the proverbial curtain. Just because you couldn't see it, didn't mean it wasn't happening.

Dale tightened his grip on the steering wheel as the road began to descend down a steepening slope. Though he silently cursed the town crew's negligence, who was he to judge, really? No more than a year ago had he held the same ignorant view of the Abenaki people who resided in the approaching trailerpark. Like so many others, all Dale had seen were alcoholics who inhabited the Buck N' Doe every happy hour. Now, after all the time he had spent among them, Dale had witnessed first hand their collective wisdom and patience. Most impressive to Dale had been their incomparable hunting skills that each man and woman seemed to inherently possess. Regardless of being a hunter since his pre-teen years, Dale realized he knew absolutely jack shit about tracking his prey, and that was after just one day in the woods with Matthew Wolfchild and his sister, Cordelia.

Like any community, be it the whitest suburb or an indigenous tribe in the far corners of Africa, the Abenaki had a few less-than-savory citizens living among them. But they were, as far as Dale could tell, a shining example of a few bad apples ruining the bunch. Oddly enough, it was one of those bad apples that Dale had come to see tonight.

During the pre-colonial days of his people, John Woodenknife would've certainly been a warrior to be reckoned with. Muscular, clever, and never without a certain intensity lighting his gaze, Woodenknife would've carried himself well on a battlefield or a hunting ground. But rather than leading a hunting party on horseback, Woodenknife led his motorcycle gang, the Forlorn Hope. And the Hope did not hunt whitetail deer or pheasants to feed their village. They ran drugs.

Dale's truck reached the bottom of the hill and continued around a sharp bend. He hardly touched the gas pedal, allowing his natural momentum to carry him down the road. Hitting your brakes in a snowstorm was never the best idea, especially when crossing an old wooden bridge like he was now. Fortunately, the rickety overpass that carried him over Copper Creek meant the trailerpark was no more than a minute away. It wasn't that Dale was that concerned with the poor driving conditions. He just wanted to get this rendezvous over and done with. That's the way he always preferred it when it came to John Woodenknife.

Woodenknife—the man was a drunk, a criminal, and a bit unstable whenever the heat increased around his collar. With so many honest, hardworking, and honorable men and women residing in all of the surrounding trailers, why did Dale seek the company of their community's lowliest representative? It was a question Dale asked himself whenever Woodenknife greeted him with a breathing mask over his nose and mouth, a sure sign of something illegal cooking in a backroom. But Dale knew the answer. It was simple, though many would not have understood.

John Woodenknife believed in the Wendigo.

Dale parked his truck just past the entrance of Brookview Trailerpark. Though Woodenknife's trailer was located on the far east side, it was better to leave the truck here to obscure Dale's destination. If Matthew Wolfchild happened to spot the vehicle, he'd most likely assume Dale was visiting Cordelia. If Cordelia happened to see it, she'd assume her brother had company. Another golden rule of visiting John Woodenknife was the fewer who knew about the meeting, the better.

Dale killed the engine and reached for his door, but found he couldn't turn the handle. His hand was shaking too much.

Oh God. Not again.

The tremors always seemed to start in his fingers and work their way up his arms, spurring every muscle in his body to spasm. As usual, Dale tried to contain the violent shakes, steeling himself the best he could. But try as he might, he could not control the rapid fire breaths that shot between his clenched teeth. The resulting sound was unmistakable, even to Dale's own ears. He was snickering.

Dale caught a glimpse of his face in the rearview mirror just before he clamped a hot palm over his mouth. The muscles in his cheeks were tightening like the rest, pulling his lips up into a maniacal smile.

He clenched his eyes shut.

Ride it out. Just ride it out. Think about fire. A nice relaxing fire.
Like all the other times before, distracting himself with

images of crackling flames did the trick. Little by little, the traffic jamming the highways of his nervous system began to thin. And just when he was sure he would hyperventilate, Dale took a long, full breath. It was over.

Only one thought raced through Dale's mind as he sat there in the truck, regaining composure as the falling flakes collected on his windshield.

What in the blue hell is happening to me?

Truth be told, this had been far from his worst episode. Previous ones had brought full belly laughs, like he had just heard the ultimate gut-busting joke. But there was nothing funny about any of this. This laughter was compulsive in the strongest sense of the word, like someone else entirely was controlling his body. Dale's voice even sounded foreign during these laughing fits, much shriller than this usual gruff inflection. And if John Woodenknife was right, someone else *was* taking up residence deep inside of Dale. Or rather, some *thing*.

The Wendigo.

A gust of cold wind greeted Dale as he finally swung his legs out of the truck. Zipping up his Carhartt jacket, he wandered off the main road cutting through the center of the park. Instead, he walked behind the trailers where the streetlights did not illuminate his journey. This dimly lit path would lower the chances of anyone spotting him, and besides, he had walked this same route so many times that stepping over rocks, tree roots, and sinkholes had become second nature. Regardless of the darkness, it did not take long to reach his destination.

Despite it being a cold November, the small lawn in front of Woodenknife's trailer was somehow still overgrown. A Harely Davidson sat parked in his driveway, covered by a heavy, black tarp. But perhaps the strongest indicator that this was John Woodenknife's home was the Foghat blasting from inside. With "Slow Ride" drowning out all other noise, Dale didn't bother knocking as he opened the front door.

Two men glanced in his direction as Dale entered, both

sitting on a couch covered in dark stains and holes. One was Woodenknife. Dale didn't recognize the other.

"Ah," Woodenknife said, reaching for the boombox that rested on the coffee table in front of his legs. He turned down the volume just as Tom Petty began to play. "White man from town. About time you got here."

Dale still regretted the time he and Woodenknife had gotten drunk on a case of Keystone Light and watched *Thinner* on cable TV. Ever since, Woodenknife had a new favorite name for his Caucasian friend.

"Fuck you, Crazy Horse," Dale said, shutting the door behind him. "Emphasis on the crazy."

Woodenknife spread his denim covered legs and grabbed his crotch. "More like Crazy Horse Cock! Just ask any bitch you know. They'll tell you."

The man sitting next to Woodenknife laughed heartily at this comment, pausing only to release a guttural belch. It was then that Dale noticed the man's yellowing teeth. They looked like corn kernels inside of his bushy, graying beard. Despite the mixing aromas of stale beer, forgotten pizza boxes, and a whole slew of chemical scents coming from the rear of the trailer, Dale could still smell the stink wafting off the man's brown chamois shirt.

"Who's this?" Dale asked, pointing at the reeking man. He took a seat in a wicker rocking chair across from the couch.

After tossing Dale a can of beer, Woodenknife slapped the stranger's shoulder. "This here's Old Joe. I ran into him at the train yard. He's trying to make his way west. Ain't that right, Joe?"

Old Joe finished another beer and crushed the can between his fingers. "That's right," he said. "Hopped a train from Portland. It's gettin' too damn cold up here, so I'm relocating to the Sunshine State."

Dale cracked his beer and sucked at the foam that immediately shot forth. With the rim clear he said, "You mean Florida? Why the hell are you going west, then?"

Old Joe looked at him cockeyed, like some vital spring or

cog inside his mind had just snapped loose. "Do I look like a fuckin' golfer to you? I'm going to California." Only he pronounced it, "Calla-forny."

"California's the Golden State." Dale took another swig and added, "Just so you know."

The radio emanated the only sound in the room as the three men went awkwardly silent. Tom Petty continued to jam out on his guitar as Old Joe stared at Dale with dead eyes.

And then he burst into laughter.

"God damn Encyclopedia Brown over here!" He smacked Woodenknife's knee. "This guy's all right, John."

Woodenknife raised his beer. "That he is, Old Joe. I said you would like him."

"Sure I do," Old Joe said, giving Dale the best example of a "shit eating grin" he had ever seen in his life. Dale only offered back a slight curve of his mouth.

Old Joe cracked another beer, a can that would soon be joining its empty friends scattering the floor. "So," the drifter said over the loud release of Co2, "How do the Lone Ranger and Tonto know each other?"

Woodenknife looked at Dale. "Mind if I take this one?"

Dale waved his hand, the universal sign for "whatever."

Woodenknife smiled and bent forward to a plastic tacklebox resting next to the radio on the coffee table. He opened it to reveal a small, ceramic smoking bowl and a plastic baggie of dried herbs that Dale assumed wasn't oregano.

"Though he may not look like it," Woodenknife said as he opened the bag, "Our friend Dale here carries a heavy burden that weighs on his soul." He paused to carefully remove a pinch of the weed. "But who doesn't, right? And like anyone else, Dale found himself in need of someone to talk to. As it turns out, that someone was me."

A chuckle escaped Old Joe's mouth just as he was taking a gulp of beer, resulting in foamy suds running down the man's chin. "So, what? You're his therapist?"

When Dale's gaze suddenly met with Woodenknife's, he knew the man must be thinking the same thing: no one had ever put it that way, but it was surprisingly accurate.

"I guess so," Woodenknife said, bringing his attention back to his task. He stuffed the pot into the bowl and added, "Though traditionally speaking, my people might have referred to my role as 'a sin eater.' Sounds a bit more bad ass, doesn't it?"

Old Joe ignored the question and offered one of his own. "Hey, you're going to pass that peace pipe, right?"

If Dale hadn't been looking in just the right direction at that exact moment, he would've missed it for sure. It happened as fast as any muscle twitch and lasted just as long. But there it was—John Woodenknife's signature look of crazed intensity. His eyes seemed to focus on nothing, growing wide as his eyebrows arched downward. Anger as hot as hellfire practically ignited the blackness of his pupils.

And then it was gone. Woodenknife was smiling again, his face completely stress free. But Dale had seen it, he was sure. Old Joe's off-color "injun" talk was finally getting to him.

"Of course I am, " Woodenknife said. "In fact, you get the first hit." He handed Old Joe the bowl and produced a lighter from the pocket of his leather vest. Old Joe greedily accepted the items, reminding Dale of a misbehaved dog snatching at a milk bone.

Their new friend took a monstrous drag, letting the smoke linger in his lungs before slowly releasing it through his nostrils. He looked like a steam engine coming to rest at a train station. Dale thought the comparison to be appropriate, considering where Woodenknife had found him.

"So what's wrong with you?" The train man said, his eyes fixed on Dale. He still hadn't let go of the piece and made no move to pass it along. "Are you suffering from depression? Life not turn out how you wanted it to? Maybe some daddy issues that need to be resolved?"

The image came strong and sudden: Dale springing forward,

slamming the heel of his work boot into the bowl just as Old Joe took another hit. The piece would either shatter, slicing both lips and gums, or shoot straight down the bastard's throat. Both outcomes were equally satisfying in Dale's imagination.

"Nah," Woodenknife said. "That could all be taken care of with a handful of happy pills. What Dale has is something far less..." He paused to find the right word. "...Suburban. Tell me, Old Joe, have you ever heard of the Wendigo?"

After another string of smoke had left his lips, Old Joe shook his head and said, "Nope. But it sounds like a red man thing."

Woodenknife smiled but there was nothing warm about the expression. "Correct. My people, the Abenaki, spawned from the Algonquin Nation. The Wendigo is an Algonquin legend, a spirit who is the embodiment of hunger. Once the Wendigo possesses a man, he can never satisfy his appetite. And the Wendigo has a very a particular diet."

Woodenknife once again reached into the small box. From somewhere within the container, came a quiet clicking noise.

Click. Click. Click.

Old Joe raised the bowl once again and gave Dale another rotten-toothed grin. "So you have an eating disorder?"

Woodenknife narrowed his eyes at Dale.

"Exactly."

Like a magician pulling a rabbit from his hat, Woodenknife yanked his hand out of the box. Wrapped in his fingers was a box cutter, its blade already extended.

The clicking noise.

Woodenknife's hand became a blur as he drove the box cutter into Old Joe's throat. His hands occupied with lighting the bowl, Old Joe could do nothing to stop the blade from plunging into his esophagus.

Blood immediately burst forward, spraying onto the coffee table. Dale threw his hand up to shield himself from the torrent, but the bloody splash failed to spread past the table's midsection. Still, it coursed like a waterfall from the homeless man's throat, soaking his stinking clothes.

Woodenknife looked down to the wet, crimson shirt and laughed. "Who's the red man now?"

Old Joe could not answer. His mouth gaped like that of a dentist's obedient patient, but not a sound escaped his lips. Nor did the smoke from his last drag, which had found a much quicker exit from his body. It drifted out of the ragged slash in his throat, turning Old Joe into a human chimney.

At first, the man's crazed eyes darted back and forth between Dale and Woodenknife with the speed of a professional tennis match. But they soon began to slow, until his gaze stopped between the two men. His head slumped forward, his body falling to the left onto the arm of the couch.

Old Joe was dead, leaving another stain on the dirty furniture.

"God damnit," Woodenknife muttered. Dale turned away his attention from the corpse to see his companion looking at the floor. "I forgot to put plastic down. Let me grab some before you start cutting." He threw the box cutter onto the table. "Cut off what you want tonight. We'll put the rest of him in the freezer."

Dale remained quiet and nodded. This wasn't the first time they had done this, but that didn't seem to matter. Dale still found himself speechless and hardly able to move.

With a few steadying breaths, he reached for the box cutter. It felt like it weighed fifty pounds in his hand. God, was he tired. Maybe he would ask Woodenknife to brew up a pot of coffee as he did his gruesome work.

Old Joe with a cup of Joe.

Sounds like a breakfast special. We should open a diner.

The joke was anything but funny. In fact, nothing was funny these days. But as Dale went to slice off Old Joe's right pinky finger, he began to chuckle. Quiet snickering at first, but it did not take long to grow into loud, boisterous laughter.

He just couldn't help himself.

CHAPTER ONE

It had just started to rain when Leigh Swanson's cell phone began to ring. She was driving along a winding road, a wall of trees lining each side. The giant trunks and full boughs of the pines cast dark shadows over the pavement. Now, with the blackening thunderclouds, it may as well have been night.

The good news was that she was getting close to her destination. Though the car didn't come equipped with a GPS, she knew she was getting close. She could feel it. In just a few minutes she would reach—

Crazy he calls me...

Had it not been for the seatbelt secured across her chest, the sudden ringtone would've startled her off her seat. She looked to the passenger seat to see her phone vibrating as the Billie Holiday tune began to play.

When had she set that as her ringtone?

Puzzled, she stared at the illuminated phone. In the dim lighting of the car, its screen glowed green across the entire roof. The effect made it look like some sort of alien technology, like a handheld communicator on a Syfy TV show. She reached for its shaking body...

And a deafening thump rattled the entire car.

Leigh's eyes darted back to the road just in time to see a dark shape roll over her windshield and vanish behind her. She heard it thud across the roof, the percussion much heavier than that of the falling rain.

Leigh slammed her foot on the brake. With the high squeal of skidding rubber, the car's backend swung hard to the left. Leigh screamed along with the tires as her vehicle fishtailed, still screaming when the car came to a dead stop horizontally across the road.

Heart racing in her chest, she slowly brushed the hair out of her face to look out the window. She knew what she would see before her gaze landed on the sprawled, limp body.

Oh God, no. I hit someone.

She hadn't even been aware of her hand unbuckling her seatbelt or opening her door. Before she realized it, Leigh was already halfway to the unconscious stranger.

"Hello? Can you hear me? Are you all—"

Her feet froze in place. It couldn't be.

A green vintage army jacket. A faded Montreal Expos cap. Shaggy brown hair sticking out from underneath.

It was Sam Tucker.

Leigh's voice came as a whisper. "Sam?"

The boy she had once knew did not respond. In fact, he did not move at all.

Leigh took a step forward and hesitated. This was the wrong move. Though a million questions surged through her head, wasting time to get a better look might cost her friend his life. If Sam was indeed still alive, Leigh's only hope of saving him would be to get help as soon as possible.

Her hand went to the right pocket of her jeans, then to the left. Both were empty but of course they were. Her phone was on the seat in the car.

"Hold on, Sam. I'm going to get help." Leigh pivoted on the ball of her foot, readying herself to spring back to the car.

But the car was gone, vanished into the thick, moist air.

Not even the faintest tire mark remained on the road. Where the car had once sat blocking both lanes, a man now stood. Or rather, something that resembled one.

It took Leigh a moment to recognize him, his body bloody and broken and hardly standing upright on his ruined legs. It was like looking at an old scarecrow hanging lopsided on a pole, its artificial flesh pecked away by hundreds of beaks.

"...Sam?"

Sam's smile was missing several teeth, turning his face into a Jack o' Lantern. His eyes had gone black, blood oozing from their corners like crimson tears. He raised a broken arm, somehow managing to point the twisted limb at something behind her.

"Hey, Leigh," he said. Though he stood several feet away, Leigh could hear his voice as if he was whispering right in her ear. "Can I get a ride?"

No longer in control of her own body, she could not stop herself from turning around to see what Sam was pointing at. About twenty feet away, a large, green sign stood at the side of the road. Despite the growing darkness, she could read its words perfectly. It read:

Welcome to Embry!

"No," Leigh whispered. "Not here."

Again, her body acted independent from her will. She again turned to face Sam, only this time, he stood perfectly straight. Not a scratch on him, healthy as a horse.

Leigh should've been overjoyed to see her friend experience such a miraculous recovery, but her sigh of relief caught in her throat when she saw what he held in his hand: a stick of dynamite, its lit end spraying bits of light like a sparkler.

He raised the stick. The fuse was almost out.

"I never thanked you for this, Leigh."

Leigh shouted at the top of her lungs but she could not hear her own voice.

"No, Sam! Throw it away! Throw—"

And then Sam exploded.

***

Leigh was sitting up in her bed before her eyes completely opened. Had she been screaming? She hoped not. The last thing she wanted was to wake her roommate for the thousandth time. In the morning she would, of course, tell Leigh it was no big deal before asking she wanted any coffee. But it was all an act in the name of politeness. How could it not be? Sharing an apartment with a girl who suffered from night terrors would eventually drive anyone crazy.

Leigh threw the blankets off her bare legs to see that her limbs, like the rest her body, were covered in sweat. This was to be expected following such a vivid nightmare, but the lack of surprise never reduced her discomfort.

Swinging her feet over the bed, she headed to the bathroom to clean up. As she paced across her bedroom floor, she plucked her damp t-shirt away from her body. The moist material clung to her skin, itching her all over. The idea of taking a shower crossed her mind, though she would have to keep the water pressure low to minimize the noise. Still, the thought of cool water on her burning skin was too nice to resist.

She crossed through the bathroom door's threshold, her hand immediately going for the light switch on the wall. Leigh had done this action countless times before, usually in the morning while still half-asleep. Groggy or not, her fingers found the switch every time without the use of her eyes.

Except for this time. Her fingertips felt only blank wall. Leigh brushed her entire hand over the wall where the switch should be, feeling absolutely nothing in the darkness.

Sighing, she felt her way to the sink. A second switch was located just above the faucet, one which would activate the vanity lights surrounding the mirror. This one was impossible to miss as the space of wall between the mirror and counter was very short and thin.

Leigh's waist bumped the edge of the sink. She stretched

her hand outward, felt along the narrow space of wall, and felt a nub of hard plastic.

Finally!

She flicked the switch. The round bulbs surrounding the mirror illuminated all at once.

And Leigh looked into the eyes of a monster.

She tried to scream but air refused to move through her throat. A green carpet of fungus covered every inch of her face and neck like an oversized Halloween mask. Strands of it dangled from her lips, eyebrows, and nostrils. Mushrooms grew out of both ears, their toadstool heads stretching down to the lobes.

Before she could take in another detail of the green carpet spreading across her face, a burning sensation erupted in the pit of her stomach. Just as she felt it moving upward into her chest and throat, tentacles of the fungus shot from her mouth in a never-ending waterfall of green mold.

One of the vines pouring to the floor entangled her leg. She tripped, sprawling backward. Her hand shot forward to grab the counter, the sink—anything to stop her descent. But her fingers touched only air and she fell.

And fell...

Back issues of several magazine toppled to the floor as Leigh's hand struck the pile. An elderly man sitting a few seats down in the waiting room looked up from his newspaper. Her cheeks burning red with embarrassment, Leigh mouthed the word "sorry," and picked up the scattered magazines.

She was just putting the last copy of *People* on the stack when the woman at the front desk called, "Ms. Swanson? Dr. Joyce will see you now."

"Thank you," Leigh said, still feeling self-conscious that she jolted awake so violently. But the nightmare had been so real. As real as every other time it had plagued her sleep. The night terrors were, after all, one of the reasons Leigh had continued to see Dr. Mallory Joyce.

Leigh approached the doctor's office door and paused to straightened her hair and dark red blouse. She noticed a wet spot on her shoulder and with a brief jolt of repulsion, realized she had drooled while asleep. Fortunately, a quick adjustment to the black scarf wrapped around her neck concealed the spot completely. With a final deep breath, she knocked.

"Come in," a soft voice said from behind the door.

Leigh opened the door to see Dr. Joyce already sitting in the sea foam green arm chair that rested parallel to a black leather couch. As she motioned to the couch she said, "Hello, Leigh. Please, have a seat."

Though she had been in this office many times before, Leigh was still impressed by the amount of degrees and certificates lining the wall behind Dr. Joyce's desk. Even more eye catching was the photo that sat next to a bubbling water cooler in the corner. Leigh's therapist shook hands with none other than Dr. Phil, the celebrity smiling from ear-to-ear. From previous examination, Leigh knew the black scrawl across the photo's surface read, "Thanks for the all the help! Your friend, Phil."

"And how are we doing today?" Dr. Joyce asked as Leigh took a seat.

"I'm well," Leigh said.

"Glad to hear it." Dr. Joyce waved a hand in front of her own face and added, "But are you sure? You just look a little flushed is all."

Leigh tried to straighten up on the couch, as if it would make any difference to her appearance at all. "Oh, it's nothing. I just dozed off in the waiting room."

Dr. Joyce narrowed her eyes. "And you had another nightmare, didn't you?"

Though shame reheated her cheeks, Leigh knew better not to lie. Outside in the "real world," she could make up excuses or dance around the subject. But in here, complete and utter honesty was what she was paying for.

"Yes," she muttered. "And I bet you can guess what it was about."

"Mmm," Dr. Joyce muttered, taking a moment to write a quick note on the pad at her lap. As she scribbled, Leigh took in her features for the thousandth time. Having long entered middle age, Dr. Mallory Joyce had kept many of her youthful features. It was safe to say her makeup concealed a line or two on her face, and there were a few strands of gray streaking her shoulder-length black hair, but otherwise, Dr. Joyce could've passed for several years younger than her driver's license revealed. From the days of their initial ice-breaking conversations, Leigh knew the psychiatrist to be an avid tennis player, who avoided most vices, such as smoking. In her words, her only weak spot was for a perfectly cooked hamburger or steak, though judging her looks, it seemed she kept that high calorie habit under control.

Leigh had first entered her office looking for a quality therapist. She had found exactly that, but even more so, a new role model. If Leigh could ever get her life back on track, Dr. Mallory Joyce was the type of woman she would aspire to be. Healthy, successful, and perhaps most important of all, helping others.

"So," Dr. Joyce said, finishing her note with a click of her pen. "Your subconscious dragged you back to Embry once again."

Leigh nodded. "Unfortunately, yes."

"And based on the fact you were nodding off in the middle of the day, I take you didn't get much sleep last night either."

Again, Leigh nodded. "I'm starting to wish I had a tank of nitrous next to my bed so I could just knock myself out. I didn't dream when I got my tonsils and wisdom teeth removed. Just started counting backwards from one hundred and the next thing I knew I was waking up. Now that would be nice."

Dr. Joyce smirked but didn't laugh. "How about when you're not asleep? Everything still going okay?"

"Absolutely," Leigh said without hesitation. "I heard back from UConn. I can start this fall."

Now Dr. Joyce smiled a full tooth-bearing grin. "That's wonderful, Leigh. I'm still so proud of you for taking this step and going back to school. With that degree in hand, you'll make an excellent psychiatrist one day. Trust me, I think I know what I'm talking about."

Leigh laughed, savoring the surge of genuine happiness warming her belly. It had taken her over a year start feeling emotions as pleasant as this. And she knew exactly knew exactly who to thank for that.

"I couldn't have done it without you, Dr. Joyce. I can't imagine where I would be right now. I think nightmares would've been the least of my concerns."

Dr. Joyce shook her head. "As a former student of psychology, you know darn well that you did all the work. My job is simply to hand you the oar. You're the one who did all the rowing while I kicked back in this comfy chair. What can I say? It's a great gig."

They shared a laugh over that comment but Dr. Joyce's face soon became serious again. "As much progress as you've made, the fact remains that you are still having these nightmares. And if we don't address a way to get rid of them, I'm afraid they'll start affecting your day-to-day life. I mean, just today you passed out in my waiting room. What will happen when you start school in the fall? What if your grades start slipping?"

Leigh pictured herself knocking over the stack of magazines and added, "What if I wake up screaming in the middle of a lecture?"

"Another good example, if not a bit extreme. The point is, Leigh, is that you've made too much progress to let this final obstacle hold you back. The good news is that I think I may have an idea."

Leigh's ears perked up. "What's that?"

Dr. Joyce leaned back in her chair and looked Leigh straight in the eyes. "Are you familiar with the concept of exposure therapy?"

Leigh thought for a moment, flipping through her mind's rolodex labeled, *Psychology Studies.* "It's the treatment of exposing a patient to a feared object to overcome anxiety brought on by said object."

Secretly, Leigh was impressed by her almost word-for-word recital of the textbook definition. Apparently she was more prepared to return to her studies than she thought. Based on the look on Dr. Joyce's face, she too was impressed.

"Very good, Leigh. I see a year off of school hasn't dulled your knowledge a bit. Tell me, when you studied this form of treatment in class, what were your thoughts?"

"Well." Leigh bit her lip as she tried to mentally recall her notes. "I remember the numbers were pretty convincing. Something like 90% of patients showing significant reductions in fear, while like 60% or so actually get over their fears completely."

"That's about right," Dr. Joyce said. "In fact, most psychologists agree its the most validated treatment known for phobias."

"Hmm," Leigh mumbled as she considered this statement. "Even so, I suppose it all still depends on the patient in question."

"That's true." Dr. Joyce leaned forward in her chair. "So do you think you're the right type of patient?"

"I…"

Leigh's chest tightened. The air within the office was now thick and hot. The couch under her crawled against her legs.

"I don't know," she finally managed to say.

Dr. Joyce offered a warm smile. "Said every patient ever to sit on a therapist's couch."

Leigh tried to chuckle but it came out far too sharp and high pitched. After clearing her throat she said, "I just don't know if I can say I'm ready for something like that. I moved back to Connecticut to start my life over again. I'd rather try to forget the first twenty-three years of my life ever happened."

"Please listen to me, Leigh." Dr. Joyce crossed her legs and stared at Leigh with the sincerity only Dr. Joyce could seem to muster. "I have spent the last year attempting to form a relationship with you based on mutual respect and trust. If you feel I have succeeded in this, then you can trust me when say you are ready."

Leigh swallowed hard. "You really think so."

Dr. Joyce shook her head. "No. I know so. And I know this because objective reality tells me that Embry, VT is only a town. It has roads. It has buildings. It has trees."

At this, Leigh had to speak up. "There not just trees. There was something horrible living in them."

"That part of the forest is gone. You know this as much as I do. That whole spread of woods was burned to the ground. What did the news call it again?"

Leigh knew it was probably a rhetorical question but she answered anyway. "The Ashes."

"And that dreadful family? The Cedars?"

If anyone else had dared mention that name, Leigh would've screamed, punched them in the face, or both.

"They're all dead."

"But they're not dead, are they? And neither is the fungus that claimed so many lives, some that very dear to you. They both live on, up here," she paused to point at Leigh's forehead, "terrorizing you day in and day out as memories that won't go away. Unless you go back and see that there is nothing there that can ever hurt you again, your mind will never be able to convince yourself that the danger is gone."

A single tear rolled down Leigh's left cheek. She used her scarf to wipe it away.

"I know what you're saying makes sense. And I know what the studies show, that this sort of thing can work wonders for people with PTSD. But Dr. Joyce, one of the key components of exposure therapy is a controlled environment, where any sort of actual danger is taken away. If I was trying to get over a fear of dogs you wouldn't just bring in a Rottweiler and say 'Have at it.' A professional trainer would be here, and he'd keep a hold on the dog the entire time I was petting it. But in my case you can't really do that."

Leigh inhaled deeply, realizing she had just said that entire rant in one breath. She stared at Dr. Joyce, utterly terrified she had offended the doctor in some way. Instead, Dr. Joyce nodded in contemplation, tapping her pen against her chin.

"Actually," she said, "That's a fantastic idea, Leigh. A professional should go with you for support. There's no reason you have to do this alone."

Leigh wiped at her widening eyes. "You mean, you would go with me?"

A frown bent Dr. Joyce's lips. "I'm afraid that's not possible. My schedule is fully booked, and I couldn't abandon all my other patients, even for one of my favorites. However..."

Dr. Joyce tapped her pen a few more times on her chin. It was tick Leigh had noticed many times before.

"How would you feel about Evan accompanying you?"

"Evan..." Leigh chewed at her bottom lip. "You mean Mr. Dixon?"

Dr. Joyce gave a half-hearted laugh. "I believe he would prefer if you call him Evan, but yes, my assistant. He's extremely close to finishing his doctorate, which means his days of working for me are soon coming to an end. This trip would be a fantastic way to cap off his time here, and besides, I can't think of a better substitute for myself. What do you think of Evan?"

"I like him quite a bit," she answered without hesitance. However, the reply wasn't completely true. There was nothing really *wrong* about Evan Dixon—he was polite, professional, and had an obvious future as a physician of mental health. The *thing* about Mr. Dixon—Evan—was that he was awkward, plain and simple. Not to say Leigh could ever pass judgment on someone shy or lacking social skills. She had a rich history of bashfulness and timidity and could entirely emphasize with anyone suffering from the same.

But spending several hours in a car with him alone? And on a trip to a place that already made her anxious just thinking about it? Leigh knew she just couldn't do it.

"The thing is, Dr. Joyce..."

"I know. He's not much for conversation, is he? One of the most brilliant people I've ever had the pleasure of working with, but I think it's pretty safe to say he lacks the people skills needed to be a one-on-one therapist. There's no question he's more fit for a lab environment, observing subjects through one-way glass. Though I've told him many times, if this doesn't work out, he should try for the NBA."

Leigh couldn't help but laugh. One of Evan's most striking features was his excessive height. She guessed he had to be at least 6'6". Still, she couldn't help but chuckle when she pictured the lanky, thick-lensed glasses wearing Evan sprinting up a basketball court.

"Anyway," Dr. Joyce continued, "I would understand if you were uncomfortable with that scenario. I want to remind you, however, that Evan has a direct line to me. If a situation were to occur that he felt he couldn't handle, I would only be a phone call away."

Leigh considered this too. Jokes aside, Evan was a nice guy, and certainly knew what he was doing. His thesis was on the treatment of PTSD, focusing on cases of domestic trauma. Maybe she could deal with some awkward silence if it meant the chance to overcome a crippling fear. Who knows? Maybe Evan was a far different person out of the office. Perhaps he was nervous around Dr. Joyce, afraid to "let his hair down" in fear it might make him look unprofessional. Maybe...

An idea came to her.

"What about C.?"

Dr. Joyce put down her pen and interlocked her fingers. Her elbows rested on the arms of her chair. "As in Cecelia?"

"Yes," Leigh answered. "My roommate. What if she came along?"

"Well," Dr. Joyce said, "No offense to Ms. Little, but I'm not sure she would be the best choice. Don't get me wrong, I like her very much. I mean, it was I who suggested you two room in the first place. But she's not a trained professional like Evan. Again, he would be my first choice in lieu of myself."

"No, you misunderstand me. I meant what if she came along with the two of us. Myself, C., and Evan."

"Oh." Dr. Joyce's voice raised in surprise. "That's an interesting idea. And I think I like it. Yes, I'm sure I do. A trained professional that you could rely on, and a close friend for emotional support. I have no doubt C. would help keep your spirits up."

To this Leigh was in full agreement. Though once plagued with severe depression, Cecelia "C." Little was even further down the road to recovery than Leigh considered herself to be. Sure, her affinity for corsets and tall leather boots might've suggested a "goth chick," but C. wielded a razor sharp sense of humor that always kept Leigh in stitches.

Leigh looked down at her hands to find she was wringing them like a soaked dishrag. She released them, her palms white from the pressure. Taking a deep breath, she looked her therapist in the eyes.

"I still don't know if this is a good idea, Dr. Joyce." She released her breath. "But I do know I trust you. So...okay. I'm going to do it."

She closed her eyes.

"I'm going to go back to Embry."

When she opened them, she saw that Dr. Joyce was smiling.

CHAPTER TWO

Had Jake Spire's phone not rung during the commercial break, he probably wouldn't have bothered to pick it up. He hated to miss a second of *American Dead*, having been addicted to the television show since its first episode. But the phone had rung during one of those annoying car insurance ads, so he figured "What the hell?" He was confident he could say "goodbye" before the zombie action began again.

As he put his beer down on the end table and lifted himself from the couch, he figured it was probably just another harassing telemarketer. Who else would call him at this time of night? Well, Eddie was a strong possibility too. He always seemed to call at the worst times, always wanting another of the never-ending favors he insisted Jake owed him. Jake would've told him to get lost months ago if it weren't for the fact that Eddie was right. Jake owed him big time.

But which favor was he calling in tonight? The job he landed Jake at the campground? The "prescription" to Demerol he'd procured for when Old Milwaukee wasn't enough? Or maybe the fake I.D. and birth certificate to help him lie low for the rest of his life? At the end of the day, Jake Spire, or rather, "Walter Parker," owed an awful lot to the wheelings and dealings of Eddie Lee.

Jake made it to the corner of his kitchen counter where the phone continued to ring. Kitchen, of course, being a misnomer—technically speaking, the kitchen, dining room, and living room were all one space. Trailers were often like that. He grabbed the receiver and threw the TV another glance. Another commercial, this one advertising a new soft drink, lit up the screen. It wouldn't be long though before Rich Gould, hero of *American Dead*, continued his endless battle against the undead. Jake would have to make this quick.

He whipped up the receiver to his ear. "What?" he said, expecting to hear Eddie's voice.

"Uncle Jake?"

Until this very moment, Jake Spire had always assumed the phrase, "heart skipped a beat," was just that—a clever little phrase to describe surprise. As it turned out, he had been wrong.

"...Mary?" he said.

The voice on the other end was quiet and soft. "Yeah, Uncle Jake. It's me."

Outside his trailer, parked in the rear of the Tall Pines Campground, a gust of wind whistled between the trunks of the surrounding trees. Inside his trailer, a commercial for body spray blared from the TV. But Jake Spire could hear none of this. The world had gone utterly silent, all but the voice on the other end of the phone.

"How are you?" the voice asked.

At first, Jake could not respond. It was such a simple question but the answer was anything but. By the looks of his cluttered trailer, or the unkempt beard continually growing from his cheeks and chin, or the near empty orange plastic bottle of Demerol that lay hidden behind his bathroom mirror, one could summarize Jake's life with two words: not good.

But that is not what Jake said after several seconds of "Uhs" and "Ums" and throat clearing.

"Fine," was what he said. "I'm fine. How are you, Mary?"

Stupid. What a stupid asshole I am.

Jake had to agree with his inner voice. What kind of question was that to ask the daughter of his deceased mentor and friend? He hadn't even had the guts to attend Phil's funeral. What he should be saying is, *I'm sorry, Mary. I'm sorry for the part I played in your father's death. I'm sorry I couldn't face you and tell you the truth, that you're dad went off the deep end and helped kill a lot of innocent hikers and campers. But he was a good man, Mary. In his heart, he really believed he was helping the greater good. And if I hadn't gotten in the middle of things, maybe he'd still be alive.*

"Well," Mary said, inhaling deeply. "Let's just say I'm less than fine. I didn't know who else to call so I thought I'd cash in on the offer you left me."

Though more than a year had passed, Jake knew exactly what she was referring to. On his way out of Embry for the last time, Jake had stopped at a blue metal mailbox and dropped in a single postcard. On the front was an aerial shot of Embry, taken from a high vantage point in the surrounding hills. On the back was a short, concise message:

Mary,

If you ever feel the need, give me a call. I loved your father very much and never got the chance to repay him for all that he did for me. I will send you my contact info from wherever I end up. All I ask is that we keep this between us.

Uncle Jake

Jake would've been lying if he said he wasn't scared to death the moment he let his fingers release the postcard into the slot. But it seemed Mary Carson had honored Jake's request as no one had bothered Jake since he made a new home deep in the Adirondack Mountains of upstate New York. His address and phone number were both listed under the Michael Keene alias, so Mary was the only person on earth who knew where Jacob Spire was hiding from the world. Eddie Lee of course knew who Jake really was, but Eddie was of no concern. He had more reason to hide than even Jake did.

"What's wrong?" Jake said. His voice sounded so hoarse to his own ears. A window above the kitchen sink reflected his own face back at him. God, when had he grown old? There hadn't been so much gray in his facial year last year.

"Everything," was Mary's response, and Jake felt that about summed it up. All he had to wake up to his new home of Jade Lake, NY was a beat-to-hell trailer, a dead-end job working maintenance for a cheap campground, and an addiction to pain pills. Mary's score consisted of a father had taken his own life, and...

"My mother," Mary said. "It's my mother. I have to get away from her."

Jake brought his fingers to the bridge of his nose and squeezed. The beginnings of a monster headache were forming like acupuncture needles working their way into his skin. He knew he should side with Mrs. Carson. For God's sake, she had a lost a husband. But the honest truth of the matter was that Jake had never cared for Tricia. It wasn't that she was a "bible thumper" as his own dad would've called her. As far as Jake was concerned, you could worship the devil for all he cared, as long as you kept it to yourself. Problem with Tricia Carson was that she never did. Her favorite hobbies, as far as Jake could tell, was baking, gardening, and reminding you as often as she could that you were going to hell.

"Look, sweetie." Jake squeezed his eyes shut, willing the headache to go away. As usual, he would've had more luck wishing for a million dollars to show up on his doorstep. Demerol Man was the only one that could save the day. "I understand that you and your mom have differences. But you have to remember that she's scared and needs you more than ever."

Jake steeled himself and braced for the teenage outburst that was sure to come. But just as he was about to take his first step towards the bathroom to retrieve yet another miracle pill, he realized what he was actually hearing on the other end.

Mary was crying. And not the melodramatic sobs that only angst-filled, energetic youth can muster, but quiet, mournful weeping. The kind you would expect from an old widow after cancer defeats her marriage. Or a divorced father losing custody of his children. This was what the absence of hope sounded like. Jake knew this all too well. He had made this sound himself, more than once.

"Mary," he said. His headache was growing but for once the pain could wait. "Talk to me, honey."

"She doesn't love me!"

Jake winced as Mary yelled into the phone but he doubted the girl heard.

"How do you know that?"

"Because she told me."

Christ.

The words stabbed Jake's chest like a lawn dart. Heartbreaking loss or not, there was no excuse for saying that to your child. Ever. Jake was fully aware that, of all people, he was in no position to pass judgment on anyone. But some things were just sacred, and that included the unconditional love a parent was supposed to have for their offspring. Even the mothers of serial killers stood behind their psychotic sons.

"If that's true," Jake said, trying to keep his voice as steady as possible, "then I know she didn't mean it."

Mary sniffed on other end. "Yes she did."

"We all say things we don't mean when we're angry, kiddo." Jake marched to the bathroom as he spoke. His headache could be ignored any longer. "Were you two fighting when she said this?"

"Yeah."

"Can I ask what about?"

Jake reached the bathroom and flicked on the light. In his reflection of the bathroom mirror, Jake saw that he was shaking his head. He couldn't help but smile at the absurdity of the current role that had suddenly been placed upon him. How in the world had he ended up playing the part of therapist?

Mary must really be desperate.

"I told her..."

Mary hesitated, obviously unsure whether or not to finish her sentence. Instead of prodding her, Jake let her think as he swung the mirror door open and saw the glorious orange bottle of pills. He felt like Indiana Jones discovering a golden idol.

"I told her I was gay."

The pill had been halfway down Jake's throat when she said it. His throat constricted in shock, his airways instantly seizing on him. Fortunately, the first strong gag brought the pill up and out of his mouth. Unfortunately, he couldn't stop his coughing in time to prevent the pill from falling down the drain.

Shit.

"Jake? Are you okay?"

Jake twisted the knob for the cold water and brought his lips to the torrent that came pouring out. After a few sips, his throat spasms settled, and he was able to say, "Sorry about that. I choked on a...popcorn kernel."

Mary chuckled. Though the sound was soaked with sarcasm, it was the closest thing to an amused noise she'd made the entire conversation. "Yeah, right," she said.

"Okay," he said after swallowing one more mouthful of water, "so I take it she didn't take the news very well."

"She called me a sinner. She said I was going to hell unless I repented."

For a brief moment, Jake reconsider what he was about to say, but then decided that honesty good or bad, was the only thing he could offer to this upset girl.

"I really don't mean any offense, but I can't say I'm surprised."

Again came that sarcastic laugh. "Of course not. It's exactly what I expected her to say. But that wasn't the worst of it."

Gritting his teeth, Jake asked, "And what was that?"

There was a pause to allow a deep breath, and then Mary said, "She said my father would've been ashamed."

"That bitch."

Jake stared at his own wide-eyed expression in the mirror. Had he really just said that out loud?

Uh oh.

But to Jake's utmost relief, he heard Mary laughing on the other end. And this time, the laughter came without a trace of irony.

"Couldn't have said it any better myself. But all jokes aside, I'm really losing my mind here. And on top of that, I have to get back to school. Classes begin again after this weekend."

Jake said nothing back. He didn't like the sound of where this was going. He bit at a cuticle on the corner of his thumbnail, silently debating what he should say next.

"Jake?"

"Yeah, sorry, I'm here. So I take it your mom doesn't want to give you a ride back."

"You got that right. She blames college for my *condition.* She thinks I should drop out and start going to church again. She even suggested one of those camps where they try to *fix* you. Pardon my French, but fuck that."

Now it was Jake's turn to laugh. "What about a bus? I can send you some money for a ticket if you need it."

Jake could picture Mary shaking her head as she answered, her dirty blonde hair whipping back and forth. "Thanks for the thought, but the closest bus station is in Scoutsville, so I'd still need a ride to there."

Jake didn't mean to sigh but he did anyway. "I suppose you're right about that."

"And that brings me to why I called."

The moment Jake was dreading had finally arrived. He shook another Demerol into his palm, threw it back, got a mouthful of water from the sink, and swallowed hard. There. That was one going nowhere but his bloodstream.

"I don't know, kid," he said. "I'm not crazy about the idea of going back to Embry."

That's one way to put it.

What he should've said is that it was full out dangerous for him to return. After he had completed what he had to do at St. Andrew's Hospital, Jake hadn't gone to the police station liked he had been asked. He didn't even return to his apartment and wait for them to call. After making sure the girl...

Leigh...

...was okay, Jake had got into his truck and simply drove away. He had no idea where he was going at the time or how far he would aimlessly drive. All he knew was that he was dodging countless interviews, testimonies, and court appearances. He had no illusions of getting away with the getaway. He knew he would have to return sooner or later the moment an authority figure summoned him back.

Only that moment never came. He never did meet another officer, or detective, or Federal Agent. Instead he had met Eddie Lee, a slimeball if there ever was one, but a slimeball who knew how to make people disappear. Eddie had done the magic trick himself years ago, after ratting on a very dangerous man in New York City. These were the secrets runaways only shared with each other, at the corner tables of dimly lit dive bars.

To return to Embry now, Jake would risk exposing himself. He wasn't sure what the penalty was for his little vanishing act, but he was sure he didn't want to find out.

"Besides," Jake added, "I'm positive that your mom doesn't want to see me. I'd only end up making things worse for you."

"But you wouldn't have to see her. I left after our fight. I'm staying at the Little Northern Inn. Do you know it?"

Jake scoffed. He had been away more a year, but he had still lived in Embry for almost ten. "Course I do. Embry's not a big place."

"You could pick me up there. My mom would never know. As far as she's concerned, I'm already back at school. Not that she cares."

Jake's head continued to pound and the ache was moving down into his shoulders. Did the pills always take this long to take effect?

"Even so, kiddo, that's not the whole issue."

There was series of noises that sounded like Mary was swallowing over and over. No doubt an effort not to cry again. Finally she said, "I understand, Uncle Jake. It wasn't fair of me to just spring this on you. I'm sure you're really busy."

"Yeah, well..."

Jake trailed off as he let his gaze wander around the trailer. Yeah, he was really busy, all right. November was such a booming time for campgrounds. Tomorrow would be spent wandering around the grounds, looking for things to do. If he was lucky, he might find a walkway that needed shoveling or a heater that needed repair. Then at quitting time, he'd head to the Old Oak Tavern until Eddie inevitably showed up to annoy him. The night would end with him going home to pass out in front of the TV, after he'd medicated himself for the third or fourth time.

What a life.

"I guess I'll let you go now. Thanks for listening me run my mouth. I really got to learn to shut it one of these days. Stupid thing keeps getting me in trouble."

Jake snapped to, blinking his eyes several times in rapid succession.

No.

That was the last thing Mary needed to do. The kid was everything Jake was not: brave, honest, and good. While Jake had tried to run from his fears, Mary had faced them head on. She must have been terrified to come out, especially after everything that had happened to her family. But she had done it anyway. And now she was paying the price.

Meanwhile, Jake drank his life away in a drug-filled haze. Still hiding, still avoiding the truth. He even made a habit of evading the campground manager, afraid he would tell Jake to go clean the public restrooms. Other than that, there was very little reality Jake had to face on a day-to-day basis. When you lived under a rock, the real world seemed to pass you by without a second thought.

Jake's vision panned over the trailer. Yeah, this was definitely the under side of a rock. He could feel its weight crushing down on him everyday. It was why he took the pills.

"Now hold on," Jake said, "I didn't say I wouldn't do it."

There was a pause.

"You mean you will?"

"I guess I could—"

"You'll come get me?"

Christ.

"Yeah, sweetie. I'll come get you. I'll come back to Embry."

Between the laughter and tears, Jake heard Mary say "thank you" about ten times. After some heavy sniffing, she asked, "You're sure this is okay? You don't have to do this, Uncle Jake."

Jake closed his eyes.

Yes I do, Mary. I owe it to your father. That's just how it goes when someone you love kills himself in front of you. Their burden doesn't die with them. It just changes hands.

"It'll be fine," he said. "But you be ready to go when I get there. This is going to be an in-and-out operation."

"Sounds good to me," Mary replied.

After a few more thank you's and even an "I love you," Mary said goodbye and Jake hung up the phone. *American Dead* had come back from commercial break but Jake didn't care anymore. In fact, the volume of the TV seemed much too loud. The noise hurt his ears, but the ache didn't compare to the painful thought that repeated itself over and over like a knife stabbing his brain.

I'm going back to Embry.

Jake turned and walked back to the bathroom, the phone falling from his hand. He needed another pill. Just one more.

Or maybe two.

CHAPTER THREE

They were getting close. Leigh hoped no one would notice when they passed the green roadside sign that read, "EMBRY 20," but the wish went unfulfilled when Evan asked, "You want me to take over, Leigh?"

Despite Evan's pleas to let C. and himself handle all the driving, Leigh insisted she contribute her fair share. Though Evan had fought her on this idea, she eventually won by reminding him that the purpose of this entire excursion was to reclaim control of her own life. Driving would help her feel like she was taking action, and not just being dragged along as a passenger.

He had agreed, though not before pointing out the painful obviousness of the metaphor.

"You want to take the wheel," he said. "Okay, I get it. I would just hoped that years and years of schooling and endless student loan bills would've added up to a little more than the slogans of motivational posters."

At this C. had laughed. "All those hours in therapy and I could've just bought that poster of the cat in the tree that says, 'Hang in there, baby.'"

To Leigh's surprise, Evan and C. had gotten along very well. While Leigh had trouble breaking through Evan's wall of timidity, C. didn't seem to notice it at all. The two had struck up a conversation the moment they had pulled away from the C. and Leigh's apartment, and they hadn't stopped chatting since. It had all begun when Evan noticed C.'s necklace.

"That's interesting," he had said as he pointed to the object that hung from the base of C.'s throat. *Interesting* was about the most polite way one could put it. A razor blade dangled from the silver chain.

Leigh had barely listened to C.'s response, having heard the explanation many times before. C. had once been, what is called in modern slang, a "cutter." Plagued with a numbing depression in her teen years, C. had found solace in the blade. The faint scars on her arms and legs were the result of self-inflicted wounds. Too shallow to cause any serious damage, but just deep enough to awake her senses.

With the help of Dr. Mallory Joyce, C. had allowed herself to feel again, and no longer relied on physical pain to remind herself of her humanity. On Dr. Joyce's suggestion, C.'s final step was wearing the object no longer controlled her.

"Dr. Joyce told me that if I wanted to prove to myself that I was the one in control, that I should try wearing this. If I can have a razor blade this close to my own skin had still not feel the urge to use it, than I know I'm no longer the person I once was."

Evan had nodded this explanation. "Dr. Joyce is a firm believer in exposure therapy and I can see why. If we don't normalize the things we fear, they'll always have an affect on us. A smoker would always be one of Pavlov's dogs whenever someone whipped out a pack of cigarettes."

"Exactly," C. said. She lifted the blade hanging at her chest. "But now I see this as just a piece of metal. Nothing more, nothing less."

The conversation had progressed to other topics, everything from music tastes, to celebrity gossip, and classic road trip games including, "I Spy," and "Twenty Questions." At the moment, C. was inquiring about Evan's unexpected hobby: pugilism.

"Don't take offense," C. said from the backseat. "But I just wouldn't have pictured you as a boxer."

In the passenger seat, Evan laughed. "No offense taken. I'm sure when most people imagine a boxer, they're more likely to picture someone like Muhammad Ali than a medical school bookworm. The thing is, being as tall and lanky as I am, I have quite an advantage over a lot of opponents. One of the first things I learned when I was just starting out was never to underestimate a fighter's reach."

"So do compete professionally or...?"

"I wouldn't call it professional by any means, but I've had a few matches at some local festivals."

At this, Leigh couldn't help but join in.

"Festivals? Don't you mean tournaments or...?"

"SherlockFest," Evan said. "It's an annual festival near Hartford that celebrates the greatest detective of all time. One of the events is bare-knuckle boxing."

C. leaned forward between the two front seats. "Bare-knuckle? They allow that?"

Evan shook his head. "Well, we wear gloves so it's not technically bare-knuckle, but we fight in the original fisticuffs style. I've participated there and at FullSteam in Rhode Island. That's a steampunk convention, before you ask."

In the rearview mirror, Leigh saw C. roll her eyes when she said, "Naturally."

Evan apparently picked up the sarcasm in her voice and turned around to face her. "I think you'd like it, C. It's a great place to pick up a new corset."

Like a typical straight-A student, Evan possessed a good memory. Though C. currently wore a black t-shirt portraying the 80s new-wave band, The Cure, fashion preferences had been one of the many topics discussed on the trip.

C. gave Evan a wink and said, "What about watching a tall drink of water enter the ring?"

Leigh raised an eyebrow.

Was she flirting with him?

She swore she could feel the heat radiating from Evan's face as he blushed. Turning back around he muttered, "I don't know about that."

But C. persisted. "Don't tell me you've hung up the gloves. What I promised to buy my ticket to next year's event the moment we get home. Would that get you out of retirement?"

Though Evan faced his window, Leigh could see spot the edge of his smile when she threw at a glance at him. "I suppose there'd be plenty of time to train before the event."

"So what do you say?"

Up ahead on the left, Leigh could see an approaching gas station come into view. It looked to be a small, independent store, with old-fashioned pumps and a charming water wheel connected to the side of the building.

Before Evan could answer C.'s question, Leigh flicked on her turning signal.

"You're pulling over?" Evan asked.

"Just for a minute," Leigh said. "We could use some gas and I'm of kind of thirsty too."

"I could use a drink," C. added. "Something to eat too."

Leigh pulled up alongside one of the two pumps and shut off the engine. She turned to look through Evan's window and saw a sign above the store's door that read, "Abel's & Mabel's General Store."

"Cute," C. said, opening her door.

The trio got out and stretched their arms and backs in unison. A chilly wind blew across the back of Leigh's neck, making her shiver. Thankfully, the driving conditions hadn't been bad, despite a snowstorm that had supposedly blown threw the area a few nights before. They had encountered only a light dusting in the last hour, but nothing to make the roads dangerously slick. Still, the low temperature had surpassed brisk, prompting Leigh to zip up her dark green fleece.

"Brr," Leigh said. "Might have to make that drink a hot coffee."

Evan walked around the rear of the car and opened the metal flap that covered the gas tank. "Why don't you to two go inside?" he said. "I think it's my turn to gas up." He walked over to Leigh and handed her a couple of twenties. "Tell the cashier to put forty on pump 2. I'll get the change when I come inside and buy something to eat."

"You got it," Leigh said, accepting the cash. "Thanks, Evan."

"See you inside," C. said, waving to the man as she and Leigh walked away.

When Leigh was sure they were out of earshot, she turned to C. and said, "You and Evan are sure getting along."

C. grinned, mischief lighting her eyes. "What can I say? I've always had a thing for tall guys."

They reached the door and Leigh held it open her friend. "I'm sure Dr. Joyce would have an explanation for that."

"Well, she'd be wrong. My father is almost as short as I am."

They both laughed as they entered the store. As it turned out, the inside of Abel & Mabel's was as rustically charming as its exterior. Old rifles and taxidermy littered the walls. A pickle barrel rested next to the deli counter in the rear. To the girls' left, two rocking chairs sat next to a blazing wood furnace, a half-played game of checkers between them. The store even displayed several signs with quaint phrases like, "I'd rather be fishing," and "Don't feed the locals."

The latter made Leigh's chest tighten at once.

You don't need to feed them. They're already full.

They already ate my friends.

"Leigh?"

Leigh flinched at the sound of her name. C. was staring at her with worried eyes.

"God, I'm a really shitty friend, aren't I? You're doing one of the bravest things I've ever seen, and I'm over here trying to get a date." She frowned. "I'm sorry. I don't know what the hell I was thinking."

Leigh couldn't shake her head fast enough. "No, no, no.

That's not it at all. I'm glad you're having a good time. It's the whole reason I wanted you to come, to lighten things up. The last thing I want you or Evan to do is treat me with kid gloves."

"Still," C. said, "I'm here for you. And not to shift blame or anything, but Evan should know better too. He's the professional here, after all."

Leigh smiled. "I think we should give him a break. I'm actually happy to see him coming out of his shell. He may benefit from this trip more than I will."

C. put her hands on her hips. "And do I get anything from being here?"

Putting on the most serious face she could, Leigh pointed past C.'s shoulder and said, "If not for this trip, you wouldn't have met him."

C. spun around and instantly shrieked. Her face couldn't have been more than a centimeter from the nose of a stuffed otter bearing its two front teeth.

"God damnit," C. said through her laughter. "Okay, you got me."

The two continued to chuckle as they walked to the front counter and gave their gas money to an elderly lady with snow white hair and a warm smile. The one and only Mabel, perhaps? The transaction completed, the two friends went to the extensive drink coolers that lined the right wall of the store. Though she had previously been leaning towards a hot beverage, an iced green tea on the top row caught her eye. Leigh was just reaching for its clear plastic bottle when she heard a familiar voice shout from the other side of the store.

"Hey, you guys!"

They looked to see Evan standing in front of a machine that rotated hotdogs under a pair of heat lamps. Apparently, he had finished fueling the car and had already collected his change. He pointed to the hot links. "Either of you want one of these?"

C. leaned close to Leigh and said, "I guess he doesn't realize you're a vegetarian."

Leigh smirked. "Even if I wasn't, I'm not sure those things qualify as meat."

"Hey." C. nudged her with an elbow. "I like those things."

"Then be my guest."

"Thanks," C. said, walking away. "I'll keep an eye out for a bag of radishes."

"Bitch."

The two exchanged equally beaming smiles before C. joined Evan at the hotdogs. Now standing alone, Leigh began scanning the racks of snacks. Just because she had sworn off meat, that didn't mean she couldn't enjoy being bad once in awhile. Surely Abel & Mabel's had to offer a nice, salty bag of potato chips.

To her delight, Leigh found this to be true as several varieties were scattered among the shelves. She picked up one labeled, "Buffalo Mac N' Cheese," and flipped it over to read the description on the back. She was trying to decide whether she should ignore the list of multisyllabic chemicals listed in the ingredients when she heard the voice behind her.

"I'm a vegetarian too."

Based on that phrase alone, Leigh expected to see a college student with dreaded hair. Or an aged hippie wearing tie-dye and Birkenstock. Or a heath-nut cyclist in spandex. Anything but the man who faced her when she spun around.

He was on the taller side with dark skin and even darker hair that curtained his face in long, straight strands. Leigh assumed he was of Native American descent, based on these most superficial details. His race, however, was hardly a thought as she stared into his rather intense eyes. Her only concern was what he wore: a black leather jacket sporting the insignia of his gang.

The Forlorn Hope.

He must have noticed her shocked expression as he took a cautious step back.

"I'm sorry," he said, throwing his hands up. "I didn't mean to startle you. I shouldn't have even been eavesdropping."

"That's okay," Leigh said. Her voice came soft like she had something stuck in her throat. She cleared it and added, "My friend was the one yelling across the store, after all. Kind of hard to ignore."

"I just thought you could use some back up," the man said. "I heard your friend teasing you about your eating choices. I know what that's like. The guys I roll with rag on me nonstop."

Leigh forced a smile. "I bet. I mean, I wouldn't expect to find many vegetarians in a biker gang."

Her throat seized up as the last two words left her mouth.

"I mean, motorcycle club." She muttered.

The man laughed, bearing his teeth. One of them, an incisor, was gold, or at least a metal golden in color. "Gang, club, whatever," the man said. "We call ourselves all of the above. But our official name is The Forlorn Hope." He pointed to the badge above his left breast pocket. It looked like a combination of a smiling skull and a jagged snowflake.

Leigh swallowed a bit harder than she had intended. "Is that in reference to the Donner Party?"

The man's smile grew larger. "Very good! Some of our own members don't even know where get our name. But I suppose bikers never claimed to be the sharpest tools in the shed."

Leigh nodded but she couldn't take her eyes on that smiling skull.

Things that aren't sharp can still be dangerous.

"Anyway," the man said. "My name's John."

He extended his arm to offer a handshake. Leigh accepted it, and with her other hand, she pointed the name sewn into the leather jacket on the chest.

"Don't you mean, 'Big John?'" She asked.

He looked down and then gave her a sheepish grin. "Only to those under me."

"I guess Little John was already taken." She hoped the man would get the reference to Robin Hood. The last thing she wanted was for this man to think she was making fun of his size in anyway.

"True," John said. "And besides, Little John was second-in-command in the Merry Men. I outrank him."

"Always nice to be the boss," Leigh said, shrugging. To her it sounded like an idiotic thing to say but John seemed to think otherwise.

"Most of the time," he said. "Being in charge does help shut'em up when they start getting on my case about the vegetarianism."

"Huh," Leigh said. She was feeling more and more awkward by the second. Where was C. and Evan? Did they even realize they had left her alone with a member of the Hell's Angels?

No, she corrected herself, *the Forlorn Hope. Even worse.*

"Well then, maybe I should start my own motorcycle club."

"It worked for me," John said, offering another laugh. "Excuse me one moment."

Before Leigh could respond, John approached the drink cooler she had just come from and swung open the door. After a moment of staring at the top row, John furrowed his brow and sighed.

"Shoot," he said. "They're out of my favorite green tea."

Leigh looked down to the bottle she gripped in her hand.

This guy drinks green tea?

When she looked back up, John's intense eyes were meeting her gaze. Still smiling, he pointed at her drink.

"Guess we have something else in common."

"Y-you can have it," Leigh stammered. She extended the bottle towards him but John put his hands up, palms out.

"No, no," he said. "You were faster on the draw than me and the early bird gets the worm. You enjoy that."

"You sure? I don't need it."

"I insist," he said. "I could use something stronger anyhow. I think there's a cup of coffee over there with my name on it."

"Well," Leigh said, retracting her hand. "Thanks. I was actually going to get one of those myself, but I should really cut down."

"Moderation is always a good idea. Just leave all bad habits up to me. I'm a professional."

Leigh lifted her iced tea. "This doesn't seem like the worst choice you could've made."

"That's cause I'm off the clock." He threw a quick glance at his wrist. Despite the absence of a watch he said, "Speaking of which, time for me to get back at it. Enjoy your tea." He leaned in as if to share a secret. In a low voice he said, "And don't let them give you any shit. Vegetarians unite!"

At first, Leigh didn't know what to make of the fist he brought up to chest level. For a moment that felt much longer than it actually was, Leigh just stared at his curled fingers in utter confusion. Then, clarity struck her like a hammer to the head.

Fist bump.

Leigh returned the gesture, feeling utterly unlike herself. She wasn't normally one to offer high fives, low fives, or any of their related variations. When Leigh's knuckles connected with John's, the man opened his fist and made an exploding sound with his mouth.

Blowing it up. Right.

Leigh did the same about a second later, like a dancer lagging behind the practiced choreography.

John smiled all the same and then went on his way.

Leigh paid for her drink, all the while scanning the store for her two companions. She didn't see them anywhere and assumed they must be waiting for her outside. As she rezipped her coat and made her way to the door, she considered the unexpected dialogue she had just encountered.

Though she wanted to deny it, Leigh couldn't help but feel awfully guilty about her initial reaction to John's presence. She liked to consider herself open-minded and tolerant, but she would have been lying if John's appearance hadn't intimidated the hell out of her. But the reality? John enjoyed green tea and avoided meat. In these ways, Leigh had more in common with a leader of a biker club than the two people waiting by her car.

You just never know, Leigh thought. *A tough looking biker could be a yoga enthusiast.*

She paused just outside the front door of the store. Cold wind blew across her face, but it wasn't the gust that chilled her insides. It was her next thought.

And sometimes an average college guy can be the related to backwoods cannibals.

"You ready?"

Leigh jumped, looking in the direction of the call. Evan and C. stood at the hood of their car. Even from where Leigh stood, she could hear the car's engine running. This meant it would already be nice and warm inside. Spurred by this thought, Leigh jogged to the car.

"Took you long enough," C. said, a sly smirk on her face.

"Sorry," Leigh said. "I was talking to..."

The three of them flinched in unison as a loud grumbling noise approached from behind. Like a rehearsed dance, they spun together to see John slowly riding by on his bike.

Over the rumbling of the engine he said, "Happy trails, guys."

Leigh gave him a smile and a wave. "Thanks, John. Nice chatting with you."

"You too, Leigh."

John revved his engine and merged back onto the road. In an instant, he was gone, having vanished the upcoming bend in the road.

As the echo of his bike faded away, Evan looked to Leigh and said, "Make a new friend?"

"Call him a truck stop acquaintance," she replied.

C., who still stared in the direction of where John had rode off, said, "Kind of scary looking, wasn't he? Did you see his jacket?"

Leigh started walking to the driver's side of the car. "You know you shouldn't judge a book by its cover. One look at you and I'd say your favorite band was My Chemical Romance."

"Screw you," C. said.

Ignoring her friend, Leigh held up a hand to Evan. "Keys?"

Evan shook his head. "Nah, why don't you take shotgun? I've got it from here."

"I really don't mind."

"Yeah, but it's almost my turn anyway and I just checked the weather on my phone. A good sized storm is coming in very soon. Trust me, I'm doing you a favor."

To this, Leigh had to agree. She had never enjoyed nor been very skilled at driving in snowy conditions. Another gust of wind stung the tip of her nose. "Okay," she said. "Let's just get in the car. It's freezing out here."

To this there were no objections. The three took their seats, buckled up, and Evan shifted into drive. Fueled up and drinks in hand, they were on their way again.

It wasn't until Leigh was almost done with her iced tea that the troubling thought raced through her mind. She was just thinking how much she had enjoyed the lightly sweetened beverage and how lucky she was that she had beaten John to the drink, when it hit her.

You too, Leigh was the last thing he had said.

But she hadn't told him her name.

CHAPTER FOUR

There were many words that might've described the lobby of the Little Northern Inn, but none would've been more accurate than *quaint*. Though Jake would've much preferred a grander meeting place, the town of Embry didn't offer anything more than a two-star hotel within its city limits. So instead of blending in among rushing bellhops, excited tourists, and a Maitre d giving orders, Jake stuck out like a sore thumb in the small, empty area.

He did, however, have two things going for him at the moment. One was his "disguise." Had he been one of America's Most Wanted, his new look probably wouldn't have rescued him from the clutches of authorities. An FBI agent would've surely seen through a pair of dark sunglasses, a semi-thick beard, and a Vermont Lake Monsters cap. But so long as he didn't run face-first into a police officer, Jake figured he would be okay. And a rookie deputy probably wouldn't recognize his face from the photo featured on TV news stations a year ago.

His other advantage was the elderly couple checking in at the front desk. In typical senior citizen fashion, they spoke slow, moved slow, and had many questions for the woman working behind the counter. This was good—it took all attention from the lone stranger pacing near the front door. The last thing Jake wanted was for any of the inn's staff to see him and ask, "May I help you, sir?" The more ghost-like Jake could be here, the better.

Still, Jake couldn't help but nervously rub his hands together. Time-consuming or not, the old folks would eventually run out of questions and make their way up to their room. And then the clerk would have no one to look at but him.

Come on, Mary. Get your ass down here.

Jake tried to relax by taking a few slow, deep breaths, but the act failed to make much of a difference. Instead, he tried to distract himself by taking in the details of the lobby. He couldn't remember the last time he'd stepped forth into the Little Northern Inn, but it was exactly as he had remembered it.

A warm, glowing fire cast shadows across the extra large, oval-shaped rug that covered most of the lobby floor. The fireplace itself was made of bluish-gray stone, and no doubt built many years ago by hand. The giant head of a moose was mounted above the mantel, and if not for the wooden plaque behind it, it would've looked like the animal died busting through the wall. Jake never had a taste for taxidermy. It only reminded him of death whenever he saw a stuffed animal posed in a mockery of life. Tourists, however, probably ate the stuff up.

Not that there were many of those, these days.

In fact, when Mary had told him where she was staying, Jake had been downright shocked that the Little Northern Inn was still in business. Through newspapers, TV, and especially the internet, Jake had kept up on Embry's dwindling tourism industry. As it turned out, most people didn't want to camp in a place once home to a flesh-eating fungus. Despite official statements from the EPA that the disease has been contained, and no matter how reminders the town provided that there were acres and acres of untouched woods to enjoy, there was just no denying one simple fact.

Embry was a dying town.

Of course, there was no surprise there, at least not to Jacob Spire. He had predicted this outcome the moment he passed the "Thanks for visiting Embry!" sign for the final time. Or rather, what he thought was to be the final time. Making a comeback tour was the last life event he would've ever expected.

Jake laughed silently to himself.

I guess that makes these two old fogies my opening act.

He looked to the front desk again. They were gone.

Uh oh.

His breath caught in his lungs. Should he turn away from the clerk? No, that would look suspicious. Head outside then? It was rather cold out, but concerns about the temperature didn't compare to the threat of being spotted. He had to do *something*. Any moment now the clerk would look over this way and...

"Wally?"

At first, Jake thought the woman at the desk had called him out. It was a ridiculous thought. There was no way she could ever know his alias. The voice hadn't even come from her direction. It had come from Jake's right, towards the staircase that led to the second floor. It had come from Mary.

The teenage girl walked toward him, a suitcase in each hand. As he watched her pace across the lobby, Jake just had to smile. He couldn't believe this was the same little girl who had visited her dad at the ranger station during lunch break. Her sandy blonde hair was no longer tied in childish pigtails, but pulled back like a professional adult. She wore a warm looking pea coat, its dark red color mostly concealing a white sweater dress underneath. Black leggings adorned her bottom half, ending with a pair of Uggs, the winter footwear choice of college girls everywhere.

College girl. Jake let the phrase repeat itself in his head. He still couldn't believe she had reached such an age. Then again, Jake was sure Mary was wondering who this old man was waiting for her in the lobby. These days, Jake knew he looked much older than thirty-something.

"Sorry I'm late," Mary said. Before Jake could reply, she was dropping her suitcases and wrapping her arms around him in a tight hug. "Thanks again for this."

Any frustration Jake may have felt at having to wait for her immediately dissipated in Mary's arms. It was the most genuine human contact he had felt in over a year, and the gratitude in her voice was nothing short of sincere. Best of all, Mary had remembered to avoid calling him Jake. Though he had previously called her from the road to inform her of his preferred handle, Jake had spent the rest of the day worrying she would forget or fall into habit. As it turned out, his worries were for not.

"Ready to go?" he asked.

"After you, Wally." She gave him a wink.

"Then let's do this."

As they walked out into the cold, Jake threw a final glance at the front desk. The woman there was on the phone, her back turned, facing a filing cabinet. It appeared she hadn't heard or seen a thing.

Perfect.

"Wow, it's really coming down."

Mary said this just as Jake was turning up his window wipers to their fastest setting. The heater, too, was cranked to the max, making the inside of Jake's 1987 AMC Eagle much toastier than the weather outside. Roaring winds blew giant flakes in all directions, covering the ground in a white sheet of snow that kept growing thicker. It was as if Embry had once been an intricate painting but now was being erased to a blank canvas again.

"Was it supposed to snow this hard?" Mary asked, wiping the moisture from her window.

Jake shook his head and gritted his teeth. "Not according

to the jackasses that work for the Weather Channel. They called for possible flurries, but the brunt of this storm was supposed to hit east of us. Maine was expected to get the worst."

"Then I can't imagine what it's like there." Mary turned from her window and looked at her driver. "Are you okay to keep going in this?"

Jake nodded. "Sure. This hunk of junk may not be my old Ford, but she's tougher than she looks. We'll be okay. Besides, we're heading west. I'm sure once we get a little further across the state it will start to clear up."

"I hope so," Mary muttered. "God, it's not even December and look it at out there."

"Well," Jake said. "That's Vermont for ya." He reached for the knob of his radio. "Let's see if the good people at the weather service have any updates for us."

They drove on in silence, listening to advertisements for a car dealership and an after school program for winter sports. All the while, Jake stewed in a mixture of nostalgia and regret. Ever since the subject came up, he couldn't shake the image of the dark green F150 he'd purchased last year. It had been such a shame to give up that truck, especially for the horrible trade he had to accept from none other than Eddie Lee. Eddie had certainly come up on top in that deal, but Jake just couldn't risk driving anything connected to his old life in Embry. He supposed he could've got some bogus plates, but that wasn't good enough for him. Forest ranger Jake Spire drove a Ford F150. Wally Parker, campground maintenance man, drove an Eagle wagon.

"Don't look so down," Eddie had said, his trademark smirk curving his lips. "She's a classic."

"A classic P.O.S.," had been Jake's reply. "Don't you have anything you can offer me that was built in the 21st century?"

But Jake just shook his head. "Trust me, you can't find American craftsmanship like this anymore. This car's a beast." His eyes had narrowed when he added, "And more importantly, her paperwork is all in order."

That last line sealed the deal.

So here Jake was: driving through a snowstorm in a car made the same year that *RoboCop* and Michael Jackson's *Bad* were released, secretly praying to anyone who may hear him that the Eagle would fly straight and get them out of town. At least he had sprung for snow tires a couple of weeks ago.

"God, they're so depressing, even in the winter."

Mary's voice brought Jake's attention back to the present. To his delighted surprise, he realized he had already driven them out of the village while his mind wandered. They were only about two miles from Crow's Crossing, the covered bridge that marked the official entry/exit to Embry.

"What's that?" Jake said, turning off the radio. The weather report had never aired, or if it had, Jake hadn't been paying enough attention to hear it.

Mary pointed out her window.

"The Ashes."

Jake shot a glance out Mary's window and saw that they were indeed passing the charred remains of blackened tree trunks and stumps. To think that Jake had once patrolled those woods every day, that he had known them as well has the average person knows the rooms of his own house. This forest, after all, had been his home. But not anymore.

These are not my beautiful woods.

And the days go by...

"You would think," Mary said, "that with all the leaves gone now, that the Ashes wouldn't stick out as much. But nope. You can still tell what they did here."

Jake mumbled a "yeah," in response, having nothing more to add to the comment. He could only imagine what the Ashes must look like in the middle of summer, when all the surrounding forestland was as green as Ireland in storybooks. Or worse yet, during the autumn. This stretch of woods would be a black stain against a backdrop of red, yellow, and orange. From a plane passing overhead, it must look like the earth has a big, black spot of cancer.

Like it has a disease.

Mary sank back into her seat. "I know it may sound dumb compared to how many people lost their lives, but it's still a tragedy that they had to destroy all those trees."

"Agreed," Jake said. "But you know they had to do it. It was the only way to make sure the town would be safe."

"No, you're right about that. But they killed far more than trees and bushes when they set that fire."

Jake raised an eyebrow. "What do you mean?"

"I mean Embry's done for. Hell, the Ashes are the first thing you see when you're driving in. They might as well put a sign up that says, "Better turn around. This place is fucked.""

"That's the unfortunate truth." Jake offered a half-hearted laugh. "But at least you're leaving, right?"

"Yeah."

Though Mary agreed, Jake could tell by her tone that a whole sea of doubt churned within herself. As if to confirm that suspicion, Mary said, "A part of me is going to miss this stupid town."

Jake kept his eyes trained on the road but he still could feel Mary's stare.

"Do you ever miss it?" she asked.

He squeezed the steering wheel and swallowed hard. "No."

It didn't take a jumping needle to know Jake was lying, but in an act of unbelievable mercy, Mary didn't push the subject any further.

Seeing an opportunity to change the subject, Jake cleared his throat and asked, "So, have you picked a major?"

It wasn't the smoothest transition in conversational history, but Mary went with it and answered, "Not officially, but I'm thinking about graphic design."

"I guess that shouldn't surprise me. You've always been pretty artistic, even when you were a little kid. Hell, I remember a picture you drew when you were only five years old of your dad and me in our ranger uniforms. I think I was petting a deer in it, like I was Snow White or something. Did you know your dad kept that picture on a tack board next to his desk all the way until..."

He stopped himself.

Christ, I was going to say "until he died." Nice, Jake. Real nice.

"Jake..."

He cut her off as he looked to her. "I'm sorry, Mary, I know. You don't have to say anything. I'm an idiot. I shouldn't be—"

"No, Jake, lookout!"

Jake swung his head back to the road as panic stabbed his chest. His foot slammed down on the brake, sending the Eagle into a diagonal skid. Immediately, recognizing his mistake, Jake let off, pumping the breaks and turning with the skid. Many practiced years of driving icy roads became evident as Jake straightened the car back out and brought it to a complete stop.

Accident averted, Jake could now only stare at the wreckage just a few feet in front of their own vehicle. A tractor trailer had apparently lost control and careened sideways into the covered bridge. It's massive body blocked what was left of the crushed entrance, which now resembled a caved in tunnel.

"Shit," Mary said, and while Jake agreed with the sentiment, he didn't feel the single word fully captured the reality of their situation.

Crow's Crossing, their way out of Embry, was gone.

CHAPTER FIVE

Though the snowfall had increased to an all out blizzard, Leigh seemed to be the only one who noticed. Evan piloted their vehicle as if driving on a perfectly sunny day, hardly slowing at all to compromise the heavy precipitation. More than once did Leigh consider asking him if the roads were getting slick, but she didn't want to interrupt the nonstop conversation between her two companions.

Since leaving the store, the attraction between Evan and C. had only seemed to grow. They had chatted about a variety of topics, but Leigh had noticed C. kept bringing the focus back to Evan's competitive fighting. Apparently, she found the hobby to be even more alluring than Leigh had assumed.

"So, wait," C. said, leaning forward from the backseat. "Is fisticuffs an effective style of fighting? Like, let's say I got into a fight on the street. Would it really be the best choice?"

Evan laughed. "Well, when it comes to street fighting, I'd recommend you use a tazer. That would solve most of your problems without having to choose a martial art."

C. playfully hit his shoulder. "Screw you! I wouldn't need a tazer. I'd just kick you in the balls."

Evan nodded. "That works too."

In any other circumstance, Leigh would've been laughing right along with the two of them. Even in her increasingly growing state of tension, she recognized the flirtatious banter between her fellow passengers was rather entertaining. But Embry was getting closer by the minute, and no conversation, no matter how funny, could distract her that from fact. Whenever the road curved around a blind turn, Leigh expected a "Welcome to" sign to appear on the shoulder.

Just like in my dreams.

"But really," Evan continued. "Though outdated, fisticufts is still actually pretty effective when it comes to defense." He shot a glance in the rearview mirror. "Try to mimic the pose of an old style boxer and you'll see."

C. considered this for a moment and then extended her arms away from her body. She raised her hands in to the level of her face and made them into fists. "Like this?"

Evan spared a glance in the rearview mirror and said, "Yes, exactly. Now check out the walls you've made with your arms. It would be pretty hard to get a punch through that, wouldn't it?"

C. examined her own arms as if they were foreign objects. "No, my arms are twigs. They'd snap in half if you punched them." They both shared a laugh and C. added, "But I get your point."

"Modern style is, of course, more effective in protecting yourself from body blows. but fisticufts still has its merits if used correctly."

"Then what's the right way to throw a punch?" C. asked, her arms still raised.

Evan continued with his lesson but Leigh had already tuned them out. She instead brought her attention to her side view mirror. Not that the reflection provided much of a view— the mirror was splotched with water from the falling flakes, and besides, all Leigh could see was white passing behind them. Had either of her companions bothered to look in her direction, they would've surely asked what she was looking at. The truth was nothing at all.

Lost in her thoughts, Leigh wondered if bringing C. on this trip was a good idea after all. Or Evan for that matter. Her intention of including both of them had been to prevent any awkward silences, but the plan was working far too well. She still insisted that she didn't need anyone to dote on her. After all, she wasn't was some porcelain doll that needed to be handled with extreme care or kept under shatterproof glass.

But this feeling she was having right now...it was all too familiar. This feeling of being the odd one out. She had been feeling this way on the day it all happened, when her life had taken a severe turn down a dark road with seemingly no end. She had been the fifth wheel that day, like an unwanted extra in a movie about two couples. That is, until Sam had gotten into their car. Suddenly the movie was all about her. She had met her match.

Only, the movie hadn't been a romantic comedy.

It had been...

A single headlight pierced the snowy haze in the side view mirror. At first, Leigh believed it belonged to a car missing one of its front lights. It wasn't until she heard the roar of the engine that she saw the vehicle's true form: a motorcycle.

"Whoa," Evan said, looking in the mirror on his side, "Not exactly bike weather. Bet that guy is wishing he'd checked the forecast."

C. craned her head around and looked out the rear window. "I don't know if it would've made a difference to this guy. Man, he's coming up fast."

Her friend's words couldn't have been more true. The bike was fast approaching, as if the snow didn't matter at all to its driver. Though the heavy precipitation muted the sound of their own car's engine, the noise of the motorcycle cut through the air and filled Leigh's ears with a loudening growl. It was if a hungry lion was closing in on an unfortunate gazelle that had wandered from the pack. It wasn't, however, the predatory sound of the Harley Davidson that made Leigh inhale with a sharp gasp—it was the sight of the man steering the bike.

Long black hair whipping behind him, the man from the store smiled as he gunned the engine and came even closer.

"Pass me already," Evan said, his vision focused in the rearview mirror. "Here, I'll slow down. Is that what you want?"

Panic squeezed Leigh's heart even tighter when she felt their car decrease in speed. A part of her wanted to scream at Evan to floor it, to ignore the blizzard and put the pedal to the metal.

But why?

It was this question that made her bite her tongue. There wasn't really any reason to fear the man coming up on their tail. Yes, he had said her first name when they had departed at the store, but was she one-hundred percent sure she hadn't told him? He had told her his name, after all. It was John. Big John, leader of the Forlorn Hope.

"Hey, Leigh," C. said. "Isn't that your friend?"

Before she could answer, Evan asked, "Why isn't he going around me?"

And before Leigh could venture a guess to that question, C. spoke again. "Maybe he doesn't pass in this weather."

"Then why is he driving like a bat-out-of-hell?"

The two continued to discuss the man tailgating behind them, but Leigh didn't hear their exact words. Her mind was too busy thinking about the name John's motorcycle club. Back at the store, she had been too distracted by John's sudden appearance to pay the name any close attention, minus the fact it was borrowed from the Donner Party incident. But now that she thought about it...

The Forlorn Hope. It was the name given to the pack of settlers that tried to snowshoe their way to salvation after the Donner Party became stranded. They got lost in the blizzard and they ran out of food. They began to die of starvation and exhaustion. And that was when the surviving members became...

The thought finished just as she saw John reach behind him with one hand and retrieve something off his back. Something he pointed directly at their car.

Cannibals.

An image suddenly flashed in front of her eyes. It was of her favorite character from the hit TV show, *American Dead.* Both she and C. never made plans on Sunday nights so they could be sure to never miss a new episode. With the object in his hand, John looked just like Darren, the brooding backwoods survivor who had yet to be killed off since season one. The object was Darren's signature weapon-of-choice.

A crossbow.

"Look out!"

Leigh yelled the words to no one in particular. She couldn't tell who John was aiming at, only that he had their vehicle in his sights. A second later, she got her answer. The left rear tire exploded.

"Shit!" Evan screamed as the car lurched to the right. C. shrieked as she went flying across the backseat, slamming into the window behind the driver's seat. The sudden momentum also yanked on Leigh, but her firm grip on the handle above her door kept her place.

The muscles in Evan's long forearms hardened like rocks as he squeezed the steering wheel. "Come on!" he yelled, trying to steer the car back onto the main road. But uneven tire pressure, combined with the slippery road, continued to pull them to the right. Leigh's eyes widened as the car edged towards the deep bank lining the highway. Without guardrails, it would be mere seconds before they careened headfirst into the ditch.

She squeezed her eyes shut and braced for impact.

"Evan! There!"

Leigh's eyes popped open to see C.'s hand right next to her face. Her friend was leaning forward and pointing to a dirt road just ahead.

Evan yelled, "Hang on!" as their tires went from the slick pavement of the highway to the dirt side road. Potholes sent violent shudders through the framework of their car, but they did nothing to stop Evan from speeding up. Their one remaining back tire sprayed snow and gravel behind them as they lurched up the ascending road.

The near crash averted, Leigh spared another glance in her side view mirror. John was turning onto the road as well, though with a much slower pace then they had managed. In his decreased speed, Leigh could see how the man had been able to drive so fast in the falling snow.

Thick, steel chains wrapped both tires of his bike, giving him advanced traction and control. The earlier analogy of a lion chasing a gazelle still applied, only now it was like a lion with cybornetic limbs pursuing a gazelle with a broken leg.

"Fucking psycho!" C. screamed.

"Just keep your heads down," Evan yelled. "And somebody call 911!"

C. frantically scrambled for her phone which had fallen underneath her seat. Leigh, however, remained in her hunkered position, already knowing what C. was about to discover.

"Oh no," C. said, as expected. "I don't have any service!" She tried anyway, bringing her phone to ear in an effort of total desperation. Her black eye shadow began to leave dark streaks on her cheeks as tears fell from her eyes. "Please," she said. "Work, you piece of shit, work!"

They jerked in their seats as the road took a sharp turn to the right. Despite the fact the heater was running on almost its lowest setting, sweat rolled off of Evan's brow.

"Don't worry," he said. "This road will lead somewhere. This guy can't follow us forever."

The car fishtailed, its back bumper hitting a tree stump that lined the narrow road. Fortunately, the small collision only served to straighten them out.

"He won't have to follow us forever," C. shouted, "If you don't keep us on the fucking road!"

"I'm trying!" Evan roared back.

Keeping her head low, Leigh turned in her seat to look

behind her. C. lay across the backseat, her arms shielding her head. Through the back window, Leigh could see John in pursuit, though he wasn't cranking back on the accelerator as he was before. She also saw that he had returned the crossbow to his back, its shoulder strap crossing his chest in a diagonal line. The sight brought a new thought to Leigh's mind.

He could catch us if he wanted to, but this isn't a chase.

A quiet moan passed through her lips.

He's herding us.

With his chains and superior vehicle, it would take only seconds for John to touch their back bumper. This wasn't a lion tracking a gazelle after all. John was a sheepdog. One with rabies and a taste for blood.

The road descended in a steep grade, causing the car's ABS system to rumble and grind as Evan pressed down on the brakes.

"Not so hard," Leigh said. "You'll send us into a skid."

Evan gave no verbal response but did let up with his foot. The antilock brakes ceased their grinding as the car gained speed. Leigh's heart rate increased to that which comes after a full on sprint. If a sharp turn lay ahead, Leigh doubted they would be able to make it all the way through.

From her almost fetal position, C. cried, "Why is this happening?"

Though the bottom of the hill was fast approaching, Evan turned his attention from the bumpy road to glance in Leigh's direction. With a surprising note of casualness, he asked, "Do you know?"

Leigh looked at him, completely dumbfounded. "What?" was all she could say in return.

"I mean does this have anything to do with..."

He paused to negotiate the slight turn that came at the end of the road and then added, "Your past?"

C. sprung up from the backseat. "You know that guy back there?" Her voice came with a combination of shock and anger.

"No!" Leigh yelled. "I have no idea who he is!"

"I shouldn't be here," C. said, shrinking back into the seat. "I shouldn't have come. Why did I say yes? Why?"

Are you kidding me?

For a brief moment, Leigh forgot all about her heart clenching fear, it now replaced with a sudden loathing for the girl in the backseat. How quickly her "friend" had forgotten how much it meant that she accompany Leigh on this difficult journey. All those nice words about how she felt Leigh was doing the "bravest thing she'd ever seen," had gone right out the window the moment her own safety was compromised.

What if it had been her on that ill-fated trip through the woods last year? Would she have risked her life to sneak into the cellar of the Cedar homestead to rescue Alex from their clutches?

To Leigh, there was no question about it.

She would've left her to die.

Leigh realized she was shaking her head as the road straightened out and Evan said, "What's he doing back there? I can't see him."

When C. made no move to lift her head from where it was buried in her hands, Leigh knew it was up to her to answer that question. She grabbed the dashboard with one hand to better brace herself to turn around.

And that's when she saw it.

Even with all the ensuing chaos, it would've been impossible to miss the vehicle's electric blue color. About twenty feet ahead on the left side of the road, a ATV sat parked at the base of a dead tree. The tree stood in a diagonal angle, no longer attached to the ground by its roots, but rather held up by the branches of a healthier neighbor.

"Do you see...?"

Her words fell short when another man peeked out from the other side of the suspended tree. While there was no time to take in the entirety of his features, Leigh did recognize three things.

The first was his leather jacket, almost identical to the one John was currently wearing as he relentlessly pursued them from behind. The second was the eye patch covering one of the man's eyes, immediately bringing to mind classic images of pirates. And the last was the long object that the man held with both hands, either an axe or a sledgehammer. Whichever it was, the man was swinging it at the base of the dead tree.

And the tree began to fall right in their path.

"Look out!"

Right before Evan swung the wheel to the right, Leigh realized it was the second time she'd yelled the words in less than five minutes.

The tree crashed into the ground, stretching across the entire road. Acting solely on reflex, Evan steered the car away, missing the massive trunk by mere inches. Unfortunately, the narrow width of the of road didn't allow for a such a drastic change in direction. Leigh had just enough time to close her eyes before the car slammed into a bank of ice and snow.

Her body lurched forward, her seatbelt biting into her chest against a force more powerful than she'd ever experienced before. A deafening crunch overtook her sense of hearing, drowning the grunt she released as the jolt rocked her entire being.

Leigh had never been hit by a train before, but she still felt it was a fair comparison.

Slowly opening her eyes, the world came back in a dull focus. Her vision spun slightly, as if she had just gotten off a dizzying ride at the state fair. She could tell, however, that the windshield had spider-webbed into a tangled series of cracks, quickly being covered by the falling snow.

She turned to Evan, her entire body aching. He rested his forehead in his palm as if suffering from a major headache. Leigh tried to turn to check on C., but her seatbelt had not released tight grip on her chest. It pinned her to her seat like a boa constrictor.

"Evan," she groaned. "Are you okay?"

He lifted his head from his hand to look at her. She saw his nose was bleeding, most likely an injury sustained from the airbag that had inflated upon impact.

"Yeah," he said, weakly. "I'm—"

He went silent and turned towards his window. Against the ringing in her ears, Leigh could hear what had suddenly grabbed his attention. The sound of not one, but two engines were coming closer.

Despite her nausea, Leigh shook her head.

I was wrong. John isn't a lion or a sheepdog. He's a wolf.

The two engines cut off simultaneously, filling the air with a immense silence. It then replaced with John's booming voice.

"Get out of the car, and don't even think about running. We got you surrounded on all sides."

And wolves...

She felt the heat of a single tear leaking from the corner of her eye.

Wolves always hunt in packs.

CHAPTER SIX

Think.

That was all Jake Spire asked of himself.

Think. Think. Think. There must be another way out of this town.

Jake had lived in Embry for many years, more than enough to know all possible exit strategies. But as he and Mary drove back the way had came, Jake's memory completely seized up. If was if his mind was a factory and one of the floor workers had punched the button to stop the line.

"Where are we going?" Mary asked, breaking Jake's intense concentration.

"I'm not sure yet." He reached to turn down the heat. It felt like it was a hundred degrees inside the car. "Wait, hold on."

Ceasing the constant heat wave blasting his face seemed to clear up his head immediately. He looked to Mary.

"Miller's Road. That takes you right out to the highway, right? We can take that."

Mary grimaced as she shook her head. "Afraid not. They closed Miller's Road last year. It goes straight through the Ashes."

"Damn," Jake muttered. "What, is it chained off?" A glimmer of hope sparkled in the back of his mind. Depending on the quality of the chain, they may be able to break their way in. Something so illegal would certainly ruin the low profile he'd so far succeeded at maintaining, but hopefully they would be long gone before anyone discovered the vandalism.

Unfortunately, Mary shook her head again. "Nope. Big ol' gate. They really don't want people going through there."

"Shit." Jake slapped the steering wheel. "Okay, that's out. What else?"

As he drove on, his grip on the wheel tightening, Jake felt like a human GPS. Street signs, road names, and town landmarks whipped through his brain at lightening speed as he searched his inner databases for a solution. Mary stayed quiet the whole time, seemingly aware that any utterance might break the man's concentration.

Her silence paid off when Jake snapped his fingers.

"Hey!" he said. Then squinting, he added, "No. Well, maybe. It's a longshot but it might work. Probably not. But maybe."

Mary, giving a half chuckle, finally asked, "What? What do you got?"

"I just remembered an old logging road on the other side of town. Embry shares it with Scoutsville and it connects the two towns. Scoutsville's in the wrong direction, but if we could make it there, we could then get backtrack to the highway."

Mary flashed a thumbs up. "Then let's do it."

"Well," Jake said, gritting his teeth. "I'm afraid it's not that easy. That old road is going to be pretty gnarly in this weather. Anything other than a truck or a jeep is going to have a hell of time getting through it."

Mary smacked the dashboard. "You don't think this beast can handle it?"

Jake shrugged. "We've got studded snows and four-wheel drive going for us, but I'd feel a lot better with some chains on our tires."

"Then let's get some."

Though Jake admired Mary's proactive attitude, he couldn't help but grit his teeth at her proposed course of action. It was bad enough that he had to enter the Little Northern Inn, but at least the hotel hadn't been one of his usual haunts while he was still a resident of Embry. But stopping to purchase snow chains? Those would only be sold at a few places in town, places where Jake had to frequently visit during his forest ranger days. One was a tractor supply store called Sanford Supply that Phil always sent Jake to pick up chains for their ranger service vehicles. The other was Embry Auto Works, the garage Jake preferred whenever his own truck needed a tune-up. Despite his new look, Jake was sure both Stu Sanford and Gus Kaufman, the owner of Auto Works, would recognize Jake with ease. Sure, there was a chance that neither proprietor would be at their respected establishments, but Jake couldn't take such a risk.

"Jake?"

The moment Jake turned to answer his passenger, the solution came to him as sudden as a slap to the face.

"Right," Jake said, accelerating just the slightest bit faster. "We'll get some chains. I'll do the paying." He let go of the wheel with one hand to point a finger at Mary. "And you do the talking."

"Me?" Mary let loose a quick laugh. "I don't know anything about snow chains. Or even tires for that matter."

"You won't need to. Sanford's has plenty of employees that are trained in just this sort of thing. And last I knew, Stu hires a lot of high school seniors and guys on college break to help out around the holidays. You can bet they'll be lining up to help the prettiest girl in Embry chain up her tires."

Mary slapped his shoulder. "Oh, please."

The two shared a quick laugh before Jake cleared his throat and lowered his voice so show Mary he meant business. "But seriously, we need to play this safe. I don't want anyone to recognize me and that's sure to happen if I take a step into Sanford's."

Mary nodded. "Sure. I'll go in. You can wait in the car."

"Not good enough," Jake said. "I wasn't kidding before.

Even if you tell them you've got it under control, I'm sure Stu will insist one of his guys helps you put the chains on. I might as well go in myself if someone's going to follow you back out to the car."

"Then what's the plan?"

As far as Jake could tell, there was only one answer to Mary's question. "I'm going to get out and wait for you somewhere. You'll drive to Sanford's, get the chains, and come pick me up."

Though Mary replied with an "Okay," her hesitation suggested she was anything but. Jake threw her a glance to see lines of worry wrinkling her forehead and the sides of her mouth.

"Don't worry," Jake said. "I know it's nasty out there right now, but I'll get us really close before you take the wheel. You'll only have to drive for a minute or two, I promise."

Mary seemed to relax at the mention of this new proposal. Her frown straightened and she said, "Sounds good. I'll be fine."

Jake gave her a smile. "No sweat. You'll be in and out." He brought his attention back to the road. "Now all we have to figure out is where I'm going to wait."

If need be, Jake was prepared to stand out in the snow if they couldn't find a discrete place for him to hold tight. Of course, he would much prefer a shelter of some kind, though not at the cost of anonymity. But did such a place exist between here and the supply store?

"What about the Little Northern?"

At first, Jake was so lost in his brainstorm that he didn't hear Mary's suggestion. But when it finally sank in, he still couldn't believe his ears.

"What?"

"The hotel. You could wait there."

Jake bit his tongue to contain the laugh he wanted to give in reply. "I don't think so, kid. Maybe you didn't notice, but the Little Northern Inn isn't exactly hoppin' right now. A stranger hanging around in the lobby would stick out like a sore thumb."

73

Mary shook her head. "I'm not suggesting you wait in the lobby. You can wait in the same room I stayed in last night."

"You..." Jake trailed off, utter confusion holding up his words. "You want to pay for your room again just so I can wait for a few minutes?"

"Nope."

Jake inhaled to ask her to clarify but stopped when he saw her going for something in her pocket. After a few seconds of digging, she revealed a credit card sized piece of plastic.

A room key.

"I was so excited to see you," Mary said, "that I forgot to check out. And since The Little Northern Inn's checkout time is noon, that means the room is mine for another hour."

Mary pointed to the radio. Jake looked to see the display read "11:04."

"Hmm," he muttered, considering Mary's idea. It felt a little strange to drive all the way back to the inn, but still, the total privacy of a hotel room was more than a little enticing.

"I don't know," he said. "I'm still not crazy about being seen by the front desk clerk."

Mary smiled from ear to ear. "You won't have to," she said. "When I checked in, the front desk told me all the room keys open a door in the back of the building. It's so that if you park in the rear lot, you don't have to carry your luggage all the way around to the front."

"Well then," Jake said, another laugh building his in chest, "you've thought of everything. How can I say no to such a solid plan?"

This time, Jake allowed the laugh to come, though now it was directed towards himself for doubting the young girl for a second. Mary had certainly inherited her father's wily intelligence. Just like Phil, it seemed she was perpetually two or three moves ahead of those around her. It was exactly this kind of tactical thinking that had made Phil such a good leader and cemented his position as head of their department.

Then again, it was also this type of thinking that had come

up with the idea to partner with the grisly Cedar family, to let them have an unfortunate camper or hunter once in awhile.

Or to make sure you never went a single morning without a cup of coffee in your hand, a little blood mixed in with the cream and sugar...

A sudden wave of nausea hit Jake with full force. It felt like his stomach was a hot tub with its jets turned to full blast. He gripped the steering wheel tight and swallowed, simultaneously willing away the phantom taste of Phil's coffee from his mouth. He figured the sick feeling would pass the moment he stopped dwelling on the awful memory.

But another sickly wave washed over him, this one even stronger than before. It made him gag, calling Mary's attention to his convulsing state.

"Jake?"

Before he could offer any sort of reply, the road ahead of him blurred out of focus. Than there were two roads, splitting apart from one another as his vision doubled. He felt the car start to drift to the right.

"Jake!"

The fear in Mary's cry instinctually brought his foot slamming to the brake. The car's rear began to slide to the left as the two passengers lurched forward against their seatbelts. Fortunately, it fish tail stopped before the back tires could cross over the double yellow line. Luckier still, there hadn't been any traffic coming up from behind.

Their car now completely stopped, Jake flung off his seatbelt and ripped open his door. He just barely got his head outside before vomiting a thick torrent of partially digested eggwich and ruby red grapefruit juice. The citrus of his morning's breakfast burned as it made its violent way up his throat.

Somehow, over his rather loud retching, he heard Mary continue to cry his name as she struggled to undo her belt. Jake managed to wave a hand up to signify "stop." He gagged twice more, spit a few times, and took his first full breath since getting sick.

"It's okay," he said. His voice came low and hoarse. "I just need my pills. There in the glove box in front of you."

This explanation was not just for Mary's benefit. Jake knew exactly what had brought on this spell, having had the displeasure of experiencing it many times before. This was demerol withdrawal, plain and simple. Normally his symptoms consisted only of severe headaches, but with all of today's excitement, he had gone much longer than usual without a fix.

A couple pills will fix me up. It'll take awhile for them to kick in, but then I'll be as right as rain. As fit as a fiddle. As...

"Uhm, Jake?"

When he turned to face Mary, the world did not keep up. The image of the girl spun as he stared at her holding an orange bottle.

"Is this it?" she asked.

"Yeah," he said, holding out his hand. "Give'em here."

"It's empty, Jake."

For a moment, the only sound was the wind whipping the branches of the trees that lined the road.

Then Jake said, "Shit." And then, "God damn it, son of a bitch, fuck." And then nothing more. He was puking again.

This time, Mary waited for his heaving to be over before she spoke again. "What should we do? Should I take you to the hospital?"

World spinning or not, Jake found the strength to throw both hands up and shout, "No!"

Mary jumped in her seat.

"Sorry," he said, noting the wetness of her wide eyes. "I didn't mean to shout. But no hospitals. No doctors."

He rested on the steering wheel as another powerful wave of vertigo washed over him. He felt water leaking out of the corners of his closed eyes. His nose, too, had begun to run.

Christ, how long has it been since I dosed? I guess I was so fixated on getting out of town, I didn't notice the signs.

From the darkness, Jake heard Mary ask, "Are you going to be okay?"

"Yeah," he said, after a moment. "But I'm going to need refill that bottle." He pointed to the glovebox. "There should be a white slip of paper in there, under my registration and proof insurance. For the love of god, please tell me it's there."

He eyes still closed, Jake heard Mary shuffling through the assorted documents. It couldn't have taken more than a few seconds, but it felt like an eternity. Finally, she said, "Is this it? Looks like a prescription."

Oh thank god.

"That's it. Just need to get it filled."

"We can do it right in town," Mary said. "At Casey's Rexall Drugs. It's right on Main St."

Jake chuckled. "I know where it is," he said. "I used to live here too, remember?" He opened his eyes and slowly brought his head from the steering wheel to see Mary biting her lip.

"Of course," she said. "Duh. Sorry, I'm just a little freaked out."

He forced a weak smile. "It's okay. Really, I'll be okay. I just got to make it to the pharmacy. So let's go."

But when Jake reached for the door, the world decided to drop out from under him. If he hadn't managed to grasp one hand around the steering wheel, he would've surely fallen to the slush covered road.

"Whoa, Jake," Mary said as she grabbed his shoulder and gently pulled him back in. "You're in no shape to drive. Come on, let's switch seats. I'm driving now."

There was no use in arguing. The girl was right.

Though it took no lack of effort, Jake managed to get around the car to the passenger side, using the hood of the car to steady himself as he went. He paused once when he felt he might vomit again, but the sensation quickly passed. After what felt like an epic journey, he slid back into the car and shut the door.

"First thing's first," Mary said, putting on her blinker to merge back onto the road. "We're dropping you off at the Little Northern."

"Mary—"

"Don't argue with me, Uncle Jake. I'm the captain now. You need to lie down. Besides, it may take awhile for the pharmacy to call in your prescription."

Jake nodded. This was most likely was going to be the case, as the doctor in which Eddie had set him up with didn't keep regular hours. Jake didn't doubt the doctor would confirm the refill, but they may have to wait for him to get back from "lunch." This was his preferred term for his midday trips to the local strip club.

With their course of action determined, Jake could do nothing more but sink into his seat and close his eyes. He knew he could ride this out until they got him what he needed. All he had to do was focus on his breathing and try to relax.

And whatever you do, don't think about the fact we're heading in the wrong direction. Back into the belly of the beast that is Embry, VT.

Sweat ran down both sides of Jake's face. He knew it would be too dangerous to ask Mary to drive any faster. But he wished to God she would.

CHAPTER SEVEN

Leigh tried to command her muscles to slacken but they didn't want to listen. With her entire body locked in a frozen state of tension, the seatbelt continued to squeeze against her chest. She took the deepest breath the belt would allow, closed her eyes, and let the air slowly escape through her nostrils. As Leigh had hoped, her shoulders dropped, her neck loosened, and the seatbelt finally went slack.

Not wasting a second, Leigh shot her hand down to the belt's release. It flung away, its metal buckle crashing against her cracked window, splintering it even more. The release couldn't have come any later. Leigh immediately tensed again at the voice booming outside.

"This is last time I'm going to say this before we come get you: Get out of the car. Now."

"All right," Evan croaked. Leigh looked to him as he added, "Don't shoot. We're getting out."

Evan's words resonated as Leigh twisted to check on C. Did they even know if they're assailants were armed? But then she remembered the crossbow. Even if that was the only arms they bore, it was bad enough. Besides, it was safe to assume that they were packing much more.

Pain stabbed Leigh's left side as she turned. She looked down to the area just above her waist expecting to find a jagged piece of glass sticking out of her like a knife. She was probably bleeding out and didn't even know it, shock having spared her the initial pain.

But no, her side looked fine. The pain was most likely the result from the biting seatbelt. She would no doubt have a long, dark bruise tomorrow morning.

If I live that long...

Trying to ignore that thought, Leigh brought her attention to her friend in the back. C. was looking the other way, out the rear window. Thanks to the piling snow, there wasn't much to see, though Leigh could make out three dark shapes through the white blanket covering the glass.

Apparently, C. could see them too. She spun back around, reached for her door handle, and began to frantically pull on the handle. A thin trickle of blood was running from C.'s hairline down the side of her face, but Leigh didn't think she noticed. C. was too busy trying to escape the car, but the door wouldn't budge.

"C.!" Leigh said, reaching a hand to her friend's shoulder. "Calm down. We're okay."

"No!" C. did not return Leigh's look as she shrieked, but kept her eyes trained out the back window. "They're coming! They're coming for us!"

"They're not going to hurt us," Leigh said. Even she was impressed at how natural the words left her mouth, considering she believed them to be a blatant lie. "They just want our stuff. That's all."

It was then that Leigh noticed the lock had been engaged on C.'s door. She kept this knowledge to herself, not wanting her desperate friend to go running off into a hail of bullets.

"C."

When Evan said her name, C. went both quiet and still. In other circumstances, Leigh may have been jealous at the way her friend ignored the advice of her closest friend but instantly followed the words of a near stranger.

"Listen to Leigh," Evan said. He stared in the rearview mirror as he spoke, but Leigh knew he was looking past C. at the approaching figures. "Just stay put and let me talk to them."

Before anyone could object, Evan brought his hand to his door handle. He pushed forward but nothing happened. Outside, a bank of snow was pushing back.

"All right," the voice from outside said. Though it was no longer just a voice. With her wits returning, Leigh identified the voice as John Woodenknife. "Here we come."

"Wait!" Evan's voice cracked as she shouted. "My door's jammed. Give me a second."

Wincing, he shoved his shoulder against the door, opening it halfway. In an instant, freezing air invaded the car. The jolt of cold hit Leigh like a splash of water to the face, washing away whatever daze still remained. Cold meant reality. Cold meant this wasn't a dream.

Evan got one of his legs out the door and reached both his hands out, palms open. "See?" he said. "I'm coming out, nice and slow."

When John replied, his voice sounded even closer. "Okay, but I said all of you. Out."

"Give them just a second." Evan said. He quickly added, "Please. They're working on it but they're a little shook up."

There was a pause. Then a scoff. Then, "I don't care if they're as shook up as Elvis. Get the fuck out of the car!"

The sound of footsteps crunching the snow quickly approached the passenger side of the car. From the backseat, C. let out a single whimper. It was all it took for Leigh's body to take control. An undeniable urge to protect her friend took over, and before she knew it, Her hand was darting for the door handle and pulling. Unlike Evan's door, hers swung open with ease and she followed on its tail, practically jumping out of the car.

The movement was much too fast. The world spun as if on a turntable, and a second, Leigh thought her feet would come out right from under her. But the sensation passed quickly, mostly due to the frigid air that now bombarded her from all sides.

Her bearings returned, Leigh saw that she was looking into the eyes of a stranger standing only a few feet away.

No. Not eyes. Eye.

He was dressed similar John Woodenknife, including a leather jacket with the Forlorn Hope logo sewn across the breast. However, one blaring difference caught Leigh's attention at once, and that was the black patch concealing the man's left eye. Leigh bit her lip to stifle a laugh that seemed to come from nowhere. Absolutely nothing was funny about their current situation, but how perfect was this new detail? Like buccaneers hijacking a cargo ship, these men had driven them off their course and were now at liberty to take what they wanted. All the man was missing was a peg leg and a parrot.

"What are you staring at?" the man said. Leigh immediately dropped her gaze. The man brushed away a lock of the straight black hair that curtained his face and took a step closer. "What, are you shy?" When Leigh failed to respond, the man added, "Well, that's okay. Perhaps your friend has better manners."

He made a move for the rear door and Leigh's body acted on its own once again. She sidestepped, blocking the man's approach. His single eye, the color of the gray sky above, looked at her with almost impressed surprise. From this close, Leigh noticed the name sewn onto his jacket.

UNO.

It seemed this man had embraced his ocular handicap, rather than resist the constant jarring that would be sure to come from his fellow bikers. He even had an oversized 1-ball sewn onto his right shoulder. The yellow pool ball practically glowed against the black leather.

"Well then," Uno said. "What do we have here?" He gestured with a shotgun gripped by both hands. Leigh had been so distracted by his clylopian facial feature she had failed to notice the weapon until now.

Mustering as much strength as she could, Leigh returned the man's one-eyed stare. "Leave her alone. I'll get her out of the car, okay?"

Uno waved a hand with no lack of flourish and said, "Be my guest, darlin'."

As Leigh turned to face the backseat door, her eyes darted in all directions, trying to gather as many details as she could. Directly across from her on the other side of the car, Evan was being led by yet another biker. This one was bald and slightly pig-faced. With thick, black rimmed glasses bordering his eyes, the man almost looked liked he should be working tech support for a large office building. But the image was ruined by not only his black leather jacket and the pistol in one hand, but the menacing look in his eyes as he pulled Evan along by the cuff of his coat.

A few feet behind the vehicle, John Woodenknife stood, his arms folded across his chest. Even without their previous conversation in the general store, Leigh would've known this man was the leader. The one who commanded and observed always was.

"Bring him over to me," John said, referring to Evan. He then looked to Uno. "And hurry up with those two."

Knowing that was her cue, Leigh reached down and pulled the door's handle. She did this as gently as she could, trying to mask the fear that was building inside. If she was to get C. to cooperate, it would take no less than an Oscar-worthy performance.

Leigh bent down and peered into the backseat. C. sat completely frozen, clutching her knees to her chest. Leigh extended her hand.

"Come on, C.," she said softly. "Take my hand. It's okay. If you get out of the car, they'll let us go."

C. said nothing. She just shook her head.

"Trust me," Leigh continued. "Just stay by my side and you'll be safe. I promise."

"Is there a problem?"

From behind her, Leigh heard Uno taking a step forward. She threw a hand up and said, "No problem. Just two seconds, okay?"

There was a beat of silence before Uno replied, "You got one."

Leigh brought her attention back to C. "Come on, don't

make me face them alone. What do we always say?"

When at first C. did not respond, Leigh braced herself for the rough embrace of Uno's arms tearing her away to grab the girl himself. But after a five count that felt more like fifty, C. whispered, "There is no me without Leigh."

Leigh smiled. "And there's no Leigh without C."

She extended her hand once again. This time, C. took it.

Leigh made sure to keep herself between C. and Uno as she led her friend out from the backseat and into the darkening outside world. They walked, huddled together, to where Evan waited with John and the other stranger.

"On your knees," John said, wasting no time. "In a nice, straight row."

C. gave Leigh a fearful look but Leigh returned it with a calm nod. "It's okay. Do what he says."

With much reluctance, C. let go of Leigh and slowly knelt to the cold earth. Leigh did the same, purposefully placing herself in the middle of their row. If given the chance, she wanted to make sure C. had the most direct escape route to the forest.

"Look, guys," Evan said, his voice quiet and careful. "We've cooperated with you, haven't we? We've done exactly as you asked without any trouble at all. And we'll continue to do whatever you want, but we need to know what that is."

John Woodenknife squinted his eyes, apparently puzzled by Evan's words. Not unlike a football player listening to a speech from his coach, John took a knee. His eyes were now exactly level with Evan's.

"What's that, again?"

Evan swallowed hard, his breaths coming short and fast. Still, his gaze did not falter. Somehow managing a steady voice, he said, "Why are you doing this?"

"Ah," John said. "That's the million dollar question, isn't it? Well, guess what?" John blinked and suddenly his gaze was superheated, as if his staring eyes had been instantly flash fried to 1000 degrees.

"I don't owe you shit," he said. He blinked again and at once the heat was gone, his eyes coldly serene once again. He looked to Leigh. "You, however, deserve an explanation."

Leigh flinched as John scooted over to her. She couldn't help it.

"Easy," John said. "I just want to talk, just like before. Remember? When we chatted in the store?"

Leigh did not answer. She couldn't bring her eyes from the forest floor.

"Sure you do," John said. "I mean, we made a connection, didn't we? We're both vegetarians!"

Standing a few feet away from where John knelt, Uno began to chuckle. But the low, grumbling laughter came to an immediate stop when his leader snapped his fingers. Uno fell dead silent.

Continuing, John said, "I want you to know, despite everything that's happened, I wasn't lying about that. I really don't eat meat. I haven't since I was twelve years old. How long has it been for you?"

Leigh shook her head, as if John had asked a "yes or no" question.

"Can't recall?" John said. "Been that long, huh? Well, I suppose it doesn't matter. Everyone's got their reasons. My reason goes back to my old man. You see, my father raised cattle. I mean, that's what he did when wasn't drinking or beating his son for being a 'White man's whore.' Yep, that was me, all right. All because I wanted to attend their schools and a get a job in their town. How dare I turn my back on my own people, right?"

When John paused, Leigh couldn't help but look up. His eyes had glazed over, his thoughts obviously taking the long way home down memory lane. For a split second, Leigh swore she could see a wave of sadness wash over the man's face. But then it was gone, vanished with the quickest twitch of John's left eye.

"So," he went on, "there I was: too red for the white man's club and too white for my father's love. As you can probably imagine, I didn't have too many friends. None that were human, anyway. Nope, my only friend in this entire world was a little calf that I named Shorthorn. 'Shorty,' as I called him most times, saved me for getting trampled by one of the bigger steers. One day this big ol' bastard got it in his thick cow head that I was impeding on his territory. He would've ran me down for sure if Shorty hadn't stepped in between us. I'd never seen a calf do anything like that before, and I swear I never have since. I can't explain it, but there it was. Shorty was my best friend in all the all the world."

"Sir?"

At the sound of Evan's mutter, John's head darted to the left like a whip crack.

"Please, we're very cold and—"

A loud *smack* echoed through the trees as the back of John's hand connected with the side of Evan's face. The slap had been as fast a bullet, its path impossible to trace with the human eye. One moment Evan had been halfway through a sentence, the next he was rocked back sent to the ground.

"Interrupt me again, boy. See what happens."

From Leigh's right, Evan nodded and spat blood. From Leigh's left, C. began to silently shiver.

"Ain't that a bitch?" John said, looking back to Leigh. "No matter what we do, we all become our fathers, don't we? But speaking of fathers, my old man eventually got wise to my friendship with Shorty and he didn't like it one bit. No sir, no way, no son of his was going to be best pals with future beef. He was raising steers, not queers. So, from his booze-fueled viewpoint, there was only one solution. My father put a rifle in my hands, brought me out to a field behind our house, and forced me to shoot Shorty right between his eyes. Ka-BLAM!"

Leigh jumped at sudden sound of narration. C. actually shrieked. John, however, ignored both of these reactions.

"But even that wasn't enough for Pops. Do you even have to guess what we had for dinner that night? That's right. Salisbury Shorty. And when I puked up my first plate, that mother fucker made me have seconds. Then it was a few lashes with the belt and up to my room I went."

John straightened up and returned to his feet. He brushed patches of clinging snow off his knees.

"By morning, I had sworn to never eat another sliver of meat for the rest of my life. Beef, pork, whatever. As it turned out, you lose your taste after you consume someone you care about."

As Leigh had thought herself to be speechless, when she spoke, she couldn't believe the sound of her own voice.

"I'm sorry. I'm sorry that happened. I'm sorry, that's horrible. I'm sorry. I'm—"

"Shh," John said, throwing up a hand to silence her. "That's kind of you to say but it's entirely uncalled for. So it may have taken me about twenty years to figure it out, but I see now that my old man taught me a valuable lesson that day. It's a lesson I can now share with others. Thanks to my father, I finally realize how can I save my friend."

Leigh's head shook out of her control. "I don't understand."

"As I once did, my friend has a taste for meat. Only, the hunger is not actually his. The Wendigo has taken control of his own appetites, forcing him to crave what no man should ever consume. If he is to have any chance to regain his humanity, we most force that humanity to come forth. He must partake in an act of consumption he will always regret."

Before Leigh could reply, John turned his back and took a few paces away. As he walked he said, "Shorthorn's sacrifice changed me forever, Leigh." He turned and stood facing his three captives. Uno and the other man joined him on either side. "And now," John said, "your sacrifice will do the same for my friend."

Leigh inhaled to speak but found she couldn't breathe.

The world was somehow speeding up and slowing down at the same time.

Is this really happening? What exactly is happening? How did we get here?

Her constant and solid grip on reality, that hold she took for granted every second of every day, had begin to slip between the cracks of her consciousness. Oddly enough, the sensation wasn't exactly alien to her. It had happened only once, but she had felt this way once before.

When Rob had revealed to be a blood relative of the Cedars, everyone's favorite family of cannibals.

Cannibals...

That's what John Woodenknife was talking about, wasn't it? He was talking about Leigh being sacrificed.

No.

Consumed.

His friend, the one that was to supposedly partake in this ghastly ritual—he wasn't referring to a one of the Cedars, was he? But they had all died. The father, Seymour, had been shot by the forest ranger, Jake Spire, the same man who had saved Leigh from the business end of an axe. That was shortly before Spire snuck blood into her grape juice to cure her of the deadly fungal disease, thus saving her twice before vanishing without a trace.

That had left the mother, Clementine, and her children, son Bugger and daughter Grizzly. Mother and daughter had practically been vaporized along with Sam...

Oh, Sam...

...when he had blown them all to kingdom come. And Leigh had seen Bugger die with her own eyes, stuck with a pitchfork like silverware skewing steak.

There couldn't be another one.

Could there?

After all, Rob had revealed himself to be part of the Cedar clan. For all her higher education, she hadn't seen that one coming at all. After that revelation, the idea of a long, long Cedar shouldn't have surprised her at all.

"Sir."

Leigh's train of thought went flying off the tracks at the sound the utterance from her right. At first, she thought it was one of John Woodenknife's troops addressing their leader. She was more than a little impressed when she realized it was Evan. Despite the blow to the face, he had yet to lose his nerve. Leigh would even admire him for it, if she didn't think it would get him killed.

By the look of John Woodenknife's face, it seemed he too was taken back Evan's second interruption.

"You don't learn well, do you boy?"

When Evan shook his head, Leigh felt tiny hot droplets of blood splash her cheek. "Not right now, it would seem. But I have learned a lot about mental illness in my lifetime. It's what I do for a living. And by the sound of what you are describing, I agree with your diagnosis. It sounds to me like your friend definitely is suffering from Wendigo Psychosis."

The man whose name Leigh didn't know said, "What's he talking about, boss?"

Evan didn't wait for the boss to reply. "It's a rare condition, but it's not unheard of, even today. There are ways to treat it and your friend should definitely seek treatment. But sir..."

Evan trailed off, his eyes going glassy as he stared off into the trees. John Woodenknife watched him, his brow furrowing with curiosity. Evan seemed to be in a daze, his head slowly shaking back and forth. Finally, when Evan spoke again, all he said was, "Not your way. Not your way."

Leigh braced herself to witness another smack, or worse, slam against Evan's head. But to her surprise, John Woodenknife did not react in anger. Both his face and his voice remained perfectly steady and calm.

"My way," he said to Evan. "Existed long before your people came and rewrote the story of our world. And now, people like you, read fiction as textbooks." He took a step towards Evan.

Oh god, here it comes.

And stopped. "But I mustn't blame you for your ignorance. If my life has taught me anything, it's not to judge people for the sins of their fathers."

To this, Evan had no response. It was impossible to know what had caught his tongue—Woodenknife's words...or the rumbling noise that was getting closer with each passing second.

All three of their captors turned at once just as headlights appeared in the distance, their beams cutting through the spaces between the trees. Someone was coming.

A shriek from Leigh's left came so sudden that her legs almost left the ground when she jumped. C., who had been catatonically silent this entire time, minus the lightest whimpering, suddenly was screaming at the top of her lungs.

"Hey! Over here! Help! HELP!"

"C.!" Leigh said, her voice lost to the high pitch of her friend's yelling. "Quiet! You don't want to piss them off!"

Leigh darted her eyes back to the men, fully accepting to see at least one, if not all three, charging at full speed to shut the girl up. Oddly enough, not one of the bikers seemed alarmed at all. If anything, Uno looked slightly annoyed.

"Ah, shut up," he said. "Save your breath. It's only D—"

Whatever he was going to say next was cut off by Woodenkinfe's jab to his shoulder.

"How about you shut *your* mouth?" Woodenknife said. Anger had returned to his eyes. After Uno nodded without saying another word, Woodenknife added, "Wait here and watch them."

The other man stayed behind with Uno as their leader paced back to meet the approaching vehicle. The blinding headlights made it impossible to identify the car's make and model, but the deep growl of the engine, combined with the height of the lights, suggested it was a pickup truck of some kind. Leigh watched as the silhouette of Woodenknife raised a hand for the truck to stop. Next came the sound of a door opening.

"You can kill the engine," Woodenknife said. "But put your mask on before you turn off your lights."

Mask?

The grumbling engine went silent just in time for Leigh to hear a new voice utter, "You really want me to put this thing on?"

"It's not about what I want," Woodenknife answered back. "You *must* wear the mask."

"Why the hell is that?"

Did Leigh know that voice? She strained to pick up any details she could, but the man's quick, short sentences gave her very little to go on. Still, she couldn't ignore the strong sense of déjà vu overcoming her.

"It's an integral part of the ceremony," Woodenknife said. "It's tradition. But more importantly, I don't want her seeing your face. And neither do you. It's going to make this far easier for you if she doesn't know who you are."

At this, Leigh squinted as hard as she could, desperately trying to see through the headlights' unforgiving glare. But the light was just too harsh, and when they extinguished a few seconds later, it was too late. The lights shut off like two fireflies meeting a sudden end, leaving a lingering spot of white in Leigh's vision. It blotted her sight as the two men approached, but by the time they reached her and her friends, the light stain had lifted away. Leigh could see perfectly.

And what she saw made her scream.

CHAPTER EIGHT

Most would compare dreams to movies, experimental films that rarely make sense. Scenes are often out of sequence and missing reels only add to the lack of coherent plot. Hell, sometimes the projector plays in reverse and instead of waking up right before the thrilling conclusion, your eyes pop open just as the dream was about to begin. Still, more often than not, dreams consist of motion pictures.

But this was not what Jake Spire awoke from, gasping like a caught fish thrown to the floor of a boat. He had dreamt in still images, as if his subconscious had opted to flip through a photo album instead of flipping on the movie-of-the-night.

He came to with only a vague recollection of the strange, dark pictures presented to him while he slept. He could recall very few in vivid detail, but the ones that remained were haunting enough to burn themselves to the walls of his mind. They were like the white shadows the dead left behind after the

Hiroshima bomb.

An axe buried in a stump.

A hand scratching at the earth, green fuzz embedded in its fingernails.

A grinning Phil Carson, long deer antlers sprouting from his forehead...

It was this image that finally startled Jake to consciousness, a scream stuck halfway in his throat. Even with his eyes open, Phil's malicious grin remained smeared across Jake's vision, those terribly gnarled antlers bordering it on both sides.

He shook his head. The image floated away but was replaced with skull splitting pain.

"Oh, man."

Jake brought a hesitant hand to his temple. Something throbbed under his touch. Slowly, his eyes began to adjust to the room's dim light. He could barely remember entering the hotel room before crashing onto the bed. A glance at the pulled blackout curtains brought with it the memory of Mary drawing them closed before feeding him some aspirin.

Mary...

Fighting the urge to move too quickly, Jake looked to the bathroom, the only place Mary could be. The door, however, was wide open, allowing him to see that she was no longer in the room at all. Still, Jake could not stop himself from saying, "Mary?"

Of course, he did not receive an answer. The room was not a suite, just a standard sized room with two double beds. The other bed appeared completely undisturbed, not a pillow or sheet out of order. Apparently, Mary had not joined Jake during his nap time.

Jake swung his legs over the beds, pausing the world spun for a brief but disturbing moment. There was no doubt he was still in bad shape, full well knowing that only Demerol would cure what ailed him. Though it only brought more pain, Jake strained to remember his last conversation with Mary.

I asked her to bring me to the pharmacy but she insisted I wait here. Yes, that's right. She said we didn't know how long it would take to call in my prescription so she would drop me off at the Little Northern while she...

Again, the quick movement brought with it both sharp pain and dizziness, but Jake hardly noticed either when he looked to the bedside clock. It read 12:32PM.

What time had it been when Mary brought them back to the Little Northern? For the life of him, Jake couldn't remember. *No, wait.*

It was coming back to him now. Mary had still had her room key on her because she had never checked out. Check out was at noon which meant her key would still work for at least another hour. But now it was half past, which meant—

There was a clicking noise to his right. Instinct took control and led his hand to the bedside lamp with the speed of a bullet. It was the same twitch response well practiced in the great outdoors, when tracking a prize buck or flock of turkeys. The light switched on, temporarily blinding him just as the door slowly opened.

"Mary?" His voice came out like a bullfrog's croak. His throat was as dry as the Mojave.

His call was replied to with a startled "Oh!" The voice was female but definitely not Mary's. With his vision quickly returning, Jake could now see a housekeeper standing in the doorway.

"My apologies sir," she said, her hand still pressed against her chest in surprise. "I didn't expect for anyone to still be here. Are you aware checkout was at noon?"

"Sorry about that," Jake said, standing up from the bed. He bit his lip as a wave of dizziness washed over him, but he managed to maintain his footing. "I dozed off before I could set an alarm. Just give me one minute and I'll be out of your hair."

The woman nodded. Circles ran under her middle-aged eyes, fatigue clearly marking her face. Still, her voice retained a pleasant tone as she said, "Take your time, sir. I can work on the room next door while you gather your things."

"Appreciate it," Jake said in a raspy voice. He cleared his throat as the woman turned to leave.

"Wait," he said. The woman turned around. "You didn't by chance happen to see a young woman in the lobby or the stairwell? About yea tall, hair down to here or so?" He provided the appropriate hand gestures but the housekeeper still shook her head.

"I'm sorry, I don't believe so. But I've been up here changing rooms for the last half-hour, give-or-take."

"Sure," Jake said. "Thanks anyway."

The woman gave a polite, tight lipped smile and left the room.

After testing the sturdiness of his steps, Jake made his way to the bathroom and turned on the sink's faucet. The cold water he splashed in his face jolted him awake, just slightly easing his headache, if only for a moment. He tried not to look at his own reflection, knowing that bloodshot eyes and a sagging face would greet him for sure. He only caught a glance before clicking off the light and exiting, but it was enough to confirm his prediction. He looked almost as awful as he felt.

The housekeeper had given him time to gather his belongings, but everything Jake had brought with him on this trip was still in the car. He would be able to make a swift exit from the Little Northern Inn, as soon as he located Mary, of course. Where was she, anyway? If she had left for the pharmacy soon after he passed out, that would mean she had been gone for at least an hour. He supposed it could've taken her that long to retrieve his medication, but only if the pharmacy had been particularly busy and were backed up with customers dropping off prescriptions. The chance of that, however, seemed awfully slim. It wasn't like the Embry Pharmacy attracted the business of a downtown Walgreens.

Confused and still gathering his bearings, Jake exited the hotel room and made his way down the stairs to the main lobby. He still had no desire to be seen in public, but the lobby was the only place he could think of that Mary may be waiting. Perhaps she hadn't wanted to disturb his sleep so was biding her time by the fireplace? Maybe she'd even offered just the right smile to the front desk to buy him some additional post-checkout nap time. Embry was practically extinct these days, but there had to be some small-town hospitality left somewhere.

The staircase leading down to the lobby gave him a bird's eye view, and about halfway down, Jake knew for sure that Mary was nowhere to be seen.

Damn it.

He stopped before he reached the final step. He knew a lone man standing on the stairs would eventually attract attention, but someone working in the factory of his mind had just pressed the emergency button to stop the line. His thoughts came to a screeching halt.

What to do next?

Moving forward was his only option since he could no longer go back to the room. He could wait in the lobby as he had when first arrived to pick up Mary, but like before, he really didn't want to stay in one location for a prolonged period of time. Perhaps he should head to the pharmacy and see if he could find Mary there, or walking back.

Wait...

Did she walk? Or did she take the car?

Spinning on the ball of his right foot, Jake turned around and bounded back up the stairs, taking the steps two at a time. At the other end of the hall from which he came, a glowing red EXIT sign glowed in the upper left corner of the wall. He quickly paced to the sign to discover another door just around the corner. Pushing it open, he found it led to another staircase, this one in a bland, cinderblock stairwell. His memory tuned to a hazy image of himself and Mary making their way up these stairs to her room. These were the stairs that connected to the rear parking lot.

Jake's steps echoed in the chamber-like stairwell as he rushed down them as quickly as he could. His head was pounding again but the pain was distant now, a secondary concern. Most of his attention was too distracted by the suspense of what he would find waiting for him outside.

After several clomping steps, he reached the bottom door and pushed it open. Icy wind and snowflakes hit him in the face. He squinted against both, preparing to scan the entire parking lot for his vehicle.

He did not have to look long. His car was parked two spaces from the left of the door.

"Huh."

Jake had been so eager to find out if his car was still here or not, but now he didn't know what to make of the answer. So had Mary been too intimidated by the slick roads and braved the snowstorm on foot? Or had she left with the car and came back?

There were impressions in the snow behind the rear tires, but the tracks had been filled in by the falling flakes. Though it was impossible to say for sure, something in Jake's gut said they were their original tracks when Mary had drove him back to the Little Northern.

"Brrr," Jake said, a sudden chill making him shiver. Jake couldn't believe Mary had decided to walk instead of drive. Sure, the roads were becoming slippery, but the pharmacy wasn't too far into town. At a slow and steady pace, the Eagle would've gotten her there without any trouble at all.

Another shiver coursing through his body, Jake shoved his hands in his pockets. Something small, hard, and cold prodded his palm.

What the hell?

He brought the object from his Carhartt—his keys.

Forgetting all about the frigid temperature, Jake stared at the metal object in his hand. Why did he still have his keys? Mary had driven them back to the inn. Had she put them back in her pocket while he slept?

"Wow," he said to himself, his voice swallowed by the wind. He had awoken with all his clothes still on, jacket included. If Mary had somehow stuffed the keys back in his pocket without waking him up, it just proved how knocked out he had been.

His hand covered with wet dots of melting flakes, Jake stuffed his keys back in his pocket. It was then he felt another object hiding within, and when he retrieved it, he cursed himself for not thinking of it before.

His cell phone.

"Duhhh," Jake said in a self-mocking tone. Here he was acting like Sherlock Holmes when he could've solved the mystery with a single phone call. Shaking his head in disbelief, Jake scrolled to Mary's number on the illuminated screen, clicked her name, and brought the phone to his ear.

Jake gritted his teeth against another gust of wind. At least the uncomfortable air was distracting him from the pounding in his—

Mary's voice spoke in his ear.

"Mary, it's Jake. Where are..."

He trailed off as Mary continued to speak. It was her voicemail message. Worse yet, Jake was realizing that he hadn't heard a single ring before the recording begun to play. That meant Mary's phone was either out of range or turned off.

"Shit."

He hung up and returned the phone to his pocket. Staring at his car, Jake contemplated getting in and driving to the pharmacy. It was a tempting idea, especially at the thought of cranking the heat all the way up. But he quickly reconsidered when he thought about the route Mary would've taken to the drugstore. It wouldn't have made any sense for Mary to exit the inn through the back. The pharmacy was just down the street and going right out the front would've been the shortest walk. After all, Mary wasn't the one concerned with whether the front desk spotted her or not. Up until a half hour ago, she had been a legal guest of the hotel.

It was far too easy to picture Jake driving away from the inn just as Mary returned, like some comical game of cat-and-mouse. No, the smart move was to check the lobby at least one more time before went anywhere. Turning around, Jake grabbed the knob of the stairwell door, its cold metal stinging his fingers. He pulled.

The door didn't budge.

It was just then he noticed the black plastic card reader installed on the wall just to the right of the door's handle. The door had locked from the other side and reopening it would require a room key. Reflexively, he jammed his hands in the pockets of both his jacket and pants. As expected, they come up empty.

Jake lowered his head, bringing his hand to his brow. And started to laugh.

"Son of a bitch," he said between chuckles. Murphy had always been nothing less and his law was even worse.

This is what you get for coming back here. Just grin and take it, asshole.

With a loud, extended sigh, Jake began to trudge to the corner of the building where he would turn towards the front entrance. As he walked, an unexpected memory illuminated in his mind's eye like a camera flash.

It had been during his early years at the forest service. He hadn't yet shed his rookie status, which meant the less desirable jobs fell on his shoulders more often than not. One of those tasks was a chore Phil insisted on every Christmas season: stringing lights on the Timber Ridge fire tower. The tower stood on an overlook high above Embry, and when lit up with hundreds of green lights, it could even be seen at the village center. Parents told their young children that the all green lighted tower told Santa Clause where to find Embry when he was flying through the night sky on his sleigh. Once that legend cemented itself in the annals of Embry lore, Phil never failed to make sure the kids saw their Santa beacon shining bright on Christmas Eve.

Of course, putting up all those damn lights was never actually Phil's responsibility. That honor was entirely Jake's and whoever he could rope into wrapping yards of light strings around the beams of the tower. One particular year it had been a college intern, one Chad Wilcox. While stringing the lights through one of the lower parts of the tower, Jake had yelled to Wilcox to throw him a new coil. Wilcox's throw fell short, and when Jake had overextended himself to grab it, he lost his footing on the beam and plummeted towards the ground. Fortunately, the lights twisted around his ankle somehow, and stopped him from crashing onto the frozen ground below. Unfortunately, however, Jake was now stuck upside down and totally at the mercy of his fellow rangers. And once Phil had somehow gained control over his belly laugher, he had made sure to snap a photo to immortalize the moment. The Polaroid remained tacked to a bulletin board at their main headquarters for the rest of Jake's days as a forest ranger.

The smile curving Jake's smile lasted only momentarily, as the recollection made him laugh but also miss his old friend immensely. Such was the bittersweet nature of the past, but at least his trip down memory road had lasted exactly as long as his trip around the Little Northern Inn. Brushing snow from his shoulders, Jake entered the front entrance for the second time that day.

Disappointment greeted him the moment he crossed the threshold. Panning his gaze over the lobby a single time was all it took to determine that Mary still wasn't here. Again, the gears of his brain began to turn. He could almost here them grinding together, bringing back that painful throb.

So what were the possibilities here? One: Mary was still at the pharmacy or returning from there. Two: She had gone back up to the room, not knowing that Jake had been already been asked to leave. Or three...

Well, three wasn't really a single possibility but a collection of more dire scenarios that Jake wasn't going to allow himself to consider just yet. Without cellular communication as an option, it seemed to him the smartest thing to do would be to head to the drug store, the only destination he knew had been on Mary's agenda.

But even smarter than that...

There was one more thing he could do but Jake didn't care for the idea at all. He could speak with woman working the front desk and see if she had seen Mary, or better yet, if Mary had left a message with her. One quick conversation could solve this whole mess in a matter of seconds, but still, Jake hesitated. Was he being paranoid? There was a good chance. An average civilian would have to be pretty damn observant to place his face to a picture they probably saw only one time in the newspaper while they were eating their breakfast and trying to rush to work. And that was over a year ago.

Despite that clear logic, Jake's pulse was still increasing by the second. His heart pounded harder than his head. He took a deep breath to steady himself.

To hell with it.

He had to find Mary, that was the long and short of it. And even if the clerk did suspect she knew him from somewhere, he would be out of town before she could put the puzzle pieces together. His mind made up, Jake walked over to the front desk. On his way there, he retrieved a pair of sunglasses from his breast pocket. They may have made him look a little bit too much like the police sketch of the Unibomber, but concealing his haggard eyes made him feel far more confident.

Jake cleared his throat. "Hello, there."

The woman looked up from a folder, a smile already plastered on her face. Jake knew the expression must have become automatic a long time ago, identical to the ones she gave every customer that approached her.

"May I help you?" she said. Her voice had a husky quality to it that made Jake realize she was older than he had first assumed. Her face had a hardened quality to it, with strong cheek bones and chin. Though her hair was a deep red, her eyebrows were a dark brown, almost black. As insignificant as it was, Jake still caught himself wondering if she dyed her hair.

Dismissing the arbitrary thought, Jake cleared his throat

a second time and said, "Yes, I'm hoping you can. I'm trying to locate my..." He hesitated, not knowing how to finish the sentence. "...Niece. It seems we had a bit of a miscommunication and I was wondering if you had seen or spoken to her."

"Is she a guest of the hotel?"

"Yes, or rather, she was. She was supposed to check out at noon."

The woman pursed her lips and shifted her eyes to the right. "Hmm," she said. "I haven't had many checkouts today. There was an elderly couple, but that's all I can remember off hand."

"She's in her early twenties. She may not have actually checked out, but I was hoping maybe you spotted her in the lobby. She was wearing a peacoat, leggings, and those boots so many girls her age seem to love. Oh, what are they called? Not eggs but..."

The woman gave an amused smile. "Uggs."

"That's it."

The smile on the woman's face faded. "I'm sorry but that still doesn't ring a bell. But hold on one moment and I'll see if the computer can tell us anything."

At this the woman stood, surprising Jake with her height. At 5' 10", Jake was by no means a tall man. A woman of roughly the same height though was a different story. In fact, had they been standing back-to-back, there was a chance that she was even taller than Jake. Of course, the floor behind the counter could've been elevated slightly, but the name tag pinned to her blouse was almost eye level with him. It read *NADINE.*

Nadine walked over to a computer at the end of the counter and Jake followed. Standing in front of the keyboard she asked, "What is your niece's name?"

"Carson," Jake said. "Mary Carson."

Nadine fingers danced on the keyboard. Though Jake could not see the screen, whatever Nadine saw made her strong brow furrow.

"I'm not seeing that name in our records," she said.

At first, Jake was taken back. But just as he about to question Nadine's spelling of the last name, a thought occurred to him. Mary may have used a false name, perhaps in order to avoid detection from her mother. She could've used any alias, and Jake didn't have the time to play guessing games forever.

"That's odd," Jake said, trying to hide the anxiety building inside of him.

"Well," Nadine said, brushing her hair away from her face. A single strand stuck to her cheek, stuck to the large amount of makeup applied there. "Do you know what room she was staying in?"

"Um," Jake muttered. He hadn't bothered to check when he left, feeling rushed by the presence of the housekeeper. "Unfortunately, I don't. But I do know it was on the second floor."

"Okay, let's see." The woman tapped a few more keys. Her eyes bounced back and forth as if she were watching a game of pong on the screen. She muttered names to herself, most likely unaware she was even speaking out loud. Jake could just make out them out as they passed through her lips.

"Clegg, Golden, Smith, Spire, Strand..."

Jake's eyes went wide behind his sunglasses.

"Wait," he said. "I'm sorry, did you say Spire?"

The woman turned from the screen. "Um, yes. But first names are indicated by an initial, and it isn't M as in 'Mary.'"

Jake swallowed. Hard.

"Is it J?"

The woman glanced back to the screen. "Why yes, it is. J. Spire." She looked up at him. "Does that name mean anything to you?"

"Uh..."

For a moment, the well defined lines of Nadine's makeup job blended together in a hazy blur. Nausea hit Jake not in a wave, but a sudden punch to the gut. For one terrifying instant, he thought he was going to lose whatever remained in his stomach. Somehow he regained his composure and his vision cleared.

"It may," he said. "It's a name she uses for security reasons.

You know, young girl traveling by herself and all. Her parents are a bit protective."

Nadine nodded. "I understand."

"Anyway, that must be her. Thank you for your help."

Jake did not wait for Nadine to reply. He was already turning to walk away from the desk as fast as he could. Not only was panic growing inside of him, but anger boiled as well. How could Mary have been so stupid to check-in with his name? He had been very clear how incognito he wished to remain. Hell, she had even remembered to address him by his fake name of Wally Parker.

"I'm sorry, sir?"

He wanted nothing more to keep moving, but the habits of polite society took over. He automatically answered when addressed.

"Yes?"

"I don't think that's her room."

With slow, tentative steps, he walked back to the desk. "How can you be sure?"

Nadine's face tightened, the telltale sign of someone who has to deliver bad news. "If I'm understanding you correctly, you believe she was staying here under a fictitious name. But she only could've done that if she had paid with cash."

Jake stared at her, waiting for any sort of point. "And?" he said.

"Our records show this Spire paid with a credit card. And in order to do that, the card holder would've had to provide identification with the same name."

"So you're saying..."

Nadine nodded. "Spire is exactly who they said they were." She then gave him a shrug. "I guess it was just a coincidence."

"I guess so."

Jake was hardly aware he was talking. His mind was an inner city riot. A World War II battlefield. A bouncy house filled with hyperactive eight-year olds. It was pandemonium inside Jake's head, but someone had managed to click on his autopilot. There was absolutely no way to tell that Jake Spire was dangerously close to losing his shit.

"I'll tell you what," Nadine said as she scooted away from the computer towards a mug holding pens and a yellow pad of post-it notes. She grabbed one of the writing implements and began scribbling on the top note. "I'm going to give you the number of the inn. In about an hour or so, my coworker should be swinging by, and if your niece was staying with us, he's the one that would've checked her in. I'm sure he'll be able to get to the bottom of this for you."

She slid the piece of paper to him. He picked it up and repeated, "An hour?"

"Yes. But hopefully you will have found her by then anyway." She gave him her best smile yet.

Jake was nodding far more than he should have but he couldn't seem to stop himself. "Thank you," he said. "Thank you for your help, Nadine."

"My pleasure, sir. And please be sure to bundle up if you go out. The wind has teeth today!"

Jake said nothing more, only offering the weakest smile as he walked away. Before he knew it, his feet had carried him outside of the hotel. Just as Nadine had said, the wind bit into his flesh like a thirsty vampire, but he barely felt a breeze. His attention was entirely focused on Mary. Wherever she was in Embry, the town hadn't bothered using teeth at all.

It had swallowed her whole.

CHAPTER NINE

Leigh knew she was lucky that a smack to the head had been her only punishment for screaming so loud. Had any of their assailants pointed a firearm at her face and pulled the trigger, Leigh wouldn't have been at all surprised. The last thing you did in situations like this was lose your cool. Screaming only made people nervous, and when people with guns became nervous, they were known to pull the trigger, intentionally or not.

But when Grizzly Cedar emerged from behind the blinding headlights, Leigh could not help herself. The image of that mask had been burned into her very soul. It had become a permanent resident of her nightmares. Countless times she had woken in a cold sweat just as the bear-masked killer was about to embed a dull axe into her skull. Sam Tucker may have killed Grizzly when he had taken his own life, but the behemoth daughter of Clementine Cedar lived on in the darkest corners of Leigh's mind.

Only this wasn't a nightmare. This was real. Grizzly was standing right in front of her. So Leigh screamed.

Smack!

"Pipe down," Uno grumbled. "Shit, that's like nails on a chalkboard."

The blow knocked Leigh's head forward, forcing her to look away from the monster who had risen from the grave. She stopped shrieking at once, the blow to the head silencing her scream like a needle ripped off a spinning record. Swallowing hard, Leigh slowly raised her head again.

Grizzly was gone. The person standing before her was indeed wearing a mask, but it wasn't made from the head of a black bear. Her mind had added that detail itself, memory overtaking what she was actually seeing. Though Uno's smack had cleared her thoughts, what she now saw was no less terrifying.

The man wore a deer's skull over his face. Long, multi-pointed antlers reached from the top like gnarled branches. Had this buck been killed during hunting season, it would've earned the shooter much praise for sure. Now it had been fashioned into the most ghoulish headpiece Leigh had ever laid eyes on. The long bone of the creatures snout extended down to the base of the man's throat. Due to the low light of the snowstorm, Leigh could not see the man's eyes behind the skull's deep sockets.

"I feel ridiculous."

The statement had been so underwhelming that Leigh did not realize it had become from the behind the deer skull. She would've thought a man wearing a mask like that would say something like, "Your time has come," or "This is where you die." But no, the man was complaining and looking at John Woodenknife.

"I don't care," Woodenknife said. "Leave it on and let's do this."

The deer man stared at Leigh. She saw he was shifting his weight from foot to foot.

"I don't know if I can do this," he said.

Woodenknife ran a hand down his face, pulling at the flesh under his eyes. He sighed. "What do you mean? We've done this a hundred times before."

"I know." The stranger pointed a finger at Leigh. "But this one's different. She's not like the rest."

Woodenknife walked over to the stranger's side, placing his hand on the man's shoulder. Standing side-by-side, the two men looked very different, and it wasn't just the bizzarre headwear. This new member of the group did not wear biker's clothes like the rest of the gang. Minus his mask, his attire was rather mundane: dark blue jeans, a brown canvas jacket, and a pair of leather work gloves.

"That's entirely the point," Woodenknife said. "It's supposed to difficult. It's supposed to be so difficult that you'll never want to do this again."

It was now Woodenknife's turn to point at Leigh. "If this goes how I expect it will, you will see that face every time you feel the urge to feed again. And you'll think about what that face means to you. You'll remember how she saved your life."

What?

Leigh's fear was instantly forgotten, replaced by pure, concentrated confusion. She no longer felt like she had been abducted by mad men, but rather, that it was the world itself that was truly mad.

Woodenknife leaned even closer into the man's ear. "Those who save your life never taste good going down. Believe me, I know. When this is all over, you'll never have the taste for this again."

The tip of the skull's snout moved up and down as the man nodded. "All right," he said. "I understand." He motioned to C. and Evan. "But what about them?"

"Don't you worry about it," Woodenknife said. "They have nothing to do with your healing. We'll take care of them."

With that, he looked to his men and gave his head a quick nod. Leigh heard crunching for snow just before Peen grabbed C. from behind. C. shrieked as Peen held her held down, bending C. into a position resembling the child's pose. Just beyond C., Evan was too was being grabbed by Uno, who held the young man's arms behind his back.

"Hey!" Evan yelled. "What are you doing?" He tried to struggle against Uno's iron grip, but it only resulted in Uno throwing him down and placing his boot on the back of Evan's neck.

Woodenknife brought his index finger to his lips. "Shh. This will only take a second." He looked to his crony looming over C. "Peen, time to do your thing."

Leigh watched in horror as a lecherous smile stretched Peen's doughy face. He threw one side of his leather jacket to reveal a carpenter's belt circling his wide waist. All of the loops were unused, minus one exception. And when Leigh saw what hung there, she instantly understood the biker's namesake.

A ball-peen hammer.

The efficiency in which Peen retrieved the tool proved he had practiced this action many times before. Wasting no time, he raised it above his head.

"Leigh..."

C. did not scream the name. She hardly spoke above a whisper.

Leigh made eye contact with her friend's desperate gaze. She tried to tell her not worry, tried to tell her that everything would be okay. But she could not mutter a single word. C.'s hair had somehow changed color. It was now bleach-blonde. C.'s eyes had changed as well to a brilliant bright blue. In fact, her entire face had transformed into someone new, a face as recognizable as it was the last time Leigh had seen it.

Alex, her old college roommate, stared at her in absolute terror. It was the same look she had the night Leigh had found her strung up in the Cedars' basement. It was how she had looked right before she died.

And now it was going to happen again.

No. Not this time.

Bearing her teeth like a feral cat, Leigh planted her hands in front of her to push herself up. She would be on Peen in an instant, punching, clawing, biting his face if that's what it took.

A blinding red light shot into her eye. Natural reflexes made her squeeze both eyes shut, immediately stopping her momentum. She could still see that piercing red dot light like a cigarette burn on her eyelid.

What...?

Throwing a hand up to shield herself, she looked in the direction of the light, expecting to see Woodenknife aiming a laser pointer at her. What she saw was far worse, its image freezing her in an awkward pose.

Woodenknife pointed his crossbow at her, an attached laser sight guiding his aim.

"Uh uh, Leigh," Woodenknife said. "You stay right where you are or I'll put one right in your gut. It'll hurt so bad you'll wish I had killed you. But it takes a long, long time to die from a gut shot."

He lowered the crossbow, guiding the dot of red light down her chest until it came to rest on her stomach. She locked eyes with him, searching his gaze for sincerity. It seemed the honor of killing her belonged to the man in the mask, but something about Woodenknife's expression told her he wouldn't hesitate to pull the trigger.

"Please," Leigh said, not taking her eyes away from the gang's leader. "Don't do this."

For a brief moment, Leigh swore she saw something that resembled remorse wash over John Woodenknife's face. His pressed lips softened a bit, his tight brow going lax. It was the unmistakable expression of a man having second thoughts.

But when he looked to his friend in the deer skull, the stern intensity returned at once.

"The Wendigo," he said, "must die." He looked away from the skull's dead stare to Peen. "Quick and painless," he said.

There was a blur of movement in Leigh's peripheral vision followed by a dull *thwack*. It oddly resembled the sound of a tennis player delivering a powerful serve.

40-Love.

C.'s body slumped onto the cold earth and began to twitch. Her eyes had rolled back into her head, making them as whiter than the snowy ground. Blood rushed from the back of the C.'s head, staining the ground a deep, dark red. With every twitch of C.'s body, the blood would fly a bit farther and splatter the snow like a Jackson Pollack canvas. In time, the sliver of wet skull that Leigh could see peeking out from her friend's hair would be whiter than the forest floor.

Leigh's entire body locked up as she watched C.'s death spasms. It was if she had been wrapped in an invisible straight jacket and strapped down to a gurney. Surely this was what it felt like to go insane, right before they sent you off to the loony bin. But what asylum could offer insanity any greater than this? *This can't be happening. This can't be real.*

C.'s body finally stopped twitching and she went completely still. An utter quiet overtook the entire forest as everyone, assailants and victims alike, stared at the body in a shared silence. It was the ultimate proof that this wasn't just some crazy nightmare. Dreams were too chaotic, the result of an overactive mind while the body was at rest. Only reality could offer such utter stillness.

When the moment of peace was broken, it was by the most awful sound that Leigh could ever imagine.

Someone was laughing.

At first, Leigh assumed it was one of Woodenknife's cronies getting some kind of sadistic joy from hurting innocent people. She expected to turn and see the one-eyed Uno with a big shit-eating grin spread across his face. To her surprise, both he and Peen wore almost identical looks of somber apathy. They could've easily been factory workers or farmhands instead of murderous bikers. To them, dispatching Leigh and her friends were just part of the job.

Due to the deer skull concealing the totality of his face, Leigh did not realize that it was the masked stranger laughing until his quiet chuckling turned to almost childlike giggles. It reminded Leigh of nights spent in with C. watching Netflix and drinking wine, when one girl's laughter would infect the other until both roommates were gripping their sides in gleeful pain.

"Christ," Woodenknife said. He slapped the man's shoulder. "Get it together. We're almost done."

"I..." The man tried to speak but another bout of laughter stole his words. "I know. I-I'm try-trying." More laughter, this fit shaking his shoulders. "I d-don't know what's wr-wrong with me."

Woodenknife pointed to the man but looked to his underlings. "This," he said, "Is the Wendigo. This is not the laughter of a man but one of a beast. It takes pleasure in this man's suffering. We must end this now."

The goons nodded in unison, their eyes actually showing signs of sorrow for the laughing man. Knowing their leader's wishes, the men proceeded to carry out their orders. In one fast motion, Uno wrapped his hands around Evan's arms and placed them on the back of Evan's head, successfully locking Evan in a Full Nelson.

"Hey!" Evan yelled, shifting his weight back and forth in a desperate attempt to free himself of Uno's hold. The hold, however, was a favorite of wrestler's everywhere for a very simple reason: it worked very well.

Peen, meanwhile, positioned himself in front of Evan and prepared to deliver the same killing blow that he had given C. just moments ago.

"Wait!" Evan said as Peen lifted the hammer. "I know what's wrong with you! I know why you can't stop laughing! I've seen this before!"

"Stop!"

The voice boomed from behind the deer skull. The stranger paced forward to Peen's side. "You have?" he asked.

Evan looked directly into the skull's black sockets. "Yes, that's right. I'm a psychiatrist, you see? Or rather, I'm training to be one."

"Hey," Woodenknife shouted. "Don't listen to this garbage. He's just trying to buy himself time. He doesn't know anything."

Evan continued, "I studied degenerative brain conditions

in school. Hell, I wrote my dissertation on them. So believe me, I know what I'm talking about here." He stared deeper into the mask's eye holes, searching for the man underneath. "I think you have Kuru."

From behind him, Uno snorted. "What the fuck is Kuru?"

"It's a neurological disorder found in the tribal regions of Papua, New Guinea. The tribes there call it "the laughing sickness" because that's exactly what it makes you do. You laugh uncontrollably, just like you are now."

"Bullshit," Woodenknife said.

"No," Evan said, a surprising amount of calm in his voice. It was the sure and steady tone that could only come with someone who has complete authority over their subject. "It's science. Kuru is caused by prions and—"

"What ons?"

It was Peen who spoke up now. Whether he realized it or not, he had lowered the hammer.

"Prions," Evan repeated. "It's an infectious protein that eats away at the cerebral cortex of the brain. The condition is called 'spongiform' because the brain gets so many tiny holes in it, that, if viewed under a microscope, it looks like a sponge."

Though Woodenknife continued to shake his head. "Do you really want your last words to be a TED Talk?"

Evan ignored the question, still speaking directly to the man in the mask. "It begins with headaches and joint pain, but soon develops into involuntarily shaking. The shaking eventually worsens to loss of muscle and speech control, which brings upon bouts of sporadic laughter. Emotional instability and depression soon follow. And still, the victim will laugh."

Evan paused to take a breath. His eyes narrowed as he asked, "How's my aim?"

The masked man's hands balled into fists, an obvious attempt to control him. "That sounds righ—"

"Enough!" Woodenknife said. He swung the crossbow from Leigh to Evan, it's red laser sight landing on the boy's

Adam's Apple. "You want to talk about aim? I'm downright surgical with this thing."

Perhaps it was because Evan had accepted he would die regardless, or maybe he had just gotten too lost in his own thoughts to stop now, but the trained weapon did nothing to stop Evan's speech.

"But what I don't understand," he said, "is how you could've ever contracted such a disease. Kuru is most often found in tribes that practice mortuary cannibalism. They eat the departed's flesh as a way to return the life force of the deceased back to the community. But you..."

Evan's voice trailed off as his eyes went wide. It was the look of someone receiving either electric shock or a life-changing revelation.

"Wendigo," Evan whispered. "Oh my god." He tried to inch away from the man in the mask but Uno held him tight. Evan's jaw quivered, his eyes glassing over with the start of tears. "You're a...you're a..."

"He's not a cannibal!"

Leigh's jumped at the sound of Woodenknife's outburst. She would've also shrieked if she hadn't been biting her tongue hard to draw blood.

"He's not a cannibal," Woodenknife repeated, this time much quieter having found his composure. "It is the Wendigo that craves the flesh of man. It is the Wendigo that must be banished forever. But as they say, first thing's first. Peen?"

Like a loyal soldier, the hammer wielding henchman step forward at once, his blunt weapon ready. But before he could get within striking distance, the masked stranger was holding up a blocking arm.

"Wait," the man said. "I may want to hear more."

"Hear more what?" Woodenknife said. "Bullshit sounds as bad as it tastes. He's just trying to save his own skin, man."

But Evan didn't sound like a desperate man. To Leigh, he only sounded earnest. Genuine. True.

"Trust me," he said, "There is no doubt you are suffering from

Wendigo Psychosis. But killing us won't make anything better. You could give up cannibalism this very second but your symptoms will only get worse if you don't seek medical treatment."

"He's clutching at straws, man."

"Christ, John, just shut up a second. I need to think."

"What's there to think about? What, you don't trust me anymore?"

"No, that's not it."

"Then what—"

"I said I just need to think!"

Though the shouting among the men grew louder, it was nothing to how it sounded in Leigh's head. The voices had become the cries of ravens, huge ghastly birds filling Leigh's mind with their endless squawking. She just couldn't take it anymore. She just couldn't...

Wait.

What was that? In the bloodstained snow, just to the left of C's head. It caught the sky's remaining light, glinting against the crimson ground. It was small, rectangular, and metal.

It was the razor blade hanging from C.'s necklace.

The crow's squawking died down at once as terror and panic were instantly replaced by an even more powerful emotion: grief.

In the grand scheme of things, Leigh had not known C. for very long. They had not been childhood friends or even old college chums for that matter. They had met much later in life, but somehow, that had failed to matter in the slightest. C. had been there for Leigh at a time when words like "hope" and "trust" had seemed like the stuff of fiction. Sure, C. had listened to Leigh when she needed to share her worries and doubts. And yes, C. had offered her own tales of sorrow and misery so that Leigh had not felt so much alone in her struggle.

But C. had also been her friend in other ways. She had cracked jokes at the perfect times when all Leigh needed was a good laugh, just like Alex had in school. And her optimism had inspired Leigh to look ahead the same way, much like the departed Sam Tucker had made her feel even in their darkest hour.

C. had been strong. She'd overcome her demons, the proof always hanging around her neck. But the charm could only do so much. It couldn't offer protection from these new demons, the ones that looked and dressed like bikers and woodsmen.

Or could it?

Leigh stared at the blade. The voices around her still shouting, still arguing among themselves.

It was no flaming sword, but it still shared the same sharp edge. It could cut. It could hurt. C. had learned this, at one point exploring her own flesh with the blade. But she had come to learn that was wrong. This wasn't for her. It never had been for her.

THIS...

Leigh pulled back her lip, unaware that she was snarling.

THIS WAS FOR C.

Had Leigh given herself any time to think, she would've stopped herself for sure, stopped her hand from reaching for the necklace, stopped her arm from ripping the chain clean off C.'s neck, stopped herself from lunging at Uno.

But she didn't think. She just attacked.

Her swipe was wild and undirected but it the blade couldn't have found a better mark. Screaming like a blood-lustful warrior, Leigh slashed the razorblade directly across Uno's remaining eye. With his arms preoccupied with Evan's hold, Uno could do nothing to stop the attack. His scream mixed with Leigh's as blood and other viscous fluid shot from his eye, his hands instantly releasing their grip on Evan. Even during this moment of absolute chaos, Leigh's memory couldn't help itself from recalling a silent Salvador Dali movie she had watched in a college film class.

The assault had been so sudden, all the other men could do was freeze in their steps, seemingly unbelieving of the ocular mutilation occurring right before their eyes. There was only one man immune to this trance, and fortunately, it had been Evan.

Like a defensive lineman charging forward to block the other team, Evan rushed forward into Peen, slamming into the biker's midsection. Peen, taken completely off guard by Evan's charge, flew from his feet and onto his back with a loud "Oof!" escaping his lungs.

It was then that Woodenknife snapped out of his state of total surprise and lifted the crossbow at Evan's chest. Had he acted a second sooner, the crossbow's bolt would've surely planted itself into Evan's heart. But Evan had already grabbed Peen's lost hammer and hurled it at Woodenknife like the Mighty Thor of Norse mythology and comic books alike. The hammer struck the crossbow, knocking it from Woodenknife's hands.

"Shit!" Woodenknife yelled. "Dale, get'em!"

The man in the deer skull advanced on Evan but Leigh reached out and found one of his mask's gnarled antlers. Though she lacked the strength to pull his entire body away, her yank did succeed in twisting the skull on the man's head. With his eyes no longer lined up with the skull's sockets, the man blindly swung his arms out for Leigh but he felt nothing but air.

Suddenly, a hand *was* gripping Leigh's waist, and for a split second, she believed the man had found her after all. But the hand belonged to Evan who was already pulling her along as he yelled, "Run!"

Woodenknife was retrieving his weapon. Peen was getting back on his feet. Deer Skull was rearranging the mask on his face. And Uno continued to yelp as he held his face in his hands. With the exception of the last, each of these actions would only give Leigh and Evan a lead of a few steps at most.

So Leigh ran, hand-in-hand with Evan, as fast as she could. Woodenknife ordered Peen to chase after them and for the other to look after Uno. The unmistakable sound of an engine coming to life as one of them started their ATV. Her own heart pounded in her chest harder than a punk rock drummer kicking his bass drum.

But Leigh heard none of this. All she could still hear was Woodenknife's voice shouting that name that was all too familiar to her.

Dale.

Leigh had only known one Dale in her life—Dale Preston, the poor hunter who had not only contracted Embry's favorite fungal disease, but been captured by the Cedar clan along with Leigh and her friends. She had witnessed with her own eyes the wonders of the Cedars' miracle remedy as they had force fed Dale body parts freshly hacked off a young forest ranger. The forest ranger had been Douglas Graham, another name Leigh would never be able to forget.

Had Evan noticed Leigh's maniacal smile as they sprinted through the trees, he would've no doubt concluded that she had gone mad. In a way, Leigh knew that wasn't too far from the truth, as this was her fracturing psyche's way of acknowledging an outstanding irony.

Dr. Joyce had sent her to Embry to go looking for her past. As it turned out, it had been hunting her all along.

CHAPTER TEN

If life had taught Jake anything, it was that death wasn't something to fear. Whether you believed it came from nature or God, in the end, death was a gift, not a curse. Life could be painful, dark, and unrelenting. Death, on the other hand, was the sweet release from all of it. Death, by definition, was peace. This was why such a large portion of Greek mythology centered around Gods who punished not with death, but rather, forever denied it from the condemned.

When Sisyphus chained up Thanatos so that humans would never die, he was condemned to roll a boulder up a mountain over and over again for all of eternity. But that was nothing compared to the punishment of Prometheus after he gave fire to humankind: His liver was eaten by birds only to have it grow back so he could endure the same painful process for the rest of time. After one round of that, *anyone* would beg for death to come. And that was the entire point: It wasn't death you should be afraid of.

It was dying.

A drive through Embry, Vermont was all the proof you needed. It had yet to become a full-fledged ghost town, a fact which only added to its desperate state. In this country, abandoned townships were often appreciated for their historical significance, many of them granted second lives in the form of tourist destinations. But what Jake Spire saw from the windows of his car as he crept down Main Street was nothing to be celebrated.

Some stores had been boarded up, pieces of plywood covering their front displays. Other business owners had simply locked their doors and walked away, allowing any passerby to see the total emptiness of their vacant spot. To a newcomer of Embry, it would've been impossible to know what kind of store or shop had once occupied these buildings.

Jake, however, was not granted this ignorance. Like lost spirits, his memories haunted these storefronts, making him feel like some sort of medium between the living and the dead. He could still smell the delicious aroma of Alonzo's Pizzeria. He could still hear the punk rock coming from Rare Vintage Vinyl. And the annual Christmas display still illuminated the display window of Green Mountain Gift Shop. They had all once fed off the wallets of seasonal tourism, their bellies fat and full at the end of every fiscal year.

And now...

Nothing. After the stories of deadly disease and tales of local cannibalism fell under the public eye, the river of consumerism had dried up in no time at all. It was only now, passing one failed business after another, that Jake realized a disturbing truth. A tourist town was a cannibal in itself. Take away the people and watch it starve.

Of course, some businesses were still clinging on by a thread. Tractor supplies and feed stores still serviced the surrounding farms. Bars and taverns remained open too, as watering holes often continue to thrive in times of communal despair. And the Pharmacy, where Jake was driving, had also been able to keep their doors open. Perhaps doubling as a grocer had helped them hang on, or maybe there were just a lot of sick people in these parts.

Jake gave a single chuckle at this thought.

Well, there certainly had been a year ago.

The pharmacy came into view on his left, the warm light from its windows glowing in the darkening daylight. Jake signaled as turned into the parking lot, more out of habit than any real need. There was no behind him or driving ahead. Besides his own car, the street was entirely empty. As was the lot, giving Jake his pick of any of the parking spaces. He chose the closest to the front door that wasn't designated for the handicapped, and shut off the ignition. With the engine no longer running, an eerie quiet filled the interior of the car. The snow outside had become wetter, turning to a sleet that beat against the roof like tapping fingertips.

Jake sat there, his hands still on the wheel, and took long, deep breaths. He knew he was stalling, that he should be opening his door and heading inside, but fear had finally caught up with him. It had been creeping at a determined pace since Mary first disappeared, making ground with each of his failed attempts to find her. His only defense against the growing panic had been to remain proactive. Now, as he sat in the parking lot, his stomach knotting, his head pounding, he realized he had come to the of the line. If Mary wasn't inside, he would have no clue what to do next.

She'll be in there or she won't. Either way, you'll find her.

Usually, Jake's inner voice sounded just like him, existing as confidence that mirrored his external determination. Now it sounded like small, scared child, a voice Jake hadn't heard in years. Even when Phil had pulled on a gun on him, admitted he was an accomplice to murder, and blown his brains out all over the cabin's wall, Inner Jake had kept his cool. Inner Jake had pulled up his bootstraps, focused on the college kids who still could be saved, and used a signal flare to burn away Jake's bindings. Against all odds, Jake had escaped, all thanks to his inner self who hadn't given up.

Now, all Inner Jake wanted to do was hide in one of the many dark corners of Jake's mind.

No.

Jake squeezed the steering wheel, his knuckles protruding against the flesh of his hands. He hadn't come all this way back to Embry just to fall to pieces in an empty parking lot. Yes, things had definitely gone south. "Fubar," as Phil would've said, a keepsake from his days in the military. But for Mary's sake, for Phil's sake, Jake would keep it together.

All right. Let's go inside. If Mary's not here, I'll ask if they've seen her. If they haven't, I guess I'll either go back to inn or give them a call. That woman at the desk said I should talk to her co-worker. So that's what I'll...

His mind ceased in an instant, as if the conductor driving his train of thought had released the dead man's brake.

What exactly had that been about at the inn? There's no record of Mary checking in? And furthermore, a guest *had* checked in with his last name and first initial. That was the most disturbing mystery of all, one which Jake had yet to solve. Perhaps Nadine had been right. It could simply be a strange coincidence.

Later, Jake thought. *Pharmacy first.*

He let go of the wheel.

Right.

He opened the door and was immediately greeted again by the miserable precipitation. Walking at a brisk pace, he wasted no time making his way to the pharmacy's entrance. A bell chimed directly above his head as he swung open the door, its sound intensified by his relentless headache.

Allowing his eyes to adjust to the harsh light of the fluorescent bulbs above him, Jake gave the store a once over. The check-out counter sat to his immediate right, a teenage boy sitting behind the cash register. The boy had his face buried in an issue of Rolling Stone, though judging by the glazed look in the boy's eyes, it seemed the magazine was doing very little to entertain him. The kid's jaw moved in a perpetual rotation as he worked the gum in his mouth like a cow chewing cud. The bored employee was just another symbol of Embry's inactivity, and Jake couldn't help wishing again that someone would just tie the entire town to a tree and put it out of its misery. Unfortunately, there wasn't much in the way of euthanasia when it came to townships. If only they would flood this place in the name of hydroelectricity.

Taking his first steps into the store, the kid made no move to greet Jake as he walked down the nearest aisle. Since Mary would be too short to see over the shelves and display racks, Jake planned to walk up and down each aisle until he was sure she wasn't here. He considered shouting her name to save time, but he figured he had drawn enough attention today already.

As he wandered down aisle 1, passing canned and dry goods, faint music emanated throughout the store. At its low volume, Jake had to strain his ears to identify the song. He wished he had just ignored the tune the moment he recognized the melody. It was "Who'll Stop the Rain" by Creedence Clearwater Revival.

There was a time in Jake's life when he would've easily considered CCR to be his favorite band of all time. But he hadn't listened to a single track by the band in over a year. All he could think of when heard John Fogerty's voice was cruising in his truck down the back roads of Embry. And that never failed to make him sick to his stomach.

"Can I help you?"

Jake jumped at the voice. He had been so focused on the Fogerty singing about finding shelter from the storm that he hadn't noticed the man in the white coat looking at him from the pharmacy counter. Though Jake had frequented the pharmacy back when he counted himself among the residents of Embry, he had since forgotten the layout of the store. The pharmacy itself was in the back, behind the grocery section. Lost in his daze, Jake had practically walked right up to the counter when he reached the end of the aisle.

"Excuse me?" Jake said. He was glad he was still wearing

his sunglasses so the man could not see his startled expression.

The man smiled. "You seemed like you looking for something."

Jake glanced the man up and down, his tired mind working as fast at it could. Did he know this guy? Or more importantly, did this guy know him? Jake was fairly certain the answer to both questions was "no."

Jake returned the man's smile. "Just browsing," he said.

"Well, let me know if I can help you with anything." The pharmacist returned to a clipboard he had on the counter and scanned his pen along a printed document. Jake pretended to read the back of a box of cereal, all the while continuing to look at the man from the corner of his eye. He was on the taller side, had short, brown hair, and a bushy mustache of the same color. Regarding these details, Jake was confident enough that he had never met this man before in his life. As long as he kept it brief, he should be safe to ask the pharmacist a few questions.

"Actually," Jake said, returning the box to the shelf. "Maybe you can help with something."

The pharmacist looked up from his clipboard. "What's that?"

"I was wondering if you'd seen a girl in here recently."

The pharmacist raised an eyebrow. "A girl?"

Jake nodded. "Yes, about eighteen years old, wearing a peacoat and leggings." When the pharmacist's eyes narrowed, suggesting equal parts confusion and suspicion, Jake made sure to add, "She's my niece."

"Ah," the pharmacist said. "And you were supposed to meet her here?"

"Not exactly." Jake approached the counter. "She was picking up a prescription for me. I would've come myself but I wasn't really in any shape to drive. She was supposed to come right back, but then it started to snow..."

"I see," the pharmacist said. He bit his bottom lip and looked past Jake's shoulder. Jake didn't bother looking in that direction, knowing that the pharmacist wasn't staring at anything in particular. He was familiar enough with the expression reserved for those lost in thought.

Jake said nothing as he allowed the pharmacist ample time to recollect anything of use. Unfortunately, the pharmacist's spacey stare came to an abrupt end as he shook his head and said, "Sorry, I'm fairly certain I don't remember anyone fitting that description."

"Damn." Jake knocked the counter his fist. The blow was gentle, more of a gesture of his frustration than an outburst of any kind. Still, it was hard enough to rattle a plastic container of pens next to the cash register. "Sorry," Jake said, quickly returning his hands to his side.

But the pharmacist only shook his head and smiled. "Let's not throw in the towel just yet. I still may be able to help you out." He gave a little wave of his fingers. "This way."

Jake followed the man down to the end of the counter to a desktop computer. Wasting no time, the pharmacist grabbed the mouse and click. In an instant, a glow washed over his white lab coat as the screen came to life.

After a series of clicks, the man said, "All right, let's if she really was here or not. What is your name?"

Jake's breath caught in his lungs like a sputtering engine. "My name?"

"Well, yes," the pharmacist said. "So we can see the status of your prescription. If it's been filled than we'll know your niece was here."

"Oh, right. Of course."

Jake mentally scolded himself. This man wasn't looking for Jacob Spire, ex-forest ranger and runaway witness. The name he wanted was—

"Wally Parker."

No, wait.

"I'm sorry, Walter Parker."

"Walter Parker," the man repeated with accompanying taps to the keyboard. "And do you have a photo I.D. on you?"

"Right. One sec."

As Jake reached into his pocket for his wallet, an all too familiar sensation hit his nervous system like a bullet to the brain. It was the same jolt of panic one received when you were halfway through your morning commute only to realize you left an important document on the kitchen table. Or when the current date on the calendar seems important all day, but you remember it's your anniversary when it's too late to secure dinner reservations.

His fingers finding the smooth worn leather of his wallet, Jake's mind was a frenzy of activity. It had become a newspaper office running behind deadline, staff writers and editors running around and screaming at one another, taking each other out as they collided between the cubicles.

Would Mary have even been able to pick up Jake's prescription for him? Wouldn't Jake had to have called his doctor and let him know Mary was acting as his caregiver? Had he done that?

Jake retrieved his wallet and flipped it open. The face on his phony I.D. stared up at him. It was his face. But it wasn't.

"Here you go," Jake said, handing over the identification of one Walter Parker. Meanwhile, Jake's brain continued to buzz. He felt like a sports commentator running through a play-by-play.

Mary had the prescription, he remembered giving her that much. So she would've given it over to the pharmacist who would've called the doctor on the slip to confirm that Mary was authorized to pick it up. Lastly, he would've asked for a form of identification from Mary herself.

But that middle step.

The more he thought about it, the more Jake was convinced that there was no way he had made the appropriate phone calls. His memory of what occurred between driving back to the Little Northern Inn and waking up in the hotel room's bed was a bit more than hazy, but it seemed very unlikely that would've blacked out entire conversations. Besides, how would he have been able to operate a phone while either puking his brains out or passing out?

The answer, as it turned out, was somehow. Somehow he had.

Because the pharmacist then said, "Ah, Mr. Parker, there you are!" He pointed to somewhere on the screen that Jake couldn't see.

Jake's eyes went wide behind the dark lenses of his shades. "Really? Are you sure?"

The pharmacist nodded. "Unless I'm looking at a different Walter Parker. What was your prescription for?"

Jake lowered his voice as he answered. It was practically a reflex at this point, a result of the stigma of overuse and abuse connected to the drug. "Demerol," he said, preparing himself for the subtle yet sure expression of "Ah, I see," to tweak the pharmacist's face. It would last half of a second, but that face would say all it needed to in that minuscule amount of time. "Oh, you're one of those," it would say.

But instead, the pharmacist's expression was one of only pure excitement.

"Yes, there it is." He kept his eyes trained on the monitor. "It just goes to show you, never take a man's memory for the gospel. I have to admit, I'm kind of dragging today, so I'm not surprised that..."

When the man didn't finish his sentence, Jake asked, "Something wrong?"

"Not necessarily," the man said. "It's just that, according to the computer, your prescription was dropped off and filled. However, it was never picked up. We still have it back here."

"Oh."

It was all Jake could muster to say. Another crippling headache was threatening to bring him to his knees. He could feel it begin to crawl through his skull, like creeping spiders with razor blades attached to each of their eight pointy legs.

"My guess," the pharmacist continued, "is that she went to get a bite to eat while she waited."

Jake gritted this teeth, willing himself to ignore the advancing pain. "Does it usually take a while to get prescriptions filled here?"

"No, but unless I had some shopping to do, I probably wouldn't wait around here either. I'd at least take a walk down the street."

Jake rubbed his temples, trying to massage away the growing ache. "In the middle of a snow storm?"

"Good point."

There was an awkward silence, filled only with the low music of the store's speakers. Mercifully, the pharmacist broke it by saying, "Give me one minute and I'll grab your prescription."

"Thanks."

The pharmacist walked away, leaving Jake alone with increasingly discomforting thoughts. Though he'd never actually read the book, he'd seen multiple film adaptations of *Alice in Wonderland*, and felt just like the titular character now. He was falling down a rabbit hole and couldn't stop his descent. Though unlike Alice, who stumbled and plummeted in one fast fall, Jake felt like he was being dragged down at a painstakingly slow pace. Just when he thought his fingers had found a loose tree root to stop him from sliding, the root would break and he would continue down.

Down, down, down...

"Here you go."

The pharmacist dropped a small white bag on the counter. It took Jake everything he had to stop himself from ripping the bag open to get to the orange bottle of salvation he knew to be inside.

Instead, Jake just said, "Thank you. I appreciate it."

"No problem," the pharmacist said "Sorry I couldn't be more help."

"Nah, it's okay. I'm sure you're right. She probably just grabbed some lunch. Maybe I'll swing by Sammy's Subs and see if I can find her there."

"Um." The pharmacist scratched his face, an obvious nervous tick. "I hate to keep being the bearer of bad news, but Sammy's closed last year."

Jake sighed. "Of course it did. Well, either way, I'll find her.

Thanks again."

He grabbed the bag and walked away, doing everything he could not to run for the door. Though it could've taken no more than twenty steps to reach the exit, the journey felt like it lasted decades. It didn't help that Jake hesitated when his eyes fell upon a gallery of employee head shots organized next to the store's front register. His gaze lingered on an elderly woman with white curly hair, thick glasses, and a generous smile.

It was Mrs. Fields, the store's manager. Jake remembered her toothy grin like he had just seen her yesterday. She and her late husband had frequented Jake's favorite diner, and many mornings had he spent chatting with them about the season's best fishing spots. Apparently Mrs. Fields had yet to retire, which didn't really surprise Jake in the slightest. After all, a good captain always goes down with the ship. Jake found himself once again hoping that Embry would just keel over and die, if for no reason than for Mrs. Fields to enjoy a much deserved retirement in Florida or Hawaii or anywhere else that was both warm and very far away.

But thank god she wasn't working today. No way my lame disguise or fake name would've fooled her.

Finally, his shoulder found the glass door and he nudged it open, greeted once again by a cold gust of wind. He jogged over to his car, being careful not to slip on any patches of ice hiding beneath the snow. Having forgotten to lock his car, Jake swung open his door and dashed inside.

At once he opened the bag, not bothering to remove the tape sealing it shut. It ripped open, the orange bottle within practically flying out like a piñata prize. Fingers shaking, Jake cursed the childproof lid as he struggled to twist it off. When it did come loose, he brought the bottle directly to his lips, allowing two pills to pass through his lips, over his tongue, and down his throat. This was in direct contradiction to the bottle's label which advised to take only one pill with water, but that was the least of Jake's concerns.

As he sat there, listening to the muted wind and wishing the pills would take effect at once, Jake found himself thinking of sweet Mrs. Fields again. Perhaps it would've been for the best if she *had* been working today. She would've outed Jake in a second, and what would've been Jake's options then? It would've forced him to bite the bullet, to come clean and reveal everything. It might've landed him some boiling hot water, but he would've also gained some assistance in solving this Mary mystery. Instead, here he was: sitting in his car, utterly unsure of where to drive it.

Bite the bullet...

The expression replayed itself in Jake's head. No, Mrs. Fields hadn't forced him to confront the truth, but there was something else he could do. And while, oh God, it was the last thing in the world Jake wanted to do, it was perfectly clear now that Jake had no choice.

It was time to call Tricia Carson.

Though it wouldn't have seemed the least bit likely this morning, there was now a significant possibility that Mary had returned home. And the more Jake thought about, the more sense it made. Upon seeing Jake's condition, the reality of what Mary was doing would've come crashing down. She would've thought about her actions, reconsidered if leaving home and writing off her own mother was really the best life decision. She could've easily returned home and tried to patch things up. Their mother/daughter relationship could've been already mended by now.

Jake shook his head as he brought his cell phone from his pocket. *Still, Mary, you could've left old Uncle Jake a note.*

As the phone began to ring on the other end, Jake rehearsed what he was going to say. He decided he would immediately ask for Mary, hoping Tricia would hand over the phone without asking who was calling. It was a long shot, but a man could dream.

"Hello?"

Jake had been so lost in his thoughts that he at first didn't register that someone had picked up.

"Oh, hello," he said, clearing his throat. "Is Mary there?"

There was a pause. And then, "I'm sorry, I think you have the wrong number."

Jake inhaled to speak but hesitated. Though it had been over a year, he could still easily recognize Tricia's voice and knew he was speaking to her.

"Um," he muttered, "I'm looking for Mary Carson."

An exasperated sigh came from the other end. "I'm sorry, but I don't know anyone by that name."

Jesus Christ.

Perhaps it was the Demerol starting to take effect, or maybe it was just that Jake had come to the end of that line we call "patience." Either way, in that moment, all the fog and dull pain clogging the channels of his brain instantly cleared. A renewed sense of energy and focus fueled his words. He no longer cared about clandestine operations or secret identities of any of that stuff. He knew one thing and only one thing.

He didn't have time for this shit.

"Listen, Tricia. It's Jake. Y'know, old Jake from the forestry department? I know you may not want to speak with me, and that's fine. But this is important. I really need to know if your daughter is there."

Another pause.

"Daughter?"

When Tricia spoke, her voice did not come with the anger or venom or surprise that Jake had expected. Instead, it sounded only confused.

"I don't have a daughter."

It was Jake's turn to speak but he could only utter a sound that resembled, "I...wha...?"

"Like I said, you have the wrong number. Goodbye."

There was a click. And then nothing.

Jake slowly brought the phone from his ear to his lap. Outside, a heavy gust of wind practically rocked his car, but Jake hardly noticed. He was too busy falling.

Down, down, down...

CHAPTER ELEVEN

As Leigh struggled to weave her way through the tangled trees, she realized she should be much better at this. She could only assume she had more experience running from psychopaths than most people. It seemed like just yesterday that she had sprinted through the woods in a final attempt to get away from the blood thirsty Rob. She hadn't done much better then, the chase concluding with her stepping right into a snare trap. She could still feel the lightening fast grip of the snare squeezing her ankle as it yanked her upward into the trees...

Evan caught her just in time as her foot slid on a damp tree root. In that brief moment of lost balance, she was sure another trap had claimed her again.

"Come on," Evan said. His voice came in a strange combination of both a whisper and a shout. "We have to keep moving."

Leigh found her footing again and nodded. "I know. I'm okay."

The rev of an approaching engine made them look back in unison.

"They're right behind us," Leigh said, speaking more to herself than to Evan.

Her companion grabbed her shoulder and turned her to the right. "Over there," he said. "The trees are thicker. There's no way they'll be able to get their ATV through all that."

Instead of replying, Leigh led the way, running as fast as she could towards the thicket. She was fully aware that the tighter trunks and branches would also slow them as well, but it was still a good idea. Or rather, it was the best idea they had.

As she continued to run, Evan just behind her, Leigh tried to force her mind to focus on a single thought: escape. Despite the very real and immediate threat hot on their heels, her brain refused to let go of the image that infinitely looped inside her head.

The hammer came down C.'s skull over and over. That hideous muffled thump. The life leaving C.'s eyes as her spilled blood grew from a puddle to a pool to an ocean. Even more drops of blood to add to that of all her fallen friends.

How many people must die because of me?

The thought stopped Leigh in her tracks. An inner voice screamed at her to keep moving, but she could hardly hear it at all. The only voice claiming her audience was the one suggesting she turn back. If she gave herself over to her intruders, would that bring an end to all of it? No one else would ever have to wind up as collateral damage simply because they happen to know Leigh Swanson. How many lives would she save by giving up her own?

"Leigh!"

Evan practically tore her shoulder out of its socket as he pulled on her arm. "What are you doing? Let's go!"

"But...I..."

"There's no time! They're right behind us!"

In an instant, sense and logic cleared Leigh's mind like a vacuum cleaner sucking up cobwebs. The look of fear in Evan's eyes was all it took for her to reclaim her will to flee. Giving herself up to Woodenknife and Dale wouldn't save Evan. The Forlorn Hope would still finish him off in order to guarantee there would ne no witnesses to their murderous acts. Leigh's surrender would only leave Evan alone to fend off this pack of wolves. And she wouldn't do that to him.

"Right," Leigh said. "We have to get back to the main road somehow. It's our only chance."

Evan grimaced. "It's back the way we came from. Back towards them."

"Maybe we can hook around and come out further down where we turned in."

"No," Evan said, shaking his head. "They'll know." He pointed down.

Leigh followed the line of his finger. The snow had become deep enough that their steps were leaving footprints. With every step they took they were leaving behind a convenient map for their pursuers.

"Shit," Leigh whispered.

Evan looked up, squinting against the snowflakes falling in his eyes. "Maybe we can climb a tree and wait for them to—"

"Wait," Leigh said, throwing up a hand. "Do you hear that?"

Evan glanced to their back. "The shouting? I think they're arguing about how to get their machine in here."

"No," Leigh said. "Something else." She strained her ears. The trees and snow did strange things to sound out here, silencing even the loudest crash. But still, she could hear it, a constant white noise in the background that she could only notice when they were standing still. It sounded just like running—

"Water."

Evan had beat her to it. A stream or river was nearby.

It was now Leigh's turn to grab Evan's hand. "Let's go!"

"To the river?" Though obviously confused, Evan still allowed himself to be pulled along.

"Yes," Leigh said, using the hand not gripping Evan to swat away low branches. "We'll follow the river by walking in the water. We won't leave footprints that way, and maybe they'll think we crossed to the other side."

Evan remained silent for a moment as the two moved along as fast as they could. Finally, he added, "But what if the river is too deep to wade through?"

"Then I guess we'll just have to swim and hope for the best."

"Christ, Leigh, that water is going to be freezing."

"I know."

What she didn't voice was that she was actually hoping for this. Rushing, frigid water would perhaps deter Woodenknife and his gang from suspecting that Leigh and Evan would do something so foolish. If nothing else, such a stunt may force Woodenknife and Peen to split up, sending one down river while the other crossed. In that case, Leigh and Evan would only have to escape half of their assailants.

Besides, I'd much rather drown or die of hypothermia than be eaten.
She could only assume Evan felt the same way.

The ground took a sudden downward slant and that was good. This must mean they were getting closer to the running water. Unfortunately, navigating the woods had become even more difficult, as Leigh's feet wanted to slide out from under her with every step. She found herself almost skiing on her shoes as she and Evan slid down the steepening slope. Over the sliding of the snow, she could hear the water getting louder.

"I think we're almost there," Evan said from behind her. "Hope you're wearing a wetsuit under those clothes." He then preceded to laugh at his own joke.

While the majority of her concentration was claimed by her unsteady legs and feet, Leigh couldn't help but notice the unnerving giggle that emanated from Evan's lips. It was far from uncommon for someone to use laughter as a coping mechanism against intense fear or stress, but the high pitch tone of Evan's laughs did not exactly inspire confidence. He had proven himself fully capable under pressure, first buying them some time with his lecture on Kuru, and then springing into action when he attacked Peen.

Still, there was one fact that Leigh could not ignore, something she perhaps knew more than anymore. As much as she wanted to count on Evan no matter what, everyone had their breaking point.

He'll be fine. If you can still handle this, then he definitely can too.
She rounded the trunk of an especially large oak tree and

caught the first glimpse of the rushing water. It moved quickly, rolling over stones and creating white caps in a few areas where the river rocks were larger. It was still difficult to tell if the river would be shallow enough to walk, but they would know soon enough. All that remained to separate Leigh and Evan from the stream was the cluttered remnants of a fallen maple. Once through that, they would have their answers, one way or another.

"Evan," she called back. "It's just ahead. Do you see it?"

Only it was not Evan that replied. Though heaving with exhaustion, her breath caught in her lungs when a different voice came from behind her.

"Hey."

It was just a single syllable, but to Leigh, it spelled death. *How did they catch up so fast? How did we not hear them?*

Slowly, Leigh turned around.

At first, her terrified mind wanted to believe she was facing the monstrous image of John Woodenknife. Long black hair, strong facial features, and a stern-eyed stare all aided in tricking her that Woodenknife had caught up to them. But then she registered the details that made all the difference. This man was not wearing a biker's jacket, but rather, a dark blue wool jacket. Combined with the wool cap he wore over his lenghty, straight hair, he looked like he should be working on a dock than roaming through the woods. And while there was a weapon in his hands, it was not a crossbow, but a standard looking rifle used for deer hunting.

The man stared at them, concern creasing his brow. His eyes danced back and forth between Evan and Leigh. Finally, he asked, "What are you doing out here?"

Leigh inhaled to answer but then Evan was yanking on her arm.

"Leigh!" he said. "Come on!"

"Evan, wait."

"He's with them!"

The man stepped forward. "With who?"

Leigh shook her arm free of Evan's grasp. Her instincts had

led her astray before, that could not be denied. When a fellow classmate and key member of your social group turns out to be a treacherous cannibal, it's hard not to doubt yourself. But her instincts were all she had this moment, and the confused look in the man's eyes convinced her he was not with the enemy.

"It's okay," she said to Evan before turning to the man. "Please," she said to him. "We need help. There are men chasing us. They've already killed our friend."

Though the man had not been pointing his gun at them, it still came as a relief when he lowered the weapon to his side. "Who? Who killed your friend?"

"Some gang," Evan said. Apparently the man's hesitance to harm them had convinced Evan he was on the level. "Bikers. The leader calls himself—"

"Woodenknife."

Leigh could sense that the same shock that froze her body also struck Evan.

"That's right," she said. "You...you know him?"

The man grimaced. "Unfortunately, yes. We live in the same campground." He gritted his teeth, his lips curling in disgust. "I always knew he was scum."

Using one arm, the man slung his rifle over his shoulder. With the other, he gestured with his hand for the couple to follow. "My name is Matthew Wolfchild. Follow me, I'll get you out of here."

"Do you have a phone?" Evan asked. "Can you call for help?"

Matthew shook his head. "I do, but it's useless out here. No signal. But don't worry, my camp is nearby. We'll be able to reach the police there."

"Okay," Leigh said. "But we have to hurry. They're right behind us."

As if on cue, the rumble of the four-wheeler erupted though the trees.

"Shit!" cried Evan. "They're here!"

Matthew pointed to the mess of the downed tree. "There,"

he said. "Get behind that."

Leigh glanced at the pile of horizontal branches and then back to Matthew. "What are you going to do?"

"I'm just going to talk," Matthew said. If he felt any fear, his voice certainly did not betray him. "I know these men. They're not going to give themselves away if they think I don't know anything. Now hide!"

Again, Evan pulled on her arm. This time, she let him, as the two scrambled into the concealment of the tree. Fortunately, it appeared the tree had fallen before it had lost most of its leaves to the changing of the season. The dead foliage that remained curling at the end of the branches helped hide the two from view.

Lying on her stomach, Leigh tried to ignore the pointy twigs poking at her sides and cheeks as she stared through the bramble. There was just enough space between two of the branches for her to see Matthew planting his feet in the snow. His shoulders rose and fell as he breathed heavy.

In a matter of seconds, the single headlight of the four-wheeler came into view. It approached slowly, carefully traveling down the slippery slope that Evan and Leigh had just descended. Matthew stood his ground as the 4x4 came up to his side, and its driver, the murderous Peen, killed the engine.

"Wolfchild," Peen said. "How goes it?" Leigh could not believe how casual the man sounded. Only moments ago had he ended the life of a innocent girl. Now he spoke as if merely shooting the shit with an old acquaintance.

"Peen," Matthew said, nodding. "What brings you out this way?"

"Uh..."

Leigh saw Peen work the handles of the four-wheeler, wringing them as if he could get water to come out if he squeezed hard enough.

"Oh, you know," Peen said, his voice raising an octave. "Just doing a little—"

"Hunting?" Matthew placed his arms across his chest. "You know you can't do that out here."

"Well, the thing is..."

"I don't think I have to tell you," Matthew continued, "that this is protected land. Unless your birth certificate says Algonquin, it's illegal to hunt any wildlife or take any vegetation out of these woods."

Peen nodded frantically. "No, you're right, Wolfchild. You're absolutely right."

Matthew took a step forward. Leigh couldn't help admire the way he was taking control of the conversation, aggressively closing the space was a way to claim his territory. As his namesake suggested, Matthew was subtly communicating that he was the alpha wolf here and this was his territory.

"Does Woodenknife know about this?" Matthew asked. "Is he here with you? I'd like to speak to him."

"Um," Peen mumbled. As he glanced around the forest, it was hard to tell if he was looking for Leigh, Woodenkinfe, or just trying to avoid contact with the intimidating Matthew Wolfchild.

"Well, he's not right *here*," Peen said.

"But he's with you?"

"Not...exactly."

Matthew brought his hand to his face and rubbed his eyes. "Look, Peen, I get it. You think if you're with a real gosh-darn Indian than no one can bust you for poaching. And technically, if no one can prove it wasn't Woodenknife walking out of here with a prize buck, than you're absolutely right."

Peen raised his hand. "But that's not what I'm doing."

Matthew raised both his own. "Hey, it doesn't matter. Seeing as I don't see any trophies tied to that machine of yours, I don't feel like there isn't any reason I need to report this." He then pointed in the direction in which Peen had come. "That being said, you need to get on your way. Cause if I see you again out here I'll be forced to call it in. Okay?"

Peen wrung the handles again, scanning the trees with his eyes.

Matthew leaned forward. "*Okay?*"

Peen sighed. "I can't leave yet."

"Oh, no? Why not?"

"I'm looking for a...um..."

"A dog?" Matthew placed his hands on his hips. "Did you bring a bloodhound in here? Oh, this just keeps getting better."

He then pointed to the snow around him. "Well, Peen, as you can see, there aren't any dog tracks around here. So your wherever your mutt ran off to, he didn't come this way. If I were to make a bet, I'd say he probably went back to your truck. So why don't you just—"

"Whose tracks are those?"

Leigh held her breath as she watched Peen point to the snow too. Matthew looked down again and shrugged. "I don't know, Peen. You tell me. Apparently the whole world is out here today ignoring Native law. But then again, what else is new?"

But Peen was still looking at the tracks. His expression had turned from that of a frightened child to a scolding parent.

"You haven't seen anyone out here?"

"What? Besides you?"

"Yeah, besides me."

"Why, Peen? You looking for someone?"

The conversation had increased to the speed of a tennis match, each player wailing the ball back and forth, hoping to catch the other off guard.

"I'm just asking if you've seen anyone else come by this way."

"And I'm just asking what's it to you?"

Peen was muttering something about it being the business of his organization and that he didn't have the authority to discuss. Leigh only caught the first half of what he said because at that moment, an icicle broke off from a tree limb high above their heads. It could've been from a breeze or from the weight of a landing bird, but regardless of the reason, a dagger of ice now plummeted to the earth. It was only slightly longer than a pencil, but it had gathered enough speed in its decent to become a mini missile. One that somehow found its way through the mess of tangled tree branches. One that struck

Leigh in the tender flesh of the bottom lid of her left eye.

It wasn't so much the pain than the surprise that made her cry out. It wasn't a loud, drawn out scream, just the quickest, little yelp. But it was enough for Peen to suddenly jerk his head at the direction of the fallen tree.

"What was that?" he said.

Matthew turned his back to Peen to look at the pile of wood and leaves. "Beats me. Must be a squirrel living in there."

Leigh could feel a trickle of blood running down her cheek from her eye. Had the icicle struck her any higher, and it would've surely punctured the eyeball itself. Considering what she had previously done to Uno, it would've been a literal example of "an eye for an eye."

But Leigh did not pay that thought any attention, nor the slight sting of her fresh laceration. All she could focus on was Peen and how he was reaching for his belt. With his back to biker, Matthew did not realize Peen was retrieving his trusty hammer.

"Matthew! Look out!"

Leigh cried out at the top of her lungs, completely forgetting she was trying to hide. Her warning came a second too late, as Matthew had just begun to spin around when Peen brought the hammer crashing down. Matthew's twisting motion did, however, spare him from taking the blow to the back of the head. Due to his half turn, the hammer instead struck his collarbone. A loud crack mixed with the *umph!* sound that shot from Matthew's mouth as he fell to the ground.

Not knowing yet if she was going to fight or flee, Leigh struggled to escape the snarled weaving of the tree branches. Whether she could help Matthew or not, Peen would soon be moving onto her next. The tree limbs were not cooperating though. Somehow they had crossed over her legs, pinning her just behind the knees.

She spared a second long glance from her legs to see that Peen had jumped off his ATV and was approaching the fallen Matthew. He lifted his hammer.

No...

Suddenly, an explosion of white bloomed in Peen's face. He yelled and staggered back, instantly bringing a hand to his now wet and reddening cheek. Leigh's confusion lasted just as long as it took for her to look to Evan, who now stood over her. Evan, who had thrown a snowball and hit a bull's-eye.

His bottom lip bleeding, Peen stared wide-eyed at Evan. His expression said it all:

Where did you come from?

The following thoughts that entered Peen's mind were also easily read by the tell-tale signs of his face. First surprise, then relief that he had successfully found his prey, and then the greatest revelation of all: his opponent was only armed with balls of snow.

Grinning, Peen twirled the hammer in his fingers.

"There you are, mother fu—"

Peen doubled over as Matthew swept up the butt of his rifle right into Peen's gut.

"Ooph!" Peen yelled, clutching his stomach. He had very little time to dwell on his midsection and Matthew sprang to his feet and slammed the rifle stock into Peen's forehead.

Peen stumbled backwards, tripping over his heels and landing on his back. Bleeding and no doubt dizzy, Peen still clawed at the cuff of his pants on his right leg. Pulling up the material, he revealed a small revolver.

He had just wrapped his fingers around the handle of the gun when Matthew pulled back the hammer of his rifle.

"No," Matthew said. "Let it go."

Peen froze, locking his eyes with the rifleman. With the fight at a standstill, Leigh returned to the task of wriggling out from underneath the tree. As she slipped her legs from under the branches, she heard Matthew say, "Good. That's good. I don't want to have to shoot you."

With one final pull, Leigh's foot came free. Slowly, she stood up, raising everything from her waist up above the tree.

Now in plain view, Peen looked to her. Their eyes met.

Leigh never would have thought Peen was so loyal to his leader that even now he would still try to complete his mission. Whether it was from a strong sense of duty or not, Peen seemed to forget all about the rifle aimed at his chest. Like a bull seeing red, he caught one glance of Leigh, and went for his gun.

Matthew thrust his rifle forward. "Peen! Don't!"

Peen didn't seem to hear. He snatched his revolver and tore it from his leg. He pointed it at Leigh.

"No!"

Leigh would never know if the word came from her mouth, Matthew's, or both. The word was drowned by the report of the rifle as Matthew pulled the trigger. Peen's gun flew from his hand as the bullet ripped through his chest, puncturing his heart. In an instant, Peen was dead.

As the ringing in her ears faded, the sound of the river's rushing water slowly returned. For a moment, all three of them, Leigh, Evan and Matthew, remained perfectly still. All around them, the snow continued to fall.

After a silence that felt immeasurable, Matthew finally asked, "Are you two all right?"

Thankfully, Evan answered right away. Leigh still wasn't sure her voice would work yet.

"Yeah," Evan said. "What about you?"

Matthew brought his fingertips to his collarbone and winced. "He got me pretty good, but I'll live. If it wasn't for the adrenaline, I don't think I would've been able to raise my rifle."

Leigh cleared her throat, forcing herself to speak. "Well, thank God you did. You saved our lives, Matthew."

Matthew smiled through his pain. Leigh could tell it was a forced expression but genuine nonetheless. "Don't forget to thank the quarterback," he said, motioning to Evan. "That crack shot saved my ass."

Evan just shook his head. "Luck," he said.

"Yeah, well..."

Matthew trailed off as he shifted his rifle sling from his bad shoulder to his good side. "All right," he said. "You two have a lot of explaining to do, but not now. When we get back you can fill me in on just what in blue hell is going on. But now, let's just move."

"Sounds good," Evan said.

"Yeah," Leigh agreed. "We're right behind you."

Matthew nodded and forced another smile. "This way, then. Everything's going to be fi—"

Matthew's neck exploded. Leigh screamed.

Falling to his knees, Matthew reached for the bolt that now protruded from his throat. Blood pumped out in a steady rhythm, soaking his jacket before pooling on the forest floor. With wide, wild eyes, Matthew looked to Leigh and tried to speak. Only a series of gurgles passed though his lips.

Leigh ran forward to help but Matthew threw up a hand, palm out. She stopped in her tracks. He then curled all but his index finger which he pointed at the ATV.

She looked to the vehicle, then back to Matthew. Through the blood and pain, he nodded.

"No..."

Leigh tried to speak but she could only whisper. They couldn't leave Matthew behind, not after he had helped them. There was still time. Perhaps they could...

"Leigh!" Evan yelled. "Move!"

"What about him?"

But Evan was through talking. He ran at Leigh, wrapping his arms around her waist. He was already a strong individual, his size was enough to prove that. But panicked and adrenaline fueled, he was all but unstoppable. Leigh could nothing but cry out as Evan carried her to the ATV and slammed her down on the seat.

She straddled the seat, facing backward towards Evan as he sat behind her and reached for the handles. Over his shoulder, she could see Matthew falling to his back.

"Matthew!" She cried. "Hang on, we'll get help!"

She wanted to say more, to reassure her bleeding ally that they would return, that he wouldn't die.

But when she inhaled to shout again, a mini firework exploded just inches from her face. She shrieked over the high pitch wail of metal slamming into metal. Even in the midst of the total chaos, her mind somehow remained clear enough to register what just happened. The ATV had just been hit with another bolt. A bolt from a crossbow.

John Woodenknife was shooting at them.

"Hang on!" Evan yelled. He squeezed the ignition, the ATV jerking forward. Leigh couldn't tell what she was squeezing harder—her arms around Evan or her own eyes shut.

Evan swung the four-wheeler around, turning the machine in a wide arch. Feeling the world spinning behind her closed eyes, Leigh opened her eyes if only to prevent the nausea washing over her. It was a huge mistake.

Her eyes open, she saw Woodenknife emerge from the thick forest. He stepped over Matthew's body and took aim at the ATV getting farther and farther away. With Evan driving in a straight line, they were an easy target for the experienced shooter.

Her body tensed for the impact.

But then Woodenknife was stumbling, his aim no longer trained on his fleeing prey. Matthew was using the last of his strength to pull at Woodenknife's leg, just below his knee.

Yanking the wheel to the left, Evan brought the four-wheeler back up the hill from which they came. Leigh had just enough time to see Woodenknife kick free of Matthew's grip and point the crossbow at his face. And then the trees obscured them and they were gone.

Evan yelled something over the roar of the engine but Leigh couldn't make it out. She probably wouldn't have heard of him even if they had been immersed in total silence. All she could think about was the question she had asked herself just moments before.

How many...

A tear ran down her cheek, burning hot against the cold, evening air that blew across her flesh. She sobbed.

How many must die because of me?

CHAPTER TWELVE

Despite everything else, Jake was feeling better. The pills had done their work, satisfying his body's addiction and washing away the pain that had been splitting his skull in half. No longer feeling like Humpty Dumpty post-wall fall, Jake embraced this new feeling of clarity. He was still more confused than ever, but at least he no longer had to contend with a cerebral thunderstorm. Now, he could figure this out.

To keep the looming sense of panic at bay, Jake found himself harkening back to his college days. While earning his B.S. in Forestry, Jake had taken many biology courses. Truth to be told, he probably didn't retain half as much from his lessons than he should have, but one reoccurring term had been permanently branded into his brain.

The Scientific Method.

Now driving back down Main Street, Jake realized he had been practicing this old classroom standby since Mary had first disappeared. Step one: ask a question.

Where happened to Mary?

Step two: research.

This he had done when inquiring with the woman at the front desk if she knew anything about Mary's whereabouts.

Regardless of the fact that his findings only served to further perplex him, Jake had no choice but to move on to step three: construct a hypothesis.

She went to pick up my prescription at the pharmacy.

This had led him to step four: test the hypothesis. So he had traveled to the drugstore only to reach another dead-end. But if his many college labs had taught Jake anything, it was that experiments more often than not rendered negative results. And when that happened, the scientist moved onto to the next step.

Step five, refine your idea.

He could hear his old Natural Sciences professor, Dr. Anderson's voice as if it was coming from the passenger seat just to his right.

"Well, Mr. Spire. Let's review your work thus far. You tried calling Mary's cell phone and received no answer. You spoke with the front desk at the Little Northern but the clerk said her room was checked in under your name. Your prescription was filled out but no one at the pharmacy could recall Mary dropping it off. And finally, Mary's own mother denied the very existence of Mary herself. So, Mr. Spire, what does it all mean?"

Jake took a hand off the wheel and began picking at his thumbnail with his bottom teeth. It had been a habit of his since he could remember, the click of his lower incisor rubbing against his thumbnail always audible when he was deep in thought.

"Mr. Spire," the imaginary voice insisted. "I'm waiting."

Jake's hand whipped from his mouth and slammed the steering wheel.

"I don't know!" he shouted. "I have no idea what is going on in this fucking, god-forsaken town!"

A dull pain throbbed in his hand. "Christ," he muttered. He took a deep breath, trying to calm himself, but it seemed Dr. Anderson wasn't quite done.

"Now that you've got that out of your system," he said with that unfailing sense of irritating certainty he had brought with him to every class session, "May I suggest we take a step back?"

Jake, completely aware he was talking to himself like a crazy person, made no attempt to stop himself. "Which step?" he asked.

Dr. Anderson scoffed, stating the answer as if it were painfully obvious. "Collect more data."

A single "Ha!" shot from Jake's mouth. "More data?" he said. "Where in the hell am I going to get more—"

And then it dawned on him. Imaginary or not, Dr. Anderson's closed lip response of "Mmm," translated into a very clear, "I told you so." Had he actually been Jake's passenger, Jake would've been doing anything to avoid looking at his condescending smirk. He'd seen enough of it in four years of school.

Reaching for his phone, Jake had to shake his head. With all the twists thrown his way, not to mention the near-blinding pain of his previous headache, he had completely forgotten to check back in with the Little Northern. According to Nadine, the clerk he had spoke with before, a different employee had checked in the mysterious "J.Spire." With any luck, the employee would be back on shift, and maybe, *just maybe*, Jake would get at least one answer.

He pulled the car over to the side of the road as he punched in the hotel's phone number. As the phone began to ring, he turned down the heater to better hear whoever picked up on the other end. It rang once. Twice. Three times.

"Hello?"

Jake's heart sank into his gut. It was woman's voice. It was Nadine.

"Hi, Nadine," he said, solemnly. "This is Wally Parker again. We spoke not long ago."

"Of course, Mr. Parker." Jake wanted to kill her for sounding so chipper. "I suggested you come by a bit later."

Ignoring the sudden rage, Jake cleared his throat and said, "Yes, that's right. I was hoping the other desk clerk you mentioned had started their shift so I could speak to him."

Nadine's voice lowered. "Oh, I'm sorry, not quite yet."

Jake gritted his teeth. *Thanks for the news flash.*

"However," Nadine said, her voice once again becoming so sunny that it could burn your skin. "I do have a message for you."

Jake almost dropped the phone. "Really? Who's it from? What's it say?"

On the other end, Nadine laughed at his anxiousness. "One moment, Mr. Parker. Let me retrieve it and I'll be happy to tell you."

There was a brief pause, but to Jake, it felt like nothing short of eons.

God damn it, woman. Hurry your ass up.

Finally, Nadine's phone returned to his earpiece. "Okay, Mr. Parker. The message appears to be from a Mary Carson."

Jake's breath caught in his throat.

"It says she'd like for you to meet her at Macky's Pub."

"Macky's? Jake said, incredulously. "You mean, the bar?"

"Yes, I believe that is right. It's on 2nd and—"

"I know where Macky's is, thank you." For the millionth or so time in his life, Jake returned to his thumbnail to his teeth and started to gnaw.

Why the hell is she at that dive bar?

It didn't surprise him in the slightest that Macky's was still in business. When times were tough and businesses were dropping like flies, pubs, bars, and taverns tended to thrive. Especially, the cheap ones.

"...Hello? Mr. Parker, are you still there?"

The voice startled Jake to life. His mind had been drifting away, taking him along for the ride.

"Is there anything else I can do for you?"

Jake winced as his tooth came down on his cuticle. "Shit," he whispered.

"What was that?" Nadine asked.

"Nothing," Jake said, spitting out a fragment of fingernail like a piece of shrapnel. "Someone's got a lot of explaining to do, but it's certainly not you. You've been a lot of help. Thanks."

"My pleasure, sir," Nadine said, the response sounding awfully rehearsed. "Do have a nice day."

"It may be getting better," Jake muttered. "But you too. Goodbye."

"Goodbye, Mr. Parker." She hung up.

Jake tossed his phone onto the passenger seat and shifted the car back into drive. As he pulled back onto the road, he couldn't stop shaking his head. He hadn't the foggiest idea where this journey had been leading him, but Macky's was the last place in Embry he would've ever guessed.

He turned up the heater to max again, but the blowing air did nothing to stifle the imaginary voice of Dr. Anderson.

"Well then," his old teacher said. "It would seem we've reached our final step. "Draw a conclusion and—"

"Yeah, yeah, yeah," Jake said, shooing the voice away. "Report the results. Give me a minute to get there, will ya?"

There no reply. Jake, after all, was all alone.

A hazy cloud of smoke blew into the outside air as Jake swung open the door to Macky's. Though the light was growing low in the late afternoon, the inside of the pub was still much darker. Letting his eyes adjust to the new dim lighting, Jake took a moment to observe his surroundings.

It wasn't quite happy hour yet, that much was obvious. Only two people sat at the bar, each on opposite ends. An old, burned-out looking woman chatted up the bartender, a bald, brawny guy in a white button-up shirt with the sleeves rolled to his elbows. At just a glance, Jake could tell the bartender was only listening to every other word the woman was mumbling. He pretended to occupy himself by washing the same glass over and over. She didn't seem to notice, continuing to chit-chat as she took occasional drags from a cigarette in her left hand. Both her arms were decorated with faded tattoos, warped by her wrinkling skin.

On the other end sat another old-timer, this one probably a retired logger or truck driver judging by his denim jacket and cap pulled over his eyes. He kept his gaze trained on the television mounted in the upper right corner of the bar, absently staring at a football game.

Nope, no Mary there.

Turning his attention away from the bar, Jake frowned as he saw that no one else occupied any of the various tables and booths scattered around the room. From the stage in one corner to the glowing jukebox in the other, the pub was all but abandoned.

Maybe she's in the restroom?

If this were the case, Jake would simply have to wait. This was the last thing he wanted to do, having been dragged along this insane journey for far too long.

"Hey, man."

Jake turned towards the bar. The bartender was looking at him. Judging by the way he smiled just a little too wide, he seemed elated to have another customer to distract him from the yammering woman.

"Can I get you something?" the bartender asked.

"Uh, sure," he said. He didn't really feel like drinking but it would feel way too awkward to just sit and loiter. "I'll whatever's cheapest on draft."

The bartender gave a thumb's up. "You got it. Have a seat wherever you'd like, I'll bring it to you."

"Appreciate it," Jake said. He figured this wasn't a service the bar staff at Macky's usually provided, but just another ploy to get away from the irritating customer. "I'll just be over here," Jake said, motioning to a booth in the back. He figured it was close enough to the restrooms to notice if Mary came walking out, plus he would be able to keep an eye on the front door.

The bartender brought over a sudsy glass of beer just after Jake slid across the booth's vinyl seat.

"Here ya go," the bartender said. "Two dollar PBR's tonight."

"Great," Jake said, reaching for his wallet. He slapped a five on the table. "That's all yours if you can help me out with something."

The bartender raised an eyebrow. "What's that?"

"Have you seen a girl in here recently?"

"Well," the bartender said, nodding towards the bar. "There's her. But I don't think she's been allowed to call herself a 'girl' for a very long time."

Jake forced a laugh. "Nah, I mean like a college girl."

The man's smile curled to a smirk. "Oh, I see. She stand you up?"

"Something like that," Jake said, losing more patience by the second. "Have you seen her?"

"Sorry, pal, but if there was some nice, young thing in here, do I really think I'd be letting that hag over there talk my ear off?"

"So that's a no?"

Jake stared at him. The man's smile dropped.

"No," he said. "I guess neither of us will be getting any tonight."

Jake's eyes narrowed. "And I guess my *niece* just hasn't gotten here yet."

The bartender looked away and scratched the back of his neck. Shifting his weight from one foot to another, he pointed to the five-dollar bill. "You still want me to keep that?"

A smile of his own suddenly formed on Jake's face. "On second thought, why don't you bring your friend over there another beer? It looks like she could use it."

The bartender went to say something else but Jake picked up his glass and added, "But the leftover buck's all yours." He turned away and began to take a long drink.

The bartender stared for a moment longer before snatching up the five and sulking away. Jake could hear him muttering something under his breath but couldn't make out the exact words. He didn't care. In fact, he felt better than he had in the last twenty-four hours. As the cool, cheap beer ran down his throat, he momentarily forgot all about Mary's unknown whereabouts. After such a long time of internalizing frustration, confusion, and plain old pain, if felt more than satisfying to stick it some rude asshole.

Unfortunately, Jake's problems were waiting for him once he placed the glass back down on the table. In fact, he couldn't help but feel a little guilty for giving a working stiff such a hard time. He expected the bartender didn't exactly kick up his heels before every shift and whistle his way to work.

To hell with it. You've got your much bigger things to worry about it. For instance, where in the flying fuck is Mary?

After the initial relief passed of knowing the young girl was okay, Jake planned to really give her the business. He was already practicing the talk he would give her, emphasizing that he had been doing her a huge favor and taking even a bigger risk in coming back to Embry. With every person he encountered within the town limits, the risk of being identified increased. Granted, he wasn't too worried about that in here. On the rare occasions when he had gone out drinking in Embry, Macky's had never been his choice establishment. Usually he found himself knocking a few back at the Buck N' Doe, or if he was out celebrating, he'd spring for The Freemont Club. But thanks to Mary Carson, here he was, choking back cheap swill at a place that felt beneath him, even as a pill-addicted fugitive.

But speaking of pills, isn't that why Mary went missing in the first place?

Jake took another drink, swallowing hard. "Shit," he whispered. His inner voice of reason was entirely right. Had it not been for his own weakness, Mary would be safe-and-sound by his side. He would be far away from Embry by now, without a single reason ever to return. Knowing this, he couldn't even justify raising his voice to Mary. This was all his fault.

Time passed, marked only by his decreasing beer. Taking a final swig, Jake finished the remaining yeasty suds that covered the bottom of the glass. Mary had yet to arrive.

With his beverage finished, Jake reached into his pocket and retrieved his phone for what felt like the hundredth time that day. He wasn't used to being on his cell so much, preferring to leave the device in his trailer while he was out working the park. He practically felt like a Wall St. trader today, having checked to see if Mary had called or texted every ten minutes or so.

He was doing exactly this when the man slid into the seat across from him. Jake didn't realize someone had joined him until he had clicked off his cell's screen and returned it to his pocket.

Startled, he flinched as he first saw the small, smiling man who stared at him with intense, eyes. "Whoa," Jake said. "Um, buddy, can I help you?"

The man's smile parted to expose very white teeth. There was something soft and gentle about his expression, his small mouth almost feminine with its big, full lips. In fact, Jake was now noticing that "feminine" was an accurate way to describe all of the man's facial features. A small, narrow nose. Almost pencil thin eyebrows. Smooth, angular cheeks. Only the man's dark brown hair suggested anything masculine, simply because of its short cut. That and his attire: a dark blue Adidas track jacket and black corduroy pants.

"Hello," the man said. As expected, his voice too, was soft. "Mind if I join you?"

Jake chuckled at that man's absurd forwardness. "Uh, yeah. As a matter of fact I do. I'm actually waiting for someone."

The man shook his head as he were a game show host and Jake had failed to answer a question correctly. "Not anymore. I'm already here."

Jake had to give it to the guy: he had confidence. If only Jake had been so assertive with his approach to women, perhaps his life would've turned out differently.

Trying to keep the strange situation as civil as possible, Jake faked a laugh and said, "That's a good one. I may even have to use it myself. But, um, don't take this the wrong way, but I think you're barking up the wrong tree."

The man squinted for a moment, as if puzzled, and then snapped his fingers. "Oh! I get it. Like if I were a homosexual.

No, no, Mr. Spire, you misunderstand me. I'm sorry, that's my fault, completely."

Jake nodded—as if that cleared things up at all—and stole a glance around the room. The bartender pretending to do work again, his back to the old woman as he "restocked" his wall of liquor bottles. The woman, now with a fresh beer, didn't seem like she had plans to leave anytime soon. And the retired trucker or logger had taken a break from the football game, apparently dozing as he rested his head on the—

Wait.

Jake turned back to the mysterious man. "What did you just call me?"

The closed his eyes, as if exhausted, took a deep breath, and reopened them. "I know you've had a long day and I do not wish to waste anymore of your time. I just want to talk."

When Jake's vision blurred, he thought another migraine had shown up uninvited, pills in his system or not. But when the pain did not accompany the symptom, he realized it was simply anger coursing through his body.

He lifted himself off the seat but only got an inch above the bench before the man raised a hand and said, "Please, Mr. Spire. Believe me when I say it's very much in your best interest to remain seated."

Jake froze, not knowing what to do. Half of him wanted to reach across the table and grab this man by the cuff of his track jacket, but the other half, the smarter half, knew exactly how foolish such an action would be. With great hesitance, he lowered himself back onto the seat.

"Who are you?" he said, and not waiting for the answer, added, "What do you want?"

The man leaned back, relaxing. "Let's slow it down, shall we?" He motioned towards Jake's empty glass. "Would you like another drink? It's on me."

Jake gave a single shake of his head. The man shrugged.

"Okay, then. In that case I suppose I'll pass as well."

"Mary," Jake said through gritted teeth. "Where is she?"

"My, my." The man raised his narrow eyebrows. "Yet another question. All right, let's work backwards. Mary is fine, utterly and completely fine."

"Where." The word came from Jake's mouth more as a demand than a question.

"Somewhere safe," the man said. "For now, anyway. And that's all you really need to know on that particular subject. Your other questions are actually far more important, so let's address those."

"No," Jake said. His hands were balling into fists, his fingernails pinching his palms. "I'm going to beat you to death you death with my own two hands if you don't tell me where she is right now."

"Now, Mr. Spire..."

"Five seconds, asshole." Jake wiped his mouth. He was drooling like a rabid dog. "You have five seconds before I drag you outside and beat it out of you." He nodded his head towards the bar. "And don't think for a second that those people will help you. The old timer's not waking up anytime soon and that bartender will look the other way for ten bucks."

The man looked the bartender, nodding in agreement. "No, I don't doubt that."

"So," Jake said. "Start talking."

The man took a deep breath. "Mr. Spire..." He paused, pursing his lips. "Can I call you Jake?"

Jake shrugged and shook his head. "I don't know why you would. My name is Wally Parker."

The man laughed quietly. "Of course." He pointed to the other bar patrons. "But fear not, those folks over there can't hear us."

Slowly, one of the man's hands went to the zipper of his track jacket, the other presenting Jake with a single finger, as if to say, "one moment."

"I'm going to show you something," he said. "Don't worry, it's just a photograph. But I will warn you, it's going to be upsetting. Still, I'm going to need you to remain calm. Can you do that?"

Jake inhaled, studying the man's eyes. There was something unsettling about them. Not anxiety, or anger, or anything at all incendiary. On the contrary, the eyes were practically emotionless. Dead.

"If it gives me answers," Jake said, "then yeah, I suppose so."

"Good. That's good." The man looked away for a second to remove a Polaroid picture from his inside pocket. He took it out and stared at it, its white, glossy back facing Jake.

"The...centerpiece, if you will, is going to command your attention, but I want you to take in all the details of the photo. In particular, the date on the newspaper, and even more importantly, the walls in the background. And the hose, don't forget the hose."

Jake covered his mouth his hand as to not attract attention. "What the fuck are you talking about?" He practically hissed through his fingers.

"You're absolutely right. You need to see the photo."

With that, he placed the photo on the table, image down, and slid to Jake's side. Without a moment's hesitation, Jake snatched up the photo and looked at it.

He felt his heart plummet into the bottom of his gut.

In the picture, someone was tied to a chair, their arms bound behind them. A canvas bag had been placed over their head, one of those reusable kinds that conscientious grocery shoppers often opt for instead of paper or plastic. A newspaper had been propped in their lap, its front page easily visible. Even in his shocked state, Jake heeded the mysterious man's words and noticed the paper's date. It was today.

Jake forced his hand to steady as the photograph began to shake in his grip. Though the person's face was obstructed, the leggings and peacoat told Jake all he needed to know.

His eyes crept from the photo to the man starting blankly at him from across the table.

"Tell me where she is," Jake said, his breath coming hard. "Or I'll kill you right here, I swear to God."

"A justified reaction," the man said. "I would've expected no less. She is, after all, a completely innocent party in all of this."

Jake drew the photo into his hand and curled his fingers around it. The photo crinkled in his fist.

The man winced at the sound of the photo crumpling. "If you're going to destroy that," he said, "I hope you noticed the details I pointed out. Did you happen to see the water?"

Despite his almost overwhelming urge to pummel this man where he sat, Jake was able to resist enough to unclench his fist and take a second look at the picture. There was indeed water pooling around Mary's feet. In fact, it had almost reached her ankles.

As previously instructed, Jake looked past Mary to the photo's backdrop. It was then he saw the ledge just above the top of Mary's head.

She's in a pit of some kind. A swimming pool, maybe?

Examining the photo even further, he spotted the source of the collecting water on the far right edge. A hose, slightly larger than one used to water a garden but smaller than one you'd find on a fire truck, lay over the ledge. A stream of water came from the nozzle, splashing as it hit the pit's floor.

"I forgot to point out," the man said, motioning to the photo, "that she is tied with chains, not rope. That's going to weigh her down if the water rises above her head."

In an instant, the man's collar was in Jake's tight grip. His other hand, balled in a fist, was raised and ready to deliver a knock-out punch. It was like they were inside a film reel that was missing several frames. Jake didn't even register the transition from holding the photo to shaking the man by his shirt.

"Where is she?" Jake yelled.

But the man wasn't even returning Jake's gaze. Instead, he was looking past him to the bar. Jake turned to see both the bartender and old bar fly staring at them.

"It's okay," the man said to the couple. "We're fine."

The bartender squinted, his upper lip curling. "I don't want any trouble in here."

The man shook his head, completely ignoring the fact that Jake still gripped his shirt. "No trouble. We're just fooling around."

The man looked back to Jake and lowered his voice to a whisper. "If he calls the police, you'll never find her. Let them throw me in jail, I don't care. I won't tell them a thing. And how are you going to get anything out of me if I'm behind bars?"

The two locked eyes as if in a staring contest.

God, help me.

Jake released the man's shirt. He looked to the bartender. "Sorry about that," he said. "He was just messing with me."

"Whatever, just keep it down, will ya?"

The bartender didn't wait for a reply but went back to wiping the counter. Jake lowered himself back into the booth, remembering to keep his voice nice and quiet. It wouldn't be easy.

"What do you want? Who are you?"

The man folded his hands together on the table. Like the rest of him, is fingers were small, narrow, and delicate. "You'll be happy to know that those are two questions I'm entirely willing to answer. So let's start with me."

He placed a hand on his chest.

"My name is Norman Floyd."

Somewhere, in the darkest, farthest corner of Jake's mind, the tiniest light sparked like two wires struggling to connect. For some reason, the name sounded awfully familiar.

Norman Floyd, Norman Floyd...

The man must have read Jake's face as he tried to unearth the memory. He said, "I'll spare some trouble. Though you and I have never met, I believe you briefly met my son."

Son?

Norman bit his bottom lip. "Very briefly."

And then it hit him. Harder than a bullet taking down a prize buck, the revelation slammed into his brain.

"Your son," Jake said. He could hardly hear his own voice. "Your son was Rob."

Nathan nodded. "That's correct. Robert *was* my only child. Until you shot him."

Jake reached out and gripped the side of the table. How was everyone else in the bar not toppling over? Didn't they feel the world spinning like he did?

"Listen, Mr. Floyd..."

He paused to swallow, his mouth having gone as dry as the Sahara.

"I didn't want to kill your son. Believe me, I wish it could've gone any other way than how it did. But he left me no choice. He—"

"Jake." Nathan raised a hand to silence him. "Please, none of that is necessary. You misunderstand me. I don't blame you for ending my son's life. This isn't about you."

Jake searched the man's eyes for deception but found nothing to suggest lies or misdirection. "You're not...mad?"

At this, the man actually laughed. "Oh, believe me, *mad* doesn't even come close to how I've felt everyday for the past year. It's probably impossible to express exactly how I feel to someone who has never had children of their own, but that's not really important. What is important is that you understand that what I'm feeling isn't targeted at you."

"Um." Jake still couldn't help but feel like he was on the wrong end of a very sick joke. "It's not?"

"I have approached this from every possible angle, Mr. Spire. And I have concluded that you were simply doing your job. I mean, if you were a train conductor, and my boy had jumped onto the tracks, would you really be to blame for running him over?"

There was an awkward moment of silence before Jake understood that the man actually wanted him to answer. "I'm not sure. I guess not."

"Of course not. And that's essentially what happened that day. You came upon my son just as he was about to commit murder, yes? If I'm not mistaken, he was even wielding an axe like some psycho in a slasher movie."

An image flashed in front of Jake's eyes, one that he had

been trying to forget for the last 365 days and failing on every one: Rob swinging that axe back like a clean-up hitter about to clear the bases.

The kid was a psycho. There was a no "like" about it.

"As a ranger," Nathan continued, "it was your duty to protect anyone who ventured into those woods. You weren't shooting Robert Floyd, my twenty-two year old son, who had a family, and a life, and a future. You were shooting a threat. There was nothing personal about it. I get that."

"Good."

For a moment, the monosyllabic word was all Jake could say in response. Sometime while Nathan was speaking, the world around Jake had taken on an intensely surreal tone. This man who had kidnapped Mary and was holding her in some type of water based death trap, was speaking to Jake as if they were old friends.

"Good," Jake repeated, trying to clear his head. "Because it's the truth. I didn't know who Rob was. I just saw a guy with an axe and raised my rifle. If I could've talked him down I would have, but there wasn't any time. And trust me, I've been paying for it ever since. That day ruined my life."

Jake shut his mouth and when realized he was rambling.

The man nodded again. "And that is why I don't blame you."

"So, then..." Jake picked up the photo. "If *this* isn't about revenge, then why are you doing it?"

"Revenge." The man stared at the table as if the single word had just fallen from his lips and was resting in-between them. "I suppose some would call it that. But they'd be wrong." He looked up from the table at Jake. "This is about *justice*. And whether you like it or not, you are going to help me get bring to justice the person who is really responsible for my Robbie's death."

Nathan leaned forward. When he spoke the name, he grimaced as if the words were laced with poison.

"Leigh Swanson."

"Oh, yeah!"

Jake jumped at the shout. He looked to the bar to see that the old man had not only awoken, but was cheering on his football team of choice at full volume. Apparently he just needed a catnap to recharge his batteries.

He turned back to Nathan who looked at him with unblinking eyes.

"Leigh?" Jake asked. "What does she have to do with this?"

"Everything. If not for her, Rob would still be alive. I don't know how that *bitch* outsmarted my son, but had she just died like the rest of them, we wouldn't be sitting here today under these unfortunate circumstances."

Jake gently lifted his hands off the table. He placed them in front of himself as to say, "Let's pump the brakes. You'll let *me* off the hook, the guy who actually pulled the trigger, and instead you're blaming someone for fighting back to save her own life?"

Had Jake not been staring directly at him, he may have missed the lightening fast motion of Nathan wiping away a tear.

"You don't know the whole story," Nathan said. "She didn't survive because she fought and won. Rob spared her. He made sure she didn't end up like the others. And why? Because he loved her."

Jake's jaw dropped like a fifty pound weight hung from his bottom lip. "Wait, what...?"

"He and I didn't talk that much near the end. But in one of our last conversations, he told me all about the girl of his dreams, Leigh Swanson. He spoke of her like he planned to marry her one day. And what did she do in return?"

"Nathan, look—"

"She got him killed. I may not have been a good parent to my son while he was alive. I didn't give or do much for him when I still had the chance. But this...this I can do. Rob did not have Leigh in this life, but they will soon be together in the next."

Jake knew he shouldn't say what he was about to say. But

God damn it, there just weren't any other words.

"You're insane."

Nathan smiled, as to confirm Jake's statement. "No," he said. "And you should consider yourself lucky that I'm not. If I were crazy, Mary would be dead by now. But I'm a reasonable person. I don't want to hurt Mary because I don't have a reason." His eyes narrowed. "Not yet, anyway."

"Okay, Nathan. I read you. So how do I keep you from finding a reason?"

"You are going to find Leigh Swanson and bring her to me. Once you have delivered her, I will give you back Mary Carson, without harming a single hair on her head."

When Nathan Floyd had first sat down at his table, Jake could tell something was off about him. When he showed him the photograph of Mary tied to a chair, Jake knew he was dangerous. But now this man had become something else entirely, something that Jake had encountered once before. The way in which Nathan spoke, talking crazy yet in a manner of absolute righteousness, reminded Jake of someone else. His name had been Phil Carson.

"Christ, Nathan," Jake said. Though there was nothing funny about any of this, he couldn't help but laugh at the pure absurdity of it all. "How should I know where to find her? Where would I even start?"

Nathan snapped his fingers. "That's the easy part. I happen to know she's coming to Embry, if she isn't here already."

Leigh's in Embry too? What is this, a nuthouse reunion?

"How do you know that?" Jake asked a moment before an even better question came to him. "How did you even know I was in town?"

"Well," Nathan said, "you I recognized, fake name or not. I'll admit, I wasn't sure until I got a good look at you in the lobby."

"You were at the Little Northern Inn?"

Jake tried to recall when he had been waiting in the lobby for Mary to come downstairs. Had anyone else been there? There was the old couple—he could still picture them perfectly—but that had been it. Well, not counting the woman at the front desk.

"Of course," Nathan said, interrupting Jake's trip down memory lane. "We spoke, face-to-face. According to the guestbook, Leigh and two others were scheduled to check in today as well. But when they didn't show, I came up with a Plan B."

He pointed to Jake's chest.

Jake's lips parted to speak, but utter confusion stalled his words. "We spoke?" he muttered. "When? I've never seen you before in my..."

Nadine.

It wasn't a particular detail of Nathan's face that clued him in. Like a light switch being flicked on, the revelation came in an instant, all at once.

"Oh my god," Jake whispered. "It's you."

Nathan framed his face with his hands. "It's me." He smiled, bearing all his teeth. It was the same grin the front desk clerk had on hand for every guest who checked into the hotel.

"Surprised?" Nathan said. "You should see your face."

Jake didn't exactly know what he looked like right now, but he imagined it was something close to the permanent expression a lot of patients wore day in and day out as they stood and stared out in the window of the asylum rec room. He wished to God somebody would cart him away right now, so he too could take his place among the loonies, this dumbfounded look forever frozen on his face.

"This rabbit hole has no end, does it?"

Nathan, or rather Nadine, gave a chuckle. "No, it does, and it ends with Leigh Swanson."

This time, Jake didn't even bother opening his mouth. It wasn't that he was struggling for words—there were just no words left. Gripping his empty beer glass in his fingers, he rolled it from one hand to the other. Though he did not look up, he could still feel Nathan's burning gaze as the kidnapper spoke.

"I can see you're really struggling to make sense of all of this. But trust me, I know how you feel. In fact, in the end, you and I are not very different."

"Are you kidding me?" The glass made a loud *clink* as it fell from Jake's grasp, barely remaining in one piece. "Am I abducting innocent girls? Am I blackmailing a total stranger? Do I dress up like a woman and—"

"I *am* a woman!"

Nathan's shout cut off Jake's words like a knife through butter. Immediately, he glanced to the bar, fully expecting the bartender to be racing over with a shotgun or whatever blunt object he kept behind the bar to deal with troublemakers. Luckily, the bartender didn't seem to hear the outburst, too distracted by the phone conversation he was presently having. Jake hoped it wasn't the police on the other end.

Nathan placed his palms on the table and took a deep breath. "My apologies. Yelling will only attract attention, I know this." His stare then became dagger sharp. "But I will not abide anyone telling me that my life is make believe."

"Nathan, look—

"Let me tell *you* something. What I'm wearing now? *This* is dressing up. *This* is a disguise. I haven't dressed like this for years, and when I did, I vowed it would be the last time. But I'm willing to make this sacrifice, to become Nathan once again, in order to bring justice to my son. It doesn't matter that his mother left me after I stopped being afraid of who I really am. It doesn't matter that I hardly got to see my boy, and when I did, his mother made me dress like *this*. It doesn't matter that, in the end, our conversations were limited to phone calls and letters I had to sign, 'Your dad, Nathan.' No, none of that matters. Because my name is Nadine. And Robert was my son."

Jake didn't realize he had been holding his breath until a great pressure forced him to expel it from his lungs. A dull throb was forming deep in his skull, a headache just starting to knock on the front door of his brain. He would need another pill soon.

"Nath—"

Jake cleared this throat, beginning again.

"Nadine. I'm sorry. Really, I'm truly sorry, but..."

Nadine nodded. "I know. That's what I meant when I said we're very much alike. We've both had our seemingly normal, everyday lives derailed by unforeseen circumstances. That's why I hate that I must put you through this."

Nadine suddenly shifted in her seat, sliding across the vinyl to exit the booth. "Then again," she said. "I'm glad it is you because I know you'll do the right thing."

She stood. Jake made a move to grab her arm but missed. "Wait," he said. "Let's talk about this."

Nadine shook her head. "No more talking, just listen. I am going to ask the bartender on my way out to bring you another beer. You deserve one, that's for sure. But I want you to take your time drinking it, because if you walk out of this pub in less than twenty minutes, Mary Carson will die."

Jake made a move to stand but Nadine motioned him to remain still.

"Twenty minutes, Jake. That will give you some time to think about how you're going to locate Leigh Swanson. After that, you will be free to leave the bar and begin your search."

She reached into her pocket and removed a small cell phone, the flip kind. She placed it on the table.

"Once you have found her, I want you to call the only number you'll find in the contacts. I will then give you further instructions. Do you understand?"

"I..."

Jake didn't know what to say. He didn't know what to do. Attack this person? Call for help? Follow her once she leaves the bar?

No.

No to which one?

No to all of them. Nadine may be bluffing, but you can't risk Mary's life. You're just going to have to play along for now.

A final thought hit Jake like a sucker punch to the gut, an emotional cheap shot delivered by his own hand.

You have to do this for Phil.

His voice low, Jake said, "I understand."

"Good. I have to go now. I need to drain the water before it gets too high."

Nadine must have seen the horror enlarging Jake's eyes because she added, "Don't worry. I'm positive it's not too high yet. And I made sure to keep the temperature nice and warm. Just think of it as a soak in the tub."

With that, Nadine tapped the phone once more, and walked away. Jake watched her go, stopping by the bar just as she said she would. When she mouthed some words and pointed to Jake's table, the bartender grimaced, no doubt unpleased he had to serve Jake once again.

And then Mary's kidnapper walked right out the front door.

A few moments later, the bartender brought over another glass of frothy beer.

"Here ya go," he said, taking little care as he practically slammed the pint glass on the table. "Courtesy of your friend."

Jake looked up to the bartender with dull, expressionless eyes. "I have no friends," he said.

The bartender scoffed. "You're breaking my heart," he mumbled as he walked away.

Jake took a sip of beer. It was just as cold as before but now tasted bitter and flat. As he sat there and absent mindedly gripped his beverage, he knew he had lied to the bartender.

I do have friends. Two of them, actually.

And to save one he would have to kill the other.

CHAPTER THIRTEEN

Leigh couldn't feel her fingers anymore. As much as she wanted to put her hands in her pockets, or tuck them under her arms, or better still, blow on them like her mother used to do when she was little, none of these were options. With the way the four-wheeler jerked and bounced as it rolled over the forest floor, she needed to keep her fingers interlocked around Evan's waist. And she wasn't about to tell Evan to slow down. She would let her hands turn black from frostbite before she did that.

As if he could read her mind, Evan asked, "Are you okay?" Maybe he had just caught a glimpse of the discomfort distorting her face. She still sat in front of him, facing him as he steered. It was the same way models in 80s music videos used to sit on motorcycles while they made out with the lead singer of a hair band. Something told Leigh that MTV viewers wouldn't have found anything sexy about it right now.

"Yeah," she yelled, over the engine. "Hands are just a little cold."

Evan nodded. "Hold on. I'll stop."

"No!" Leigh squeezed him tighter to stress the point. "I'm okay. Just keep moving,"

"It will only take a second. When I stop, jump off and get behind me. You'll be able to stick your hands in pockets of my jacket."

Though she still wanted to get as much distance as possible between her and their pursuers, Evan's idea was just too tempting to pass up. She would be far more comfortable and she wouldn't have to risk losing any of her fingers. Besides, Evan was right. It would take less than ten seconds.

"All right," Leigh said. "Let's do it fast."

Evan released the throttle, jerking Leigh forward as the ATV came to a sudden stop. Though Leigh had demanded they move quickly, she found her body didn't want to cooperate with that command. She had been tensing her body since boarding the vehicle, and the cold had stiffened the muscles in her arms and legs. Groaning, she forced her numb hands to become unlocked, wincing as she swung her locked knee over the seat.

She almost fell as her feet hit the forest floor, pins and needles radiating all the way up her legs. Ignoring the strange sensation, she climbed back onto the ATV, sitting on what little remained of the seat behind Evan.

"Okay," she said, re-wrapping her arms around Evan's waist. "I'm good. Let's go."

But Evan did not move. Instead, he stared out to their left, a look of concentration steeling his face.

A initial jolt of terror seized Leigh's insides as she believed Evan had spotted the men who relentlessly hunted them. But then she saw that Evan's expression had turned to one of relief, almost joy. After the horror they had endured, the emotion had become so alien that Leigh barely recognized it. Whatever Evan saw, it was actually good news.

"What is it?"

Evan stretched one of his long arms and pointed. "Is that a trail sign?"

Sure enough, a wooden sign had been nailed to a tree about fifty feet from where they parked. An arrow pointed to the right of the tree trunk where a smooth path extended into the woods. Next to the arrow was the word, VAST. She didn't know what the word meant, but the illustration behind the letters told her everything she need to know. The silhouette of a snowmobiler framed the four-letter word.

Excitement ignited Leigh's voice as she said, "It's a snowmobile trail!"

To Leigh, the snow covered trail might as well been made of yellow bricks. Not only would the maintained path provide them with a much smoother ride, but better yet, the trail was sure to lead them out of the forest. Though it was impossible to say how long it would take, eventually the trail would have to come to an exit of some kind. Whether it be a state park, or parking lot, or main road, salvation would be waiting for them at the other end.

Not wasting another second, Evan gripped the throttle and away they went.

It did not take long for Leigh to realize that the previous pain in her freezing fingers may have been a gift of sorts. With her hands now protected in Evan's pockets, her mind was no longer distracted by the intense cold numbing her flesh. Now her thoughts could drift, and what took the place of the distracting frostbite was much, much worse. An image replayed itself over and over that she could not force way no matter how hard she tried: Matthew Wolfchild's final moments.

She saw Woodenknife raise his crossbow, take aim at Matthew's face, and then trees blocked her view. She saw Woodenknife raise his crossbow, take aim at Matthew's face, and then trees blocked her view. She saw Woodenknife raise his crossbow, take aim at Matthew's face, and then...

Stop it. STOP IT!

She squeezed Evan a little harder, hoping he wouldn't notice. She could only wonder if Evan was also dwelling on the murders they'd both witnessed, but Leigh had her doubts. Evan, after all, had to focus on keeping the ATV on narrow trail, slowing when they took sharp corners and regaining speed when they straightened out. Leigh thought she had never been more jealous of anyone in her entire life. She would give anything to escape the pictures within her head. Because when she actually did manage to block out Matthew's demise, C.'s death was waiting in line.

She considered taking her hands out of Evan's pockets and letting the cold air bite her skin again. But what would be the point? Even if she did manage to keep her horrible thoughts at bay, Matthew and C. would be waiting for her the next time she went to sleep. They would both join her friends who already had reoccurring roles in the cast of her nightmares. She could almost see them walking into a big room with a long table in the center. Around it sits Marshall, Alex, Eliza, and of course, Sam. Rob would be there too, since you can't have a good nightmare without a boogeyman.

"Welcome you two," Sam would say. "Pull up a chair and grab a script. We've got to rehearse before that bitch falls asleep tonight." And C. and Matthew would smile like the rest of them, knowing that they would get their revenge against the one that doomed them to die.

Then again, they might not get the chance if Leigh didn't make it out this alive. Leigh was reminded of the possibility of that outcome when she felt the ATV slowing before it came to a full stop.

Though Evan kept his grip on the handles, he no longer squeezed the throttle. Instead, he stared out to his left, much like when he had spotted the snowmobile trail sign.

"What is it?" Leigh asked.

"The trees."

It was all Evan had to say. When Leigh turned she saw that the entire forest before her consisted of nothing but blackened trunks. The dark wood stood out against the white falling snow like struck matches. A comparison, Leigh thought, that was entirely accurate. After all, this whole area of woodland had been set ablaze in a controlled burn, the state's method of choice to irradiate Embry's lethal fungus.

"The Ashes," Leigh said, leaning forward to speak into Evan's ear. "Somehow we drove right into the Ashes."

Evan said nothing back, only nodding a response. He apparently didn't need further explanation, which didn't surprise Leigh at all. Embry's forest fire cookout had been huge news when it occurred. She herself had seen the news coverage on TV. She remembered C. quoting Robert Duvall in *Apocalypse Now*, though with a slight modification.

"I love the smell of fungus in the morning."

It was supposed to be a lighthearted remark to cheer Leigh up as C. must have known full well the terrible memories the newscast was surely bringing to the surface of Leigh's mind. Leigh had faked a laugh, keeping her eyes trained on the screen. She half expected the flames to turn green from all that god awful fuzz lurking in the woods. Even then she knew, deep down inside her, that mere fire wouldn't solve the problem. It was just too damn simple to be the actual solution.

One year later, and not a single new sighting of the disease. Looking out at the charred remains of the woods, Leigh had to admit she had been dead wrong. Fire had saved the day after all. Unfortunately for the town of Embry, they might as well have been burning money. The town's economy would forever be in the same state as these trees—burnt to a crisp. Dead.

Evan shook his head. "It's wild, isn't it?"

"Yes," Leigh replied. "It's something else."

"Well." Evan glanced back at her. "Let's keep going. Hang on."

And just like that, as if on cue, the ATV's engine stuttered to a dead stop. Without the grumbling noise of the idling machine, the forest fell to a dead silence.

"Evan?" Leigh's voice sounded much to loud against the total quiet. "What happened?"

"I don't know. The engine just died."

Evan looked to both sides of the vehicle before he found

the engine's pull string. Checking behind him to make sure he wouldn't hit Leigh with his elbow, Evan gave the string a hard pull.

The engine made its expected growl but didn't catch. He pulled again, harder this time. Still nothing. Evan pulled again, this time adding a "Come on!" as he yanked. The ATV did not follow his command.

"Shit!" Evan let the cord snap back out of his grip.

"Are we out of gas?"

"I don't know," Evan said. Based on his last outburst, Leigh expected Evan to shout his answer at all, maybe throw an "F-bomb" in there for good measure. But his voice sounded tired, as if he was on the verge of defeat. "It doesn't make any sense. We haven't been driving for that long."

"Maybe it didn't have a full tank to begin with?"

Evan didn't say anything back but Leigh didn't blame him. This guessing game would do no good for anyone. Even if they could determine the cause of the problem, what could they do to fix it? They were out in the middle of the woods without any tools or extra fuel. Still, Evan seemed to determine to take action as he asked Leigh to slide back so he could step off.

"I'll check the tank," he said. "If there's gas, maybe I just need to give it this thing a few more yanks."

Leigh got off the ATV and followed Evan back to the rear of the machine. Upon locating the gas cap, Evan unscrewed it and peered inside. Although Leigh could not see insider herself, Evan's sour expression told her all she needed to know.

"Bone dry," Evan said. He let the gas cap fall to the ground as he looked at her with tired, sunken eyes. "We're fucked."

Ignoring the quickening pace of her heart, Leigh strained to keep her face from drooping as well. "Okay," she said. "So we walk."

Evan waved a hand in the direction they were heading. "And for how long? That trail could go for miles for all we know."

"What, then?" Leigh said, throwing up her own hands. A part of her knew she was steadily losing her cool but she couldn't seem to help herself. "You know we can't turn back!" She turned towards the way they had come. "The only thing waiting back there is..."

She let her sentence be carried off in the wind. It was just angry ranting anyway, nothing constructive would come of it. What was more important was the strange, dark trail running along the center of their tire tracks. It was slightly off-white in color, tinged with a bit of yellow. Juvenile as it might've been, she couldn't help but compare the color to urine.

It's like the ATV was taking a really long piss as we drove.

"Oh shit," Leigh said. That was exactly what had happened.

She immediately fell to her hands and knees, feeling the cold bite of the snow as it leaked through her pants. Not knowing exactly what she was looking for, she peered under the ATV as if she were an expert mechanic.

"What are you doing?" Evan asked from above her.

Before she could answer, Leigh spotted a long, silver rod sticking out from under the ATV's chassis. Though she couldn't have identified any of the parts scattered among the underside of the vehicle, the fletching she saw told her that this particular item didn't belong. Cold metal stung her palm as she wrapped her hand around its base. With a grunt, she pulled the piece free, revealing its arrow-shaped end.

"Leigh?" Evan called. "What is it?"

Leigh crawled out from underneath the ATV, brushed the snow off her pants, and placed the crossbow arrow in Evan's hand. He stared at it like it was a piece of alien technology. When it dawned on him what had happened, his looked up with big, wide eyes.

"Holy shit," he said. "He hit our fuel line."

In an instant, Leigh recalled the bright bloom of light that had erupted at the back of their four-wheeler as John Woodenknife fired at them while they sped away. She pointed to the sharp end of the arrow. "Few inches higher and that would've gone right into my back."

"No," Evan said. He looked back down to his hand. "You were sitting in front at the time. This would've killed me."

Leigh dug her nails into her palms. Somehow the idea that Evan would've been the one to get hit was even worse. Once again, that horrid question broke its way into her mind.

How many must die because of me?

Evan gave the arrow one last look before throwing it aside. "But we're both still alive. That's what counts."

Before Leigh could say anything back, a huge gust of wind ripped through the well-cooked trees. Both she and Evan lifted their arms to guard their faces, closing their eyes against the stinging snow.

"Okay," Evan said, the moment the gust subsided. "You're right. We don't have a choice. Let's just hope to God that this trail leads somewhere soon. If not, we'll probably freeze to death."

"Compared to our other options," Leigh said, walking past Evan, "that's the best news I've heard all day."

Evan said nothing back, but Leigh knew he agreed when she heard him following her, his footsteps crunching in the snow.

They didn't walk five steps before they heard John Woodenknife's voice no more than five feet away.

"Omega, check in. Over."

Leigh shrieked, the noise erupting from her as a total reflex. She spun to see Evan doing the same, but no one stood behind them.

"Omega Wolf, this is Alpha Wolf. Come back. Over."

Evan looked back to Leigh, his brow furled, his lips slightly parted. "What the hell?" he said.

Leigh shook her head, too startled to speak. At first, the voice sounded like it was right on top of them, but now its muffled quality suggested it was actually coming from *underneath*.

Walking like there were landmines hidden under the snow, Evan carefully tiptoed back to the ATV.

"God damnit, Omega Wolf. Pick up! Over."

Leigh copied Evan's movements, also returning to the ATV with careful, measured steps. When she reached Evan's side, he was already lowering his ear to the source of the sound.

"I'm here."

There was a second voice now, but it sounded as muffled as the first. Now that she was closer, Leigh also could hear an almost robotic quality to it. The voice was tinny, metallic.

There was a pause, and then, "Er...over."

"Where the hell have you been? I've been trying you forever. Over."

Evan's gaze shot up and met Leigh's. "Holy shit," he said. "It's coming from under the seat."

Sure enough, when Evan explored the edge of the seat with his hands, he discovered it lifted at one end, revealing a shallow compartment. In it lay a industrial flashlight, a Leatherman multi-tool, and the source of the conversation: a walkie-talkie.

"Sorry, I left the walkie-talkie in the truck. I just grabbed it. What's going on? Over."

"The rabbit got away. Repeat, the rabbit got away. Over."

Leigh and Evan shared a glance. There was no mystery to what that meant.

Another pause and then, "Shit. What do we do now?" Pause. "Over!"

Evan picked up the walkie-talkie so that both of them could hear it better over the whistling wind. "First of all," Woodenknife's voice said, "Calm down. We're fine. They took off on Beta Wolf's four-wheeler, but I'm pretty sure I know where they're going. I need you and Lone Wolf to..."

Woodenknife paused, the airwaves going dead for a moment. And then, "How is Lone Wolf? Can he travel? Over."

"Um..."

Now it was the other voice's to go silent.

Dale's voice...

"Negative, Alpha Wolf. Lone is out of commission. Over."

"What? You mean...?" There was a click of the transmit button being released. When Woodenknife finally came back he muttered, "Christ. All right, here's what you're going to do.

Put Lone in the back of the truck and make sure he's covered in something. You've got a tarp? And bungees? Over."

"Yeah, over."

"Good. Once he's settled in, take my bike and ride to Susan's Swamp. You know where that is, right? Over."

"Sure I do. But what for? Over."

"I think the rabbit is on the VAST trail that dumps out right there. I'm in pursuit on foot, but you're going to head them off. Understood? Over."

Evan inhaled quickly, just short of a full gasp. "Oh shit," he said.

In the walkie-talkie, Dale was practically yelling. "That's it? For God's sake, they're on an ATV! You'll never catch them and I'll never get to Susan's Swamp fast enough. Over!"

"I don't think so," Woodenknife said. The words came through with such a wicked confidence, they chilled Leigh far more than the winter air. When the sicko known as Bugger Cedar had her cornered during her first nightmarish visit to Embry, Leigh had heard the voice of evil with her own ears. It had sounded just like this.

"Their horse is bleeding, if you get my drift, and it will be dead soon. I'm following the blood trail as we speak. Do you understand? Over."

There was one more pause, as if Dale was contemplating what he had just heard. "Finally," he said. "Some good news. I'm on my way. Over."

"Excellent. Over and out."

The radio waves fell silent, turning the walkie-talkie into nothing but a block of plastic and wire. Evan stared at it as if it might come back to life at any moment.

"Okay," he said, finally coming out of his trance. "What do we do now?"

Leigh pointed to the walkie-talkie. "For starters, we keep that. Let's try every single frequency until someone answers."

Evan nodded with enthusiasm. "Yeah, that's a good idea. I

mean, someone's got to pick up, right? And they can get help." The bright look in his eyes suddenly darkened. "We can't stay here, though. Even if we do manage to reach someone, there's no way they'll get here before you know who."

"You're probably right," Leigh said. "But it doesn't look like we should stay on this trail any longer."

Evan kept nodding as if the gesture now more of a compulsion than a deliberate action. "I would say we could chance running into another snowmobiler, but you can tell this the first real snowfall of the year. Most people would wait for a few more inches before bringing their machines out here."

Leigh pointed to her right with one hand and the left with the other. She felt like the scarecrow in the Wizard of Oz when he first encounters Dorothy, but she ignored the feeling. "Then which way?"

Evan pointed to his right, or Leigh's left. "We took a few twists and turns, but I'm pretty sure that river we heard before is that way. I think we should go back to our original plan. If the river can't hide our tracks, it still may lead us out of here."

Leigh lowered her arms. "I don't know if it's a good plan, but it's a plan. Let's do it."

Evan reached down into the under-seat compartment and retrieved the flashlight and Leatherman. He pocketed the multi-tool and handed the flashlight to Leigh. "These could come in handy. I'll hold onto the walkie-talkie and keep trying it as we walk."

Leigh accepted the flashlight. Its weight felt comforting, as if she were brandishing a weapon with an attack far stronger than a simple beam of light.

Evan led the way, Leigh following behind in his literal footsteps. She figured it couldn't hurt to minimize their tracks, not to mention it would make her travel much easier if the snow before her was already padded down.

She turned back one last time to give the ATV a final glance. Its dark finish was already obscuring it in the lowering light. It reminded her just how early night came in the final months of the year. Before they knew it, total night would be upon them. Leigh silently prayed that they would be out of the woods by then, that this nightmare would be coming to a close by the time the sun made its final descent behind the horizon.

But something deep down in her gut, call it intuition, told her that would not be the case. Just then, the famous line by the poet Robert Frost came to her, and Leigh knew it had never been more true.

I have miles to go before I sleep.

CHAPTER FOURTEEN

The phone rang in Jake's ear as he drove away from the central part of town.

"Come on, Eddie. Pick up!"

Jake had followed Nadine's instructions, remaining in the bar until his beer was finished. It hadn't gone down smooth to say the least, but when the glass finally emptied of everything but the white suds running down the side, Jake headed right for the door. At first, he thought he might throw up on his way to the exit. Two beers had never had this effect on him, but there was enough stress twisting his belly to give him stomach cancer. Fortunately, the nausea passed as quickly as it came, and Jake stepped outside.

They say when it rains, it pours. Apparently, this also applied to snow. As if things couldn't get any worse, Jake found that the snowstorm had actually intensified during his time in Macky's pub. There was no sign of Nadine, not that spotting her would've been easy in the swirling flakes. With absolutely no plan whatsoever, Jake stumbled to his car, if only to gain shelter from the snow and wind.

He had driven absent mindedly for the first five minutes. It was as if his mind had decided to check out, telling him it would be back when all of this blew over. Till then, he was on his own, a zombie crawling down Main Street in an Eagle wagon. Jake kept asking himself, "What the hell am I going to do?" But there was never any answer.

Jake drove by more closed stores, more vacant lots occupying nothing but ghosts of the past. This time, however, he barely noticed. A trip down memory lane was the last thing on his mind. All he cared about was the future. Mary's future.

But where to go? What did Nadine really expect he could do? This was the most desperate plan he could ever imagine. Sure, Embry was a small town compared to a lot, if not most places in the United States. There were much larger haystacks in which to find a needle, but this was still such a longshot.

What does that nutjob think I'm going to do? Just call information and ask if...

It was then the idea occurred to him. He would call the one person he always called when he was in a jam. His hookup when he needed a fix. His fixer when he needed to skirt laws or regulations. Jake would call Eddie Lee.

"For crying out loud," Jake muttered when the phone continued to ring. "You know it's me. Pick up, already!"

As if on command, Eddie's voice materialized on the other end.

"J-Man, what's crackin?"

"Eddie!" Jake said, startled. He had all but given up on Eddie answering. "I need you to do me a favor."

"Of course you do," Eddie said. Though several miles away, Jake could still see Eddie's smug face as clear as day. "Why else would you call me?"

"Fair enough," Jake said. "But I'll make it worth your while once I'm back in town. I promise."

Eddie coughed, most likely after taking a drag on a cigarette. "Ooh, you promise, huh? I don't know, man. Can't really pay the bills with promises, know what I'm saying?"

"Shit, Eddie, come on!"

Jake hadn't meant to yell. It just sort of came out.

"Easy bro," Eddie said. "I'm just bustin' your balls. You know I take care of my loyal customers. And know you're good for it."

"Sorry," Jake said, without hesitation. "It's just been a long day."

"In that case, Dr. Feel Good knows what you need. You looking for a local distributor? I can make some calls."

Jake shook his head as if Eddie could see him. "No, man, I'm all set in that department. I'm actually calling for some information."

"Information?" Eddie paused to take another hit from his cigarette or joint. There was an equal chance it could be either. "Not exactly my forte, but I'm listening."

Jake let off the accelerator a bit. He had reached the highway leading out of town where the speed limit increased. He found himself having to resist the habit of pushing his foot harder on the gas. Flying off the road wouldn't help anything.

"I've got no time to explain, but I just need you to go with me on this. I'm still in Embry and the shit's really hit the fan. I need to find someone as quickly as possible but it's snowing like a bastard here."

"So what are we talking here? A disappearance? A kidnapping or some shit?"

Jake paused. The question took him completely off guard. Should he tell Eddie about Mary's kidnapping? No, he decided. It would only complicate things.

"Nothing like that," Jake said. "At least I don't think so. I really just need you to see if you can find anything on any accidents up here that have happened today. Don't know if you've got any contacts in this neck of the woods, but you can at least surf the web for me."

Eddie belched. Apparently he was drinking as well. "I'd have to consult my rolodex to see if I know anyone up there. As for checking the net, sure thing. But I doubt I'll find anything until tomorrow morning's news hits the stands."

"Just call me back when find anything, and I do mean *anything*. I'm heading to store just off the highway to see if they've seen or heard about any serious crashes. In case I lose service, the store is called 'Abel's & Mabel's.' Look up the number and call there if you can't reach me on my cell."

"Abel's & Mabel's," Eddie repeated, though it was impossible to know if he was actually writing it down. "Got it. You sure you can't fill me in here?"

"Sorry, man, but I got to stay focused. You're just going to have to go with the flow for now."

Jake heard the sound of a beer can crinkling, another dead solider joining the ranks. "Whatever," Eddie said. "But hey, speaking of staying focused, you sure you've got enough medicine?"

Jake was actually reaching into his jacket for his pills at that exact moment. He pulled the orange pill bottle from his pocket and shook it. "Definitely," he said. "Practically have a full bottle."

It occurred to him now that he probably had Nadine to thank for that. After nabbing Mary, she must have gone to pharmacy to make sure Jake's prescription would be waiting for him. After all, Jake would've been of little use to her had he still been suffering from withdrawal.

"Aight," Eddie said. "I'll call you back." Without waiting for Jake to respond, Eddie hung up.

The phone call hadn't made Jake feel better like he had hoped. If Eddie did manage to drag his lazy ass to his computer, he was probably right about the chances of finding anything useful. Even if Leigh had been in an accident worthy of news coverage, it wouldn't be released until tomorrow. It wasn't like this was New York City or Los Angeles, where there were millions of people with millions of phones just waiting to capture the next viral video. Hell, if Leigh really had lost control and flown off the road, her car could be buried in snow by the time another vehicle came driving by.

Speaking of car trouble, Jake was now coming upon the remnants of some which occurred earlier today. Though almost filled in by the falling snow, swerving tire tracks were still visible on both sides of the road. Jake slowed his own car to get a better look at them, as his eyes couldn't quite tell what he was looking at. It seemed like the vehicle had an odd number of tires based on the number of tracks. But when the tracks split, two of them careening up a side road while the third continued straight, Jake realized he was looking at the tracks of a car and a motorcycle.

Both sets of tracks shot out of view as they disappeared up a side road. It appeared the motorcycle had not kept up the car, as it passed the road before turning around in a dramatic sweep. Jake guessed that the car had lost it on some ice and bailed onto the side road to keep the bike from crashing into its rear. After a close call, the bike pulled a "u-ey," to make sure the car was okay. It wasn't an uncommon courtesy in these parts, and Jake knew he would've done the same.

Of course, I wouldn't have been caught dead on a motorcycle today.

Moving on, Jake accelerated, but not too much. He was anxious to get to Abel's & Mabel's, but had no intentions of repeating the mistake of the travelers who had come before him.

Even at a slower pace, it wasn't long before he reached the general store and gas station. As expected, the parking lot was almost entirely empty, as most folks around here were probably hunkered down already and waiting out the storm. There was, however, a pick-up truck and station wagon parked alongside the building, which Jake hoped belonged to the employees. Judging by the sign in the door still flipped to "OPEN," it seemed that was the case.

Jake took the closest non-handicap space to the door and shut off the ignition. He gave his phone a quick check before to find he still had two bars of service. Knowing that would be enough for Eddie to reach him, Jake pocketed the phone, stepped out of his car, and ran inside.

A small bell jingled as the door swung open, calling the attention of an elderly man behind the counter. Jake took one glance at the man and instantly thought this was what Jim Henson may have looked like had he not died at the young age of 53.

"Greetings," the bearded man said. His voice even had a nasally, Kermit-esque tone to it. "She's really coming down out there, ain't she?"

Jake brushed off his jacket and stomped the snow from his boots as he made his way to the counter. "You got that right," he said. "I think we can officially call this one a blizzard."

Elder Jim Henson gave his beard a scratch. "Oh, yes, we left 'flurries' a long time ago. You're on your way home, I hope."

Jake reached the counter, trying not to drip melting snow onto the wooden finish. "Just about," he said. "But before I do, I need to find someone first. She went out in this weather, and, well..." Jake leaned forward as if he and the old man were co-conspirators. "She's not the best driver, if you know what I mean."

The old man smiled revealing a full set of teeth that may or may not have been dentures. "You sure you're not looking for my wife?" The old man practically started hooting as he laughed at his own joke. "Women," he said. "You can't live with 'em, and they can't drive." This was followed by more hooting.

Jake faked a laugh, doing his best to play along. "Yeah, well, that's a story for another day. The woman I'm looking for is in her mid-twenties, dark hair, average height..."

Jake trailed off, struggling to describe someone he hadn't seen in a year's time. He considered for a moment telling the man exactly who she was, thinking that the old shop keep would recall her name from last year's news reports. But he instantly dismissed the idea, not wanting to risk the elderly man recognizing him as well. Though the old timer sounded like he was knocking the dementia's doorstep, you never knew when a spark could ignite in someone's memory.

"She's from out-of-town," Jake said, recomposing himself. "So she would've had out-of-state plates, most likely."

"Hmm," the man said, stroking his beard again. "You

know, there was a time we got so many tourists in there parts, that your description would've been as useful as a screen door on a submarine, if you don't mind me saying."

Jake shook his head. "I've never been good with details."

"However," the man said, dropping the "r" at the end of the word, "Things have slowed to a death's pace around here, with the outbreak and all. In fact, I can't even say with full confidence if we'll open next year, if I'm being completely honest."

"It's a shame," Jake said. From under the counter, he balled his hands into fists.

Get to the point, old man.

"Yes sir," the man continued. "The world's just not to same place as it used to be. One day people are eating sandwiches from my deli, the next day they're eating each other."

"It's crazy, all right." Jake ran the back of his hand against his brow. When it came back wet, he knew it wasn't from melting snow. This guy was literally making him sweat. "But that being the case, are you saying you do remember the person I'm looking for?"

The man stared at him, one eyebrow arched.

Did he really forget what we were talking about?

He snapped his fingers, startling Jake so much he twitched. "Right," the man said. "The girl. Well, the thing is, I wasn't working the counter today. I was in the back most of the day, fixing up our water heater."

Christ. What a waste of time.

"I see," Jake said, already backing away. "Well, I thank you for your time anyw—"

"But my wife may have seen her. She was probably out front when your girl came in. Hold on a second." The man turned around.

Oh no, not another one.

"That's okay, sir. You don't need to trouble her."

But it was too late. With more volume than Jake would've ever guessed the old timer could manage, the clerk yelled,

"Mabel! I need you up front!"

It probably didn't take more than ten seconds for the old woman to emerge from a curtained doorway in the back of the store, but to Jake, it felt like a millennium.

"You say something, Abe?"

"This fella here is looking for a friend of his. Said she might have come in earlier today."

Mabel made her way down an aisle of canned goods as her husband spoke. "That so? What she look like?"

Jake took it from there, believing he could describe Leigh much faster than waiting for the elderly Abel to spit it all out. If left to him, the old man was likely to start talking about the fishing in Alaska or the rising price of gas or who knew what else.

Mabel listened to Jake's description of Leigh, and though he was still lacking on details, she was smiling by the time he was done.

"Oh yes," she said. "I do believe that exact girl was in here earlier today. Pretty young thing she was." Her smile suddenly dropped. "Though I didn't care too much for the company she kept, if you don't mind me saying."

Jake raised an eyebrow. "Company?"

"One of those biker fellas," Mabel said. "You know the type. Leather jacket covered in flames and skulls and what not. Tattoos covering 90% of their body."

"A biker?" It was now Jake's turn to scratch his beard, though it was not nearly impressive as Abel's. "Are you sure?"

Mabel nodded with vigor. "Yes, sir. In fact, I may not have remembered your friend if it wasn't for him. Don't get me wrong, I don't mean to say she's plain or anything, but men like that tend to stand out in a place like this."

"Bikers," Jake said, clarifying.

"Well, yes." The old woman's eyes shifted a bit when she added, "But he was also an Indian."

Though rather confused by this new information, Jake did not fail to notice the woman said, *an* Indian, rather than just Indian.

"You mean, American Indian?" He shook his head, correcting himself. "I mean, Native American."

"Whatever you call them, yes. He was quite striking, I will say that much. I can see why she would be attracted to him. Besides, young girls always tend to like the bad boys, don't they? It's as true today as it was in my time."

Abel gave his wife a nudge with his elbow. "It certainly worked on you."

"Oh, please." Mabel smacked his shoulder. "The closest thing you ever drove to a motorcycle was a tractor."

The two continued to squabble, leaving Jake to stand there and do his best to hide the fact he was wincing. As it turned out, this had all been a huge waste of time. A native American biker? What in the world was this old bat talking about?

The phone within his pocket vibrated, alerting him of a text message. The old married couple continued to speak amongst themselves as Jake retrieved his cell to see the text was from Eddie. It read:

MAY HAVE FOUND SOMETHING. CALL BACK.

"Well," Jake said, dropping the phone back into his pocket. The two senior citizens looked to him in unison. "You've both been a lot of help, thank you. But I really should be heading home now before it gets any worse out there."

Mabel turned to the window in the front of store. "Let's hope it doesn't get any worse than this!"

"It certainly could," Abel said. "Remember the ice storm of 97? Now that was a doozy. I remember there was..."

"Thanks again!"

Jake didn't know if the old man continued on his story or not. He was already dashing out the door, the bell ringing one last time as he slammed it behind him.

Yikes. That was a mistake.

Jake considered going for his phone, desperately hoping that Eddie had some good news for him. With time running out as every second passed, Jake needed a lead more than ever. But a strong gust of wind prompted him to get his car first where he could dial with fingers he could actually feel. Besides, the sooner the he pulled away, the sooner he could eliminate any chances of the either of the old shop keeps following him outside.

Turning up both the heater and windshield wipers, Jake pulled onto the road and headed back towards town. There was no reason to keep going the other way—all that lay ahead in that direction was a collapsed bridge from the tractor-trailer accident. With his car steady on a straight away, Jake hit redial on his phone put it on speaker mode. A moment later, Eddie's tinny voice filled his car.

"Yeah, boss."

"Eddie," Jake said, keeping his eyes on the road. "What do you got for me?"

Eddie's reply was not the first thing Jake wanted to hear.

"Not much."

Jake took a deep breath before speaking again. "But something?"

"Maybe." Eddie's voice changed, as if he was speaking through clenched teeth. Jake figured he must be holding a cigarette in his mouth. "As expected, I couldn't find anything on any major accidents. Well, I did find something on a semi taking on a bridge, but I assume your friend wasn't driving a big rig."

"Well done, Sherlock. What else?"

"Sherlock, huh? I guess that makes you my bitch, Watson." Eddie released a half-cough, half-laugh that confirmed Jake's cigarette theory.

"What else, Eddie?"

"All right, all right. After I hit the dead end with the accident reports, I made some calls to a few connections I have up your way. I didn't expect much since they're all small time lowlifes, but I did find out who runs the most drugs up there."

"Drugs?" Jake turned down the whirring heat to better hear the conversation.

"Yeah, I know. Not exactly human trafficking but I thought you still might be interested. If anything shady happened to your missing person, I'm willing to bet these guys would have at least heard about it."

Jake considered this for a moment. It was yet another long shot but those seemed to be the only shots he could take lately. "So who are they?"

"Hold on a sec, I wrote it down." Jake heard the wrinkling of paper and then, "Some biker gang. Call themselves the Forlorn Hope."

Jake's Eagle fishtailed as his foot came slamming down on the brake. It stopped about halfway from completing a three-hundred-and-sixty degree loop, leaving Jake gasping for breath, his hands squeezing the wheel like a vice grip. He now stared at the guard rail, his car resting horizontally across both lanes.

"Jesus Christ," Eddie said. "What the hell was that?"

"Nothing," Jake said, slowly releasing his hands from the wheel. He was surprised to find he hadn't bent it half. "Just hit some black ice, that's all."

It was one of the biggest lies Jake had every told in his life. Not only had the shock of Eddie's answer spurred him to slam the brakes so carelessly, but also what he had just been passing when Eddie spoke. It was the side road, the one which had the unique tire tracks jutting up it. Though you couldn't really see the tracks anymore, the image had been branded into Jake's brain.

A car being followed by a motorcycle.

Jake shifted his vehicle into reverse to straighten himself out. "Eddie," he said. "Thanks for everything. I got to focus on the road now, but I can call you back in a bit."

"Don't bother," Eddie said. "I've got more important things to do today than talk to you, like last night's *American Dead* on my DVR."

Jake finished straightening his car and shifted back into drive. "Suit yourself." A mischievous smile formed on his face from out of nowhere. "And Eddie?"

"What?"

"T-Bone gets bitten by a zombie in this one."

There was a beat of silence. And then, "What? You motherfu—"

Jake hit END with his index finger. The line went dead.

Spoiler alert.

The joy of ruining the episode for Eddie left as quickly as it came. One look at the side road brought the severity of Jake's situation crashing back like a tsunami wave.

Okay. Let's see what's behind door number one.

The road was almost undrivable. It was obvious it hadn't been touched by a plow all day, and Jake's tires sank the instant he started up its steep grade. The Eagle's squealed and pleaded as the wheels continued to spin against the slick snow. Jake tried every driving trick in the book, pumping the gas to avoid spinning out, steering the car to the road's edge to find traction.

But it was a futile endeavor. Even in a powerful diesel truck, this road would've been a challenge. Four-wheel drive or not, Jake knew he wasn't going any further when he fell just short of the crest of a hill. He could see over the knoll that the road curved to the left before vanishing behind some low hanging trees.

He shifted the car into park and pulled up on his parking brake for good measure. He was fairly certain he would be able to back down the way he came as long as he took it slow. But for now, if he wanted to proceed any further, it was going to have to be on foot.

As Jake opened his door, he discovered that somehow the air had turned even colder in the short drive from the general store. However, the trees lining either side of the rural road were doing their part to block the high winds that were previously pulling at his car when he was driving down the highway. Still, Jake hoped he wouldn't have to venture too far ahead before he found...

Well, anything. He wasn't sure what to expect as he began to trudge along the road. A part of him wished he was packing any sort of fire arm, though a bigger part of him didn't want to even imagine a situation where one would be necessary.

He had his trusty pocket knife clipped to his belt, which was something at least, but he couldn't help but think of that old adage of bringing a knife to a gun fight.

Or maybe you're just bringing a knife to a picnic. Let's not get ahead of ourselves.

Jake did his best to listen to the voice of reason, but he didn't care for how loud the crunching snow made his footsteps. He could only hope the growing snow drifts were muffling the noise from anyone who could be listening. Once, when he was still living in Embry, an out-of-state motorist had crashed their car at the end of Jake's driveway while he was outside brushing off his own vehicle. He hadn't heard a thing until the driver yelled an obscenity, and only then did Jake look up to see the BMW smashed into the telephone pole. The crash had been dampened by the snow like a drum kit underwater.

Jake let the memory slip away so he focus more on the present. For the life of him he couldn't remember where this particular road led, though his surroundings were becoming terribly familiar. Was this the road that went to the Abenaki campground? If that were indeed true, it would explain why Jake was having such a hard time placing it. In all the years he had lived in Embry, Jake had done his best to respect the Native people's land. Unless directly invited, Jake made it a practice not to overstep his bounds as a forest ranger. To an outsider, these woods could all look the same, but it was a ranger's job to know where his jurisdiction ended, where he could enforce fish and game laws and where he could not.

Still, I think have been down here at least once before. Didn't Phil bring me down here once to show me...

The thought snapped like a broken fishing line at the sight of the fallen tree lying across the entire width of the road.

"Whoa," Jake muttered. But the spectacle of the roadblock did not hold his attention for very long. His gaze was now transfixed at the swerving tracks that veered violently to the right, straight off the road and into the trees.

Jake jogged as fast as the snow would allow, which wasn't very fast at all. As it turned out, this was nothing short of a gift sent from on high. If not for his hindered speed, Jake would've run right into an ambush, not seeing the two men before it was too late. As it was, he had time to hear their voices first, stopping him right in his tracks.

"God damn it! Son of a bitch is stuck. Can you give me a hand here?"

"Hey asshole, take a look at me. Does it look like I can help you?"

Jake fell to the ground in one motion, instantly concealing himself in a blanket of snow. Intense cold bit him all over his body as the snow found places of exposed skin, but Jake hardly noticed. In his prone position, he slowly crawled like a solider to where the car had careened off the road. It wasn't long before the tail lights of a sedan came into view, the front end of the car imbedded against the trunk of a tree. A few away, two men rested near a parked truck, a vehicle not unlike the one Jake used to drive when he worked for the Forest Service. Lying on his stomach, not moving a muscle, Jake watched the two men argue.

One was sitting on the ground and holding a handkerchief to his face. Based on the bloodstained cloth that covered most of his face, he had suffered a severe injury. Though it was difficult to see any of his facial features, his attire suggested that of a biker gang—leather jacket, chaps over jeans, and lots of chains.

"Besides," the sitting man said, "Little John wanted you to keep it on."

Jake couldn't see the other man's face either, but for a far different reason. The other man stood above his sitting companion and paced back and forth. At first, Jake though the was wearing one of those old style bird masks, the one's with the long beaks that guests often wear to masquerade balls. But when Jake saw the mask's true form, his blood ran colder than the snow stinging his flesh.

The man was wearing a deer skull over his head. He yanked

at with both hands but it seemed to be getting caught under his jaw.

"I don't care what John wants," the Deer Man said. "I just want to get this thing off of me. I can hardly see anything out of it."

The sitting man suddenly pulled his rag away from his face. Jake fought the urge to gasp when he saw the bloody mess where the man's eye should have been. Unfortunately for the biker, his other eye was a lost cause too, already covered by a patch.

"Are you fucking kidding me?" Eye Patch yelled. "*You* are having trouble seeing? I'm fucking blind over here!" He returned the rag to his face. "That bitch!"

Deer Man raised his hands in a calming motion. "Uno, relax. I'm sure a doctor will be able to fix you right up."

Uno, as his partner called him, shook his head. "Like they were able to fix my other one? Yeah, right." He pointed a finger at Deer Man, though his aim was slightly off to the right. "I'll tell you one thing. I know you're supposed to be one to finish her off, but I'm calling that shit off. That Leigh bitch is mine. You'll just have to settle for the other one."

Jake took a deep breath and held it, not knowing which revelation shocked him more: Eddie being right that these were the men who had abducted Leigh, or that Leigh was apparently still alive.

"Just settle down, okay? Let's wait for John and Peen to get back and then we'll figure..."

The man wearing the deer skull brought a hand to his chest and cleared his throat.

"We'll figure..."

Once again, his sentence fell short. His hand moved from his chest to his mouth, under the snout of the skull. His shoulders then began to move up and down in rapid succession, like he was crying...

Or laughing.

Indeed, the man began to chuckle at first, quiet chortles

emanating from behind the mask. Something had tickled this man's funny bone and he couldn't seem to stop himself.

"What?" Uno said, blindly looking from one direction to the other. "What the fuck is so funny?"

"Nuh, nuh..." Another wave of giggles hit the man. "Nothing."

"You find this funny? I'll probably never ride a bike again. Does that make you laugh?"

"N-no." Deer Man clenched his hands into fists and took a deep breath. "I'm just h-hungry. I haven't eaten since yes-yesterday."

"For fuck's sake." Uno removed the rag from his face again and proceeded to wring it out like a dishrag. The liquid that fell from the cloth dyed the snow red. "Then eat something already," Uno said, bringing the handkerchief back to his eye.

"I think I need to."

The man's quivering body suddenly grew still, his bouncing shoulders coming to rest in an instant. The laughing fit had left him as quickly as it came.

"I know I do."

Uno did not reply as the other man walked to the truck and threw open the passenger door. He then leaned inside, reaching for something that Jake couldn't see. Based on the man's last comments, Jake assumed he was retrieving an old sandwich, or a Snickers bar, or a bag of beef jerky. But he was wrong.

When the man reemerged from the truck's cab, he gripped an enormous hunting knife.

To his own disbelief, Jake almost cried out in warning as if he was watching a movie from the comfort of his own living room. He bit his tongue and watched as Deer Man closed the truck's door and slowly walked back to where Uno was sitting. Without a word, he stepped around to the blind's man back.

Uno looked around, apparently unaware that his companion stood behind him. "You find some grub?" he asked.

Deer Man nodded. "Indeed."

"So what did you find?"

Deer Man raised the knife.

"Meat."

Deer Man reached down and wrapped an arm around Uno's forehead, startling the blind man to drop the rag. Without a single functioning eye, Uno resembled a biker version of Oedipus, his mouth popping open in surprise. No words came from that mouth however, as Deer Man was already running his blade across Uno's throat.

A torrent of blood shot forward and sprayed the snow in an arching formation. It reminded Jake of a garden hose attachment, when you only partially squeeze the handle. Instead of a thick, powerful stream of water, it comes out in an almost bloom-like shape. Jake could remember playing with a hose as a child in his backyard, holding the nozzle up to the sun to see the prisms that formed in the liquid curtain.

But no rainbows could be seen in the fluid that propelled from Uno's jugular. There was only one color to be seen here.

With one hand, Uno grasped blindly for his throat, the blood shooting out between his fingers. With the other hand, he slashed out wildly, desperately trying to find his assailant. The Deer Man stood far out of reach, silently watching the strength quickly drain from his victim.

"Gaaale," Uno said, the unintelligible word barely escaping his lips. His speech had become a watery, choking sound. "You shun of a betch!"

Uno took a sudden step in the right direction, actually closing the distance between him and the masked man. Though he couldn't see his face, Jake could tell Deer Man was surprised by this movement by the way he awkwardly shuffled backwards. Uno's fingers were mere centimeters from his coat.

And then Uno collapsed with one final ragged exhale. He fell face first into a combination of snow, dirt, and his own blood. Just like that, the forest was silent again.

Jake had no time to even begin to register the outright

murder he had just witnessed. As he continued to watch from afar, the horrible realization dawned on him that this horror show had only just begun.

Wasting no time, Deer Man grabbed Uno by the shoulders and flipped him onto his back. He leaned down and pulled the dead man's shirt and jacket up to expose the skin beneath. Though Uno's body blocked his vision, Jake could still hear the awful sound of steel puncturing flesh as the Deer Man brought the knife to Uno's side. After a few seconds of what sounded like an enthusiastic diner digging into a prime porterhouse, Deer Man straightened back up. In his hand was now a palm-sized chunk of something pale, wet, and red.

Jake squeezed his eyes shut and swallowed, concentrating as hard as he could on the sole goal his life now had.

Don't throw up. Keep it together, Jake.

But that was getting harder with each passing second, as Deer Man's actions continued to grow in depravity. He now paced back to the truck, swung the door open once more, and reached inside. This time he revealed a small, butane blowtorch. If Uno were still alive, Jake's first reaction would've been to think Deer Man intended to torture his victim. But Uno's body was growing colder by the minute.

So what is he...?

Deer Man tossed the hunk of Uno's flesh onto a nearby rock, the viscera landing with a sickening *plop*. He reached into his pocket and exchanged the knife in his hand for something too small for Jake to see at this distance. He didn't need his eyes to identify the object when he heard the familiar sound of metal scratching flint. A second later, the butane torch ignited to life.

Deer Man lowered the torch's steady flame to the flesh on the rock. At that exact moment, a powerful ill-timed breeze blew through the trees, wafting the scent of cooking meat right into Jake's nostrils.

Oh God.

Risking discovery, Jake brought his hand to his face, covering both his mouth and nose. The movement was not without noise, but apparently the Deer Man could not hear over the constant hum of the torch and the sizzle of the macabre protein.

Seemingly satisfied with his job, Deer Man turned off the torch and carefully lifted the now blackened morsel into the air. Pausing only to blow on it through the opening in his mask, Deer Man brought the meat to his mouth.

He took a bite.

No...

The meat stretched as Deer Man pulled it away. Human flesh was apparently quite stringy. Jake wished he could cover his ears as well so he wouldn't have to hear the lip smacking and occasional moan of pleasure emanating from behind the mask. At least he could close his eyes as the Deer Man went for a second helping, but there's was still the sounds. Those awful, awful sounds.

And then something else. A noise so loud and sudden it almost made Jake cry out. At first, he believed the voice to belong to Uno, a zombie back from the dead who wanted to take a bite out of the man who currently consumed him. But no, the voice was too distant. Too hazy.

"Omega, check in. Over."

Both Jake and Deer Man looked to Uno's body where a walkie-talkie was strapped to the corpse's belt.

"Omega Wolf, this is Alpha Wolf. Come back. Over."

Deer Man took one last bite of his meal and tossed the remaining meat to the ground. He marched over to his prey, struggling to free the walkie-talkie from Uno's waist.

"God damnit, Omega Wolf. Pick up! Over."

Finally, the walkie-talkie came loose. It was slick with Uno's blood. Deer Man brought it to his mask and pressed the large button on its side.

"I'm here," he said. When no one replied, he added, "Er...over."

"Where the hell have you been? I've been trying you forever. Over."

Deer Man stared down at Uno as if deep in thought. "Sorry," he said. "I left the walkie-talkie in the truck. I just grabbed it. What's going on? Over."

"The rabbit got away. Repeat, the rabbit got away. Over."

Jake tensed at this last message. Somehow he knew the speaker wasn't being literal with his phrasing. The rabbit had to be Leigh.

"Shit." Deer Man muttered. "What do we do now? Over!"

"First of all," the other voice said, "calm down. We're fine. They took off on Beta Wolf's four-wheeler, but I'm pretty sure I know where they're going. I need you and Lone Wolf to..."

The voice paused, the airwaves going dead for a moment. And then, "How is Lone Wolf? Can he travel? Over."

"Um..."

Now it was Deer Man's turn to go silent.

"Negative, Alpha Wolf. Lone Wolf is out of commission. Over."

"What? You mean...?" There was a click of the transmit button being released. When the voice finally came back it muttered, "Christ. All right, here's what you're going to do. Put Lone in the back of the truck and make sure he's covered in something. You've got a tarp? And bungees? Over."

"Yeah, over."

"Good. Once he's settled in, take my bike and ride to Susan's Swamp. You know where that is, right? Over."

"Sure I do. But what for? Over."

"I think the rabbit is on the VAST trail that dumps out right there. I'm in pursuit on foot, but you're going to head them off. Understood? Over."

Deer Man practically yelled into the walkie-talkie. "That's it? For God's sake, they're on an ATV! You'll never catch them and I'll never get to Susan's Swamp fast enough. Over!"

"I don't think so," the other voice said. "Their horse is bleeding, if you get my drift, and it will be dead soon. I'm following the blood trail as we speak. Do you understand? Over."

There was one more pause, as if Deer Man was contemplating

what he had just heard. "Finally," he said. "Some good news. I'm on my way. Over."

"Excellent. Over and out."

The conversation finished, Deer Man lowered the walkie-talkie and shook his head. "Christ," he said aloud to himself. "What a mess."

Just as the voice on the other end had ordered, Deer Man went to work lifting Uno's body into the back of the truck. It was strenuous work, Jake could tell that much. Uno wasn't exactly a small man, and now he literally carried "deadweight." Still, Deer Man was able to hoist him up, and with that task done, next came concealing the body from any passing eye. Fortunately for Deer Man, he had been transporting an old, wrinkled blue tarp in the truck bed. Though it had a few holes here and there, tied with a few bungees, it did the trick.

Jake had to give it to him. If he were still a forest ranger, he would've drove right by that truck without a moment's suspicion, thinking it was a just a deer hunter who had a lucky day.

By the time Deer Man had revved up the parked motorcycle and driven away, both of Jake's leg had grown numb. He could barely get back onto his feet, the falling snow almost burying him under a blanket of white. Though his circulation refused to return to anything below his waist, he willed his body to run forward. Near hypothermia was nothing to take lightly, but it was nothing compared to shear panic.

The Deer Man had taken off in the direction of Jake's parked Eagle. In a matter of seconds, the bike would come upon Jake's vehicle and Deer Man would know he wasn't alone.

Ignoring the charred meat still steaming on the ground, Jake leaped over the pool of Uno's blood and headed for the trees. He had know idea where he was going but that didn't matter. All that mattered was getting away in case Deer Man, the Omega Wolf, decided to come back.

The thought of wolves reminded Jake of what the voice had said.

The rabbit got away.

If both he and these wolves were chasing the same prey, what did that make Jake? Was he a wolf too?

As Jake continued to run as fast as the thickening snow would allow, he decided no, he was a not a wolf at all. For wolves always hunted in packs.

And Jake had never felt so alone.

CHAPTER
FIFTEEN

Once upon time, Leigh had found herself trekking through the woods in a thunderstorm. The rain had all but pelted her as she trudged along, its intensity softened only by the canopy of trees branches far above her. With the leaves providing little shelter, Leigh and her group were soaked by the end of their journey. And what had it all been for? So her friends could smuggle a little bit of grass into the Green Mountain state. Leigh remembered quite vividly that one thought that cross her mind more than once during that trip.

It doesn't get worse than this.

Now, trudging along in thickening snow, increasing wind, and perhaps worst of all, fading daylight, Leigh realized just how wrong she'd been. At least her group had known where they were going, a nearby hunting cabin where they could hunker down until the storm passed. And they had someone leading the way who knew exactly where to go, the late great Sam Tucker.

There was very little Leigh wouldn't have done to have either of those things right now. Even if she couldn't ever have Sam back, Leigh would've settled for anyone who could tell her much farther she and Evan had to venture. Leigh held her breath around every tree that blocked her sight, praying to God that they would stumble upon the river they sought. But no such luck had arrived, leaving the two of them to blindly continue on, not knowing if they were only getting deeper into backcountry.

Leigh didn't really know much about the scope of Vermont's woodlands, but she did recall a conversation she had once had during her college days about the famous hiking route, the Long Trail, which ran right through the state. While drinking a beer by a company that bore the trail's namesake, her friend Marshall shared his interest in exploring the well-known footpath.

"I've already tamed the ocean," Marshall said, referring to his skills on a surfboard. "Now it's time to conquer the land."

Unfortunately for Marshall, his girlfriend, Alex, would rather be caught dead than spend a prolonged amount of time in the outdoors. And when Leigh had heard just how long the trail was in its entirety, Leigh couldn't blame her friend and roommate for trying to talk Marshall out of it. The trail went for 272 miles.

Could they go that long without running into nothing but trees? The rational part of Leigh's brain said "no," reminding her that even the Long Trail occasionally came to a highway crossing or a public rest stop. So while it was over 250 miles long, not all of those miles ran through undeveloped, primeval landscape. Besides, she knew for a fact that Embry and other such towns were relatively close by.

But still, that dreaded number lingered in Leigh's mind like a playground taunt.

272 bottles of beer on the wall, 272 bottles of beer. If one of those killers should happen to catch up...

When her brain had refused to let go of the image of Matthew Wolfchild being cut down by John Woodenknife, Leigh had considered exposing her hands to the cold as a welcomed painful distraction. She hadn't made this connection until just now, but perhaps for the first time ever, Leigh fully understood why C. had been tempted to cut herself with her once beloved razorblade. Even if it was temporary and fleeting, physical pain almost always overpowered its mental counterpart. Like a good friend that acts goofy when you're feeling blue, or takes you out for drinks if only to give your heartache a reprieve, pain takes yourself away from yourself.

And it was doing that right now.

It wasn't just her hands anymore. Leigh's whole body was freezing from her head to her toes. Her skin stung with every gust of wind that whipped through the trees. Her muscles ached as the frigid air seeped through her clothes and into her bones. Her feet were numb, the snow having reached a depth that soaked her shoes and socks beneath. Though she had always believed only exaggerating cartoon characters did this, Leigh's teeth chattered together if she didn't keep her mouth shut tight.

As if he had been reading her mind, Evan said, "This is bad. We should've come across the river by now, right?" He had been trudging along in front of her but now came to a dead stop.

Doing her best to keep her voice steady, Leigh answered, "I would've thought so."

Evan looked back. "We couldn't have missed it?"

Leigh figured the question had meant to be a statement, but it came out quizzical all the same. "I don't know," she said. "That trail we were on had a lot of twists and turns. Maybe we weren't facing the same direction as we thought."

"So what do we do now?"

Leigh squinted as a gust of wind blew sharp tiny granules of snow into her eyes. "I guess all we can do is stay the course. We can't go back, right?"

Evan gritted his teeth against the cold. "Yeah, okay. Let's keep going. I mean, we have to run into something eventually."

Leigh nodded in agreement but she had as little faith in that idea as Evan probably did himself. Still, they had no choice but to solider on, the forest only getting colder and darker by the minute. Whenever the cold became particularly painful, Leigh kept reminding herself that a death march would always be better than Woodenknife and the rest. It was the choice between a rock and a hard place. Or a cold place under the current circumstances.

As she walked, Leigh kept her tucked down as often as she could. She found it helped in shielding herself against the wind. It also helped her ease her fears. If she looked up, she would see the dark and scary woods, as daunting as any forest from Grimm's fairy tales. The view downward, however, was only of her feet—just one step at a time, over and over.

Leigh had been so concentrated on her own feet that she walked right into Evan's back when he came to another stop. In her almost Zen-like state, she had lost track of how long they had been traveling. She wanted to curse Evan for breaking her of her trance, as it had slightly lifted the cold and discomfort incessantly clawing at her body. Instead, she asked, "What's up? Why are we stopping?"

Evan's reply was to point to circle a finger in the air next to his head. "Look around," he said. "I just can't get over it. It's so eerie here."

When she did what Evan asked, Leigh saw what had claimed her companion's attention. The Ashes seemed even more prominent here, stretching as far as she could see. Long, charred tree trunks stood like black statues all around them. The pine and spruce trees were no longer Evergreens. Green, in fact, would never be a color found anywhere in this stretch of woods. The controlled burn had turned the pallet of the forest into one of a 1960s television show. Black and white and gray were the only colors that existed here, for these were the colors of ash. These were the colors of death.

"Leigh," Evan said. "Should we be worried about..."

Though he trailed off, Leigh knew what he was asking. "No," Leigh said. "The fires took care of it. Nothing could've survived a burn like this. In fact, we're probably safer here than any other part of the woods."

"Sure," Evan said, obviously trying to assure himself. "Good point. And the government verified the disease was gone." He continued to stare at their surroundings as he added, "Still, it's a bit unnerving being out here, isn't it? Surrounded by all this death? Knowing what was here before?"

"Trust me," Leigh said as she too stared unblinking into the mass of charred totems. "It was worse when it was all alive."

As if snapped out of a trance, Evan looked to her. "Shit, I'm sorry, Leigh. What a stupid thing to ask you. While I'm at it, maybe I should ask a 9/11 survivor if it's just a little eerie to visit Ground Zero."

Leigh forced a smile against the cold. "It's okay, Evan. No harm done. Besides, hurt feelings are really the least of my concerns right now."

Evan returned the smile and looked like he was about to say something back. But then a powerful gust of wind, the worst yet, practically screamed as it shot through the blackened trunks. He and Leigh both shielded their faces and waited for the gust to past.

"This is no good," Evan finally said once the air had quieted enough for him to be heard. "The Ashes stretch for a quite a ways. I don't know if we can make it in this."

"They run along the road," Leigh said, trying to sound optimistic. "I saw them while we were driving today..."

God, that feels like years ago.

"...We could walk through them back to Route 6."

Evan shook his head. "Okay, but which way? We choose the wrong direction and we're fucked."

Leigh glanced around, trying to get her bearings, but it was a fool's errand. They were already lost, and the fires had made the trees look like identical images of one another. She felt like she had stumbled into an outdoor maze of mirrors, where every direction looked the same.

"Looks like we have to guess," Leigh said. "We know it's not the way we came, so that gives us a one-out-of-three chance."

Evan shook his head. "No," he said. "We're not going to guess. I know where we're going."

"How do you know how to get back to the road?"

Evan looked to her. "I don't. But we're not going for the road. Not yet, anyway. We're going in there." He pointed a finger to his right.

Leigh followed the finger to see that the ground rose into a knoll about fifty feet away from where they stood. To Leigh, the rising terra firma resembled a tumor, as if the earth itself had developed a kind of cancer. Considering the once diseased woods which they now found themselves in, Leigh figured this held more than a bit of truth. However, it wasn't the rising slope that caught her eye but rather the large, circular opening in the middle of the hump.

Dark and gaping like the mouth of a great beast, the sight of the cave entrance sent shivers down Leigh's spine more powerful than those caused by the extreme cold. Her imagination flooded her mind with every sort of creature that could inhabit the space within, some which only existed in the pages of fiction. Bats, hibernating bears, fire-breathing, gold-eating dragons—in Leigh's head, they were all waiting for her inside.

"You want to go in there?" she asked, no amount of incredulity spared from her voice.

Evan was already pacing towards the mouth of the cave. Leigh caught up just in time to hear him say, "We can wait out the storm inside."

Though childish fears of trolls and witches still scratched at the back of her mind, Leigh admitted to herself that Evan's idea was not only an option, but a necessity. They were out of time, plain and simple. The sun was minutes away from setting completely and the wind was only getting stronger. And if anything was going to do them in, it would be the wind.

While living on the UVM campus, part of Leigh's morning ritual, along with taking a shower and brushing her teeth, had been to check the local weather forecast. It did not take much time living in Vermont to learn there was little you could do to prepare yourself for the state's unpredictable weather. Still, if nothing else, it did help knowing what type of jacket the temperature would require when it came to picking out the day's outfit. Almost every single time during the winter months, the weatherman would report the afternoon's predicted temperature, but then add a second prediction that included one of Leigh's least favorite phrases.

With wind chill.

"It looks to be a chilly one out there today," the weatherman would say. "With a average temperature of 27 degrees, though with the wind chill, it may reach below zero."

God, did she hate that. If it was going to be windy, as so many Vermont winter days were, what was the point of even sharing that first number? But it did prove just how much difference wind made when it came to the cold. And in these windy conditions, she and Evan may not survive.

There would be no wind in the cave, however. It would still be awfully cold inside, that was for certain, but its thick walls would block even the mightiest gust. In fact, Leigh could recall reading more than one article about lost hikers who did this exact same tactic in order to make it through a night in the woods. Some even dug their own shelters in the snow when there wasn't a natural cave to be found.

"I'm with you," Leigh said as she kept up with Evan's quickened pace.

When they reached the mouth of the cave, something hard and flat snapped under Leigh's shoe. They both looked down to see she had stepped on a large piece of wood, its rectangle shape almost completely covered by snow. Evan reached down and picked it up, brushing off its charred surface. Like everything else around them, it had been licked by the forest fire's flames, though under the cover of the cave's entrance, it had been spared much more than the exposed trees. Through the black smudges and ruined wood, Leigh could read the old, hand-painted words.

SMUGGLER'S DEN: During the prohibition era, many bootleggers travelling from Canada used this cave to hide alcohol they had illegally transported over the border.

"How about that?" Evan said, slapping the sign with the back of his hand. "This was once a tourist spot. I bet the Forest Service put this up. This is a good sign." He gave Leigh a wink. "No pun intended. But it means this cave might be a little more hospitable if it used to have frequent visitors."

Leigh nodded in agreement, trying to share Evan's enthusiasm, but her expression was mostly for show. Though Evan made a good point, the sign brought back too many horrible memories that were seeping into her mind like poisonous gas. She had once been a bootlegger herself, whether she had liked it or not, smuggling illegal substances across the Canadian border. Leigh wondered if any of these liquor smugglers had met a similar fate as her dead friends.

"Got that flashlight handy?"

Evan's question snapped her back to attention. She reached into her pocket and retrieved the torch, offering it to her cohort.

"You keep it," Evan said. "I can manage if I keep by your side." Yet another gust of wind stung the back of their necks. "You ready?" he asked.

"It can't be any worse in there. Let's go."

Side by side, the two entered the cave.

It was, for the most part, exactly what Leigh had expected, minus the scary, nasty creatures of her childhood nightmares. She couldn't help aiming the flashlight's beam at the cave's ceiling the moment they entered, but to her relief, she did not find one sleeping bat. Evan kept up the best he could, slipping on a rock here and there, but nothing that sent him crashing to the ground.

They both commented on how much better the temperature was within the cave walls. They were only a few steps in and their bodies were already welcoming the lack of wind. Perhaps it wasn't like stepping into a steamy sauna, but it was an improvement, nonetheless. If they remained in this shelter, Leigh felt confident that they could wait out the storm and then continue seeking help.

Unless, of course, Dale and Woodenknife catch up to us.

Try as she might, Leigh couldn't exorcise the thought from her head. If they came from opposite ends of the trail as they had planned through the walkie-talkie, Woodenknife and Dale would eventually meet up at the parked ATV. From then on, it was anyone's guess if the two would be able to see her and Evan's footprints leading away. By the time they reached the four-wheeler, Evan and Leigh's prints would be considerably covered by snow, and night would most likely be upon them. She could only pray for this to be true.

"If only we had some matches," Evan said, stumbling along. "We could find a spot to build a fire. Then we'd really be in business."

Leigh motioned to Evan's pocket. "You still have the pocketknife, right? The one from the ATV? Maybe we could strike against a rock and create a spark."

Evan laughed. "Who am I? Daniel Boone?"

"Who does that make me, then?" Leigh asked, joining in on the laughter.

"I don't know. Sacajawea?"

"She was with Lewis and Clarke," Leigh said. "Not Daniel Boone."

"My mistake," Evan said, just before adding a sudden, "Whoa!"

She pointed the flashlight in his direction. "You need some light?"

"Nah, I'm good," Evan said, waving her away. "Best to keep the light in front of us. There's just a slippery rock I need to get around." His voice became a little distant as he increased the space between them. "Anyway, back to the subject at hand. Let me think."

In the darkness to her left, she heard him taking a few more careful steps.

"Calamity Jane?" he asked.

Leigh let loose another giggle. "What does she have to do with starting fires by hand?"

"I don't know!" Evan said, laughing as well. "She was, like, an old-west chick, right? Couldn't all those cowboys and cowgirls do that?"

"Try again, Mr. Boone."

"Hmm." There was a pause, and then, "Okay, then how about Annie Oak—"

Evan's speech cut off at that exact point, as if Leigh had been speaking to him on a cellphone and the call had been abruptly dropped.

"Evan?"

Leigh whipped the light around but the flashlight beam hit nothing but air and the far wall of the cave.

"Oof!"

Evan's cry echoed in the chamber. It sounded like someone had punched him directly in the gut, knocking all the wind out of his lungs.

"Evan!"

Making sure to be careful, Leigh moved as fast as she could towards the direction of the sound. She had gone less than ten steps before she came to an immediate stop, her feet skidding across the slick floor of the cave.

"Whoa," she whispered. Her toes were hanging over the edge of a straight drop-off. She scanned the circumference of the hole with the flashlight to see that it was about as big as the opening of a city dumpster. Peering over the edge, she saw it was much deeper than one, but that wasn't all.

Evan lay on his back and stared up at her. Judging by the calm expression on his face, he didn't appear to be seriously hurt. His eyes were still wide with surprise but he did not grimace or show any other sign of pain. Leigh could see all of these details but it was not due to the flashlight she shined into the hole.

Evan lay atop a bed of blue, glowing mushrooms. Their bioluminescence filled the bottom of the chasm like a nightlight, all but the squashed mushrooms glowing with a gentle blue hue.

"Holy shit," Evan said, his voice echoing up to the top of the hole. "These mushrooms saved my life."

Leigh outright grinned when she was sure Evan was okay. "They're beautiful," she said. "I've never seen anything like them."

Evan looked to his right and left. "Me neither, except for maybe in National Geographic. I don't think I've ever seen bioluminescence outside of fireflies."

"It's really something," Leigh agreed. "But you're sure you're not hurt?"

"Pretty sure," Evan answered. "I think I only scraped my arm a bit."

"God." Leigh released a heavy breath. "That was lucky."

"You don't have to tell me twice." Evan reached for the wall to his left and hoisted himself up. "This hole came out of nowhere."

Leigh directed the light to better assist Evan's sight. "That sign did say this caved was used to store booze. Bootleggers probably made this hole a long time ago."

The blue light reflected off Evan's teeth, making his enamel react as if he was standing under a black light. "And now it all stores is pretty glowing mushrooms."

"Can you climb out of there?"

Evan glanced around for a moment and then said, "Yeah, I think so. The walls of this hole aren't smooth at all. I think I can enough handholds to pull myself up. But give me a minute."

"Take your time. It's not like we're going anywhere soon."

Being sure to keep the light out of Evan's eyes, Leigh aimed the light so that Evan could see exactly where he was placing each hand above him. It was slow going, but after only one near slip, Evan finally made it to the top of the hole and dragged himself out.

"Well, that was fun," he muttered. "You want to give it a

try? Those shrooms are nice and soft."

Leigh gave the hole one last look. "I think I'll pass. You probably broke most of them anyway. If I were jump down there now, I'd probably impale myself on a stalactite."

Evan raised a finger. "*Stalagmite*," he said.

"What?"

"Stalagmites grow straight up from the floor of a cave. Stalactites are the ones that hang from the ceiling."

"Hey, it's Bill Nye the Science Guy!" Leigh chuckled again. It felt good to laugh this much after the day she and Evan had endured. Even if it was all just a coping mechanism, her body's natural method of dealing with stress, Leigh didn't care. It beat screaming and crying any day of the week.

Evan shrugged. "I was really into rocks and stuff when I was kid. I even wanted to be a geologist when I grew up."

"And then you discovered mental health?"

Evan grinned. "No, then I saw *Jurassic Park* for the first time and wanted to be an archeologist. This whole psychology shit came much later." He tapped Leigh on the shoulder. "How about you?"

"What about me?"

"Did you have any childhood aspirations? I doubt your heroes back then were Freud and Jung."

Though the frigid air outside still found its way into the cave, Leigh realized she was feeling warmer than she had in hours. She didn't know if it was due to their new shelter or just the distracting conversation, but she didn't care.

"Oh, you know," Leigh said, being sure to walk slow so Evan wouldn't lose his footing. She doubted they were lucky enough for him to survive a second fall down another hidden crevasse. "My dream job was about what you'd expect."

"You wanted to be the fourth PowerPuff Girl?"

"Bingo."

Though her response was supposed to be entirely in jest, the word's meaning came when she saw what her flashlight had just then illuminated. The circle of light shown across another wooden sign, attached to a rock ledge about ten feet away. Unlike the sign they had found outside, this one was in far better condition, having been entirely protected by the controlled burn. Moreover, this sign not only included words, but some sort of illustration.

It did not take long for the two of them to understand what they were staring at. Evan voiced their discovery out loud.

"Holy shit," he said. "It's a map."

Bingo indeed.

Leigh grabbed Evan's hand to more quickly guide him to the wooden diagram. He did not resist, letting himself be led along until they were standing directly in front of the map.

A standard "X" represented the traditional marking of "YOU ARE HERE." From there, the map showed three tunnels extending from that point. Two appeared to be dead-ends, one ending at a place labeled "ECHO CHAMBER," and another leading to "UNDERGROUND POOL." To a tourist of yesteryear, both places would've held equal interest and been worthy of a visit. But for Leigh, it was only the third tunnel that caught her eye, as its destination made her gasp with something she thought she would never feel again.

Hope.

"Oh my god," she whispered, barely able to breathe. "Evan, look."

She pointed to the end of the third tunnel, the one in the middle of the other two. At its finish read the words, "MAPLE RIDGE STATION."

"What is that?" Evan said. Though he sounded confused, there was no denying the hope in his voice too. "Do you think that's a ranger station?"

Had she shown the light on her own face, Evan would've seen the smile stretching her mouth from ear to ear. "I know it is," she exclaimed. "I've been there."

"What?" Now Evan only sounded utterly surprised.

"Last year," Leigh continued. "When my friends and I were

in trouble. We walked to that station to try to find help." Her smile dropped when she added, "Not that it did any good."

She immediately drove the negative sentiment away, knowing this was not the time to dwell on the past. That there would be time for that later, though if Leigh managed to survive this night, she would have plenty of new nightmares to relive.

"But all that matters," she said, "is that we can get there without ever leaving the cave. Woodenknife and his men will never find us down here. Not before we get help."

Now it was time for Evan's smile to drop. "That sounds good, but if this station was in the Ashes, there's no way it's still standing. The fire would've definitely taken it out."

"We don't need it to be. As long as we can tell where it once was, I can use that as a starting point and lead us out of here. My friends and I entered the woods from a path leading right off the main highway. All we do is walk the same route backwards."

Evan raised an eyebrow. "Are you sure?"

"Trust me," Leigh said. "There are some things you never forget, no matter how hard you try."

Evan lowered his eyes, visibly ashamed. "Of course," he said. "There I go again. If I keep this up, I'm a shoo in for *Psychiatrist of the Year.*"

"It's okay," Leigh said. "Besides, who knows if we'll be able to see the path in this weather. But what other choice do we have?"

Evan raised his gaze, straightening his posture as well. "Well, then." He bent his arm and extended his elbow, offering the limb to Leigh. "To Oz?"

Once again, when Leigh smiled, she found she didn't have to force it at all. She wrapped her arm around the crook of Evan's elbow and said, "To Oz, Dr. Grant."

"Hey!" Evan said, also smiling. "Nice Jurassic Park reference."

Leigh was about to say something along the lines of "Maybe you would prefer Dr. Crane?" to further impress Evan with a reference to the fictional psychologist from *Cheers* and *Fraiser.*

But the words never came. She was too distracted by Evan's

smile. His teeth were reflecting blue light, just as they had when he was in the bottom of the mushroom filled hole.

"Evan?"

It was then she noticed Evan scratching at his chest. It was then she noticed the light was coming from under the collar of his shirt. It was then she saw the blue fuzz, glowing bright with bioluminescence, spreading up Evan's throat.

It was growing right before her eyes.

Evan must have seen the horror deforming her expression, as he frowned and asked, "What's wrong?"

Leigh tore her arm away from Evan so fast, the motion knocked the flashlight from her hand. The torch turned off as it hit the cave's floor, the force of its landing clicking off its switch. The area around them, however, did not fall to darkness, but remained well-lit with soft, blue light.

"Leigh," Evan said, panic raising his voice. "What is it?"

She did not have to reply. Evan received his answer the moment he brought his fingers from his chest and looked at his hand. It was almost entirely blue, glowing brighter and brighter as the blanket of fuzz continued to spread.

When Evan screamed, the sound bombarded Leigh's ears as it bounced off the cave walls all around her. The echo was so loud that Leigh didn't even realize that she was screaming too.

CHAPTER SIXTEEN

When Jake came upon the bodies of yet another biker and what appeared to be a local hunter, he was far less shocked than he should've been. After witnessing the murder and subsequent consumption of Uno, dead bodies just didn't pack the punch they once delivered.

When he had first run from the road into the forest, Jake's only goal had been to get away. Fearing the man wearing the deer skull would double-back after discovering Jake's parked car, Jake sprinted through the thickening trees without any direction whatsoever. He had been bounding through the snow for probably five minutes before he realized his tracks were not the only ones left behind on the white forest floor.

Though they were almost completely filled in with the snow that continued to fall, the tracks were still barely visible. Jake could see they were two sets, one larger than the other. Neither appeared to be left by a boot, but rather by much lighter and less appropriate footwear. Tennis or running shoes, perhaps. These weren't the prints of any one in the biker gang, which meant they had to belong to the gang's prey. For the time being, it seemed Leigh was not traveling alone.

Jake followed the tracks, losing them once for a brief

amount of time when they all but vanished into the snow drifts. Light getting lower by the second, Jake had a moment of panic when he thought he would not be able to relocate them again, leaving him standing in the middle of the woods without a single clue on where to go. Just when he thought all hope was lost, he noticed some indentations under the heavy bows of a nearby pine tree. The branches had protected the tracks underneath them from the snowfall, allowing Jake to pick up the trail once again.

When he came across the two dead bodies, he initially believed his success at tracking was all for naught. Covered by a heavy dusting of snow, Jake couldn't identify the bodies at first. The only thing he could tell was that they were dead.

Upon inching closer, a great weight lifted from his chest when he saw that neither person was female. While one of these could've been Leigh's traveling companion, there was still a chance that Leigh herself was alive. The question remained, however, who were these men?

It was safe to assume by the leather and chains that one of these men belonged to the Forlorn Hope. Jake wouldn't spend another second worrying about that one, since the biker gang had more than proved themselves to be the enemy. This was "good riddance" as far as Jake was concerned, as it was just one opponent he wouldn't have to worry about himself.

The other corpse was dressed more "normal," wearing clothes much more suitable for the weather. Based on the man's darker complexion and hair, Jake guessed that this man belonged to the local Abenaki tribe. It was difficult to say with one hundred percent certainty, as blood covered most of the man's face. It poured from his left eye socket where an arrow protruded. Only the fletching was still visible, the rest of the arrow buried in the man's skull. His one remaining eye looked up towards the darkening sky, its lens glazed over in an eternal death stare.

Jake looked back and forth between the two bodies, trying

to deduce what murderous deeds had transpired. Though Sherlock Holmes he was not, Jake thought that even the famed detective would've had a hard time figuring this one out.

Judging by the hole in the biker's chest, he had had been struck by a bullet rather than an arrow. But neither a gun nor a bow rested among the dead bodies, confusing Jake even more. Had the biker and the Abenaki shot each other at the same time? That didn't seem likely, since both hits were instant kill shots. It didn't seem plausible that both men would've been so successful at hitting their marks while simultaneously getting shot themselves. This meant a third man might've been involved. A classic Mexican standoff.

Jake looked to each man again.

Without any Mexicans.

He was just about to laugh at his own joke when the voice came from behind him.

"Don't move."

Jake obeyed with one exception. He shook his head.

God, do I hate being right.

"Turn around. Slowly."

Jake knew he would see a woman before he faced her. The voice, albeit strong and serious, carried an unmistakable feminine tone. As expected, Jake turned to see a woman standing about ten feet away. The rifle she pointed at him didn't come as a surprise as well.

Slowly raising his hands up, Jake spoke in the steadiest voice he could muster. "Don't shoot, okay? I'm unarmed and mean you no harm."

"Quiet," the woman said. She took one hand off the rifle to brush away a thick strand of black hair from her eyes. The hair tucked into the raised hood of her jacket, the hood's fur lining bordering her stern, dark face. Her complexion was in stark contrast of her jacket—an orange, puffy goose-down coat.

"Did you do this?" she asked, motioning to the bodies with barrel of the rifle.

Jake vigorously shook his head, making sure to keep his hands where the woman could see them. "No. I just found them like this." He took a breath to summon the courage to ask what could be a very sensitive question. "Do you know either of these men?"

The answer was worse than he even feared.

"That one is my brother," the woman said. Though she did not gesture to a particular body, Jake could only assume she wasn't referring to the biker.

She took a step forward and repeated, "Did you do this?"

Jake wanted to close his eyes and brace for the shot that seemed destined to come at any second, but he forced himself to look the woman in the eyes. "No," he said again. "I didn't kill either of them. I know it looks bad, me being the only one out here and standing over your dead brother, but please, look a little closer. I don't have a weapon on me, and even if I did, your brother was killed by an arrow. See his eye?"

Though the grimace contorting her face proved that it pained her to do so, the woman stole a glance at her deceased sibling's bloody face.

"See?" Jake said. "I wouldn't be able to hide a bow under my coat. Not even a crossbow."

"You could've thrown it away," the woman challenged.

"But you would've seen that, right? I only would've chucked my weapon if I thought someone was coming, and believe me, you totally got the jump on me."

Jake dared the smallest smile, hoping it would only make him look innocent and vulnerable and not offend her.

Though the woman kept the rifle aimed at Jake's chest, he didn't fail to notice her grip on the weapon relax the slightest bit.

"Who are you?" she demanded.

"My name is Wally..."

Jake paused halfway through his fake alias. The well-practiced answer had almost become automatic at this point, as it had been his new identity for over a year. But before he could speak his fictitious surname, revelation struck him like a bullet to the chest.

Or an arrow through the eye.

"I know you," he said to the woman. "Your name is Wolfchild, isn't it?"

Before the woman said anything in return, Jake knew he was correct. The surprised look in her eyes told him everything he needed to know.

"How do you know that?" she said.

"I used to live here," Jake said, letting his hands lower a little. "You and your brother had a stand at the Embry Farmer's Market. *Wolfchild Meats?*"

Though the woman did not speak, she was nodding as if she agreed. Jake took this as a good sign and offered her a smile. "I bought meat from you guys plenty of times. I really liked your cured venison sausage."

The corner of the woman's mouth perked upward, showing the subtlest hint of a smile of her own. "That was Matthew's specialty," she said.

Jake snapped his fingers. "Matthew! That's right. And that makes you..." He hesitated, trying to conjure the name off the tip of his tongue. "Cornelia?" he said, wincing when the name didn't sound quite right.

"Close," she said. "It's Cordelia."

"Like the character from *King Lear*. You told me that once. I remember now."

The rifle in Cordelia's hands lowered even more. It wasn't yet resting at her side, but at least it wasn't pointing at Jake's chest anymore. She asked, "What was your name again?"

There was no use in lying now. If Jake wanted Cordelia to believe him, it was best to come clean. At least they were in the middle of the woods, miles away from another ear.

"It's actually Jake—"

"Spire," Cordelia finished. "You're the forest ranger, the one that disappeared right before they set fire to the Ashes. I didn't recognize you at first but I see it now."

Jake felt a great weight rise off his shoulders. "That's me," he said. He lowered his hands.

"Hey!"

Jake's hands immediately shot back up. He reached for the skies like a hostage of a old west bank robbery.

"Did I tell you to lower your hands?" Cordelia looked down the sights of the rifle she had once again aimed at Jake's chest. "My brother's body is getting colder by the second, and the only one around is a man wanted for questioning by the Embry police. So you just keep those hands where I can see them."

"But I didn't do this!"

Jake knew it was never a good idea to yell at anyone who held you at gunpoint, but frustration had him at his wit's end. The longer he stood here and argued with this woman, the farther Leigh got away. The chances of her pursuers catching up with her were increasing by the minute, and meanwhile Jake was wasting precious seconds with this vengeful sibling. If he were to having any chance at reaching Leigh, this conversation had to end now. If not, Cordelia might as well shoot him.

"Listen to me," Jake said, continuing before Cordelia had a chance for rebuttal. "I'm looking for a friend of mine who's in a lot of trouble. She's being chased by a biker gang who call themselves The Forlorn Hope."

Cordelia's eyes widened. "You mean Woodenknife's crew?"

Jake shook his head. "I don't know who you're talking about. In fact, I really don't know much about them at all. But I do know it's The Forlorn Hope who is after my friend."

Jake dared to lower one hand to point at the dead biker at his side. "See this one? He's got the gang's name and insignia right on his jacket."

Cordelia looked from Jake to the dead biker, paused, and then returned her eyes back to Jake. Wagging the gun barrel, she motioned to his right. "Have a seat, right over there."

"Look, there's no time to—"

"I said have a seat."

Cordelia cocked the rifle, the click sounding like a snapping twig amidst the silence of the trees.

Without another second's hesitation, Jake sidestepped to his right and sat down in the cold snow. Frigid wetness instantly seeped into his pants and stung his buttocks, but he barely noticed. His entire attention was on Cordelia who carefully walked over to the two dead bodies, making sure to keep the rifle trained on Jake.

She knelt down and examined the biker first, eyeing the Forlorn Hope logo as Jake said she would find. Satisfied with her discovery, she moved onto the other corpse, the one who had once been her brother. Jake watched as she reached out and gently brushed the fletching of the arrow jutting out from Matthew's eye.

"Woodenknife," she whispered.

Suddenly she was standing back up and shouting at the top of her lungs.

"YOU FUCKING BASTARD!"

She turned on Jake, and in the solitary second it took for her to reach him, Jake knew this was it. He flinched, squeezing his eyes shut in preparation for the gunshot. He hoped she would kill him in one shot. He hoped he would be dead before he knew what hit him. He hoped he would see Phil and Doug and everyone else he ever cared about and loved waiting for him on the other side.

And then a strong hand was grabbing his arm and yanking him up. Jake's eyes popped back open to see Cordelia staring at him, her rifle uncocked and slung over her shoulder.

"Jake Spire," she said. "Where did that mongrel son of a bitch go?"

At first, Jake could not speak. Hell, he could barely breath. "Wait," he said, his senses coming back to him one-by-one. "So you believe me?"

"I don't know anything about any missing girl, but

you're right—that is a Forlorn Hope biker over there. More importantly, I recognize that arrow sticking out of my brother. John Woodenknife lives in the same trailerpark as me. I've seen him shooting beer cans with that crossbow of his a thousand times. He leaves those arrows all over the park."

Her lips parted and she bared her teeth like a growling dog. "And I'm going to shove every one of them right up his ass before I kill him. Now which way did he go?"

"I have no idea," Jake said, afraid of breaking eye contact with the raving woman. "I haven't seen him. But did I run into a couple of his gang members. One had an eye patch and the other was wearing a deer skull like a mask."

Cordelia raised an eyebrow. "A deer skull?"

"Come to think of it, I remember him saying something about how John wanted him to wear it. That's got to be John Woodenknife he was talking about."

"Okay," Cordelia said. "Then what happened?"

"Well, um..."

Jake swallowed hard, wondering how Cordelia would take this next part. He realized he really didn't want to relive it himself, but what choice did he have?

"The one in the deer mask killed the other one. And then he..."

He hesitated again and looked down at the snow.

"He ate him."

A silence thicker than the falling snow filled the space between Jake and the woman. From somewhere in the forest, a bird squawked three times. When Cordelia finally spoke, she offered only a one syllable word.

"What?"

"I swear to God. He carved off a piece, cooked it with a butane torch, and ate it."

Cordelia squinted, as if she was trying to tell if Jake was telling the truth. She apparently found it, as she shook her head and muttered, "Drugs. Had to have been on drugs. Like bath salts, you know?"

"Maybe," Jake said, "But I don't think so. This seemed too deliberate, too purposeful. I hadn't seen anything like it since..."

Jake stopped himself, utterly taken off guard by the completion of that thought.

Since the Cedar family. That murderous backwoods clan that consumed countless hikers and hunters rather than leaving their diseased forest home. The family that Phil helped survive, assisting them right under my nose for years.

Though Jake kept all of this to himself, Cordelia got the message regardless. The gist of it, anyway. It was a massive news story after all.

"What is it about this town and cannibalism?" she said. She didn't wait for an answer but instead asked a more serious question. "Anyway, then what happened?"

"Well," Jake said, trying to shake the haunting memory from his mind and return to the present. "Deer Mask got a call on his radio from who I presume to be Woodenknife. It sounded like Leigh somehow got herself a four-wheeler but the thing is leaking gas. Woodenknife and Deer Mask are going to try to come at her from both sides and ambush her, which is why I need to get to her first."

Cordelia turned and pointed behind her. "So these must be her tracks?"

Jake peered over her shoulder, expecting to see more of the same footprints that had led him to this scene of multiple homicide. Instead, the unmistakable tracks of a four-wheeled vehicle led away from a spot only a few feet from where Cordelia stood.

"Holy shit!" Jake said. He felt like he had just discovered the yellow brick road. "That's got to be the ATV."

Before he could take his first step towards the trail, Cordelia was already leading the way. After a few steps she turned back to Jake and said, "Are you coming or what?"

Jake paused. "Wait, we're doing this together?"

"I have a score to settle and you don't have a weapon. Besides, now it will be a fair fight. Two-on-two."

"Yeah," Jake said. "If there's only two of them out there."

Cordeila patted her rifle and smile. "I got enough friends in here to even the odds. So what do we say we give that cannibal pal of yours his final meal?"

Jake marched forward to Cordelia's side.

"I say dinner is served."

Cordelia gave her brother one last look, said something in a language that Jake did not understand, and the two of them began their trek deeper in the forest.

CHAPTER SEVENTEEN

If there was anything positive to be said about their current situation, at least Leigh and Evan no longer had to share a flashlight. Evan was doing just fine lighting his own way.

And that was it. Everything else had gone straight to Hell, to the deepest, darkest regions.

Evan's panic, for one, was growing by the second. Leigh tried to calm him, to reassure him that everything would be okay once they made it out of the cave. Help was waiting on the other side, and if they could just reach the cave's exit, policemen and paramedics would not be far behind.

She might as well have been talking to the cave walls around her. Evan would hear none of it, too busy ranting and rambling about how bad the fungus itched his skin.

"It burns, Leigh. My god, it burns so bad. It's eating me, isn't it? If I could tear this stuff off there wouldn't be any skin left underneath. It's going to eat right through my bones."

"That's not how it works," Leigh said. Though nothing seemed certain anymore in her nightmarish world, she was pretty confident about this. "It only grows on flesh."

"But what if this is different? I don't remember reading anything about this stuff glowing bright blue! All the photos, all the news report—the fungus was always green. So what the hell is this?"

"I don't know, Evan!"

Leigh clamped her teeth together the moment the last word left her mouth. She really didn't mean to yell, as raising her voice was only going to make things worse. The flames of Evan's panic fire didn't need any more fuel.

"I mean," she said, lowering her voice to the most calming tone she could, "I can't be sure, but I think this glowing effect is simply a result of our present environment. My expose to the fungus was all above ground, in the forest, where there's plenty of sunlight. Apparently, this stuff can thrive without it, and has adapted to grow in total darkness."

She must have been appealing to the highly academic side of Evan's mind, because for the first time, it seemed like he was listening to her.

"Like fish at the bottom of the ocean?"

Leigh nodded. "Exactly. What we're dealing with right now is nothing new, nothing that the authorities haven't seen before. I bet you a hundred bucks that fungus will stop glowing the moment we see the sun again."

"Oh, good." The sarcasm lacing Evan's voice was as thick as corn syrup. "Then I'll just look like Jolly Green Giant." A chuckle came so suddenly from his lips that he snorted. "Anyone want any peas? Or green beans? Who likes broccoli?"

"Shh," Leigh coaxed. The sound of Evan's laughter was making even more nervous, something she didn't think would be possible. "I know you're scared, but—"

"YOU DON'T KNOW, LEIGH!"

She tensed, Evan's shout freezing her in her tracks.

"I read all about what happened to you. You never got infected. Your friends did, sure, but you got away Scott free! Not a speck of this shit on any part of you. So don't tell me you understand. You have no idea how this feels. I..."

He took a breath. When he spoke again, his voice had returned to a normal volume.

"I can feel it *underneath* my skin. Maybe it's just my mind playing tricks on me, but I swear I can feel it *inside* of me. If it was just my skin, that would be one thing. I've gotten poison ivy before. I had chicken pox as a kid. But this..."

The look he gave Leigh shattered something inside of her. She couldn't say if the human soul existed or not, but if it did, hers just broke into a million pieces.

"It's too much, Leigh. I don't think I can make it."

Leigh stopped herself just in time before she reached for Evan's hand. Instead, she placed her arms at her side and stood as tall and as confident as her frightened state would allow.

"Listen to me, Evan. This fungus? It takes a long time for it to kill someone. You'll wish you were dead, I have do doubt about that. But I imagine it works even slower down here, away from sunlight and rainfall. You just have to hold on. We're almost there."

Evan's gaze dropped to the cave floor.

"Can you hang on, Evan? For me?"

"I..."

It was all he said. The silence in the cave was almost a physical thing, like it could choke you if you breathed in too deep.

"Evan?"

He whipped his head up, staring at Leigh with wide, wild eyes. "Augh!" he screamed, the nonsense word louder than anything else he had spoken before. "It's my hands and arms," he cried. "Where the mushrooms touched me. That's the worst part. If I could just get that part of this stuff off of me, maybe I could bear this. If I could just..."

He looked down, at what Leigh first thought was the ground. Instead, he brought his glowing hand to the left front pocket of his pants. Had Leigh had more time to think, she probably would've guessed what he was reaching for. In this panicked, frenzied moment, the appearance of the multi-tool came as an utter surprise.

Like a magician pulling a rabbit from a hat, or a cheating poker player sliding a card up his sleeve, the tool seemed to materialize from nowhere. Leigh was just about to ask, "Where did you get that?" when she remembered the secret stash they had discovered under the seat of the ATV. Along with the flashlight and the radio, the multi-tool had been among the hidden treasures. Leigh had simply forgotten about it until now.

The device offered many tools to its user, including a screwdriver, corkscrew, nail file, and tweezers. Leigh knew, however, which attachment Evan would flick up with his thumb, long before it reflected the light from his own skin. The pocket knife shimmered in that bluish hue as Evan slowly brought the blade to the back of his hand.

"Evan!" Leigh cried. "What are you doing?"

"Quiet. I need to focus." Evan sounded not unlike a surgeon prepping for a delicate operation. To Leigh's horror, it dawned on her that this was exactly what she was about to witness.

"Evan, don't. You're going to hurt yourself."

He glanced up. "More than I already am? Trust me, I'll welcome any kind of pain right now. Anything but this." He looked back down to the task at hand. "If I can just cut some off..."

"That's your skin!"

"Shh."

Before she knew it, Leigh was punching Evan's shoulder, her concern about keeping a healthy distance instantly forgotten. "Your skin is under there, you idiot! You're going to slice your own skin off."

"GOOD!"

Saliva frothed from the corners of Evan's mouth as he screamed, as if he had contracted rabies along with the horrendous fungus. Leigh had to look away as Evan began cutting, closing her eyes to reassure she didn't see anything. But she couldn't close her ears, and the sickening sound of Evan's slicing skin found its way into her head.

"Errr," Evan groaned between his gritted teeth. It was a surprisingly subtle noise, more suitable for pulling out a long sliver or extracting a wasp's stinger. Leigh wished he would cry out to mask the wet, squishy sounds of both fungus and flesh giving way. It reminded Leigh of cutting into a tomato that had gone past its expiration date—its rubbery texture oozing juice and turning to mush.

"Gyah!"

The unintelligible cry forced Leigh to open her eyes and spare a look at her self-mutilating companion. Evan had ceased cutting his hand before he was finished with the operation. A flap of skin now hung from the back of his hand, a thin stream of blood falling from his tight fist and splashing on the stone surface below. Leigh suppressed a gag at the sight of the loose flesh, trying not to think of chicken skin sliding off a drumstick.

Instead, she let her mind focus on how remarkably dark the wound was against the rest of Evan's hand. The exposed viscera underneath was the only part of the extremity not covered by fungus. It was dark, oozing patch surrounded by blue radiancy, as if a black hole had formed just under Evan's knuckles.

"I couldn't do it," Evan muttered. "It just hurt too much." He actually sounded ashamed.

Leigh swallowed back the bile rising in the back of her throat. "That's okay," she said. "So why don't you just put the knife away and we'll get out of here?"

Evan wasn't listening. He was staring at the waterfall of blood pouring from his hand, a faint smile slowly forming on his face.

"What a fool I am," he said with a scoff. "I really lost control there for a second."

Leigh tried to smile as well. "Hey, it's all right. You were just scared."

But Evan continued, completely ignoring Leigh's attempt at consolation. "Of course I can't cut off the fungus. That would never work. See?"

Evan held up his hand as if his profusely bleeding body part hadn't been in plain sight this entire time.

"I only made myself bleed." Evan's smile dropped like a heart rate monitor flatlining. "But it's not my blood that I need."

He raised the knife.

"Evan?" Leigh took a step backward, her heel stopped by a sizeable rock. "What are you saying?"

Evan shook his head. "Don't pretend like you don't know. Out of all people, you know *exactly* what I'm talking about. The fungus has only one cure, only one thing that can save my skin." He started to giggle. "Save my skin. I never thought I'd use that phrase so literally."

Leigh took another backwards step over the rock behind her foot. She caught herself just in time before she stumbled onto her back. "Come on, Evan. Don't even joke about that. I'm scared enough."

Evan's quiet giggling cut off like a severed phone line. "I'm dead serious. I'm not going to die, Leigh. I'm not going to die in some cave, in the middle of the woods, all alone in the dark. Not like this. Not like this. Not like this."

Had Leigh not spoken up, Evan may have repeated that phrase forever. "But you're not alone," she said. "I'm here with you! And I'm going to help you!"

"Yes," Evan said, taking a step forward. "You are going to help me." He flipped the knife in his hand so the blade was pointing down, out of his fist. It was the same stabbing grip reserved for such horror movie monsters like Jason Vorhees and Michael Myers.

Leigh kept walking backwards, too afraid to look away. She knew the moment she averted her eyes, Evan would strike. Even if she could manage to get a few steps ahead of him, there was no way she could navigate the rocky terrain fast enough to increase the distance between them. One slip and Evan would have plenty of time to catch up. Hell, he wouldn't even need to run.

So she kept the flashlight beam aimed at his face, as little good as that did. Evan didn't even squint against the blinding light, his illuminated eyes as wide as they could possibly be. Their pinprick pupils made him look even more insane.

"Evan, whatever you're thinking of doing..." She realized she didn't know how to end that sentence. This was all just too crazy. She wasn't supposed to be afraid of him. Evan was supposed to be her only remaining ally, the only person left in this world she could trust. They were supposed to be on the same side.

"Don't do it," was all she could say as her back connected with the wall behind her. She could retreat no further.

Evan shrugged, the gesture almost comically underwhelming for such a situation. "I have to," he said. "I must do what must be done."

"Then let me do it!"

It was apparent the statement took Evan completely off guard, based on the expression of total shock that stretched his face.

"You mean," he stammered. "You're going to..."

He mimed running the knife along his own throat.

"No," Leigh said. "That's not necessary. That's what I've been trying to tell you all along. You don't need to do that because you only need a little bit of my blood."

Evan raised an eyebrow. "How do you know how much I need?"

"Because I contracted the fungus too!"

That same shocked look remained on Evan's face. "What?" he said.

When Evan didn't clarify that question, Leigh vigorously nodded. "It's true. When I was admitted to the hospital, they found traces of the fungus on my body. I have no idea what they were planning to about it, because before I could speak with a doctor, a forest ranger named Jake Spire fed me his blood without me knowing."

In other circumstances, Leigh might've laughed at Evan's expression and perhaps would've even added, "I'm just full of surprises, aren't I?" Instead, she just waited for Evan to process this information, praying that he would listen to reason.

"How did you not know?"

"What's it matter?" Leigh shouted. She knew she was

getting closer and closer to hysteria but couldn't stop herself. "He put it in some grape juice, okay? The point is, it was so minute, I couldn't taste it at all. But guess what? It did the trick! Look at me now!"

Though just an expression, Evan seemed to take her seriously, giving her a once over with his eyes. For a moment, it looked like he understood. His eyes softened, his tight mouth relaxed.

But then he shook his head. "I'm sorry, Leigh. I just can't take the chance. There's no way you were as bad off as me. There's no way you looked like this."

Even as Leigh began to babble and beg Evan to reconsider, she had to admit he was right about that.

"Evan, wait. Please, just think about what you're—"

"I must do what must be done," Evan repeated as he advanced a step closer.

Leigh tried to press herself even deeper into the wall, as if the stone might give and encase her in a protective shield. Of course, it did no such thing, leaving her with a homicidal young man and her raving thoughts.

It isn't supposed to be this way. I'm not supposed to be here. I already survived this once. How is this happening again? Why is this happening again?

"I'll make it quick, Leigh. I promise. It won't hurt."

It was obvious that Evan was saying these words less for Leigh's benefit and more as a way to convince himself to follow through. He could've attacked Leigh at any time but he couldn't seem to stop talking.

"I'll make it quick and that will be that. Then I'll remedy my situation and make my way out of these godforsaken caverns. And if anyone asks? Well, it was you that those men were after. I was just in the wrong place at the wrong time." Evan's eyes glazed over, something within his himself turning off. "Yeah, that's all. I was just in the wrong place at the wrong time."

He had found it, the train of reasoning that would allow himself to commit bloody murder. To Leigh, it was just another rambling rant of a yet another psychopath. In her eyes, it might as well have been the resurrected corpse of Rob come back to finish the job. It had all been just like this. Rob had her cornered in the Cedar family barn. Her back had been pressed against a wall exactly like now. But just as he was about to reach her, Leigh's hand had found the handle of that hammer. She had gripped it, its heavy weight bringing a last second chance to survive. She could almost feel that weight now.

No...

She *could* feel that weight now.

Evan charged and Leigh swung the rock in her hand as hard as she could. She didn't exactly know when her fingers had found the solid stone, but she didn't care. All that mattered is that it smashed into the side of Evan's head, striking just below his right temple. He cried out as he fell away, landing somewhere to the left with a heavy thud. Leigh didn't bother to look. She was already sprinting into the darkness.

"LEIGH!"

Evan's echoing scream came at her from all directions. Leigh had struck a formidable blow to Evan's skull, but something told her he would be on his feet in a matter of seconds. Risking a life-threatening stumble at any moment, Leigh ran deeper into the cave, hoping to God she was still heading in the right direction. Although if the tunnels led her directly to Hell, Leigh wouldn't have been surprised at all.

CHAPTER EIGHTEEN

Had Jake been trying to follow the fading 4x4 tracks by himself, he would've surely lost the trail a long time ago. Fortunately, Cordelia proved to be a far superior tracker, as she was able to determine the direction of the tracks in even the most questionable areas. Though impressed, Jake wasn't at all suprised with the woman's abilities. There was a reason that she and her brother were able to bring fresh stock to their farmer's market booth every week. Between the two of them, no game animal had a chance.

The problem with having Cordelia lead the way was that Jake now had to keep up with the expert hunter. With night almost completely upon them, the toil of the day had finally caught up with Jake's body. Despite now having medication to keep his headaches at bay, other hardships were wearing away at his physical being.

Stress, for one, could only be ignored for so long. Jake didn't know which felt more tired: his muscles or his mind. He felt like he had just walked away from a terrible car accident, his muscular system a single, tight mass. It would take no less than a master massage therapist to work out the countless knots squeezing his neck, shoulders, and back.

Food was another problem. Until now, crisis after crisis had distracted him from his growing appetite. Now that he was finally able to let someone else steer the ship, he realized just how hungry he had become. A quick mental recap of his day's consumption included a handful of pills, a couple beers during his rendezvous with Mary's kidnapper, and...

Jesus, was that all?

No wonder Jake felt like he was on the verge of collapsing. If memory served, he hadn't eaten anything since last night's dinner. And while he was certain that the image of the deer man eating the one-eyed biker's flesh would scare away his appetite forever, his stomach had something different to say on the subject. The constant grumbling coming from his gut said only thing: "I need food. *You* need food."

Jake considered asking Cordelia if she had anything on her. As a veteran outdoorsman, she would know not to venture into the woods alone without a single morsel of food. A bag of granola, a candy bar, even a single Starlight mint—any of these could make the difference between life and death. Then again, Cordelia hadn't been alone this morning when she had left for her hunt. Matthew had been with her, and maybe he had been carrying the emergency snacks.

What really stopped him from calling out to Cordelia for a quick pick-me-up was that he didn't want to interrupt her pursuit. They were making good time, even in spite of the fading light and thickening snow. In the end, Jake could deal with hunger pangs and some light dizziness. But if they didn't reach Leigh in time, she would have much greater problems to deal with.

He would be okay for now. He just had to distract himself. He just had to think about something other than the hunger gnawing on his insides like some rabid animal. If he could do that, he would be fine. He would—

"Are you okay?"

Jake almost collided with Cordelia, not realizing she had

stopped dead in her tracks. The woman looked at him, a grave concern hardening her expression. "You look a little pale," she said.

Jake laughed. "How can you tell in this light?"

Cordelia ignored the joke and asked, "When was the last time you ate something?"

Shrugging, Jake said, "Don't know, don't care. We have to keep going."

But Cordelia would not take another step. "Not much sense in running into danger if you can hardly stand on your own two feet. If you're going to watching my back, I want you alert and ready to fight." She unzipped her jacket and reached into the inside pocket. A moment later, her hand emerged with a clear, plastic baggie. Inside were strips of meat.

"Venison jerky," Cordelia said, throwing Jake the bag. "My own recipe. Matthew may have been good at sausage, but jerky was always my thing. Go on, take a bite and tell me you've ever had better."

She didn't have to tell Jake twice. Once glimpse at the jerky and his stomach practically barked like a dog. Not even bothering to pull apart the sealed top, Jake tore open the side of the bag and shoved three sticks into his mouth at once.

Dear God...

It may have been his severe hunger talking, but there was no question about it: Cordelia was right. This was the best jerky he had ever tasted. Hell, it may have been greatest food he had ever tasted in his entire life.

"Phank roo," Jake said, his jerky filled mouth slurring the words of gratitude.

Cordelia smiled. "Don't mention it. Can you eat and walk?"

Instead of another distorted verbal response, Jake just nodded affirmative.

"Good," Cordelia said. "But try to finish as soon as you can. Based on the freshness of these tracks, we're getting close."

She proceeded again, her eyes trained on the ground unless to dodge a tree branch now and then. Jake did as she asked, wolfing down the jerky with ravenous bites. He wished he could eat it slower if only to savor the meat's delicious flavor. As it were, he was hardly tasting it as it went from his lips to his stomach in record time.

The last of the jerky consumed, Jake stuffed the remnants of the plastic bag into his pocket. It was truly remarkable how quick the food was working his magic, as he was feeling better already. The effect must have been entirely psychosematic, as no human body could digest food that fast. Still, just the thought of knowing his stomach was no longer a barren wasteland gave him a renewed sense of energy.

He called up to Coredelia. "Thanks, again. You were right, I needed that more than I realized. I sure do feel better now—"

Jake immediately closed his mouth when Cordelia's hand shot up. She kept her hand suspended in her air, clearly signaling for Jake to remain where he stood. After what felt like an eternity, Cordelia waved the tips of her fingers. She was summoning him to her side.

Moving as quietly as the crunching snow would allow, Jake made his way to her right. She remained silent but pointed with her other hand to a dark shape about twenty feet away. Giving his eyes a second to adjust, Jake squinted to see that the dark mass was a parked four-wheeler. Though covered in snow, its wheels were still clearly visible.

"Bingo," Cordelia whispered.

"Yeah," Jake agreed, also keeping his voice to a whisper. "But I don't see anyone. Do you?"

Cordelia shook her head. "Hard to see any footprints at this distance. I'm going to have get closer."

"Wait." Jake grabbed her arm before she could advance. "What if Woodenknife is nearby?"

The woman smirked, the expression filled with genuine amusement. "The day that bastard can sneak up on me will be a cold day in Hell." She un-slung the rifle from her shoulder and offered it to Jake. "Still, better safe than sorry, right? You cover me."

Jake accepted the weapon. Its weight felt good in his hands. It felt like power. It felt like control.

"Okay," Jake said. "Let's do this."

Without another word, Cordelia proceeded to sneak forward. She kept crouched as she moved, trying to make herself into the smallest target possible. Jake breathed a sigh of relief when she made it to the ATV without incident.

After a quick scan of the ground surrounding the machine, Cordelia looked back to Jake. She made a walking motion with the middle and index finger of her right hand. She then flashed him what looked a peace sign, and then pointed to the woods leading away from the ATV.

Two sets of footprints, heading that direction.

Jake nodded that he understood and returned his own hand gesture. He pointed to himself and then at the ATV.

Should I come to you now?

At first, Cordelia nodded "yes," but immediately raised her hand when Jake took his first step. He froze as she sniffed the air like a stalking mountain cat.

Her gaze falling to the forest floor, she examined the snow under the chassis of the ATV. A moment later, she was looking back at Jake and mouthing the word, "Gas."

Jake turned back the way they had come, but there was no sign of leaking fuel. Though the four-wheeler would've have shielded the puddle of gas underneath it, the falling snow had completely covered the liquid trail leading to its final resting place.

He turned back to the woman to ask, "So what now?"

And then turned again.

What was that?

Looking past their own footprints, Jake stared into the distant trees. He had almost missed it, as the antlers were barely visible against the tangled tree limbs. But they were there, bright white against the dark trunks of maples and oaks. Based on those antlers, Jake was staring at a trophy buck. On any other day, the Wolfchild siblings would've bagged themselves quite a prize.

On any other day...

But today was today, and that wasn't a deer. It was a deer *skull*. *No.*

It was the man wearing a deer skull on his head.

"Son of a bitch!" Jake hissed, his feet already moving. A voice somewhere in the back of his mind asked if leaving Cordelia was the best choice of action, but god damnit, he had that cannibal bastard in his sights, and this time, he had a gun.

The Deer Man gave up his statue routine and began to run away. Jake considered taking a wild shot, thinking perhaps that even a missed shot would convince the man to come to a halt and raise his hands to the sky. But no, he decided, that would be a waste of ammo. This man was in too deep to surrender that easy.

With the grounding sloping down, Jake's steps were becoming slides. He felt like he was skating after his prey rather than running. At this rate, he wouldn't be able to steady himself for a clean shot. Maybe if the ground was level, or not covered in slick snow, or while he was wishing, not littered with sight obscuring tree trunks.

Suddenly, the man came to a stop. A downed tree blocked his path and its thick branches made it to tall to leap over. The man looked right then left, unsure of which way to go.

Now.

Jake slid to a stop, feeling more like a figure skater than ever before as he dropped to one knee with an unexpected grace. He raised the rifle to his eye and looked down the sights. This would be not be a carefully aimed shot. There simply wasn't time. He would just have to pull the trigger and hope the bullet didn't strike the man in the head or heart. Jake didn't want to kill anyone if he didn't have to.

He inhaled, steadied himself, and—

From behind him, Cordelia screamed in pain.

The sound lasted only a second, but it was enough time to distract Jake to miss his shot. The Deer Man darted to the left, rounded the base of the tree, and was gone.

Shit!

Returning to his feet, Jake struggled to climb the hill he had just descended. Each step resulted in his foot sliding backward, threatening to send him to the ground. Using the rifle as a makeshift walking stick, Jake managed to maintain his balance until the ground leveled again. More secure in his footing, he rushed forward.

And froze.

Through the cover of the trees, Jake could see Cordelia sitting on the ground next to the ATV. Her body was contorted into an awkward position, one of her legs sprawled out to the side. It was only a second later that Jake understood why her leg seemed to be stuck in that pose. An arrow protruded from her thigh.

Before he could even think of what to do next, a figure emerged from the trees and approached Cordelia with a confident swagger. If Jake hadn't been already been able to guess the man's identity, the crossbow he rested over his shoulder was a dead giveaway.

As Woodenknife came closer, Cordelia tried to back away, but the slightest movement made her cry out in pain. As much as the wound surely hurt, Jake could tell by the woman's impeded movement that it wasn't just the pain keeping her in place. The arrow must have traveled completely through her leg and pinned her to the ground.

"It's a shame it's not Wolfchild season," Woodenknife said. "I would be talk of the Elk's Club with the kind of day I'm having."

Cordelia did not give a verbal response. Instead, she spat at his feet with more venom than Jake had ever witnessed.

Woodenknife chuckled. "Nice. I guess you're a family of few words. Then again, Matthew couldn't say much with an arrow sticking out of his throat."

"You bastard," Cordelia hissed. "I'm going to kill you."

"Is that so?"

Woodenknife lifted his foot, bringing the sole of his boot

onto the arrow in Cordelia's leg. A smile exposed his teeth as he began to press down.

The cry of pain that shot from the woman's mouth instantly spurred Jake to lift the rifle to his eye and take aim.

Time to say goodbye, fucker.

Hesitation, however, seized Jake's trigger finger. At the very last moment, he remembered the single word Cordelia had mouthed as she examined the four-wheeler. The area all around the vehicle was soaked in gas, which also meant the fuel tank could still be leaking now. If a single bullet struck the exposed fuel, both Cordelia and Woodenknife would have front row seats to the last fireworks display either one of them would ever see.

Woodenknife lifted his boot off the arrow and returned it to the ground. "Though I'd love to continue chatting with you, I'm afraid I just can't spare the time. My real prey is just up ahead and I don't want to be late to the dance." He took the crossbow off his shoulder and brought it level with his eyes.

Jake readjusted his grip on his own weapon and exhaled all the breath from his lungs. *Aim high*, he told himself. *That way, you won't ignite a fire if you miss.*

He gritted his teeth.

But I'm not going to miss.

He pulled the trigger.

The click that came from the rifle couldn't have been any louder than a single tap of a computer mouse, but to Jake, the sound echoed in his ears. He lowered the rifle and looked at it in disbelief. Was the gun not loaded?

No.

In his panic, he had forgotten to take the safety off.

Jake fumbled with the weapon, completely disregarding the noise he was making as his shaking hands struggled to activate the safety switch. After he finally flicked the mechanism from *S* to *F*, he gasped when he returned his gaze to his target ahead.

Woodenknife was staring directly at him and muttering, "What the fuck?"

In the second it took Jake to bring his rifle up, Cordelia had already made her move. Like a pouncing cat, she reached up and swatted for Woodenknife's long, black hair. Had the man been only a step further back, she would've failed in her attempt. Her fingers just barely found purchase, but it was enough to yank his head downward with a violent tug.

Woodenknife cried out and his body followed suit, the sudden momentum bringing him to his knees. He collapsed right at Cordelia's side, the crossbow falling from his grip. And then, from seemingly out of nowhere, a Zippo lighter was in Cordelia's other hand. She flicked its top open with its signature sound, her thumb immediately sparking its flint wheel.

Even from several feet away, Jake could see the flame reflecting in Woodeknife's wide, frenzied eyes.

"It sure was cold today."

Woodenknife's puzzled expression at Cordelia's words must have mirrored Jake's own face. But before either of them could say or do anything else, Cordelia said, "Let me warm you up."

She dropped the lighter.

A wave of heat bombarded Jake as the ground all around the ATV went ablaze. A second later, a thunderous *Whoomp!* filled the surrounding forest as the flames found the trapped vapor in the ATV's engine. With nowhere else to go, the ignited gas exploded within the machine, practically lifting the vehicle off its tires. Jake shielded his eyes from the explosion, his cry of Cordelia's name lost in the deafening boom.

When he regained his vision, a plume of jet black smoke floated up from the smoldering wreckage. Through the dark gray cloud, he could barely make out the shape of someone's arm sprawled across the forest floor.

He ran forward.

It was Cordelia, her body still pinned the ground by Woodenknife's arrow. Having been this close to the explosion, the blast must have killed her instantly. At least, that's what Jake hoped. If there was anything resembling justice left in the universe, this woman deserved a quick death for her bravery.

Woodenknife, on the other hand...

Jake scanned the ground all around the flaming mess but could not find any trace of the bastard anywhere. Panic's icy teeth sank themselves into his heart once again at the thought of Woodenknife surviving such an explosion. Had he somehow crawled his way behind a tree and was aiming his crossbow at Jake at this exact moment?

But then Jake heard it—a groan coming from directly behind him.

He turned, bringing his rifle up to start shooting. As it turned out, defending himself would no longer be necessary.

The blast had rocketed Woodenknife back into the trunk of a large evergreen tree. The man may have actually survived the explosion with only superficial injuries, had it not been for the broken tree branch that impaled his left side. A jagged, blood-soaked stick protruded from Woodenknife's body, missing his heart by mere inches. With his face charred from flames, the man looked like a vampire who angry villagers had staked and left to burn in the sun.

Woodenknife lifted his head as Jake approached. Through bloody lips and teeth, he actually smiled at Jake's presence.

"Well," he said, pausing to release a few wet coughs. "What are you waiting for? Let's get this over with."

At first, Jake had no clue what the man was talking about. It was only when he noticed that Woodenknife was staring at the rifle that he understood.

He raised the gun, aimed it at Woodenknife's heart, put his finger on the trigger...and lowered the weapon.

"The girl," Jake said. "Why are you after her?"

Between coughs, Woodenknife was able to say, "Need her."

"You need her? What for?"

Woodenknife shook his head. "Not me. My friend."

Jake paused, completely taken back by the idea of someone this murderous appreciating the concept of friendship.

"Your mean the guy in the mask? What does he want with her?"

Again, Woodenknife shook his head. "White man," he grumbled, looking away. "You wouldn't understand."

A bolt of pain hammered its way between Jake's eyes, another headache showing up unannounced. At the same time, the man before him was no longer John Woodenknife, gang leader, drug dealer, and cold-blooded killer. For a split second, a grinning Phil Carson looked back at Jake, the bullet hole still bleeding from when he shot himself in the head.

And then, just like that, the image was gone.

"I wouldn't be so sure," Jake said, ignoring his throbbing head. "I've seen what loyalty can do to man. It can kill you."

To this, Woodenknife nodded. "Speaking of which..." He gestured to the rifle with his head.

Jake slung the gun over his shoulder. "I'm afraid you'll have to stick around a little bit longer." He paused to consider his choice of words and then added, "Pardon the pun."

Woodenknife laughed, more blood oozing from the corner of his mouth. "Don't have the guts to pull the trigger?"

"Nah," Jake said. "I just can't afford to spend a bullet on you, not with your buddy still out there."

With that, he pivoted on his heel and began to walk away. From behind, Woodenknife yelled, "You might manage to put him out his misery, but you'll never kill the Wendigo inside him."

Jake halted in mid-step and looked back at Woodenknife. "Oh, you'll see," the dying man said. "In the end, the Wendigo always wins."

Jake inhaled to say something more, but decided to bite his tongue. There was nothing more to say, only a girl to find, another to rescue, and more psychopaths that needed to be dealt with once for all.

This time, when Jake turned to walk away, he did not turn back.

CHAPTER NINETEEN

Chalky dust from the cave's ceiling fell on Leigh's head as something rumbled high above her. For a moment, she felt like a war refugee hiding in a bunker as a battle raged on outside. The thunder, for a split second at least, also distracted her from the psychopath chasing her in the dark.

And then he was back.

"Leigh!" Evan screamed from somewhere in the black. "You can't run forever!"

She had no idea what could've caused the booming noise and ground shaking vibration. That, however, didn't seem that important at the moment. All that mattered was that the sound had come from above, from the outside world where Leigh could escape. The fact that she had both heard and felt the blast so well must mean she was fairly close to the surface.

All right, she thought. *Look for a way up.*

Leigh sidestepped to the wall to her right, thinking maybe it she would be able to spot an offshoot or break in the rock that she could slide through. Even if she couldn't find a chute leading up to the surface, she might be able to squeeze herself into a crevasse and wait for Evan to run past her. Then she could backtrack and go right out the way she and Evan had come in, while her pursuer traveled farther and farther into the cave.

Christ, why didn't I think of that before?

The answer was obvious enough. She had been blinded by pure terror, all logic and reasoning pushed aside to make room for her oversized fear. Not that her horror hadn't dissipated in the slightest, but it appeared her survival instinct had finally showed up to throw one final Hail Mary pass.

As she continued to run as quickly as the rocky surface would allow, Leigh kept a hand on the cave wall, feeling for any spaces her eyes might have missed. It also helped her keep her balance, as it felt like every other step threatened to pull her to the ground. The only break she had been granted in this fucked up situation was that her pursuer was as equally out of his element. If she was being chased by a coal miner or a rugged outdoorsman, Leigh had no doubt she would've been turned to mincemeat in no time at all.

As it were, it seemed Evan was having just as difficult time as she was. With crazed desperation fueling him, it sounded like he was being even more careless with this footing. Every now and then, Leigh would hear him curse or cry out as yet another jagged rock grabbed his ankle. Every one of these slips was a gift to Leigh, but she couldn't rely on them forever. She couldn't chance that Evan would slip and crack his head open before she did.

The cave continued to stretch out before her, a never ending tunnel of stone that was looking more and more to be her eternal resting place with every passing second. The wall to her right had yet to reveal any passageway that she could use, and Leigh was starting to think that maybe calling this plan a "Hail Mary" was a bit too generous. At the very least, a Hail Mary pass was attempted by a professional athlete, a skilled and practiced quarterback calling on the extent of his talent to win one for his team.

But Leigh was no expert spelunker. This was more comparable to the those near impossible half-court shots during basketball games where fans could win large sums of money. She had seen a few videos on YouTube of people actually winning that challenge, and a winner's strategy didn't look any different than that a loser. Both would just rear back, throw the ball in a long arch, and pray. Most wouldn't even come close.

The rock wall under Leigh's fingertips suddenly stopped. A breeze of cool air touched her palm. She turned to see a wide crack in the stone, just wide enough for a person to squeeze through.

But once in awhile, some lucky person walked away with an oversized check.

Once again, Leigh's heart leapt in her chest, only this time it wasn't from paralyzing fear. She hadn't experienced this emotion in so long that it felt like a first time guest from a foreign country.

It was hope.

Not allowing herself to think twice, Leigh turned herself sideways so that she could fit in the narrow space. What was left of her fragile psyche didn't miss the opportunity to remind her that she was literally between a rock and a hard place. She stifled a maniacal laugh, knowing that even a chuckle would echo in this chamber and give away her position. Besides, if she started laughing now, she knew she would never stop, even when Evan began to chop her into bits.

Though she still gripped the flashlight, the passageway didn't allow enough room for her to raise her hand and illuminate her way. That was for the best, as the entire point was to hide in darkness while Evan stumbled past her. Still, she couldn't help but be curious about what lay ahead. Where was that breeze coming from?

The question was quickly forgotten as a dim, blue light shone to her left. She didn't need to hear his voice to know that it was Evan, lighting his own way with the glowing fungus spreading across his body. The light intensified as he drew closer, the eerie azure light casting dramatic shadows on the wall.

Leigh inhaled as quietly as she could and held her breath. It wasn't easy with the rock wall pressing against her chest, but she knew at this close distance that a single breath could reveal her location.

Please, please, PLEASE don't look in here.

Mere inches away, Evan stopped in his tracks. At first, Leigh thought he was looking around, as if he had somehow acquired night vision along with the aggressive fungus. But no, he wasn't looking into the darkness.

He was listening.

Oh, God...

Her silence may end up betraying her after all. Without a single sound of her footfalls emanating in the cave, Evan was sure to figure out that she had stopped moving. And if she had stopped moving, she must be hiding. And if she is hiding, where would she be? Jammed in a crevasse, perhaps?

"I know you're near," Evan said. "You couldn't have gotten that far ahead. What rock are you hiding under?"

Evan took a step and his foot rolled across a few loose pebbles. He shot his hand out, reaching for the wall to steady himself. Had his hand been only a centimeter to the left, he would've felt the gap that was concealing Leigh.

Fighting the urge to move any faster, Leigh slowly turned her head in the opposite direction. If Evan approached any closer, the light he casted off his arms and face might reflect off her zippers, or jewelry, or perhaps even her own eyes.

Slow, she kept telling herself. *Quiet.*

Her head finished its rotation.

And her heartbeat seized at what she saw. Had Leigh been able to do so, she would've clapped her hand over her mouth. Somehow, biting her bottom lip kept the scream inside her, the one that desperately wanted to be unleashed.

Evan was inside the crevasse with her.

No, wait.

That wasn't true. That was no man standing just inches away from her, though it did glow with the exact same vibrant color. The blue fungus was growing against the cave walls in glowing tendrils that snaked like river lines on a map. Fortunately, they didn't reach into the space where Leigh was presently wedged, or else they would've no doubt been growing on her too. They did, however, stretch another direction. They were spreading upward.

What?

Evan had taken a few more steps passed the crevasse, so Leigh decided to chance it. She shuffled to her right, deeper into the cave wall, towards the dangerous fungus. With extra care, she planted her feet deliberately being sure not to step on any of the deadly plants. To her joyous surprise, the walls squeezing her in front and in back, suddenly let go. She was standing in what felt like a narrow chute. Leigh looked straight up, seeing the blue fungal tendrils climbing into the darkness above.

Was that the surface up there?

"Found you!"

Leigh shrieked as the voice amplified in the rock chamber. She turned to see a glowing, fungus covered eyeball staring through the crack. Though she couldn't see his mouth, Leigh knew Evan was grinning.

"I'm not going to die," Evan said. "I've got you now."

Leigh frantically looked around the chute as if a secret passageway would magically appear, but there was only one option for exit—the way she came in. And that option was blocked off by an insane doctor's assistant who wanted to eat her flesh.

This was it. She was dead. There was no way out.

Except...

Leigh looked up into the darkness. The chute was narrow enough that she might be able to put her back to one side and shimmy up until she reached the top. Then again, how would she avoid the fungus growing on random patches of the stone? Was it worth the risk of infection?

Leigh shrieked as icy fingers brushed her shoulder. Evan was halfway through the crevasse and was reaching for her.

"Come here, you little bitch!"

Yes. The risk was worth it.

Not hesitating a moment longer, Leigh reached up and grabbed a protruding rock high above her head. Using all her strength, she pulled herself up, instantly reminded of the indoor climbing wall she had been forced to scale in high school gym class. She hadn't been a very good climber back then, but maybe she had just been lacking the right motivation.

Before she knew it, Leigh had wedged herself in the chute just as she had planned. It was a not a moment too soon, as Evan was squeezing his way through the remainder of the crack and into the chamber. His voice practically deafened her as he cried out, the shout intensified in this natural funnel.

"Are you kidding me?" he yelled. "You know, Leigh, I was only going to kill you to save my own skin. But you're really pissing me off now. I'm actually going to enjoy this!"

Though she kept her eyes trained above, Leigh could hear Evan begin to climb.

Oh, God. Where is the top?

Jagged rock cut into her fingers but she hardly felt the pain. Dirt and wet soil rained upon her face, but turned her head away from the filthy shower and kept moving. Blue fungus glowed bright just millimeters from her eyes, practically blinding her, but she ignored that too. Had she touched it? Was it already crawling on her flesh?

Her mind swatted away those questions like houseflies, focusing on a single thought that repeated in her mind like the ultimate mantra.

Reach the top. Reach the top. Reach the top.

"Right behind you!" Evan shouted from below. He sounded so close.

She kept climbing, a task that was getting more difficult with every passing second. Though she had wanted to believe it was only in her head, Leigh couldn't deny that the chute was getting narrower. Soon it would be too tight for her to climb any higher, and she would be stuck. Evan would simply have to tug on her leg to send her crashing back into the cave where he could take his time and savor every bite.

Or maybe she'd get lucky. Maybe the chute would become too narrow for Evan to pursue and she would just remain here like Santa stuck in a chimney. Hell, maybe her mind would snap from the claustrophobia, sparing her consciousness of the final moments before she died of exposure.

That was what her definition of luck had become: not dying at the hands of an insane cannibal. Perhaps Dr. Joyce's therapy had worked after all—it had certainly changed Leigh's perspective. It wasn't that long ago that Leigh would've viewed being buried alive as a bad thing.

But then Leigh's fingers felt something cold. Only this wasn't another rock, hard and unforgiving. This was soft and fragile, so much so that it melted under her touch. She knew this sensation, as she had felt it time and time again after growing up in New England her entire life.

It was snow.

With the absolute last bit of her energy, Leigh gripped the rocks above her with both hands and pulled as hard as she could. A moment later, her head emerged from the ground, her sight blinded by the deepening snow. It suffocated her, filling her mouth and throat as she continued to pull herself up. Just as she though the frozen fluff would asphyxiate her, her head broke the surface. She gasped, wonderful, life-saving air filling her lungs.

Despite not having any feeling left in her hands and arms, Leigh managed to pull herself completely out of the hole. She collapsed into the snow at once, lying on her back as she struggled to regain her breath. She knew Evan couldn't be more than a minute behind her, but her body didn't seem to care.

I know you're tired, but get up! You have to get away!

Her mind's words fell on deaf ears. The cold of the snow was tightening her already stiff muscles, quickly changing her into a statue. But as she lay there, watching her heavy breath form white puffs of steam, she began to realize she couldn't really feel the cold at all. In fact, a pleasingly warm sensation was overtaking her entire form. Given a few minutes, Leigh had no doubt she could easily fall asleep.

"Leigh?"

Or maybe she didn't even need that much time. She could already hear voices in her dream.

"Oh my god, it's you!"

When the voice came a second time, Leigh went to open her eyes, only to find they were open already. This wasn't a dream. The voice was real.

Her muscles crying out in painful protest, Leigh lifted her head from the blanket of snow. Standing about ten feet away, a man stared at her, eyes wide in disbelief. His open jaw separated his bearded face, a snow covered ball cap covering his shaggy dark hair. Even in her near delirious state, Leigh felt there was something very familiar about this man.

"You with Woodenknife?" she croaked. "Figures, doesn't it?"

The man bounded through the snow as he rushed toward her. "No, Leigh, it's me. It's Jake Spire."

"I know that name," Leigh said, letting her head rest against the ground again. "You're the...the...ranger."

Jake came to her side and looked down at her. His clothes had transformed to those of a forest ranger—tan pants, green shirt, and the traditional hat. The snow was gone as well, replaced by crunchy dead leaves and soft pine needles. The fact that Leigh had time traveled to the previous year didn't startle her at all. It seemed completely natural that she had returned to the moment that Jake Spire had rescued her from being beheaded by the axe-wielding Rob.

"Don't move," Jake said. "Let me take a look at you, make sure nothing is broken."

As he spoke, the details of reality began to reshape. Jake's green shirt morphed into a dark jacket, the nametag disappearing all together. The beard re-grew on his face like a motion captured video.

"I can't believe I found you," Jake said. "Where did you come from?"

Though her arm felt like it weighed a hundred pounds, Leigh raised a hand and pointed to her left. Just as Jake followed the finger with his eyes, Evan's head sprang from the snow like a demonic Jack-in-the-Box.

"Leigh!" he screamed.

Jake got to his feet, and for the first time, Leigh saw that he carried a rifle in his hands. He pointed the weapon at Evan's glowing, fuzz-covered face, but didn't pull the trigger.

"Jesus," he muttered. "What the fuck is this?"

Evan appeared oblivious to the fact that he being held at gunpoint. He jerked his head left and right, desperately trying to the free his arms from beneath the earth.

"Gonna eat you," he said. "Gonna eat you and I'll feel all better."

"S-stop," Jake mumbled. "Just take it easy, buddy."

Evan was doing anything but. He successfully freed one arm, the blue appendage breaking the surface of the snow and grasping for better leverage. It was like watching the transformation scene of a werewolf movie, only this man was apparently turning into the Cookie Monster.

"I'm serious, man," Jake said, his voice gaining a newfound strength. "I'll shoot you, if I have to."

Leigh looked from Jake to Evan, and for a moment, her eyes met those of the fungus covered madman. At their eye contact, Evan stopped moving, the rage twisting his expression replaced by a solemn seriousness.

"This is all your fault," he said. "You know that, right? C., myself...it's all because of you. Dr. Joyce was wrong. You don't need therapy, Leigh. You need to be wiped off the face of the earth. You need to be squashed like a bug."

Leigh couldn't say where she found the strength to stand, but it came all the same. She felt like a puppet master was pulling her strings, lifting her from the ground and standing her on her feet.

She reached out and placed a hand on the barrel of Jake's rifle. Gently, she pressed down, urging Jake to lower the weapon. Though obviously still confused, he complied and let the barrel point at the ground.

Then Leigh walked over to Evan and stood right above him. He looked up at her with bloodshot eyes.

"Maybe you're right, Evan. I probably don't deserve to live. I probably should be squashed like a bug."

She lifted her foot high in the air.

"But you first."

Evan had just enough time to gasp before the heel of Leigh's foot came crashing into his forehead. And then he was gone, stomped beneath the snow and back down the long, dark hole. Leigh heard him scream the entire way down before his cries ended with a heavy thump.

Silence as thick as London fog filled the space between Leigh and Jake. It was finally broken when Jake cleared his throat and said, "Are...are you okay?"

Leigh, who was still staring at the hole, looked up to meet Jake's gaze.

"I'm good," she said. "How you doin?"

And then she collapsed.

CHAPTER TWENTY

There was no greater motivation in the world than having no choice. Had there been as many as two options available to Jake, he would have surely froze, both figuratively and literally. Doubt would've overtaken his thoughts, resulting only in indecisive hesitation. But as it were, his goal was singular, as were the means to achieve it.

He had to get Leigh out of the woods, and the only way to do that would be to carry her all the way back to his car.

So that's what he did.

Slinging the rifle over his shoulder so the weapon lay diagonally across his back, Jake was free to use both arms to carry his unconscious companion. He felt much like one of those black-and-white movie monsters, like the Creature from the Black Lagoon, carrying a fainted heroine back to his lair. If only he were the monstrous Gillman right now, he would be cruising around the warm climate of the Amazon, rather than on the verge of freezing to death.

As Jake trudged as fast as he could through the snow, he tried to recall as many Universal movie monsters that he could. It wasn't just the cold he was trying to distract himself from, but the looming thought that the remaining kidnapper could be following right behind. What had Woodenknife called him?

A Wendigo.

Jake didn't buy that for a second, not that his dismissal helped at all. Possessed by an evil spirit or not, the man in the deer skull was dangerous enough. Still, what could Jake do? With Leigh in her battered condition, Jake couldn't afford the time to wait the man out. All he could do was keep moving and pray he didn't find himself in the deer man's crosshairs.

All right, he thought. *There was Frankenstein, Dracula, the Wolf Man, the Invisible Man, the Mummy, um...*

He paused his mental game to focus on climbing over some fallen brush. Once he was sure he had solid footing, he resumed.

The Bride of Frankenstein, the Son of Frankenstein, the...shit. Cousin of Frankenstein?

He chuckled to himself, full well knowing he was forcing the laugh. He didn't need a degree in psychology to know he was utilizing a coping mechanism. But what was the alternative? Dropping to his knees and giving up?

Fuck that.

All he had to was put one foot in front of another. Jake had been way out in back country plenty of times in his Forest Service career. Each time he had hiked his way home, feet and legs aching, his canteen bone dry and his throat begging for a drink. This was nothing. Leigh felt lighter than a sack of raked leaves. He could do this. He could—

Something snapped behind him. He turned.

With the tangled trees, falling snow, and thick darkness, there was little to see.

"Hey," Jake shouted. The word left his mouth before he had given it any thought. "Hey asshole, you out there?"

He waited a moment. Silence.

"Christ, buddy," he said. "If you're going to do something, then just do it already. I mean, you really want this girl?"

He lifted the unconscious Leigh a little higher into the air.

"Then come and get her! And if you don't have the balls, then fuck off!"

He was shouting now.

"Because I am so sick of this shit! I've been suffering withdrawals all day, freezing my ass off, stumbling around like a dipshit tourist, and I've had enough! So if you're going to kill me, then pull the trigger! You'd be doing me a favor, you really would. I mean, if I was dead, at least I would never have to come back to this GOD- DAMN, MOTHERFUCKING, COCKSUCKING TOWN!"

"Who are you talking to?"

Jake, now heaving and out-of-breath, looked down to see Leigh staring at him with foggy, dreamy eyes.

He glanced up to check the forest one last time. Scoffing at himself, Jake had to smile.

"Nobody," he said.

Leigh went in and out of consciousness for the rest of the trip back to the car. Whenever she would ask a question like, "What happened?" or "Where are we?" Jake would encourage her to save her strength and wait till they were back. Every time she came to during their seemingly endless walk, she was a little more coherent each time. By the time they reached his Eagle, she had regained all of her wits.

"This is your car?" she said as the AMC vehicle came into view.

"Hey," Jake said, pretending to be offended. "It's a classic. Most importantly, the heater works."

He set carefully set Leigh down on her feet, giving the girl enough time to place one hand on the roof of the car to steady herself. Once it seemed she wouldn't topple over, he let go to retrieve the keys from his jacket pocket. "One sec," he said.

It didn't take much longer than a second to unlock the passenger door and assist Leigh inside. He shut the door behind her and rushed around the front of the car to the driver's side. It was then he saw the knife sticking out of the back tire.

"Shit," he muttered.

He must have cursed louder than he thought, for when he opened his door, Leigh was already asking, "What's wrong?"

Jake slid inside, closed his door, and placed the key in the ignition. He turned over the engine and a wave of cool air blasted him in the face.

"Sorry," he said, reaching for the fan controls to lower them. "The air will heat up in a moment." He turned to his female companion. "In the meantime, I have a flat to deal with."

Her eyes widened. "A flat tire?"

He nodded. "One of those men slashed my tire. Honestly, I'm surprised the car isn't up on blocks."

Leigh leaned forward, trying to see the tire just outside her window. "They only got one?" she asked.

"Yeah, by the looks of it. If it's who I think it was, the guy was in a hurry to catch up to you. I'm guessing he saw my car, had no idea what to think of it, but figured he'd slash the tires just in case. Lucky for us, it looks like his knife got stuck in the rubber after his first try. Had he not been in such a rush to cut you off, I have no doubts he would've went to town."

"Lucky us," Leigh said, a hint of sarcasm in her voice. "But you have a spare, right?"

Jake motioned behind him. "Right in the trunk."

Leigh sighed in relief. "Thank God."

"Always be prepared, right?"

She turned to him, her face wearing a small smile. "I should've figured you were a boy scout."

Jake grinned. "Nah, but I am an *Eagle* scout."

The girl just stared at him blankly.

"Eagle?" Jake said. "Like the name of this ca—" He shook his head. "Nevermind. Just wait here and get warm. This shouldn't take too long."

"You don't want any help?"

Jake shook his head. "Not with the tire, but you can do me a favor." He flicked on the car's headlights which basked the trees in front of them with bright, white light. "Keep an eye out for me. I don't want to alarm you, but there could be at least one of those men left lurking around. If you see anything, and I mean *anything*, honk the horn. Okay?"

"I can do that," Leigh said.

Jake gave her a thumbs up and reached for the handle of his door. Suddenly, Leigh's hand was on his arm.

"Wait," she said. "Now that I'm warm enough to think straight, why are you here? What's going on?"

"Tire first," Jake said, raising a finger. "Let's not spend another minute out here than we have to. Once that tire's changed, we'll be on our way and I'll tell you everything. Sound good?"

Hesitantly, Leigh let go of Jake's arm. "Okay," she said. "But please hurry."

"You don't have to tell me twice."

Jake exited the car, the cold wind greeting him at once. He reached into his pants pocket and grabbed the cell phone, immediately turning on the device's flashlight. The light showed an average-sized pocket knife sticking out of the driver's side rear tire. Jake figured the deer skull man had chosen to hold onto his larger blade, as it was surely more effective in slashing throats. Seeing as he was switching the tire anyway, Jake didn't try to pull the knife from the rubber, but instead popped open the trunk.

With the spare tire in hand and the carjack under his arm, Jake reached up and closed the trunk. He practically shrieked when he saw Leigh standing right next to him.

"Yah!" Jake yelled. "Leigh, what the hell?"

"Sorry," she said. "But I figured I'd could watch your back a lot better out here. Now I can see in all directions."

"You're not cold?"

"Of course." Leigh shrugged. "But not nearly as bad as before. Besides, this will only take a minute, right?"

"Yeah," Jake said. "Even quicker if you hold the light. Come on."

The two went to work changing the tire. As he loosened the lug nuts, Jake began to doubt the spare's abilities in the snow. Like any spare tire, it nothing more than a doughnut, lacking any sort of significant tread. Still, he kept these worries to himself. He would get them out of there, one way or another. At the least the back road slanted down all the way to the highway, which meant gravity would be on their side.

One at a time, he handed the nuts to Leigh so they wouldn't get lost in the snow. All the while he told Leigh everything, from getting the first phone call from Mary, to her disappearing, to the encounter with her kidnapper, to finding Leigh in the woods. Leigh interjected here and there, informing Jake about Dr. Mallory's therapy, Woodenknife's plan, C.'s murder, and how Evan had lost his mind in the mine.

Tightening the last nut on the new tire, Jake looked up at Leigh. "Hell of a day, huh?"

Leigh smiled. "Not my best."

"Well," Jake said, getting to his feet and brushing the snow off his pants. "I think we're good to go. Jump in while I put the jack and wrench back in the trunk."

When that task was done, Jake rejoined her in the toasty car.

"Jake?" Leigh said before he could put the car in reverse.

"Yeah?"

"What are we going to do?"

Jake took his hand off the gear shifter and looked her in the eyes. "We're going to get Mary back, but there's not going to be any exchange. I just need you to play along so we can trick this bastard, okay? Can I trust you to do that?"

Before Leigh could answer, Jake began laughing dryly. "Shit," he said. "Listen to me, asking if *I* can trust *you*. You're the one who should be asking that question. Why on earth would you ever trust me, the guy who left you high and dry to deal with the aftermath of everything that happened here."

He could feel wetness in the corners of his eyes. Sometimes when he had gone a long time without a fix, severe headaches would cause his tired eyes to water. This was not was happening right now.

"I'm sorry," he said. "I ran and hid myself away like a coward. We were the only two people to survive, and left you all alone."

Leigh remained silent.

"You know," Jake continued. "For the longest time, I judged my friend Phil for his part in the whole Embry mess. You remember him, right? You guys never met but I'm sure you read all about him."

Leigh cleared her throat and said, "He was the forest ranger who was helping the Cedar family."

"Yes," Jake said. "And God knows that was wrong, but so didn't Phil at the end. His guilt was so strong that he couldn't live with himself anymore." Jake wiped his eyes. "But at least he *tried*, you know? He ended up doing the wrong thing, but he had to do something. He wasn't like me. He couldn't just run away. He didn't just hide in the shadows and become some waste-of-life junkie. No, he stayed. It cost him his life, but God damn it, he stayed."

With his eyes closed, Jake felt something warm and soft gently place itself on top of his hand. When he opened his eyes, he saw that Leigh had put her hand on his.

"But you came back," Leigh said.

"Yeah," Jake said. "But what if I'm too late?"

"Maybe you're not." She lifted her hand from Jake's. "But there's only way to find out. Let's go do the one thing Phil never did. Let's fight back."

Leigh's eyes hardened like diamonds.

"All right," Jake said, swallowing hard and doing his best to compose himself. "Let's go get Mary."

"I'll do you one better," Leigh said. "Let's go put this fucking crazy family to rest, once and for all." She shook her head in disbelief. "Rob's father...I never would have guessed."

"Yeah, well," Jake mumbled, reaching again for his phone. "Can't say I find anything to be unbelievable anymore."

He found the number that Nathan had given him in the bar. His finger hovered over the "SEND" button.

"You ready?" he asked Leigh.

"Call the bastard."

He did. A minute later, he hung up.

"Well," Leigh said. "Where are we suppose to go?"

But all Jake could do was shake his head. "All right, I take it back."

Leigh threw her hands up. "What? Where are we going?"

Jake looked at her, a strange combination of humor and horror shaping his face.

"You're not going to believe this."

CHAPTER
TWENTY-ONE

When Dr. Joyce had first suggested that Leigh return to Embry, Leigh doubted that this was anything close to what she had envisioned. Merely crossing the town line would've marked an accomplishment, and if Leigh made it as far as Main Street, she could've considered this confrontational therapy a total success.

But returning to the Cedar homestead? No psychiatrist in their right mind would've prescribed this. Unfortunately, she and Jake had no choice.

As they approached the barn, Leigh looked over to where the Cedar house had once sat. The old cabin was long gone, having been blown to smithereens by Sam's final courageous act. The only evidence remaining of the cabin's existence was a few charred boards and roof shingles, as well as the home's foundation. If she were to creep a little closer, Leigh would've been able to look down into the exposed basement.

The cellar where Dale had survived the blast.

On their ride over, Leigh had filled Jake in on Dale's reemergence into her life. It was he who Jake called "The Deer Man." After contracting what was probably the worst case of the fungus in the disease's entire history, Dale had been fed the body parts of Jake's doomed coworker, Douglas Graham.

Leigh would never forget that name, having been forced to watch Graham be hacked apart in front of her. His nametag had reflected the overhead light the entire time.

"And now Dale's got a taste for human flesh?" Jake had asked as they drove to the Cedar property.

"He must have been practicing cannibalism ever since," Leigh said. "It's caught up with him, though. If what Evan said was right, he's contracted a neurodegenerative disorder called Kuru."

"A neuro what?"

"To put it bluntly, eating human flesh has caused his brain to breakdown. He's losing neurons, and that brings on unpredictable behavior."

Jake took his eyes from the road to throw her a glance. "Like laughing hysterically?"

Leigh's eyes lit up. "Exactly. How did you know that?"

"I saw it." Jake brought his attention back to driving. "He was laughing like a loon just before he slashed the throat of one of those bikers."

"Sorry I asked," Leigh said, grimly. "Anyway, it's kind of like mad cow disease, just without the tainted burgers." She paused before adding, "Of course, Woodenknife thought it was something else entirely."

"Yes," Jake agreed. "The Wendigo."

"Oh," Leigh said. "So he told you too."

"Last thing he said to me. As brutal as that guy was, he actually believed he was the one fighting evil."

Now that they walked across the Cedar property, Jake's words echoed in Leigh's mind. She looked upon the cabin ruins and swore she could still hear the voice of Clementine, the Cedar matriarch:

I never wanted to do any of this. So don't waste your breath telling me 'this is wrong,' or, 'you can't do this.' I know the price of what we do. I've known it most of my life. But I can do this. And I will.

Leigh flinched as Jake grabbed her arm.

"Hey," he said. "Are you okay?"

"Sorry," she said, exorcising the old woman's voice from her head. "I was just thinking about the lengths some people will go to protect the ones they care about. Clementine Cedar, John Woodenknife—"

"Phil Carson," Jake added. He looked at her. "Or us, right now."

"Yeah. It's hard to call yourself the 'good guy' when everyone else is too."

Jake looked down at his feet. "I don't know if I'm a good guy," he said, quietly. But then he spat, looked back up at Leigh with fiery eyes, and said, "But I do know I'm the guy who's going to get Mary back. How about you?"

"I'm with you," Leigh said. "I've always blamed myself for all the ones I've lost. And who knows? Maybe it is all my fault. But right now, all I care about is your friend in there."

She pointed to the barn.

"You've saved my life twice," Leigh said. "It's about time I pay it forward."

Jake nodded, his eyes narrowing. "All right, then. Let's do this."

So off they went, one foot in front of the other, towards the barn. Leigh didn't know why Mary's kidnapper had chosen this spot for their rendezvous. Maybe it was from a twisted sense of nostalgia, or a morbid sense of humor, or merely because the location was so heavily isolated. Whatever the reason, Leigh's PTSD was bombarding her at full force. She wasn't thinking about some faceless kidnapper waiting for her inside. In her mind, the only face she expected to see belonged to Bugger, the most sadistic Cedar of all. He would be standing just the past door, saw blade in hand, eyes void of nothing but madness. This time, nothing would save her, not even Rob, who had proven to be no less crazy himself. Bugger would get her. This is what would happen.

Leigh should know. She had this nightmare almost every night.

Before she could voice her apprehension, they had reached the door. "Okay," Jake whispered. "I'll do the talking. You just stay behind me, okay?"

Leigh stayed silent, nodding that she understood.

Taking a deep breath, Jake pushed open the door.

The first thing Leigh saw was the first thing she had seen the last time she was in this building—the long, curved saw blade hanging on the far wall. There it still hung, still smiling at her like the Cheshire Cat's soon-to-vanish smile. And why not? The Cheshire Cat always appreciated madness in all its gleeful forms. What place to better to find it than the Cedar family barn?

That was the first thing Leigh noticed. The second was the chair positioned in the center of the room. And the young girl tied to it. And the man standing behind her, a revolver in his hand aimed right at the girl's head.

Nathan Floyd—Rob's father.

"Jake," Nathan said. "You made it. What a delightful supr—" The man cut himself short and shook his head. "No, what am I saying? I'm not surprised at all. There was never a doubt in my mind that you would fail to deliver."

He chuckled, the laugh as light at his speaking voice. Leigh eyed the man up and down, from his black corduroy pants to his dark blue track jacket. Nathan was small, almost dainty, with sunken features that sharpened the angles of his face.

It was actually kind of funny, though in the least comical way. Had Jake not previously told Leigh the man's identity, she would've never guessed in a thousand years. Rob had always tried much too hard to portray a certain "bad boy" persona. From the patches of the punk bands adorning his denim vest, to the hardcore music always blasting from his car, Rob was incessantly trying to prove to the world that he was "edgy." After discovering his Cedar lineage, his charade made quite a bit of sense: he was trying to hide his blood connection to backwoods cannibals. Looking at Nathan, Leigh now considered that perhaps Rob was overcompensating for his father's appearance as well. That would've fit Rob's asshole personality like glove— ashamed of his own father's life choices.

"Listen Nath—," Jake said, before clamping his jaw. "I mean, Nadine..."

The man put a hand up. "I appreciate the effort, Jake, I really do. But considering why we're here, I think Nathan is more appropriate. I had yet to transition into Nadine when Rob was still alive."

"About that," Jake said, "Why don't we all just have a little talk? I'm sure we can all come to some sort of—"

"Jake?" Nathan said, pushing the gun a little closer to Mary's head. "Sorry to cut you off, but would you mind placing your rifle on the ground and kicking it away? It help me concentrate to what you're saying."

Jake's grip tightened on his weapon. "Why don't we both lower our guns? I too find yours a bit distracting." He lowered his eyes to the girl in the chair. "Are you all right, Mary? Has he hurt you?"

Before Mary could answer, Nathan spoke first. "She's fine, Jake. I'll admit, she didn't have it easy when I had her in the basement over there." He motioned in the direction of the ruined cabin. "Remember the photograph? The one with the hose and the rising water? I told you if you didn't hurry than Mary would drown when the water reached above her head. I'm afraid that was a bit of a fib. Had I kept Mary in that foundation, she would've died of hypothermia long before she drowned. I'm not even sure that cellar would've held enough water before it drained into the ground. No, that photo was all for dramatic effect. A motivational tool, if you will. She's been in here, nice and dry, the entire time."

"Well, that's good." Jake nodded. "So how about the gun? That just for dramatic effect too?"

Nathan shook his head and offered the creepiest smile Leigh had probably ever seen. "Oh, not at all," he said. "I am one hundred percent for real when I say I will not hesitate to pull the trigger if you don't get rid of your rifle." He chuckled again. "So I guess it is a motivational tool as well. Do you feel motivated yet to drop your weapon?"

Nathan pressed the barrel into Mary's temple. She gave a soft whimper.

"All right, Nathan. For fuck's sake, take it easy. I'm getting rid of it."

Jake activated the rifle's safety before tossing it down. Nathan watched him to do this with a pleased grin.

"Thank you, Jake," he said. "By the way, that wouldn't happen to be the same rifle you used to shoot my son through the eye, would it?"

"Nathan..."

Nathan raised his hand. "Forget it. It doesn't matter at all. I was just curious." He shifted up on his tiptoes as if trying to see beyond Jake. "You know," he said, "you're such a smooth talker that I just realized I haven't said a single word to our other guest."

Leigh's whole body tensed. Jake sidestepped to block her even more.

"Why don't you just keep talking to me? We're the ones making the deal, after all."

But Nathan ignored him. Through the space between Jake's left arm and his upper torso, the man made direct eye contact with Leigh.

"Hello, Leigh. We've never met before, but I hear you knew my son quite well."

"Hey," Jake said, a bit louder. "Can we stay focused here?"

"Jake, please." Nathan raised an eyebrow. "I'm trying to have a conversation." He looked back to Leigh. "Now, where were we?"

"Rob," Leigh said, stepping aside Jake's body. "Yeah, I knew him. He was a real son of a bitch."

To her right, she could sense Jake's whole body go as still as a statue. She knew he must thinking, *what the hell are you thinking?*

She braced herself, ready to receive the full force of Nathan's outrage. Instead, the man bent at the waist and laughed.

"What can I say?" he asked, once finished with his belly laughter. "I can't argue with that. His mother certainly was a bitch in the strictest sense of the word."

His facial features suddenly fell into a somber expression, his voice lowering as he added, "However, he was still my son, and I cannot allow your deeds to go unpunished."

Jake scoffed as he repositioned himself in front of Leigh. "Unpunished?" he said. "Really, Nathan? Do you know what his girl has been through ever since she met your demented son? Your family ruined her life. It all but destroyed mine too. We pay for our past every single day. And you threaten us with death? HA!"

Leigh flinched as Jake threw his head back. She looked to Nathan who stared at them with wide, uneasy eyes. Leigh could tell this wasn't going as he had previously planned.

Nathan grabbed a handful of Mary's hair, pulling her head back as he shoved the gun under her chin. The girl yelped as Nathan said, "You forget, Jake. I'm not threatening you will death. I'm threatening her!"

Jake reached out with both hands as if trying to stop an oncoming car. "Okay," he said. "I'm sorry. All I was trying to say was that none of this is necessary. We could all just walk away, leave town, and move on with our lives, no matter how miserable they may be."

Nathan smirked. "Right. As if I could just let you just walk away at this point?"

"Why not? Hell, that's exactly what Mary and I were trying to do in the first place. If that damn bridge hadn't been out, no one in this town would've ever seen us again. I mean, if I gave a flying fuck about you or anything else that goes on in Embry, do you really think I would've skipped town to begin with?"

When Nathan only stared at him in response, Jake continued. "For God's sake, I'm wanted for questioning by the police! If I were report you, I'd have to turn myself in. And you know, after the day I've had, I just don't feel like doing that. I want to get out of here, Nathan. So does Mary. So does Leigh. You've made your point. No one would ever question that you loved your son. Now we know exactly what you would do for him and no one can ever take that away from you."

By the time Jake finished his speech, his chest was heaving from exhaustion. While Leigh had thought his monologue was merely a ruse, it was clear to her now that Jake meant every word he had just said.

Meanwhile, Nathan continued to stare with his sunken eyes. It was the face of a true sociopath, completely void of any telling sign of emotion. There wasn't even any evidence to say Nathan had heard a single word that came from Jake's mouth.

Until he smiled.

"Wow," Nathan said, his voice smooth and steady. "I have to say, I am quite impressed, Jake. Tracking down Miss Swanson and delivering her to me, that was impressive by itself, but as I said, I knew you were fully capable. You're a mountain man! It's what you do! But this speech of yours?" He drew the gun away from Mary's face so he could use both hands to clap. "This is both impressive *and* unexpected. I'm impressed, Jake, I really am."

"So am I."

As if rehearsed, Leigh, Jake, and Nathan all turned in unison at the sound of the new voice. A moment later, a pair of legs and feet appeared from behind a stack of rotting hay bails. The feet were wearing a pair of woman's boots, evident by the decorative fur that lined the tops. The legs were wearing jeans, designer ones, tight and well-sewed. Leigh followed the legs up to the black, NorthFace jacket, puffy with the goose down feathers stuffed inside. Further up still, Leigh's eyes fell upon the newcomer's face as she walked into the light.

Leigh gasped, not at some alien grotesquery, but the sobering familiarity of who she saw.

"Dr. Joyce?"

The psychiatrist gave her a warm smile, the same one that had greeted Leigh at the beginning of every one of her sessions.

"Hello, Leigh," Dr. Mallory Joyce said. "How's the therapy going? Have you confronted your fear yet?"

"I...I don't..."

Leigh stumbled as the world seemed to tilt under her feet. She caught herself and tried to swallow, but her throat had gone bone dry. "I don't understand," she finally managed to say.

"Yeah," Jake said. He spoke with far less shock, but equal confusion. He looked at the newly arrived woman. "Who the hell are you?"

The woman walked to other side of Mary and placed a hand on her chair. "Dr. Mallory Joyce," she said. "I'm Leigh's therapist." She pointed at Jake. "And you must be the infamous Jacob Spire, the man who shot my son and then rode off into the sunset. Nice touch, by the way. Very John Wayne of you."

"Listen, lady," Jake said. "I don't know how many times I can say this. I'm really sorry about your—"

Jake and Leigh looked at each other at the same time, their stunned expressions an exact mirror image of one another.

Leigh turned back to Dr. Joyce. "Are you saying Rob was...?"

Dr. Joyce nodded. "Unfortunately, yes. Robert was my one and only offspring." Her eyes narrowed as she eyed Leigh with immeasurable venom. "And *you* took him from me." She looked to Jake. "Both of you did."

Leigh couldn't speak. Hell, she could hardly breathe. Fortunately, Jake could still do the talking for them, albeit with severe hesitance.

"Everybody just slow down," he muttered. "I'm getting lost here." He looked to Nathan. "When we spoke at Macky's, you told me Rob's mother left you when you transitioned into Nadine. You said she hardly allowed you to see your son. Are you telling me, that after all of that, the two of you cooked up this little scheme together?"

Dr. Joyce shrugged. "It's true, my ex-husband and I have had our differences. But when it came to our child, we were able to agree on one thing: his killers needed to be punished."

Nathan gestured with his head in the therapist's direction. "Like I said. A real son of a bitch."

"Oh, ha ha." Dr. Joyce narrowed her eyes at Nathan. "At least I'm a *real* bitch."

Nathan's voice went as flat as a cadaver's heart monitor. "Mallory, I'm more of a woman than you'll ever be." He turned to address Jake. "I take it back. Call me Nadine. That is, and forever will be, my name."

Leigh could hardly hear this banter. Her mind felt like a malfunctioning carousel, speeding up to such a speed that the world around her became a blur. She wanted to jump off, for this ride to be over, but all she could do was hang on tight as distorted colors and sounds spun around her.

She took a deep breath.

"Dr. Joyce."

Her therapist looked at her. "Yes, Leigh?"

"Why did you do this?"

Dr. Joyce pursed her lips as if puzzled. "Did you miss the part when I revealed that Rob was my son?"

"No," Leigh said, shaking her head. "I mean, why like this? Couldn't you have just broken into my house and killed me? Or hired someone?"

"Breaking and entering really isn't my style, Leigh. And as for hiring a hitman or what have you, I just couldn't afford to risk such a loose end. What if they got caught? What if they talked? But if something happened to you in Embry, how could I be to blame? I only suggested you come here as part of your therapy."

"Yeah right," Jake said, interrupting her speech. "Like it would've taken Sherlock Holmes to link all of this back to you if your ex-husband had been caught."

"Please," Dr. Joyce said, dismissing the notion with a roll of her eyes. "You don't reach my stature without gaining the ability to make certain things go away. Cutting my ties to Nathan was easier than separating myself from my sister and her fucked up family."

Leigh's jaw fell slack. "You mean...Clementine?"

"A little professional advice, Leigh. All the schooling or connections or money in all the world doesn't mean shit in this industry if you come from the wrong family. You think anyone would've taken psychiatric advice from a relative of cannibals? That was one family tree that had to be cut down."

When Jake laughed, everyone looked in his direction. "Christ, lady," he said. "I've heard of skeletons in the closet, but you've got god damn boneyard in yours."

"Whatever." Dr. Joyce sighed. "I shouldn't even have to listen to this right now. Leigh was supposed to come to Embry, check into the Little Northern, and our desk clerk here would take care of the rest." She whipped her head at her former spouse. "But then you had to complicate everything."

Nadine threw her hands up. "What? If it wasn't for my quick thinking, we'd have nothing. But now we've got two for the price of one!" She eyed Leigh and raised her brow. "Where were you, by the way?"

"Biker gang," Jake said, answering for her. "The Forlorn Hope. They beat you to the punch."

Dr. Joyce exchanged a glance with Nadine before saying, "There's one I have to say I didn't see coming. Are you serious?"

"Yes," Leigh spoke before Jake could get the chance. "They drove us off the road. They dragged us into the woods. And then they took a hammer and bashed in C.'s brains."

Dr. Joyce stared at her, obviously trying to read Leigh's face for truth. "C. is dead?"

"That's right. Because of your little revenge plan, C. now lies somewhere in the woods, buried in snow." As Leigh spoke, she could feel a warm tear leak from her eye and roll down her cheek. "Blame me if you must, Dr. Joyce. But why did you have to involve innocent people?"

Dr. Joyce's hand shot up, a finger pointed at Leigh. "Wait just a minute. *You* are the one that *insisted* that C. come along. I had no intention of involving her. That one is on you, young lady. And as for Evan, well..." She lowered her hand, relaxing a bit. "He was essential to the plan."

"You mean...?"

Her inner carousel was picking up speed again. To slow it, Leigh balled her hands into fists and dug her fingernails into her palms.

"Evan knew?" she said.

Dr. Joyce gave a low laugh. "Of course," she said. "He was my delivery driver, so to speak. And for his services, I promised him a high position at the brand new mental health center that just opened in Black Creek Junction. I don't mean to brag, but a letter of recommendation from me can open a lot of doors."

Something roiled in Leigh's stomach like soup left on a hot stove. She swallowed hard, fighting the urge to vomit. "Are you telling me he willingly participated in murder...for a promotion?"

"That's right." Dr. Joyce's nod quickly changed to a headshake. "Well, not completely right. Part of it was to help his career, but most of all, he just wanted to show his commitment to me. We both agreed it was time to take our relationship to the next level."

Leigh's hand shot to her mouth to hold back the bile rising in her throat. "You were sleeping together?"

"Please," Dr. Joyce said, scorn lacing her voice. "It's much more than that. He was the first person I ever told about Rob. After hearing what you did to him, Evan couldn't wait to put my plan into motion."

At this point, Dr. Joyce looked around, as if she had just then remembered something she was supposed to do. "Speaking of which," she said. "Where is Evan?"

Leigh hadn't meant to smile, hadn't meant to do anything that would instigate her two opponents. The grin came anyway, stretching cheek to cheek and dripping with malice. "I can tell you where he is," she said. "But I suggest you bring a miner's helmet, a pick axe, and a really good flashlight." She paused to reconsider her last word. "On second thought, forget the flashlight. I don't think you'll have any trouble finding him in the dark."

It was now Dr. Joyce's turn for her jaw to drop. "What are you going on about? Is..." Her eyes grew as large as full moons. "Is he dead?"

"I really couldn't say for sure." Leigh's smile remained on her face. "But it sure as hell sounded like it when I kicked him down that hole."

Dr. Joyce's face contorted in anger, and for a moment, Leigh could swear she was looking at a resurrected Clementine Cedar. The psychiatrist's whole body shook as she yelled, "You BITCH!"

"Hey!" Nadine yelled as well. "Would you hold it together please?"

Dr. Joyce turned on him. "What? Did you just hear what she did?"

"Yeah, and I'm really sorry you lost your little boy toy, but need I remind you this is about our son?"

Leigh wouldn't have thought it possible that Dr. Joyce's anger could rise any further, but that's exactly what happened.

"Boy toy?" she screamed. "You listen to me, *Nadine*. Evan was more of a man than you ever were!"

"Is that a fact?" Nadine replied. "And how, exactly, is a man supposed to act?"

Without warning, he tossed the handgun to Dr. Joyce, who reacted just in time to catch it with both hands.

"Christ, Nathan, what are you doing?"

Nadine ignored Dr. Joyce's question and advanced on Mary still tied to the chair, grabbing the girl by the chin.

"How about this? Is this what a man does?"

Before Dr. Joyce could answer the question, Nadine brought her lips to Mary's and kissed her on the mouth. Mary kicked in her chair and gave a muffled squeal.

"Hey!"

Jake ran forward, too quick for Leigh to stop him.

"Get off of her, you piece of—"

The insult was cut short by the sound of Dr. Joyce cocking back the handgun's hammer. She pointed it directly at Jake's chest.

"All right," Jake said, putting his hands up. "Take it easy, take it easy."

Nadine finished kissing Mary and looked to Dr. Joyce, seemingly oblivious to Jake's advance. "There? How about that?"

"Hmm?" Dr. Joyce said, mockingly. "Oh, I'm sorry, I wasn't paying attention. I was too busy ending this." She raised the gun to Jake's head.

"Come on," Jake pleaded. "Think this through. If you pull that trigger, you're going to have to live with it your entire life. Trust me, I know. You don't really want to shoot anyone, do you?"

For a moment, it seemed like Dr. Joyce was really considering Jake's words. Her face softened, her eyes looking deep into his. The magnitude of what she was about to do seemed to be hitting her like crashing wave.

But then her eyes narrowed again and she smiled. "Yes," she answered. "I want to shoot someone."

She turned the gun away from Jake and pointed it at Leigh. "Her."

The bullet hit Leigh before she even heard the blast.

CHAPTER
TWENTY-TWO

LEIGH!

Though in his mind he was screaming at the top of his lungs, not a sound escaped Jake's mouth as Leigh fell to the ground. His mouth hung wide open, though not a single breath passed his lips. He could only stare in breathless shock as his friend and companion collapsed like a knocked out boxer, the retort of the gunshot still ringing in his ears.

For a moment, no one said anything. No one even moved. The air in the barn was as still and heavy as the snowdrifts outside. Jake watched, unblinking, as Leigh remained motionless too. He silently prayed she would mutter even the weakest moan, but not a sound came from her crumpled body.

"Well," Dr. Joyce said, finally breaking the silence. "That's that."

Jake turned on her, his entire being burning with hate. The woman's voice had acted like a jumpstart of sorts, like two wires sparking to hotwire a car. In an instant, his frozen trance was broken, replaced with an animalistic urge to kill.

"You..."

It was all he could say, his mind too enraged to finish the statement. No insult or damning curse seemed worthy of this woman. Jake simply lacked the vocabulary to describe the monster holding the still smoking gun.

"You what?" Dr. Joyce asked, smiling. "You bitch? Come now, Mr. Spire. Certainly you can do better than that."

Jake shook his head. "No," he said. Though his whole body trembled with anger, his voice came dull and flat.

"No?" The doctor challenged. "How about my son? What did you call him before you shot him through his eye?"

Jake felt his legs go rigid, a steely resolve washing over his body. "Nothing," he said as a smile stretched his lips. "There wasn't any time to think, let alone say anything."

He took a step forward, ignoring the fact that Dr. Joyce was turning the gun on him.

"But if I had the time," he continued. "I would've called him a dickless, chickenshit, little panty waste..."

He paused, looking for the right word.

"Well," he finished. "Bitch, I guess."

Dr. Joyce scoffed, seemingly unimpressed by Jake's demonstration of bravado. "How cavalier," she said, cocking the gun again. "I'll make sure it's written on your tombstone."

"Ugghh..."

Everyone, even Mary still bound and gagged in the chair, turned at the sound. Leigh wasn't just groaning, she trying to pull herself up into a sitting position. She cried out before she could fully sit up, her arm giving out to send her onto her back. From where he stood, Jake could see the dark patch of blood coating the top of her left arm.

"Oh, for Heaven's sake," Dr. Joyce said. "I got her in the shoulder."

Nadine, who had remained silent as her ex-wife did all the talking, spoke up. "Nice going."

"Shut up," Dr. Joyce shot back. "It's the first time I've ever fired a gun. Give me a break."

"So are you going to shoot her again?"

Jake tensed, readying himself to hurl his body at the therapist if she tried to pull the trigger a second time. Even if he took a bullet, there was a chance he could wrestle the gun away and incapacitate both of his opponents. It was a fight he would probably lose, but he would go down swinging. He would make sure of that.

Instead, Dr. Joyce walked over to Nadine and handed her the gun.

"No," the psychiatrist said. "I'm going to use my hands. I want to feel the life leave this bitch." She pointed to Mary. "If Mr. Spire makes a move to stop me, put a bullet in this one's head. Understand?"

"Got it," Nadine said, returning the barrel of the gun to Mary's cheek.

Jake grimaced as Dr. Joyce took her time, practically sauntering over to where Leigh lay writing in pain. He knew there was nothing accidental about how close the doctor passed him, purposefully mocking the fact that he was powerless to stop her. If he as so much brushed his fingers across her jacket, Nadine was sure to blow Mary's head clean off her body.

"Please," Jake said as the doctor came within feet of Leigh's body. "Don't do this. You've made your point, haven't you? You've hurt the one who took your son."

Dr. Joyce continued to walk as she spoke. "This is nothing compared to what she's done to me."

"Then why not let her live with this? If you kill her, you'll only end her suffering."

Dr. Joyce stood over Leigh, a foot on either side of the girl's body. "Oh, her suffering's just begun. My son's waiting for her on the other side, and I can only imagine what he's going to do to her."

Dr. Joyce fell to her knees, straddling Leigh's waist. She leaned down, their faces merely centimeters apart. "When you see Robbie," she whispered. "Tell him Mommy sent you."

Jake threw a glance at Nadine and tried to gauge the distance between himself and Mary's captor. The gun was just too close to Mary's face. Even at his fastest, Jake would never be able to tackle Nadine before the trigger was pulled. At point blank range, there was no way Nadine would miss.

Hesitantly, he turned back to the two on the floor, full well believing that Leigh would already be dead. Dr. Joyce would just be releasing Leigh's throat, having squeezed all the air out of her prey like a python crushing a mouse.

Only Dr. Joyce's hands weren't touching Leigh at all. Instead, she seemed to be studying something on Leigh's neck, her brow furled in confusion. Slowly, she reached down and pulled the collar of Leigh's shirt away from her throat.

Even from several feet away, Jake could see the blue glow radiating from underneath Leigh's clothes. It was if Leigh had covered herself with glow-in-the-dark paint, the light in the barn low enough to trigger the paint's luminescent effect.

As Dr. Joyce spoke, Jake heard the same words run through his brain.

"What the fuck?"

Like a Jack-in-the-Box that had just reached the end of its song, Leigh sprung up from her lying position. She grabbed her therapist by both wrists and yanked them down onto herself. Dr. Joyce shrieked as her hands were forced upon the glowing mass on Leigh's chest and neck.

That's not paint.

Jake had seen it before, on that young man in the woods who had been pursuing Leigh, the one the psychiatrist had called *Evan.* Just before Leigh had used the heel of her boot to send him deep underground, Evan had been covered in the same glowing substance.

The fungus.

At some point during her escape from the caverns, Leigh had contracted the disease. Even more unbelievable was the fact she had hid her condition from Jake, despite how much it must have been tormenting her this entire time. It had been her ace in the hole, her secret weapon to be unleashed if things went south. Had she told Jake her plan, would he have allowed her to continue?

No way. I would have never allowed it. I would've cured her, even if it meant my using my own blood. Again.

But it was too late now. Dr. Joyce screamed and writhed as her fingers dug into the fuzzy clumps of glowing fungus. But no matter how much she thrashed like a cowboy riding a bucking bronco, Dr. Joyce couldn't break Leigh's vice grip on her wrists.

"Go on," Leigh said from underneath her therapist. "Put your hands on me. I've survived worse than you."

Jake instinctually went to advance on the wrestling women, to help Leigh in her struggle, but then remembered the other woman in serious peril. He looked back to Mary, relieved to see remained unharmed. Better still, Nadine had slightly lowered her gun, now distracted by the bizarre conflict occurring on the barn's floor.

"Mallory?" Nadine said. "What's going on?"

Now!

Jake shifted his weight to the balls of his feet, ready to push off and hurl himself at the distracted Nadine. But before he could even inhale, Mary was already in action. Using all of her body weight, Mary shoved herself towards her captor, bringing the chair along with her. She practically lifted off the ground as she slammed into Nadine, sending them both crashing to the floor. Nadine landed face down, the gun skittering across the barn's wooden floorboards.

Jake's heart seized as he saw the weapon fly loose, his mind struggling to keep up with everything happening at once. He commanded his legs to move forward but they just couldn't react fast enough. It was like being in one of those dreams where you're trying to run away, but the ground has turned to quicksand, the air has turned to water.

The gun was only inches from Nadine's fingertips, who crawled toward the weapon like a demented baby. Mary tried to pin her legs down, but she was still tied to the chair and couldn't get to Nadine in time. Neither could Jake, who found himself frozen at gunpoint when he was only a single step away from the pistol. Nadine had won the race and aimed the handgun up at his chest.

"Nice try," she said, climbing to her feet.

Jake raised his hands above him like an arrested criminal. "All right, you win," he said. "I'm backing away."

"No," Nadine said, violently shaking her head. "You're not going anywhere. This ends now."

She raised the gun to his head, aiming right between his eyes. Jake stared back at her, refusing to close his eyes or look away. For the first time in his life, he understood how Phil must have felt before he turned the gun on himself. Jake knew he should've been frightened at this moment, terrified even. Hell, he should at least care that his life was about to end. But no, all Jake could feel was relief, like a pair of strong arms had just lifted a mighty weight off his back. Of course he didn't care. Caring was not his job anymore.

"Any last words?" Nadine asked.

Jake nodded, remembering the final words to leave Phil's lips. "Non sibi sed patriae."

Nadine wrinkled her brow, clearly confused by Jake's Latin valediction. She shook it off, taking aim again. "Whatever," she muttered.

Jake flinched as the gun went off, bracing himself for the impact of the bullet. When he felt nothing, he knew the shot must have hit his brain, instantly shutting down his nervous system. He was dead but his body didn't know it yet. Any moment, his legs would give out, he would crumple to the floor, and all would fade to black.

Except that didn't explain why Nadine was looking at him like that. She should've been smiling or even laughing in triumph. But her look was not one gives a vanquished enemy. There was too much pain in that expression. Too much surprise. Slowly, she looked down to her stomach just Jake saw it too.

A patch of dark red was quickly spreading across the left side of her gut.

She looked back up, giving Jake a look that seemed to say, *How did you do that?* And then she fell, dropping like a sack of potatoes.

For a moment, Jake was too stunned to move, to exhale even. He simply stood frozen in his "don't shoot" pose, his arms still outstretched before him. When Nadine remained motionless on the floor, the pool of blood growing from underneath her body, Jake finally turned around.

A man stood at the door of the barn. A man with Jake's discarded rifle in his hands. A man wearing a deer skull on his face.

Jake and the stranger stared at each other, as if neither knew who should make the next move. Only this wasn't a stranger to Jake anymore. If what Leigh had told him was true, this was Dale Preston—local hunter and recent cannibal.

Their stalemate was broken when Leigh cried out at the top of her lungs. It was not a cry of pain or distress, but more like that of a bloodlust filled warrior entering the battlefield. Both men turned in unison at the sound.

At some point in their struggle, Leigh had managed to roll on top of Dr. Joyce and was now pinning her down. The therapist squirmed and wriggled under Leigh's weight, but to no avail. Leigh was sitting on her legs and was holding her arms down with her hands. Jake could see the blue fungus now grew on Dr. Joyce's palms, sticking up in some places like sapphire stalagmites.

From his position at the door, Dale raised his rifle and pointed it at the two women. Jake made a move for Nadine's handgun, knowing that he wouldn't be able to shoot in time if the Dale decided to pull the trigger.

Miraculously, Dale lowered the rifle before Jake could even take another step towards Nadine's still body. The masked man watched the women through his deer skull as if this was all an entertaining movie on TV.

"What's wrong?" Leigh said between bouts of maniacal laughter. "Are you scared of a little fungus? Then just consider this *exposure therapy*. Are you feeling *exposed* yet?"

"Get off me!" Dr. Joyce screamed. "You're—

"Crazy?" Leigh finished. "You should know! I mean, we've spent a year forming a relationship based on mutual respect and trust."

"I'm going to fucking kill you!"

Leigh laughed even louder. "Kill me? No, Dr. Joyce, you helped me! Or rather, you gave me tools I needed to help myself. Just like a good therapist is supposed to do."

"Nathan?" Dr. Joyce cried out, unaware that her ex-husband was down for the count. "Shoot her! Do something, for God's sake. Help me!"

"Oh, Dr. Joyce," Leigh said. "Take your own advice—no one can help you unless you help yourself. Take me, for example. I've contracted a nasty case of this fungus. And unless I administer the cure, it's sure to eat me alive. Trust me, I've seen it before. So what am I going to do?"

"Leigh, I swear to God—"

Using her firm grip of Dr. Joyce's wrists, Leigh lifted the psychiatrist off the ground and slammed her back down, knocking the back of her head into the hard floor. Dr. Joyce fell silent, staring up at her old patient with wide, fearful eyes.

Leigh smiled, exposing her snow white teeth. "I'm going to help myself," she said.

And then she bit into the throat of Dr. Joyce, tearing away a mouthful of flesh and blood. Dr. Joyce's jaw fell open to scream, but only a gurgling liquid noise came forth. Leigh titled her head back and chewed, dark red rivulets of blood streaming down her chin. Underneath her, Dr. Joyce's body shook in death spasms, as if she had touched an exposed wire. Sprays of blood shot from her exposed throat like those famous Las Vegas fountains that Jake had seen in movies. Jake could do nothing but watch, utterly transfixed by this unbelievable scene. Only when Leigh lowered to take another bite did he snap out of his trance, his mind begging him to cry out, "No!"

But Leigh wasn't bending down to go for seconds. She was collapsing as she lost consciousness, her body rolling off of Dr.

Joyce and coming to rest beside her. Whether it was from blood lost or merely her mind shutting down from stress, Jake did not know. All he did know was that Leigh had passed out, Dr. Joyce was dead, and Dale Preston still stood by the door, armed with a gun.

Dale, who had been as still as a statue, slowly turned in Jake's direction. Jake tensed, expecting the man to aim the rifle at him, but instead, Dale walked the three steps to the barn's wall. For what felt like the thousandth time today, Jake flinched as Dale suddenly slammed his head into wall.

What the hell?

An echo of a previous conversation bounced around Jake's head as he watched the man slam his head a second time. Leigh had briefly told him about Dale's suspected condition, a brain disease that slowly but surely eating at his sanity. Was this what was happening now? Was Jake witnessing the crescendo of madness, a final attempt to escape lunacy by smashing in his own brains?

The answer came after the third and last time Dale hit his head against the wall, when the top of the skull cracked in half. Dale immediately lifted a hand to the crack and tugged, pulling away the mask with a forceful tug. Even in the dim lighting of the barn, Jake could see the man's hair matted with perspiration, his cheeks red from cold, his eyes sunken with exhaustion.

Dale looked to Jake and said, "Finally. Been trying to get that damn thing off all day." He then pointed at Mary, but with a harmless finger instead of the rifle. "You should help her."

Feeling foolish, Jake placed a hand on his chest as if to say, "Are you talking to me?" It just seemed so surreal to hear Dale speaking in such a casual way, like watching a werewolf take human form, or Mr. Hyde transforming back to the passive Dr. Jekyll.

"Go on," Dale encouraged. "That blood's about to get in her face."

Jake looked to Mary to see what Dale was talking about.

As Nadine's wound continued to bleed, the pooling blood was traveling across the floor to where Mary lay sideways, still bound to the chair.

As he rushed to Mary's side, an unwanted flashback forced its way into his mind. Just over a year ago, Jake had found himself in this exact predicament as Phil's blood coursed along the cabin's floor to yet another chair that Jake had been tied to himself.

Jake grabbed the back of the chair and hoisted it to its feet. He bent down and removed the gag in Mary's mouth, whispering in her ear as he did so.

"Are you okay?"

Though she sobbed loudly, Mary was able to offer a subtle nod. "Yes," she said. "I...I think s-so."

"Good," Jake said. "Everything's all right now, but just try to stay quiet, okay?"

Again, Mary nodded.

Jake stood up straight again and walked around Mary to block her from Dale's view. "So," he said, staring the other man in the eye. "What now?"

Dale Preston told him exactly what he had in mind, while outside, the sun began to rise to greet a new day. A doe and her fawns walked across the yard on a well-traveled deer path. And the final flake of yesterday's snowstorm fell to the earth without a sound.

CHAPTER
TWENTY-THREE

When Leigh dreamed, she knew it this time. This wasn't really her home. This wasn't really her bedroom. She was far too aware of the constant haze that fills the space of every dreamscape. More often than not, this foggy quality could only be identified after she awoke, basking in the relief of that classic saying, "It was only a dream."

This time, however, the unreality of her world was as clear as day. She had once read that lucid dreaming was a good step towards recovery for people with PTSD. It served as a demonstration of power, proving to the dreamer that they were in control of their own mind, their own fears. If a monster was chasing you, you could simply remind yourself, "This is only a dream. The monster isn't real." And *poof!* The monster disappears. If you accepted the concept that all fear is an illusion created by the mind, you could apply this same practice in your waking life as well.

None of these theories mattered to Leigh in the slightest. Yes, she knew she was dreaming, but control was the last thing she felt right now. Leigh was absolutely terrified by the light coming from the bathroom door in front of her, for all of this was something she had dreamed before. She would walk into the bathroom, stare into the mirror above the sink, and scream at what she saw—a mask of fungus where her face used to be.

So don't go in there. Just wake yourself up.

Try as she might, Leigh couldn't escape the prison of her nightmare. She closed and re-opened her eyes over and over, only to find herself still sitting on the edge of her bed. It seemed the only way she would return to the land of the conscious was to shock herself awake. That had worked countless times before, whether it be falling off a cliff or walking in front of a speeding car. This time it would have to be facing her own hideous reflection.

Let's get this over with.

Pushing herself off the bed, Leigh took her first steps towards the bathroom. She was about halfway to the door when she realized she was trying to keep quiet to not wake her roommate. She had to laugh at herself, a slave to habit even when she knew this world was entirely fiction. She need not worry about disturbing anyone here. In this world, nothing existed outside her bedroom door, let alone a roommate—

Her laugh came to an abrupt end when she remembered that a roommate wouldn't be waiting for her when she awoke either. C. had been her roommate. And C. was dead.

As Leigh's hand touched the bathroom door to push it open, she asked herself why she even wanted to wake up in the first place. Even if this was a nightmare, how could it be any worse than the world waiting for her on the other side of sleep?

Well, I've come this far.

In the end, the suspense outweighed any practical logic. Sure, she could stay here in the safety of her familiar bedroom, but the unknown would forever be looming over her. What awaited her outside? What awaited her when she awoke? For better or worse, Leigh had to know.

So she opened the door.

Her body fully braced for the horrific image staring back at her, Leigh forced herself to keep her eyes open and look straight ahead. To her utter surprise, the only thing greeting her arrival was her regular, everyday reflection. No blotches of fungus created a patchwork of green on her skin. No ivy-like tendrils were trying to escape the from the corners of her mouth. It was just her.

The relief washed over her like a warm water from a shower head. Her terror had been unfounded this entire time. Perhaps the fact that this was a lucid dream meant that Leigh was already beginning to change the world around her. She didn't want to see herself covered in fungus, so she simply willed the image away.

Except...

Her face in the mirror still wore an expression of absolute dread. Her eyes were wide and white. Her jaw slowly descended in a silent scream. Yet Leigh herself did not feel the emotion displayed by her own reflection. She only felt confused, as if she was looking at someone else entirely.

"What is it?" she asked her other self. "What do you see? What—?"

And then Leigh caught a glimpse of her own hand. Or rather, where her hand should have been. Like a seed just starting to take root in fresh soil, a scream began to grow deep within Leigh's core.

Her fingers had become horrendously elongated. Long and thin like tree branches, the digits were covered in skin so pale, it was almost translucent. At the end of each finger was a nail so long and curved, they were better described as talons.

Leigh's gaze trailed up her wrist to see that her arms had transformed as well. It was like she didn't have an ounce of fat or muscle on her body. She was merely skin and bones and nothing more.

"Oh my god," she tried to say, but her mouth could only produce a dog-like growl. She brought the talons of her twisted fingers to her face, expecting to find the source of her vocal problems. Indeed something was wrong with her mouth—her lips had thinned like the rest of her body, pulled back against a set of pointed teeth like that of a shark. But when she let her hands travel upward, she felt the most startling disfiguration of all.

Two protrusions sprouted from each side of her head, rock hard and smooth like fossilized wood. They stretched from her skull like insect antenna, twisting and curving in multiple directions. Though she couldn't see them herself, her hands told her the entire stomach turning story.

They were antlers.

The scream rising in Leigh's throat finally came forth like an erupting volcano. Her reflection in the mirror, however, did not mimic the same action. Instead, it mouthed a single, multisyllabic word that Leigh didn't understand.

Her reflection said it again. And again. And again. By the sixth time or seventh time, Leigh finally made out the word just before she awoke.

Wendigo.

Leigh awoke with a startled yelp to find herself in a familiar setting—a hospital room. All the usual qualities of hospital accommodations surrounded her. A muted TV mounted in top left corner of the room played a daytime soap opera. White carnations bloomed next to her bed in a vase on an end table. And the bed itself was nothing short of a space shuttle, various buttons on her left and right that did God-knows-what.

What wasn't expected was the man who sat in a chair by the entrance door. The man had apparently been snoozing as well, for he raised his head up to look at Leigh with drowsy eyes. Even with the fatigue sagging his face, Leigh recognized him at once.

"Jake?"

Jake's brow raised in surprise, almost as if he was actually surprised to see her.

"Leigh," he said. "That you?"

Leigh's face scrunched in confusion. "Um," she said, disorientation pummeling her still awaking senses. "Yeah. It's me."

"I should get a doctor," Jake said, rising from his chair.

"Wait," Leigh said. She tried to raise a hand but her arms didn't want to move. She must had been sedated and the drug was still in her system. "Don't go. I want to talk…"

Her voice trailed off as another foggy cloud washed over her mind. She shook her head, commanding her own brain to snap to already. "What's going on?" she asked. "What happened?"

Jake stepped away from the door and walked towards her bed. "You're being cared for," he said. "You're safe now."

"But what about Dr. Joyce?" Leigh could hardly ask the question as she realized her mouth and throat were bone dry. "And the other one…the man?"

"You must mean Nadine," Jake said. "Don't worry about them. They've been taken care of."

On the table next to Leigh's bed, a plastic cup of water with a straw sticking out of it sat next to the vase of flowers. She made a move to reach for it, but again, her body wouldn't cooperate.

"Hold on," Jake said, reaching for the water. "Allow me."

He lowered the cup and brought the straw to Leigh's lips. It was, by far, the most refreshing drink of water she had ever had in her life.

Her tongue feeling less like sandpaper, she smiled at the man who leaned over her. "Are you sure that's only water?" she said. "No blood in it this time?'

Jake nodded. "Nice to see you've still got your sense of humor."

But Leigh's smile didn't last when she remembered another question she needed to ask, one of vital importance. "What about Mary?"

"She's okay," Jake said, returning the water to the table. "She's safe and sound. She was examined by a doctor, and minus a few superficial nicks and scratches, she's completely unharmed. In fact, I'm giving her a ride to the airport tomorrow. She's going to live with an aunt and uncle of hers that live in Washington state. She plans on attending a college out there in the spring."

"That's great," Leigh said, feeling the relief cover her like a soft blanket. The last she could remember, Mary was still at the mercy of her captors, her life in their malevolent hands.

And then what?

Leigh searched her memory, feeling much like an old librarian browsing through an out-dated card catalogue. Mary had been tied to a chair. Jake was trying to talk them down. Dr. Joyce revealed herself to be behind the whole thing. And then—

"I was shot," Leigh muttered.

Jake nodded again. "That's right," he said. "But only in the shoulder. The doctors were able to fix you right up."

At the mention of doctors, Leigh instantly flashbacked to first time Jake had visited her in a hospital room. Only that time, Leigh hadn't realized it had been Jacob Spire, forest ranger, who dropped by her room. He had been disguised in a white lab coat and introduced himself as Dr. Benson. No one, not even Leigh, had discovered the truth until Jake was long gone out of town. He had been wanted for questioning ever since.

So how...?

"Jake," Leigh said, staring deep into his eyes. "How are you here? I mean, aren't you afraid of being spotted?"

The man shook his head. "It's all right. I gave the woman at the desk my alias, Wally Parker. As far as she's knows, I'm your uncle."

"But," Leigh stammered, the room starting to tilt a bit. "Someone might recognize you, right? You lived in Embry a long time. Any local could pick you out, even after all this time."

Jake's gaze fell to the floor, as if he could no longer look Leigh in the eye.

"Jake? What is it?"

He lifted his chin to reveal eyes that looked to be a hundred years old. "Leigh," he said, his voice grave, "you're not in Embry."

"I'm not?" She looked around the room again. There was

nothing unique to identify the hospital. "Then where am I?"

"Black Creek Junction."

Had Leigh not been lying down, the answer would've taken her right off her feet.

"That's like two and a half hours away," Leigh said. "Was I airlifted?"

"No," was all Jake said in reply.

"Then how did I get here so fast?"

Just as Leigh finished the question, she realized it wasn't the one she should be asking.

"*Why* am I here to begin with? Shouldn't I have been brought to Saint Andrews just outside of Embry?"

Jake looked at her, his eyes becoming glassy. Were those tears?

"You *were* brought to Saint Andrews," he said. "I decided I was done running away and brought you right through the door of that hospital. It didn't take long for the cops to show up and put me in the hot seat."

Leigh's heart rate quickened at once. "Are you okay?"

Jake raised a hand. "Don't worry, it's all been settled now. An associate of mine, Eddie Lee, hooked me up with a lawyer. Real sleazebag for sure, but the guy knew his stuff. Besides, I had Mary's testimony to back up my entire story."

"So you're not in trouble?"

Jake smiled. "Once the media got a hold of the story, it was a total circus. Worked out in my favor, though. I think my favorite headline was, *The Embry Avenger Returns.* Can you believe that? They're calling me a hero."

Leigh felt a tear of her own roll down her cheek. "You are a hero, Jake."

Jake's face tightened as he swallowed hard. "I definitely don't feel like one right now." He paused to wipe his eyes. "Anyway, while I was dealing with all of that, you were moved down here to Black Creek."

Though Leigh nodded that she understood, something heavy still weighed on her mind. It wasn't that she didn't believe

Jake. He had no reason to lie to her and there was nothing in his voice or his facial expression that suggested deceit.

But something about this story didn't make sense.

"Wait," she said, closing her eyes in an effort to get her bearings. "Police investigations and legal council and news reports..." She reopened her eyes. "That would take time. A lot of time."

Jake lowered his gaze once again.

"Jake," Leigh said. Her voice was shaking now. "You never answered my question. What am I doing in Black Creek?"

Jake didn't look up as he answered. "This is where you need to be right now."

"What?" The drowsiness that been fogging Leigh's mind was almost completely gone now as adrenaline began to course through her system. "Why? What's in Black—"

She couldn't say exactly how the memory came to her at precisely that moment, but suddenly Leigh could hear the voice of her ex-psychiatrist, Dr. Mallory Joyce, echoing in her head.

"Evan was my delivery driver, so to speak. And for his services, I promised him a high position at the brand new mental health center that just opened in Black Creek Junction."

Leigh's breath caught in her throat.

Mental health center.

In Black Creek Junction.

Leigh tried to spring forward, a strong surge of adrenaline suddenly pumping through her system. She wanted to jump out of bed and demand answers, if not from Jake than from someone else. Anyone else.

The straps around her wrists, however, kept her pinned to the bed.

"What is this?"

Both wrists were fastened to the metal frame of the bed by leather belts. This whole time, Leigh had believed it was sedatives that impeded her movements. She had been so out of it she hadn't felt the leather scraping her skin.

"Leigh," Jake said, raising his hands. "Please, calm down."

"Jake?" She shook both arms in attempt to free them, but only succeeded in rattling the bed. "What the *fuck* is this?"

"I can explain everything," Jake said. His voice had sharpened to a razor's edge. "But if you don't settle down, the nurses will come in here and put you under again. Do you want to go back asleep?"

"I..."

For a second, Leigh had no idea how to answer that question. Maybe she didn't want to go back asleep. Maybe sleeping forever was the best idea she'd ever heard.

Instead, she shook her head and whispered, "No." Tears were now streaming down both sides of her face. "I just want to know what's going on. I'm scared, Jake."

"I know," he said. "But you have to trust me when I say it's for your own good."

"But why?"

Jake inhaled to answer but then hesitated to grab his chair and pull it to Leigh's bedside. He sat down, ran a hand through his hair, and gave a loud exhale.

"At the Cedar homestead," he said. "You remember being there, right?"

She nodded.

"At the Cedar homestead, you attacked Dr. Joyce. I think everyone thought you were down for the count, but you caught her off guard and..." He squinted, trying to read Leigh's face. "Do you remember any of this?" he asked.

Leigh thought as hard as she could. Somewhere in the recesses of her mind, she saw an image of Dr. Joyce staring down at her. Or was it Leigh staring down at Dr. Joyce? It was like trying to recall an old dream. She couldn't tell what was real from what her imagination was making up.

"Sort of," Leigh finally answered. "It's very hazy."

"Not for me," Jake said. "I'll never forget it. You sank your teeth right into Dr. Joyce's throat."

Leigh's mouth shot open. She wanted to retort, to tell Jake he was full of shit, but at that exact moment, a memory emerged from the depths of her brain. Unlike before, this one was vivid and undeniable.

She had been infected. Sometime during her escape from Evan's clutches, the fungus which claimed his body and jumped onto her own skin. If Leigh hadn't feasted on Dr. Joyce's flesh, that blue fungus would've surely claimed her life by now. She didn't need to see every inch of her body to know she was entirely cured.

"All right," Leigh said, swallowing hard. "I guess I lost it for a minute back there. It was a momentary loss of control, there's no doubt about it." She shook her right wrist. "But did it really warrant *this*?"

Both Jake's face and voice became even more somber. "That's not all," he said. "Shortly after you *disposed* of Dr. Joyce, you lost consciousness. That was when that guy, Dale Preston, showed up. Remember Dale?"

Leigh scoffed. "How could I possibly forget? He wanted to eat me, for Christ's sake."

"Yeah, well," Jake said. "Not anymore. He had me in his crosshairs, could've killed me and Mary both. Obviously, he chose not to, which is why I'm sitting with you here."

As she couldn't lift her hand, Leigh used her shoulder to wipe a tear away. "So what? He just suddenly came to his senses?"

"I wouldn't say that, exactly. While he did let us go, he insisted we leave behind Dr. Joyce and Nadine. He said he had 'plans' for them, and I think they were of the dinner variety, if you get my drift."

Leigh's nod quickly became a head shake. "That guy was crazy," she said as she stared up at the ceiling. "Hell, he might've been the craziest one of them all. I used to think the Cedar family was insane, but at least they were eating people to survive. Sickos or not, they resorted to cannibalism to remedy a lethal disease. But Dale? He blamed everything on an evil spirit. 'The Wendigo,' he said. Can you believe that?"

She took of her gaze from the ceiling to look at her friend. What she saw simultaneously terrified and broke her heart. Jake was sobbing into his hands.

"No," he said, lifting his head. His eyes were wet and puffy. "A week ago, I wouldn't have believed it. But then I saw what you became, what you have been until just a few minutes ago. You haven't been you, Leigh. That's what I've been trying to tell you."

"Wha," she stammered. "What do you mean? Who have I been?"

"Something else," Jake said. "Something vicious and feral and wild. They've had to keep you sedated most of the time, because when you were awake, you would attack anyone who came close."

"Jake, I don't—"

"I didn't believe it either. To me it sounded like you had contracted rabies or something. But that wasn't it at all. That's not what the doctor's called it, anyway."

Leigh's heart felt like it might explode right out of her chest and hit the ceiling. "What did they call it?" she asked. "What's wrong with me?"

Jake wiped his eyes before staring deep into hers. "Wendigo psychosis," he said.

The room began to slant upward, as if Leigh's bed were a rollercoaster car approaching a loop-de-loop. She thought that she might vomit at any second.

Leigh closed her eyes only to see her own reflection from her dream. Her face in the mirror mouthed the word *Wendigo* over and over.

"Oh my god," she moaned. "No. Please, no."

"Shh," Jake coaxed. He reached out brush the hair out of her eyes.

And Leigh whipped her head and snapped her teeth, missing Jake's fingers by no more than a centimeter.

Jake recoiled. The two stared at each other for what felt like an eternity. Finally, Leigh said, "Jake, I'm sorry. I don't know what just happened. I—"

"I should go get the doctor," Jake said, standing up. "I should have when you first woke up."

Leigh threw herself forward to stop him, but the straps held her in place. "No, Jake, don't. Please, just stay with me."

But Jake had already made it to the door and was reaching for the handle. "You need a doctor," he said. "Don't worry, they will help you."

"Jake, please!" Leigh was screaming now. "Don't go!"

"I'll be back soon," Jake said, opening the door. Though Leigh couldn't say why, there was no doubt in her mind that he was lying. Before she could protest any further, Jake was gone, replaced by a man in a white coat and a nurse following close behind.

"Jake!" Leigh screamed, ignoring the medical experts standing over her. "Come back!"

"Now there," the doctor said. "Let's calm down. You'll see your friend another time. Right now, you need your rest."

He turned away to retrieve something from his pocket. A moment later, Leigh saw it was a hypodermic needle. At the sight of the injection, she began to cry.

"Oh, honey," the nurse said in a soothing voice. "It's okay, we're not going to hurt you. There's no reason to cry."

Only Leigh wasn't crying anymore. While the nurse had been speaking, her sobs had transformed into a light chuckling.

"Something funny, dear?" the nurse asked.

Leigh couldn't answer. Her chuckling had become full fledged laughter, even as the doctor injected the sedative into her I.V. Had she been able to speak, however, she would've told the nurse that there was nothing funny about this at all.

She just couldn't help herself.

EPILOGUE

Dale Preston had heard many adages about his home state during his lifetime, but out of all the old sayings and expressions, there was one that held more truth than all the rest.

If you don't like the weather, wait five minutes.

Case in point, it was hard to believe that this same stretch of road had been covered in snow only a few days ago. By the looks of it now, it appeared someone had forgot to inform Mother Nature that winter should've already begun. High temperatures and lots of sunny days had all but melted the snow blanketing the ground, revealing the browned grass and soggy earth underneath. It had precipitated here and there since the blizzard, but always in the form of rain. Having long lost his taste for the colder seasons, Dale didn't mind the unseasonable warmth at all.

Not that any of it mattered, really. By the end of the day, the weather would never be a concern of his again. The planet could witness the coming of a new ice age for he cared. Let the world freeze or burn or flood or whatever. Dale Preston wouldn't be around to see it.

He turned the wheel of his pick-up truck to turn onto the unmarked dirt road. Locals used to call this particular route, "Logger's Lane," as it once led directly to the always bustling Embry sawmill. These days, it was as desolate the road that crosses the Mojave. It was this reason why Dale Preston had chose this exact location to end his life.

No one would bother him at the saw mill. In fact, there was no telling how long it would take for someone to discover his body. Dale imagined it would eventually be a pack of teenagers to stumble upon his corpse. Rambunctious teens were the only people to ever visit the old mill anymore, as it was a prime spot to party or hook up. Then again, were there even people that young left in Embry anymore? Dale honestly couldn't say for sure.

His truck passed underneath some low hanging branches to reveal his first view of the mill. The building had been ravaged by time, its wood siding perpetually rotting, its ceiling riddled with gaping holes. Old equipment, completely brown with rust, littered the yard around the main structure. As Dale drove closer, signs of more modern times became visible as well—empty liquor bottles and crushed beer cans, piles of ash from old campfires, and discarded cigarette packs scattered here and there.

Dale drove his truck to an empty space right next to one of the various doors. No doubt this was once a space reserved for someone of importance, a foreman most likely. Now it was merely a great spot to view the faded graffiti sprayed across the wall directly in front of Dale's truck.

FUNGUS GROWS. EMBRY BLOWS.

Though Dale had seen the lil' motto before, it still made him laugh every time.

With his door squealing, Dale jumped out of his truck and glanced around. Though the light rain of the morning had all but stopped, he could still hear countless drops falling from trees around him. Deciding this was the only sound he could hear, Dale made his way into the mill.

His plan was really quite simple. No dramatics, no fanfare, no remorseful note even—Dale was simply going to place the barrel of the shotgun under his chin and pull the trigger. He figured buckshot was the best way to go, as a bullet could easily miss his brain and leave him lying there, slowly bleeding to death and feeling every agonizing moment. But a shotgun? His brains would be splattered across the wall before he even realized he was dead.

But first...

There was one last thing Dale wanted to do before he called it quits. All efforts to excise the hunger within him had failed. Woodenknife was missing, most likely as dead as his two cronies, Uno and Peen. Regardless, Dale still could've followed through with Woodenknife's plan. One well aimed bullet through the old forest ranger's heart and Leigh Swanson would've been his for the taking. Unfortunately, Dale had seen too much. He had seen how the girl ripped into the psychiatrist's flesh, consuming both the skin and the muscle that lay beneath. He had seen the crazed look in her eyes, the total and utter loss of control. He knew this look as well as he knew himself. Consuming Leigh would not have vanquished the demon within him, as it had found a home in the girl as well. If anything, eating Leigh Swanson would've only strengthened his hunger, doubling the presence of what John Woodenknife had called the *Wendigo*.

So Dale had let them go, deciding right then and there that he was giving up. Either Leigh or Spire would certainly report Dale to the cops, and it would only be a matter of time before they found him. That was all right with Dale, as long as the police found him without his brains still in his skull.

The air inside the mill had the intense stale scent of mildew. Everything inside the building was rotting, much like the town of Embry itself. The only real difference Dale could see was that the mold growing inside the building was your standard black variety, and the Hell borne fungus that had decimated the community.

Making his way across the production floor, Dale headed for the staircase at the end of the long room. It led up to the foreman's office that had once overlooked all the other employees hard at work. It was in that office that Dale had left not only his shotgun, but his remaining business as well.

The stairs creaked under Dale's weight. He wouldn't have been surprised if they suddenly gave way, sending Dale to his grave a few minutes ahead of schedule. As before, the old steps held, and Dale reached the door to the office. His hand gripped the handle.

It was just about time. But first, he would allow himself one last indulgence. Like a death row prisoner on the day of his execution, Dale was going to have one last meal. He doubted, however, that any prisoner had ever been granted Dale's particular menu.

He opened the door.

Natural light from the hole-filled ceiling lit most of the room. Still, the office remained quite dim, so Dale walked over to a kerosene lantern he previously left an old oak desk. With the lantern lit, his dinner illuminated into full view.

When Dale had left the Cedar homestead, he hadn't left alone. The dead psychiatrist was of no use to him, as she had gotten awfully close to Leigh's infected body. Though she could've expired before the fungus had a chance to lay claim to her living tissue, it was not a chance Dale was willing to take.

The other one, however...

Dale had made sure to bring along the one in the track suit. From what Dale had gathered as he spied on the scene from outside the Cedar barn, this one had kidnapped the girl tied to the chair. This fact made Dale's choice all the easier. Satisfying his hunger one last time was really all he cared about, but if he could rid the world of a kidnapper, then it was all the better.

So Dale had brought his food to this place where he could eat in peace and die in peace. A significant part of himself wanted to eat right away, but Dale had to do something first. While it was far too risky to return to his home, he figured it would be worth the risk to visit his old hunting cabin. It seemed like a lifetime ago that he and his brother-in-law, Red, would retreat to their backwoods abode to bag trophies and guzzle beers. After Red's death, the cabin had been left to his sister, Cathy. While she didn't have much use for the property, sentimental reasons had prevented Cathy from selling the place. Dale knew it wouldn't take long after his death for his sister to find herself at the camp, where she could best remember both her husband and her brother. That was when she would find the letter explaining everything to the best of Dale's ability. It wasn't great literature to say the least, but it was the least he could do.

Letter written, Dale had driven back to the saw mill where the radio had informed him the continued search of his whereabouts. It also revealed that Leigh Swanson had been transferred to the asylum in Black Creek Junction. Well, they didn't use the word "asylum," but they might as well have. Dale sincerely hoped the girl would get better some day. For his money, being in a nuthouse was a far worse fate than being in the ground.

And if you don't get going with this, a nut house is exactly where the police will put you forever.

With his inner voice snapping him out of it, Dale approached the person tied to the chair. He had placed an old tarp over the body, weighing it down with scraps of wood he had found around the mill. Underneath, his food was securely tied to the office chair, a slab of duct tape covering its mouth. It was almost funny, actually, how naturally Dale had thought of the human being under the tarp as food. He had overheard the person being called both "Nathan" and "Nadine," and under other circumstances, this might have confused his simple mind. But the food could call itself whatever it wanted, it didn't matter to Dale in the slightest.

As he kicked away the pieces of wood weighing down the tarp, it occurred to him that the food wasn't making a single sound. Dale had left it making moaning sounds through the duct tape across its lips. It had been shaking violently, trying to free itself from its cocoon of thick ropes. Now, it sat perfectly silent, perfectly still.

Had it died of blood loss? It had been shot in the shoulder by Dale himself. The wound didn't appear lethal to Dale's eyes, though what did he really know? He wasn't a doctor.

It just passed out, that's all. It's hard to tell with the tarp still on, but its still breathing. I'm sure of it.

Dale grabbed a handful of the tarp, hoping his inner voice was right. If the food was unconscious, it would make it easier for both of them. Without a struggle, Dale could make a clean slash across its throat, and the food die peacefully in its sleep.

He yanked on the tarp.

And recoiled.

The heel of his boot hit one of the discarded scraps of wood, instantly throwing him off balance. Arms flailing, Dale toppled over, landing flat on his back. Stars washed over his vision as the back of his head connected with the hardwood floor. For a full minute, all he could was wait to catch his breath and for the world to stop spinning. When his bearings finally returned, he lay there for a minute more, not wanting to confirm what he saw. He knew it hadn't been his eyes tricking him. If he looked again, it would become real.

But he couldn't lay here forever. Hell, he couldn't even reach the shotgun from here. With great hesitance, Dale pulled himself to his feet and forced his eyes to gaze upon the food.

The food was completely engulfed in fungus. Green fuzz coated every visible inch of skin, turning the food into a single lump of mold. This person wasn't Nathan. She wasn't Nadine. It wasn't even food anymore. It was only the fungus. Dale hadn't seen such a bad case of the infection since...

My God.

Since he was infected. In an instant, Dale could feel the fungus eating away at his own flesh, penetrating his pores and feasting deep inside of him. None of it was real, he knew this. Dale hadn't gotten close enough for the fungus to latch onto him, but that still didn't stop his mind from conjuring up the worst sense memory of his life.

Fortunately, Dale's brain immediately sent the PTSD into far corners of his consciousness to make room for a more pertinent thought.

How the hell did this happen?

It was just wasn't possible that the fungus grew in this section of the forest. Every square inch of woods that the fungus called home had gone up in flames. Even if it had somehow spread to this neck of the woods, Dale himself should have contracted it. Since there wasn't a speck of green on him, he had to assume the food had contracted the fungus *before* Dale had brought it here.

But how?

Dale had never had the best memory, but he was certain that neither Leigh, nor the psychiatrist, had gotten anywhere near Nadine during their little tussle. Though Leigh had been infected and used her disease as a weapon against her old therapist, the other kidnapper had been standing several feet away. Besides, the fungus that covered Leigh's flesh had looked different than what Dale gazed upon now. Leigh's had been a shade of blue that Dale had never seen before.

Did that mean the kidnapper contracted it before? It seemed highly unlikely, as the first symptoms would've shown up long before now.

Then how could...?

As if his memory was an old VHS recording, Dale immediately pressed the "pause" button as one particular image flashed before his eyes. The still frame of the memory remained frozen in Dale's mind as he fought to accept the horrifying truth.

While he watched from outside the barn, looking in through a crack in the door, he saw the ex-spouses arguing. Dr. Joyce had accused her ex-husband of not being a real man.

"You listen to me, *Nadine*. Evan was more of a man than you ever were!"

"Is that a fact?" Nadine had replied. "And how, exactly, is a man supposed to act?" Nadine had then grabbed Mary Carson's face.

"How about this? Is this what a man does?"

Before Dr. Joyce could answer the question, Nadine brought her lips to Mary's and kissed her on the mouth.

Oh my God...

While Dale had been a captive of the Cedar family, he had learned many things about their brutal practices. They revealed that veteran forest ranger, Phil Carson, had been helping them all along. He had kept himself fungus-free by sticking to a cannibalistic regiment, mostly consisting of jerky that he would also offer to naive tourists. Dale would never forget Clementine Cedar, the family's murderous matriarch, scolding him for not trying one of Phil's meat treats before venturing into the woods. That was right before Leigh and that Tucker kid had shown up.

So here was Phil, a secret cannibal, using human flesh as an antibiotic for years and years. Eventually he has a child, a daughter named Mary. Thanks to her father's ghoulish diet, she inherits an immunity to the fungus.

But not just an immunity.

In the early 1900s, a woman named Mary Mallon became the first person in America to be identified as an asymptomatic carrier of typhoid fever. Since she showed absolutely no signs of the disease, she infected twenty-two people before being put into quarantine. Dale had seen a special about her once on the Discovery Channel. They called her, "Typhoid Mary."

If the papers were to find out about this, Dale wondered what they would call Mary Carson. Fuzzy Mary?

Dale couldn't resist smirking. It sounded like one of those fruity drinks no self-respecting man would ever order, but always secretly prefer over his bitter glass of beer.

He wondered where Fuzzy Mary was right now. Had she already infected others? Did anyone else know about this?

A distant sound high above Dale's head spurred him to look up. Through the hole in the roof, he could see the tiny dot of a airplane flying across the stratosphere. As Dale watched it leave its signature on the sky in the form of a vapor trail, a final question crossed his mind.

What if she leaves Embry?

Dale lowered his eyes back to the fungus covered body of the person once known as Nathan, and then as Nadine. He didn't know the answers to any of these questions. He didn't know what the future held for Embry, let alone for the rest of the world. He didn't even know what to do with himself. There was only one thing Dale Preston did know, and this new found knowledge finally brought him the peace of which he had been searching for so, so long.

He had lost his appetite.

ABOUT THE AUTHOR

Asher Ellis is a screenwriter, educator, and author of the novels PET, Curse of the Pigman, and Cracker Jack. He has written multiple award-winning short films, including Exit 7A, which was featured in the feature-length horror anthologies, The Portal and Conjure X. His penned short film, My Name Is Art, was featured in Amazon's first annual "All Voices Film Festival," celebrating underrepresented communities. When not writing, Asher enjoys hiking through the woods of his home state of Vermont (which he insists are not full of cryptids and cannibals).